All Friendship Brings

Michael Saxton

All Friendship Brings is dedicated to my wife Valeria,
who gave me the love, time and space to write this story.

CONTENTS

Acknowledgments

ACKNOWLEDGMENTS

Grateful thanks to:

My daughter Carlotta, my father David, and my trusted friends and allies Kate, Lise, Matt and Warren for critiquing my early drafts.

And to Simon for ruthless sub-editing and Julie at 72pt design for the jacket. You truly are an awesome couple.

DISCLAIMER

1 - PROLOGUE

Sean had taken a shine to him right from the off, said he saw something of himself in Tom at the same age; trusted him to do what needed to be done, hailed from good stock. Farmers from the County. Gaelic-speakers, proud people. That's what he said. Look at your brother, serving time. For membership. Sean spat out the words. Now, look in the mirror Tom. You, Michael, and me. We're the same. I'll teach you everything I know; when the time comes you will be ready.

Tom had learned quickly. The job at Marconi. It was an apprenticeship. The neat way he worked with wires and the circuitry. Everyone could see he had a feeling for it. The young lads reckoned he was ready, but Sean urged caution. It's not like those radios you have been building. You get this wrong, you lose a hand, or an eye, or worse. Tom listened hard and learned well. He wasn't afraid to ask questions or have Sean repeat the steps when he lacked confidence. Tom took his time and went through the process, again and again until he felt he could do this with his eyes shut.

Tom had taken the Shannon flight to Heathrow with Brendan, to find work, they told their families. Brendan made him laugh by telling folks they were in the building trade. In a way, they were. In the Fulham flat, Tom patiently constructed each device by hand. They are beautiful things, said the rest of the boys.

Sean can't visit the mainland, but his words find their way through, from friends of friends: our enemies want to crush us;

they will never give us our land, our Republic. Steel yourself; never have any doubts, Tom.

Tom had none.

Tom stood ready.

Weeks passed: then, the first instruction arrived.

They planted it where the soldiers went to drink. Not in London, but in a provincial squaddie town. The blast ripped through the place. The British media said it was worse than Ulster. They had no idea.

The unit buried itself deep into normalcy; Tom's star shined brightest of them all. He took command. The Council gave him licence to select the targets; a new idea formed. Tom asked for new recruits.

Eddie and Robbie joined Tom and Brendan in Fulham. Fresh volunteers. Clean skins. Sean had vetted them personally. Tom told the new boys to scope new targets.

After a week, they presented a list: Military Club. West End hotel. The Telephone Exchange: it made him think about his time in Cork, at Marconi. It would be an ironic twist. Selfridges, Harrods. Harrow School.

He hushed the table. Harrow School – whose idea was this one? The boys looked at Eddie. Tom was pleased. Sean would approve. Move it to the top priority.

Eddie and Robbie scouted the school. Brendan plotted. Tom was clear: there can be no injuries; they would issue an advance warning. Tom can't sleep thinking about it; we don't kill kids.

Don't think about it, Tom. Sean's words whispering in his ear. Pushing him on.

Under an Anglepoise lamp, Tom sat down and carefully laid out all the pieces on the table; the blinds drawn shut even though it was mid-afternoon, and the sun was winking out behind west London clouds. He thought about the big open skies back home, and let his hands go to work. Five pounds of explosive. You'll need to place it carefully, he stated to the boys, and then he sent them on their way.

Brendan made the call to the Press Association. The receptionist patched it upstairs to the top brass at 11.30am. Brendan knew the message by heart: A bomb at Harrow School. There is a warning this time, but if nothing is done, there won't be any more. If you don't move the kids, they will be OK.

The sons of prime ministers, of generals and majors, captains of industry. The privileged few. They set the bomb on the windowsill of the school cottage. Out of harm's way if they followed the message.

Tick-tock, tick-tock. Set for ten minutes.

Tom knew what ten minutes felt like when the clock was running down. Hold your sweet boys where they are. Sit it out. Do as you are told. Five, four, three, two, one.

The evening news was full of it. Tom watched television on his own. The boys, his boys, shared a bottle in the kitchen. Sean met the Council. They raised their glasses to the plan and its faultless execution. A blow to the establishment. They drained them and had another.

Tom smoked an ashtray full of cigarettes, going over the other names on the list until the names blurred into one and tiredness came, washing over him. In the morning when he awoke, the house was empty. Brendan had left the day's newspaper next to his bed. The headline screamed 'Terror comes to Harrow'. Tom made himself tea and settled down to think. He was only just getting started. This was his calling.

2 – UNHAPPY BIRTHDAY

Quite how Giles had come to sit the exam for the preparatory school remained a mystery to him. They had whisked him off in the Capri in the second week of the new year. He sat the entrance exam in a hot and sticky classroom, the teacher sitting quietly behind a large desk, scarcely looking up from the paperwork and books on his desk. When he did speak his voice was raspy. Giles, with his problem ears, had struggled to hear. More than once he had to ask the teacher to repeat what he had said, which had made the man irritable.

On the drive home, Frank, his father, fired questions at Giles, demanding to know how he'd got on, and what he thought about the school, and whether he would be excited to go there. When Giles mentioned the experience with the teacher, an awkward look had passed between his father and mother.

However, he must have done ok. Because a few months later, in March, the postman arrived with a large brown envelope that his mother Moira ripped open. He watched as she read it carefully. She looked surprised, perhaps sad even, and had sent him to play in the garden, so she could telephone his father at the showroom. His father had come home early from the dealership. Unlike his mother, he had a bounce in his step. The owner, Mr Henderson, a jowly, purple-faced man said the family should go out and celebrate. Frank booked a table at the carvery in town. First, though, they had stopped in on his grandmother. She doted on Giles.

The good humour evaporated on arrival. Soon, there was a strange atmosphere among the adults, which quite naturally interested Giles.

His mother, whose behaviours increasingly swung from listlessness - prone to lying in bed in the morning or dozing on the couch in the afternoon – to bouts of frantic energy, seemed coolly detached. This had the effect of making his father tetchy. Giles sat on the shag pile rug and played with his grandmother's dog. His grandmother looked unsure about how to react to the news. Eventually, she was the one who dared ask the question. "So, he will be boarding then?" She sounded tense and awkward; she hated confrontation of any kind, especially when it came to Frank. She thought any cross word with her son would have catastrophic consequences.

Frank had glanced at Giles, who was teasing the terrier.

"Giles will board monthly, Mum," said Frank with a cheerful smile. "He'll come home on Sundays." Frank squeezed Moira's leg. Giles' mother had forced herself to smile. The old woman wanted to know why he had to sleep at school. They did, after all, live within a short driving distance. His father said something meaningless. Moira visibly shrank away from Frank.

Giles dangled the soft toy in front of the dog. The terrier barked loudly and tried to snap it out of his hands. Once or twice the dog succeeded, wrenching it free and then gripping the toy between its teeth. Giles tugged as hard as he could, the dog growling. Eventually, Frank snapped like the dog and told Giles to stop. Granny eyed her boys carefully. "More tea?" she offered. Frank had his eye on the clock, itching to make tracks but it was still too early to leave for the restaurant.

Moira too would have been happy to have made their excuses. She watched her son from the corner of her eye, already starting to feel like she was losing him even though there would be months before he went to the new school. "Why don't you go and get some fresh air?" she said.

It didn't take his parents long to start on each other. Through the patio doors, Giles could hear their raised voices. His grandmother sounded distressed. Giles threw a stick into the bushes at the end of the garden so the dog would leave him alone. The terrier bounded away, while he sneaked up to the doors to listen.

"What good do you think will come by sending him away?" said Giles' grandmother.

There came the sound of crying. He stole a peep through the blinds. His mother was wiping tears from her eyes, the mascara had run, and she looked bruised. She pushed his father away when he tried to console her. This was just the sort of scene to which Giles had become accustomed. And sure enough, his father now wore the expression of the injured party. Next, he would be sure to start pacing the room like a caged beast. Giles watched on, impassively

"Ask Frank. Ask your precious son," said Moira, in response to his grandmother's question, gesturing to Frank to stop marching about.

"Please sit down, Frank," said Giles' grandmother. Her pale face looked all creased up, the big blue vein in her neck stood out like electrical wiring, pulsing every so often. Giles wondered what would happen if it popped there and then.

All of sudden Frank stopped and stared at his mother. He had a weird expression on his face, like he had a stroke. "Let's not pretend we don't know what this is about," he said, fiercely, glowering then at Moira. "We had to do something to wipe the slate clean. After what he did." It came out as a whispered hiss. Frank turned abruptly round to face the garden. Just for a moment, Frank thought he could see Giles behind the doors. But when Frank went to look, flinch-faced, Giles was lying on the hammock. Giles had sprinted away. Feeling his father's eyes upon him, he glanced up and then looked away. Frank lingered awhile, and then pulled the nets closed.

Giles gave the hammock a big push and lay back. He didn't need to have his head pressed up to the glass to know that they were talking about him, about that day, the day he turned nine, what had become known as the unhappy birthday.

The morning had started out brightly, and why wouldn't it? Having opened his big present, an expensive set of golf clubs, Giles was given the choice about which two friends to invite to the driving range. There was no question about who Giles would ask to join him.

John had been his friend forever. They did everything together. Their mothers had met at antenatal classes. John's mother Yvonne modelled herself on Twiggy. She was tall and elfin-like. Frank followed her with his eyes when he thought Moira was not looking. John had the same frame; long and lean, already an inch or so taller than Giles. The two boys wore near-identical designer clothes by Jean Le Bourget.

Marcus was a new friend of Giles. They had met at the golf club. The boy was a year younger than Giles, but it did not matter; Marcus was very good at golf, which was good enough for Giles who wanted to learn everything so he could start to play on a course as soon as possible. Giles, John, and Marcus had challenged one another to see who could hit the golf ball the farthest.

The boys had a bucket of coloured balls between them: green, yellow, and white. Twenty of one colour each. Frank had promised he would give a pound note to the boy whose golf ball landed nearest to the 100-yard target, an ugly metal bullseye set in patchy grass.

Moira thought the competition was a bad idea; it was bound to upset someone, by which she meant Giles. There should at least be runners up prizes. Frank had pooh-poohed the idea. It would spoil the *fun* – that was the exact word he had used.

As more accomplished golfers who had played at the driving range before, Giles and Marcus were in their element. The odd shot veered left and right, but as the buckets started to empty out, they were hitting the balls ever closer to the target. But then John got into a huff. When he swung, he missed the tee, or he connected poorly with the ball and it went careering into the wooden panels separating one booth from the next. Giles laughed. It was funny.

The boys took their shots in turn until the last ball. At that point, they drew lots as to who would go first.

John drew the short straw. His final shot of the day was no better than the rest: his yellow ball travelled a pathetic 20 yards before coming to rest in the grass. He stamped his feet on the ground, huffing. Giles and Marcus didn't even notice.

Marcus lined up his white ball on the tee and swung. There was a moment when it seemed to disappear into the white sky. It could have gone anywhere. Giles prayed it would; it was his birthday. The ball struck the target with a loud thud. Marcus did a dance, celebrating.

Giles's recollection is oddly fractured: some memories feeling distant and fuzzy, others as raw as on the day itself, heightened by knowing what comes next.

Marcus was putting him off and Giles shouted at him to stop larking about. That was how he had come to fudge his shot: he took a swing, missed the ball, and spun like a top. John burst out laughing. Giles hurled the club to the floor.

Marcus said play it again.

John said no. Rules are rules.

If only things had ended there.

Marcus picked up the driver, wiping the club face on his orange cords. He wanted Giles to play a clean shot.

Giles cannot remember how he expended the next few seconds. Did he say thank you to Marcus for handing him the club? Or did he snatch it out of his hands? Between placing the green ball on the rubbery raised tee and the swing was John still complaining?

There were signs dotted around the driving range commanding golfers to keep their distance when a player was at the tee. And yet, it had happened: the lightness of the swing and the swoosh as it cut through the air like a blade, contrasting with the weight, the terrible heaviness of the head of the driver as it smashed into Marcus. John ran to call the adults: he told them what Giles had done.

When Frank came, breathless, Giles was still holding the club, the metal face slick with blood. Giles stared down at Marcus. The boy whimpered and called out for his mother. People stood around, transfixed. The rumours and the whispering, they started there, the name calling came soon after; people stopped coming to the house. Finally, the accident became something else, a dreadful thing done to another by a troubled boy. The new school was a chance to put it all behind him.

Things had turned quiet in his grandmother's garden. The dog must have gone indoors. Giles settled back into the garden hammock and closed his eyes. The cushions felt warm and soft from the afternoon's sun. Giles let his mind wander as the psychologist said he should. No thoughts or memories should be out of bounds, every feeling should be explored. He knew where they would take him, and Giles had no desire to go there. He opened his eyes to push the thoughts away, reaching down for the hard lawn under the hammock. With the flat of his hand, he pushed off, setting the hammock into a steady swing. He did it again and again, until the hammock started to judder, the metal groaning, the frame buckling. He lay back and closed his eyes, thinking about the questions that psychologist asked. What do you see? How do you feel? The psychologist had warm, sweet breath.

Giles pushed down harder on the grass. He pictured himself at a ship's helm, amid a storm, the wind whipping in, the waves lashing the hull, the horizon drifting away. Giles flung himself back into the padded folds of the hammock keeping his eyes tightly shut, embracing the feeling of being at one with the waves, of being carried further from shore, of being powerless against the swell.

He must have stayed like that for a long time because when his mother gently shook him awake the hammock was still, and it was cold, and the sky had grown darker. It was an inkier shade of blue and empty save for the vapour trails of a distant aircraft, which slowly faded from view. "Are you ready for some supper?" asked his mother. Giles shrugged. The sensation of being cast away at sea remained with him. It was a strange feeling, unsettling and exciting.

Spring and summer passed slowly at The Close. There was little to do except stay in his room or visit the rec, where he played alone. Yet when the day came to leave home for the new school, it arrived out of nowhere, fierce, and bright. Moira was flustered, everything in a whirl. There had been a few awkward goodbyes to neighbours and then, finally, the packing of the trunk – shoes, shorts, ties, blazer, cap, jumpers, pyjamas, towels, swimming trunks, ironed shirts, socks in bundles, trousers pressed flat – everything going in two-by-two. Full to the brim, Frank sat on the lid to close it tight. The trunk had cost a pretty penny. Only the best for a new start.

Giles had not spent much time alone with his father except for when they played golf, and they had not played since his birthday. He wondered if his father would ever let him play again; the bag had been stowed away in the garage, concealed beneath a dust sheet.

Moira wondered why they were taking their time. There was a schedule to keep. Frank said come upstairs and see. In packing, they had managed to trap themselves inside Giles' bedroom. On reflection, it was a light-hearted moment. Eventually, they wrestled the trunk out the bedroom and down the narrow stairs.

"Don't let it drop," said Frank. However, it was heavy, and Giles was unable to prevent it from thudding down the last few steps. Moira ticked them off about the noise and the mess their shoes had made on the carpet. But her words sounded hollow, and she looked scared. It was a fleeting, unsettling image which Giles found hard to shake off.

The front door of the house was already ajar, in preparation for their exit. It framed a peerless blue sky, a bank of red-brick identikit houses, and tall trees whose branches and leaves swayed in a light breeze. If this was a holiday day not a school day, Giles would have been out there like a shot, running as fast as he could to his dens and camps and hideaways. It seemed cruel to be leaving home when the weather was playing tricks like this.

Father and son heaved the trunk out of the house, down the pathway and out to the Capri, parked up on the street in readiness. Frank and Moira had told people to stay away. They did not want any fuss, so it was just the three of them loading up the boot and packing the final bits and pieces on the back seat. Giles would have to squeeze in and be careful not to shuffle around on the journey.

"We need to have a family photo," said Frank.

Moira ducked back inside the house, leaving them to stand together in silence until she returned with the Polaroid camera. "Where shall we stand, Frank?" she asked.

While they debated this, an old woman passed by. She was an

elderly neighbour whose garden backed on to the recreational park – the rec. Giles was adept at reading his parents' body language; their awkwardness was plain to see. The woman saw the camera in his mother's hands and volunteered to take their picture. They all stood in front of the Capri, its green paintwork all shiny and pristine. "Say cheese," she said, and they smiled for the camera. The woman handed the camera and the still wet photograph to Moira, who waved it dry.

Moira studied the photograph. She could see the likeness of her father in Giles, in his pale complexion and thick hair. His eyes were all hers, like dark moss under water. "It's lovely," said Moira, holding it out so they could all see for themselves. "You take it," she added, thrusting the picture into Giles's hand, and kissing him with almost brutal force.

Giles inspected the Polaroid. They looked like any ordinary family with their interlinked arms and fixed smiles, except there was nothing ordinary about them, or that day.

"You should keep it in your tuck box with all your other special things," said Frank.

"I will," he replied, taking one last look at the house and The Close before his father gunned the engine to take them on their way to Frampton Prep, and a new beginning.

***

The Capri pulled slowly off the road and into the school driveway, tyres crunching on the gravel surface. Giles was struck by the massive proportions of the building. Its big red façade. Three floors, maybe four, rows of windows glinting in the sun.

They came to a stop behind an orange saloon. A family was busying away, emptying out luggage from the boot. On the opposite of the driveway, separated by the neat little circular lawn, two more families were doing the same. Three uniformed boys were helping to ferry the contents from the cars to the school. Giles watched on from inside the Capri. He saw the tall man approaching their car. Giles recognised him from the exam and the interview. The principal housemaster David Scott leaned into the open passenger window, startling Moira. "The Ashworths," he said, smiling.

Frank jumped quickly out of the car, stepping around the vehicle to shake the housemaster's hand. Scott held the door open for Moira. Giles took his cue from his mother, and quickly unbuckled. Frank gave Giles a reassuring wink as he stepped out of the car, while Moira straightened her blouse and skirt after the car journey.

Giles listened in while his parents made small talk. Mr Scott seemed taken with his mother. "Moira." He said her name, slowly, thoughtfully. "A lovely name. Irish?" he inquired.

"Yes, originally," she said, clearing her throat. He continued to look at Moira, expecting her to say something more, but instead she said nothing, so he turned his attention to Frank.

The conversation turned to the car journey from home – very easy, nothing on the road today – and the weather. Unusually warm for the time of the year. Blah, blah, blah. Giles wouldn't have minded if they could just get on with things. He gazed at the school and started counting the number of windows. He and John used to do it all the time when there was nothing else to do: the birds in the trees, brown-coloured cars on the road, the number of cracks in the pavement on the walk to school. They never ran out of things to count. But mostly they were never bored, they always had something to build in the woods, a camp, a den, or some other kind of hide-out.

Giles was unaware his mother had broken away from the conversation between Mr Scott and his father until he felt her hand on his shoulder. "It's a lot bigger than I remember," she said. "I hope your father is right and you will be happy here." Giles thought about this while they watched various boys scuttle past with trunks and tuck boxes.

Perhaps sensing what they were thinking or wanting to hurry things along for his own benefit, Mr Scott called over a freckle-faced boy. Dressed in dark grey shorts, a lighter grey shirt with the arms rolled up neatly above the elbows and dark knee-length socks with black sandals on his feet, the boy approached the family. "This is Hepbridge from dorm four, your pilot. He'll help you get settled in," he said. Giles had heard about this arcane tradition from his father who had pored over the school prospectus as though he was preparing to sit an exam himself.

Andrew Hepbridge said hello to each in turn with a firm and sweaty handshake.

"You'll show Giles the ropes, won't you?" Mr Scott asked with a fixed stare.

"Yes, sir," said the boy, politely.

They'd have some tea said Mr Scott, while their car was unloaded. He called over a tall gangly boy whom Giles had watched unload the orange saloon, and then he led the family into the school. The lobby was cool and dark in contrast to the light and warmth outside. The wood-panelled walls were lined with school photographs. The floor had a just-polished smell, a heady wax fragrance that Giles would always come to associate with the school. A single large writing desk stood in one corner, the only piece of furniture in the room. Frank asked what lay behind the small wooden door tucked away below the big staircase, which ascended to the dormitories and the other floors above. "That is the head's office," said Mr Scott, coming to a stop in the middle of the room.

Clasping his hands behind his back, he gave the Ashworths the opportunity to take it all in. This was something he liked to do when welcoming new boys and their families to the house; it underlined the importance of the institution. It reminded Giles of fogeyish stately homes, which his grandmother liked to visit.

A group of boys burst into the lobby. "Ah, the year fives," he said by way of introduction, waving them through. "This is the oldest part of the school," Mr Scott continued, pointing out the room's features. "Five centuries old, dating back to Elizabeth the First." Giles remembered hearing his father read this out aloud to his mother. He glanced at his father while the housemaster droned on about the Civil War and rebuilding the school. Sure enough, his father was lapping it up.

Talk finally over, the family followed Scott through the ground floor, from one sparsely furnished room to the next until they entered a light and bright room, which had been arranged for tea. Large windows faced the driveway. Giles looked outside. He could see the same year five boys who had breezed through the lobby starting to take his belongings from the Capri. They were laughing about something as they hauled the trunk from the boot.

Three large floral sofas were arranged around a low mahogany table. Mr Scott gestured to the parents to sit. The Ashworths took one, which gave as they sat, while he took the sofa opposite. Hepbridge continued to stand, so Giles did the same, fidgeting with the watchstrap on his wrist. "Take a seat, boys," said Mr Scott eventually, a frown flickering across his face. "Over here," he added, patting the floral three-seater to his left. Hepbridge edged as far away from Mr Scott as he could, wedging himself into the corner. Giles took the other end.

Conversation turned to the curriculum. Giles zoned out while Mr Scott launched into the subjects. The housemaster read the lessons from the timetable, calling out those topics which were important at Frampton: Latin, PE, RE, Chapel, Clubs and Lights out. He held the timetable up like it was a sacred book. "All that's in a normal week, of course. This first week is a little bit different as we help the boys to become accustomed to their new surroundings," he said, setting down the book. Scott yawned and stretched out as though exhausted by his efforts. He asked if they had any questions.

Moira asked Scott about the piano in the room. Giles had not noticed it. Moira said she loved the piano. The housemaster was of the same mind. "Giles is a very accomplished pianist," she said, looking proud. Scott raised his eyebrows in surprise. "Can he continue lessons from where he left off?" she asked. He was on Grade 2. He had John's mother Yvonne to thank for introducing him to the piano.

"What does he like to play?" said Scott, looking from Moira to Frank. Giles wondered why the housemaster did not ask him.

"You can tell Mr Scott," said Moira, in a reassuring tone.

"Pop stuff, mostly. The Beatles. I can play Yesterday as good as Paul," said Giles. The housemaster gave Giles a cool, appraising look. "Paul McCartney, sir."

"We don't go in things like that," said Mr Scott testily. "We'll have you playing classical pieces before term's out."

"That'll be nice," said Moira, with an unconvincing smile. She wanted to know all about lights out. "How does it work?" she asked, exchanging nervous glances with Giles and her husband.

"Giles isn't used to going to bed as early as 8.15pm," added Frank helpfully.

Mr Scott coughed quietly into his hand. "With a new school there are many things for boys to get used to, not just new dormitory boys, new routines. He'll get the hang of it. They all do," he said with a winning smile. Giles had already decided he did not like Mr Scott. Warming to the subject, the housemaster addressed the pilot. "An earlier bedtime is something all boys get used to, isn't it Mr Hepbridge?" All heads turned towards the boy. Halfway through a biscuit, Hepbridge knew he was expected to provide a clear and affirmative response, but he could not chew the Rich Tea fast enough for the housemaster's liking. The biscuit turned to a dry paste in his mouth. With considerable effort, he squeaked out a 'Yes Sir', swallowing hard to get the thing down.

Moira offered the boy some milk, pouring a glass, which he drank quickly, as though he expected someone to snatch it away. Hepbridge wiped his mouth on the back of his hand. "Explain what you enjoy about school?" said Scott. The boy looked blank.

"What do we do on Saturdays?" asked the housemaster by way of a prompt.

"Tuck and cinema, sir," the boy stammered. He looked at Mr Scott for approval. When none was forthcoming, he pressed on. "Sometimes we play British Bulldog, or Kick the Can, or war, and there's skateboarding if you like that kind of thing. I don't, I can't skateboard." By the time he had finished, Hepbridge's face was crimson, beads of sweat glistened on his top lip, which he tried to lick away.

"As I said, lots of new things at first, all of which will feel familiar soon," said Mr Scott. And with that, he brought tea to an abrupt end and suggested they said their goodbyes. They left the way they had come in.

"So, we'll see you soon," said Frank, resting his hand on the Capri. He had his free arm around Moira's waist. Giles could not remember the last time he had seen his father display any kind of open affection for his mother. It seemed unnatural. Only their car and a white estate remained in the driveway. Every other family had been and gone.

Giles stood at the porchway alongside Mr Scott. "One more thing before you go," he said, placing his arm around Giles' shoulder in a way designed to reassure Frank and Moira that their son was in safe hands. "We've another boy joining the house in year three. Hugh Burton. You may have heard of his father, Colonel Hector Burton?" Moira and Frank shook their heads. At that moment, a well-dressed man appeared from behind the housemaster. The housemaster pulled Giles to one side so the man could step by. "The very man!" exclaimed Mr Scott. "I was just explaining to the Ashworths that their son and

Hugh will be dorming together."

Hector Burton stopped abruptly and looked at Giles, "Is that so?" he asked. Giles shrugged. Hector looked the boy up and down and then ruffled his hair. Frank then stepped forward and the men shook hands. They were of similar height, but that's where similarities ended. Long and lean, Frank wore his dark hair on his shoulders, whereas Hector, stocky, barrel-chested, kept his hair short and neat, parted with a touch of Brylcreem. He looked older than Frank, with lines around his eyes and grey flecks in his hair. Hector also had the confident bearing of a more mature man.

"My wife, Moira," said Frank. Hector was pleased to make her acquaintance. Mr Scott watched on with interest. He did not remotely care for Hector Burton. Everything about the man reeked of arrogance and birthright, despite the fact he hardly had a penny to his name. By contrast, the Ashworths seemed grateful, and they were evidently not short of money.

"I think it's time we got Giles inside," said Mr Scott. Frank, Moira and Hector stopped talking. Moira wanted to give Giles one last hug, but the housemaster had his hand draped on Giles' shoulder and seemed intent on taking him inside.

"Hold on, Ashworth," bellowed Hector in a booming voice. Despite the unfamiliarity of being called by his surname, Giles instinctively glanced around.

"Yes, sir?" said Giles.

"Make sure you don't get mixed up in any of Hugh's silly games," said Hector with a conspiratorial wink.

Giles had not the faintest idea what on earth Colonel Burton meant. "Ok," he shrugged, momentarily catching his mother's eye. He could see she wanted to cry.

* * *

After the Ashworths had driven away, Hector lit a cigarette. He smoked quickly, feeling that he was breaking an unwritten rule about school standards, and then made his way back to the headmaster's study where Anthony Richardson remained patiently waiting for him. The meeting had gone well so far. The school would accept a delayed payment of the term's fees for a month, which would help him settle things with the bank. All that remained was to reassure the headmaster that Hugh had put his mischief behind him.

Carrying a hint of smoke with him, Hector sat back a little further from the headmaster, "Now, where were we?" asked Anthony, peering inquisitively at Hector, over the top of his glasses. "Ah, yes," he said, shuffling the papers on his desk into a neat pile, "we were talking about Hugh's time at Fleetwood, and why he ran away."

It was a question Hector had asked his son without receiving a satisfactory answer. While composing his thoughts, Hector caught his reflection in the glass cabinet behind Richardson's desk and was surprised by the man he saw looking back. He had grown old. When did that happen? Forty-six, but he had seen a lot of things in that time. They left their mark on people in different ways.

Instead of addressing the question, Hector decided to focus on his son's good character. "Hugh is a very straightforward and open boy, you'll have no issues with him," he said confidently.

All these things were true. However, Hugh was equally prone to making rash decisions and was easily distracted. They were the traits that Hector hoped the school would correct.

However, Richardson was like a dog to a bone. In Crown Court barrister mode, he read out loud the less than glowing reference from Fleetwood and badgered Hector about Hugh's woeful academic performance. And then there was the business about Hugh's disappearing acts. "He ran away twice?" asked Anthony, with a whiff of incredulity in his voice.

The old man in the mirror nodded in reply. Hector did not like this compliant, passive version of himself. "Yes, that's right," he replied, eventually.

"Where was he going? Home?" asked Anthony without looking up from the paperwork.

Hector thought hard before answering. "You know we are a military family. Mostly we stay in one place for a long time. But last year was very unsettling for Hugh, for *all* of us," he said. Hector's mistake, he realised too late, had been in keeping Veronica in the dark. When Hugh had absconded, he had wanted to save Hugh's mother from worrying, so he did not tell her about either occasion until later. Veronica was furious. How could she trust him? In a marriage you shared everything. All he did was lie. If he wanted to protect her, this was not the way. Any normal person could see that. She asked him to stay at the barracks. He had packed a small overnight bag, while Veronica took Hugh to the cinema. A couple of days later, Hector received a delivery at the base. It contained the rest of his things. He had instructed a couple of privates to empty out the contents of the vehicle and send back one piece, the trunk which had belonged to his father, which had been passed down to Hector. Hugh would need it for Frampton. Perhaps even now, Hugh was attending to unpacking and meeting his dorm mates. Hector would have liked to have ventured upstairs and see the dorm for himself, and help his son get accustomed to his new surroundings.

"I'm sorry to have asked these questions," said Anthony, moderating his tone. There were trustees to answer to, reassurances that he had to provide. "Personally, I am delighted Hugh is joining us. We have a proud history of military families trusting their boys into our care," he said. The school's active junior cadet force had been a factor in Hector's choice. He felt it was important to have continuity in the right things, and Hugh clearly enjoyed junior soldiering. Following in his footsteps, just as Hector had followed his father, and his father before him. Three generations. In time – four.

"Thank you, headmaster. I'm sure he will be very happy here," said Hector, feeling a sense of relief that this particular conversation had reached its conclusion. It was getting late, and he had a long drive back to regiment headquarters. "Are we all set, then?" he asked.

"We are, Colonel Burton. Let me see you out," he replied politely.

"No need," said Hector, rising from his chair. But Anthony insisted.

Outside the air was cool; the sun had dipped below the trees and the light was fading fast. September: always a month of change, as summer gave way to autumn. "Such a beautiful evening," he commented.

"I love this time of year," said Anthony, casting his eyes over the playing fields. "I feel excited for the boys. At this age they have so much potential. Great friendships are made in these years."

"Very true. I hope that can be said for Hugh," replied Hector, staring up at the grand façade.

"He'll be fine. There's another boy joining in the same dorm…"

"Giles Ashworth. I met the family and the boy," said Hector, recounting the brief encounter. "Some cars!" he added.

"The father is in the motor trade," said Richardson. "Local people, actually." Hector was surprised, he assumed boys only boarded when their families lived far away. "The Wilson government is killing off grammar schools. We're the only hope for a good education." he added, smiling.

"And what's the boy's story, why is he joining now?" asked Hector, keen to know something about Giles, knowing it was uncommon for boys to join a new school midway through prep years.

"They're ambitious people and they know Giles will thrive here," said Anthony. "It'll be a step up from what the boy has been used to, but he'll relish a fresh start. You could say the same will be true for Hugh, am I right?"

Hector nodded thoughtfully in reply. He had a good feeling about the headmaster. It was a pity that Veronica had been too upset to come. She had had enough of her son boarding. If he failed to settle at Frampton, she'd be taking responsibility for his schooling. "Look after my boy," said Hector, shaking the headmaster's hand.

"It goes without saying," replied Anthony.

Hector lingered awhile, thinking about his own time at boarding school. He'd found it easy to fit it and follow the routines. Army life was no different. Hugh would have to knuckle down, that was all there was to it. Eventually, the rules and behaviours became second nature. With that thought in mind, he squatted down by the side of the car and then dropped to his knees to inspect the undercarriage for anything suspect. It was an ingrained part of his routine. Men had lost limbs and their lives by failing to take the right precautions. Satisfied, he brushed the dust and dirt from his trousers and gave the building one final, cursory look. Hector hoped Hugh might be there, waiting at a window, but while the lights burned brightly from within, there was not a soul to be seen except for Anthony Richardson, who was once again seated at his desk ploughing through his papers. The lives of teaching staff and officers were not so different: educators and administrators, tasked with shaping the futures of their charges for better or worse.

***

Mr Scott walked Giles through the lobby and up the main staircase to the dormitories on the first floor. He was eager to introduce the two new boys, so they could start to settle in. The door to dorm three was ajar. Linda Wallace, the school's matron, was making up their beds. Hugh was standing to one side, holding a pillow and a blanket. Mr Scott ushered Giles into the room. He introduced the boys and told them to hurry along. "Matron or Mr Rhys-Davis will point you in the right direction," he said.

Matron took the pillow from Hugh and stopped what she was doing. "You look like two peas in a pod," she said. The boys had no idea what that meant. She asked them to stand side by side and face the mirror, so they would understand. There was a passing similarity between them.

"Oh, yes," said Giles. He was a little taller than Hugh, his hair a shade fairer and his skin paler. Hugh still had colour in his face and on his arms from the summer holiday. They wore their hair in the same way, cut like a pageboy. But more than that, there was something about the way they stood, hands on hips staring into the tall mirror that was quite disconcerting; they had an almost louche way about them, which made them seem old beyond their years.

After matron had finished with Hugh's bed, she asked Giles to help with his. "The other boys will be up soon," she said. "Make yourselves at home and then it'll be time for dinner."

Hugh shut the door behind her. Giles was already lying on his bed. The dormitory looked like every other dorm Hugh had slept in – flocked wallpaper, cheap lino, a couple of large wardrobes, and six beds for six boys. Each bed was separated by a small bedside table with a lamp. At the foot of each bed, a laundry box containing a boy's clothing for a week. Thick curtains designed to shut out the day framed the large window.

Hugh sat down on his bed and bounced on the mattress. It had collapsed in the middle. He felt like he was sinking. He was glad to have been given the bed nearest to the door. Hugh could not keep still. No sooner had he tried the bed, he wanted to inspect the rest of the room. Giles watched him with curiosity.

Hugh pointed out things to Giles, which he felt were important:

the window's paintwork was chipped and worn but the lock was shiny and new. He slid open the catch and pushed it up, but he was unable to raise it more than a few inches or so. "See, window locks hold it in place. We're shut in," he said. Hugh pressed his face to glass. In the gloom, there was not much to see, just a small garden below, a low brick wall, and then some more out-buildings.

Hugh closed the window and started to walk from bed to bed, randomly opening and closing bedside drawers. Comic books, pencils and pens, a cricket ball, an expensive-looking catapult. He pulled back the thick elastic band and released it with a loud thwack.

"Let's see it," asked Giles.

Hugh tossed it over. Giles turned it over his hands. It was cast in metal and had a depression for the thumb for a strong, steady grip. The cord was made of chunky rubber, securely attached to a leather sling. He'd always wanted one like this. Reluctantly he threw it back to Hugh. Dropping it into the drawer, Hugh turned his attention to the laundry box at the end of the nearest bed. He started to kick his heels against the wooden frame, gently at first, and then with more force. Rhythmically. Tap, tap, tap. Tap, tap, tap. He was already bored. Giles could see that.

They looked up when they heard voices growing nearby. Hugh brought his foot-tapping to an abrupt end. By the time the door swung open, he was lounging on his own bed, head propped up against a pillow. "Hello," said Hugh, brightly to the two boys who entered the form.

Douglas Rice and Declan Morris eyed Hugh and Giles warily. Red haired, freckled, furrow-browed, Douglas stood a good six inches taller than the brown-haired boy, who asked, "Are you Ashworth?"

"Who's Ashworth?" Hugh said, grinning.

"The new boy," replied Declan, blushing slightly.

"He's the other one, that one," said Douglas, pushing past Declan. "He's Burton."

"I am Burton," said Hugh. He beat his chest like Tarzan, and said it again, only louder and with a roar at the end, leaping off the bed to sit alongside Giles. Hugh bounced on it with his bottom. The bed squeaked as he moved up and down.

"Don't do that," said Douglas, irritated and cross. "It's not your bed."

"You'll get us in trouble," said Declan.

"I don't mind," replied Giles with a faint smile.

"I don't want to get anyone in trouble," said Hugh, settling back on his bed. "I hope we can all be friends." Douglas did not reply. Eventually, Hugh asked how long it was until dinner. He was beginning to feel hungry.

"It must be soon," said Giles. He was as bored as Hugh, and ravenous.

The strange quiet that had fallen on the dorm was eventually broken by the sound of heavy footsteps.

"RD," said Declan.

The boys turned as one towards the door. A thick-set man in a pale blue suit and tie breezed into the dorm. Harry Rhys-Davis was a flamboyant dresser. The duty housemaster – Mr Scott's number two – had picked the summer suit that morning in keeping with his optimism about the new term, as well as to account for the unseasonably warm weather. "Hugh. Giles." he said in a jovial tone. "Welcome, welcome."

Up close, the teacher's bulk was impossible to ignore; he looked pregnant, stomach protruding above his belt, his shirt buttons fighting a losing battle to hold back his pink flesh. He seemed friendly in a cartoonish way.

Giles vividly recalled the school tour Mr Rhys-Davis had given after he had sat the exam. His mother and father had fallen out over something and the atmosphere had been particularly frosty. Giles had felt embarrassed throughout.

"Tomorrow Hepbridge will help you navigate your way around the school, but now it's time for supper, and then you can meet the rest of the dorm before lights out," he said, leading the way to dinner. Walking unhurriedly, he pointed out this and that to the two new boys: dorms on one side, the house bathroom, two more dormitories down another corridor. His bedroom-cum-study was always open to them for a chat, he said. It was where he worked and slept. Giles couldn't imagine anything worse.

They took the fire exit to the ground floor, passing through the reception area and various ground floor classrooms before making their way out into the playground. Giles had a dim recollection of the playground being used as a car park on exam day. "Quite right, well remembered," said Mr Rhys-Davis, pointing to where Giles would have sat the entrance exam. During term time it was where he taught geography and history. A light was on inside, a cleaner at work polishing the wooden desks. The blackboard was still wet in patches. "Over there is the new teaching block," he asked with a foppish wave. "Four new classrooms and the gym. Do you like PE?"

The boys looked at each other quizzically. "I like swimming, sir," replied Hugh after a pause.

"We have a lot of boarders in the swimming club," said Mr Rhys-Davis, seeming pleased.

"What about you, Ashworth?

Giles shrugged, "I suppose."

"Put your names down on the list outside my room and you can join the lads for an afterschool swim," he said, as they crossed the playground towards the dining hall. "You can play ball sports over there," he added, gesturing to the far side of the playground where faint yellow paint marked out a basketball court. A mesh net drooped from a solitary rusted hoop.

"What's over there, sir?" asked Hugh, pointing to the shady area that lay at the far end of the playground.

Rhys-Davis squinted into the distance. "Oh that," he said, with a disdainful flick of the wrist. "That awful concrete mess is for skateboarding. Some new kind of American fad. I hope you don't go in for any of that nonsense," he said, somewhat stiffly.

Giles and Hugh looked at each other for the answer. Giles had a skateboard at home in The Close, but he decided to say nothing about it.

The entrance to the dinner hall was off to one side, the frosted double glass door set inside a small, covered walkway. They could hear the hum of chatter from inside. As they entered, the room quietened down. A row of five or six younger boys paused momentarily between mouthfuls, staring at the newcomers with curiosity, resuming when Mr Rhys-Davis had walked on.

In the hall, long low tables had been arranged in vertical lines, eight deep, with benches on either side, so that boys faced each other. At one end, on raised dais, was a seating area reserved for the teaching staff. The school's Coat of Arms and the motto Spes et Virtus – hope and courage – were proudly displayed on the wall behind. A solitary bell sat on a small table at the foot of the steps to the platform.

Giles and Hugh traipsed behind Mr Rhys-Davis as he picked his way through boys returning from the kitchen with trays of steaming food. A few continued to gaze at them with interest; Giles feigned disinterest. One or two caught Hugh's eyes – when a boy stared at him, he found it hard not to stare back – it had gotten him into a few scrapes in the past.

Three teachers were eating together on the raised platform. They broke off their conversation as Harry approached. The nearest man turned his chair and bent forward, so they could speak privately. The boys kept their distance. Giles was starving; he could hardly keep his eyes off the open kitchen where the cooks were serving up the evening's meal.

"They are talking about us," said Hugh. "He's the head." Anthony smiled at the boys.

"He gives me the creeps," whispered Giles.

Hugh giggled and looked away to where the food queue was

forming. "Maybe we should join before there's nothing left?"

"You go first," suggested Giles.

As the dinner line inched forward, the boys forgot about the teachers. Giles passed a tray to Hugh and grabbed some cutlery. When it came to their turn, there was a choice of fish cakes or beef stew, the chicken had run out. Giles gawped at the chafing dishes. The chef told him he didn't have all night, "What's it to be, sonny?" he said. He was a fat man with an outdoorsy complexion, his left cheek pock-marked with scars from acne in his youth.

"The stew, please." Giles liked the look of the gravy sauce.

The chef dolloped it on his plate and ladled on potatoes and peas. He eyeballed Hugh, looking impatient. Hugh asked for the same as Giles.

"Give them some pudding while you're at it," shouted a middle-aged woman from across the kitchen. Her chef's whites were splattered with fresh tomato stains, which looked like blood. The chef and the woman started bickering. Hugh continued to hold his plate out until they had finished.

"Here," said the chef and served him fishcakes. Hugh didn't have the nerve to say anything, and they looked all right, if a little dry. "Do you want pud?" asked the chef.

Hugh called Giles back. The chef gave them a large portion each. "Enjoy!" he exclaimed theatrically.

The dinner hall had thinned out. The boys took an empty bench and started to eat. Hugh prodded the fishcake.

"Don't you like it?" asked Giles, tucking in.

"It's ok, I guess," Hugh replied, nibbling away. He shuffled his food around the plate, while Giles licked his clean before downing a glass of water. Hugh fired a few questions at Giles about what he thought of things so far, which were met with brief 'yes' and 'no' answers.

"You don't have much to say do you," noted Hugh. "Are you homesick already?" Giles shrugged. He hadn't given home a single thought.

Hugh continued to chew a bit of the fishcake, waiting for Giles to say something. He decided he didn't like it after all and scooped it out of his mouth and placed it under the plate. Hugh wished that he had summoned up the courage to correct the chef's mistake.

"Seeing as they have thrown us together, why don't we get to know each other properly. You tell me something about you, and I'll tell you something about me." His mother called it an icebreaker. She used it all the time. Hugh had seen her put it to the test when he had accompanied her on visits to the Mess to meet the wives and girlfriends of soldiers who had just joined his father's regiment.

"Ok, but only if you go first," said Giles. It wasn't such a bad idea, but he hated these things. He hoped Hugh would take his time. Fortunately, Giles had met the right boy; Hugh could barely contain his enthusiasm. West Berlin. Hong Kong. Belfast. Hugh made each place sound exciting and glamorous. Giles had never lived anywhere other than The Close. Hugh scarcely paused for breath for five minutes; he hadn't even got to the pudding by the time that Giles had eaten his. "Do you want that?" asked Giles, eying up Hugh's dessert.

"Go ahead and help yourself," said Hugh, pushing the plate across the table.

"Where's Belfast?" asked Giles, tucking in.

Hugh looked taken aback. "I thought everyone knew Belfast," he said. Giles shook his head. Hugh leaned across the table. "It's where the IRA are from," he said, quietly. Giles shrugged again. "Don't you listen to the news, or watch TV? They talk about them all the time. Blowing up cars and shooting people." Giles shook his head, shovelling the last of the dessert into his mouth.

"They blew up Harrow, the most famous school in the country. I'm going there when I'm older," he said, somewhat pompously. "We all go to Harrow in my family. It's a tradition. But I don't want to," he said, quickly. "I ran away, you know, from my old school. Not once, mind you, but twice!" he said, with a proud look on his face.

At that piece of news, Giles stopped eating. "Why?" he asked, mystified.

"Just because," said Hugh in a matter-of-fact tone. "I bet you want to know how I escaped?" he asked. However, before he had the chance to explain, Anthony Richardson appeared by the table as though he had materialised out of thin air.

"Boys, have you had enough to eat?" he asked, looming over the table. The boys stared up at him. "Mr Rhys-Davis was filling me in on how you're getting on. All quite well, I gather?"

The boys nodded. "Yes, sir," said Giles.

"And you, Mr Burton?"

"I think so, sir."

"You think so," said Anthony Richardson, amused. "You are not sure?"

"I mean yes, sir. I haven't had much time to get to get to know the place," he replied, scratching his head. "We were late to school."

"Well, we don't want to make a habit of that, do we?" asked the headmaster after a pause, a smile still playing on his lips.

"No, sir," said Hugh.

"Now, let's have those plates cleared away," said Mr Richardson, pointing towards the kitchen, "and then get yourselves into the house and up to your dorm to wash and change for lights out."

The boys swung their legs out from the bench and picked up their trays. Giles walked quickly towards the kitchen. Mr Richardson stepped in front of Hugh. "Burton" he said, placing his hands on the boy's tray, gentle pressure, sufficient for Hugh to come to a halt. "Your father has asked me to keep an eye on you." Hugh looked down and away. "If there's anything you are not sure about… anything that worries you…" There was a searching look on the headmaster's face. "My door is always open. Always."

Hugh glanced around, wondering if anyone was listening in, but only Giles seemed to notice, watching and waiting by the open kitchen. "Yes, sir," Hugh replied, quietly, trying to hold the headmaster's gaze, before finally blinking away.

Mr Richardson smiled. "Good. As long as we understand one and other."

"What did he want?" asked Giles when they were alone, walking back to the dorm.

Hugh shrugged a Giles-like shrug. "It doesn't matter. Come on, let's race each other back to the dorm."

The boys sprinted upstairs, changed into pyjamas, and trooped to the bathroom. The bathroom was busy; boys coming in and out, towels and toothbrushes in hand looking for a spare basin.

"No jostling, now. Wait your turn," said Mr Rhys-Davis.

Giles ran his fingers along the tubs while waiting for a basin to become available. The tubs were deep and wide, easily big enough to fit in two boys at a time. They were fixed to the floor by massive metal bolts. When Giles had been on a ferry to The Isle of Wight, tables in the dining room had been anchored down in the same way.

Teeth brushed, faces washed, and hair combed, the boys padded back in their slippers to the bedroom. Fifteen minutes to lights out. Dorm six – the youngest boys, the seven-year-olds – was already set. Along with Giles and Hugh, they were all new to the school. Mr Rhys-Davis turned off the main light in the corridor outside their room and closed them in for the night.

"How are you boys?" asked Linda Wallace, poking her head into dorm three. Declan and Varun Singh, a quiet, studious boy, were under their bed covers, reading. She cast her eyes around the room. "Pick up your tie," she told Steven Walker. "And you, Douglas, put those smelly shoes away, and all of you get yourselves into bed," she stated to the boys, in general.

Giles looked at his watch. Five past eight. He thought about what he would usually be doing: watching TV, assuming there was a programme on the box he was permitted to watch. Otherwise, he might have been upstairs in his bedroom building a model plane to add to his collection. In his trunk, he had three new Airfix kits, going away presents from his mother.

Hugh was still pacing about, the only one who had not taken his place in bed. "What are you reading?" he asked Varun. The boy raised the book above the blanket and flashed the cover. "What's it about?" Hugh asked, perching himself on the metal frame at the end of Varun's bed. Varun drew up his feet under the blanket.

"War and stuff, I suppose." Varun spoke with a breathless voice. He sounded like an old man.

"Yeah? Is it any good?" Hugh slid off the frame and onto the mattress to take a closer look.

"I'd rather you got off my bed," uttered Varun, closing the book and sitting up. "I know you are new and all that…"

Hugh got off the bed and straddled the frame of Giles' bed instead.

"Leave off Burton and get into bed. You seem hell bent on getting us into trouble," said Douglas, irritably. The boys looked from Hugh to Douglas. "Well, he does, doesn't he?" said Douglas, glaring at Declan for confirmation. The dark-haired boy nodded. Douglas looked pleased with himself. Hugh acted as though he had not heard. "So, what are you waiting for?"

said Douglas, seemingly poised to get out of his bed and confront Hugh. "Maybe you want RD to take you outside for a good slippering?"

Declan giggled. "Burton wants a good smack," he said, clapping his hands together. Walker and Singh laughed. Hugh simply chose to smirk in reply. "Have you got nothing to say?" said Douglas, angrily. The room had fallen quiet. "What about you?" he said, directing his question to Giles. "What do you have to say about your new friend?"

Giles glanced from face to face, his gaze eventually settling on Douglas. "Hugh can do what he likes," he replied, staring straight through Douglas.

"What's that supposed to mean?" asked Douglas, tetchily.

"Just that," replied Giles, casually, offering nothing more. Hugh smiled at Giles.

Douglas grunted, looking for someone else to pick on, or something else to do. "Let me look at the book?" he said to Singh. Varun hesitated. Douglas jutted out his chin, daring the boy to refuse his demand. The boy threw it over. Grabbing it with both hands, Douglas started pawing at the pages furiously. Varun flinched at the sound of the pages being roughly handled and turned away, pulling up the blanket to his chin before switching off his bedside light.

"I'm tired as well," said Hugh. He slid off Giles' bed and got into his own. "'Night."

"Yeah, 'night," said Giles. However, Giles did not feel sleepy. He tried a book, but it only made him feel more awake, so instead began to count the cracks on the walls, and the weird blotches on the ceiling. They looked like clouds. He settled on those. He got to thirty and then lost count.

"Lights out in five," said Mr Rhys-Davies, from somewhere along the corridor.

Giles huffed and began a recount. The mattress was bowed in the middle and every time he shifted position to get comfortable, the old metal bed squeaked. Douglas tutted. Giles looked across to see if it was aimed at him. However, Douglas appeared to be immersed in Varun's book. Giles strained his eyes to spy the cover. A Tommy was striding forward with bayonet in hand, advancing on a German soldier who lay prone on the muddy ground. In the night sky, rockets flew in red and yellow. Night Attack! screamed the headline. Giles wondered whether Varun had more comics like it.

"Lights out, now," said Mr Rhys-Davis, approaching the dorm. Douglas tossed the comic to one side and rolled over, switching off his lamp in one well-practiced manoeuvre.

"Ashworth, lights out," repeated the deputy housemaster, standing at the doorway. Giles reached out and thumbed the switch. As he did so, Mr Rhys-Davis killed the overhead light, plunging the dormitory into darkness.

When Giles awoke the room was pitch black. He had always loved the silence of the night ever since he could remember. The luminous hands of his watch read three am. From the next bed he heard soft breathing.

Slowly his eyes grew accustomed to the dark. Giles crept out of bed and used his feet to find his slippers. He tiptoed across the room towards Douglas. The boy lay on his back, one arm thrown across his face, his nose nuzzled in the crook of his elbow. Giles ducked down next to his bed and quietly eased open the top drawer of his bedside table, carefully feeling around until his fingers closed around the catapult's cold, metal shaft.

Giles gently closed the drawer. Douglas mumbled in his sleep and threw back his arm. For a moment, Giles thought the boy was waking. Instead, Douglas rolled over on his side and carried on sleeping, his face turned aide. Giles paused before he crept away to where the other boy lay, a featureless shape beneath the covers.

Crouching down at the foot of Declan's bed, he carefully lifted the blanket so he could gather up the bottom sheet. He carefully untucked it, peeling back the elasticated corner. With his free hand he pushed the catapult in between the fold of the sheet and the mattress.

Declan sighed in his sleep and twitched beneath the covers. Giles kept perfectly still, until he was free to remove his hand from the bedding. Giles glanced around, taking nothing for granted as he smoothed down the sheet and blanket. Silently, he returned to his own bed, inching his body back under the covers. He smiled to himself. The catapult would make a handsome addition to the collection of special things he kept in his trunk.

3 – NEW BOYS

For Linda the first few weeks of a new term were always the hardest. Long and draining days. The boys vying for her attention. The older ones familiar and knowing; the younger ones missing their families and wanting her to be their mother.

Can it be two years already? She laid her hands on her belly where her baby should have been. When she miscarried, her mother said it was for the best. The shame of it, a single mother at your age. Rushing to grow up. Falling into bed with the first man who treats you nice. Trying to speed through life without realising that the best days are behind you before you know it. And then he sped out of her life; he felt trapped. Which only went to prove her mother was right.

However, Linda did not really care that they were no longer together, although she thought about him from time to time, and wondered what he was doing now, and where he lived and if he was with another woman, and … No, she decided she would not let herself think like that. She had wanted a child and now, she had fifty to take care of. But still, none to truly call her own. Is that why she stayed at the school when she could have left last summer? She looked at herself in the mirror as though it might provide an answer, but the woman gazing back with clear blue eyes had none to give. Linda brushed her hair with a soft brush; her mother's colour: hazelnut with a hint of sunlight, but the style was all her own. She had never liked long hair, and the new cut was boyish and practical. Linda leaned into the mirror, pursing her lips together to apply a natural lipstick. She was blessed with a full and sensual mouth. Wasted on these boys, she thought.

After she had finished applying her make-up, she threw open casement window to drink in the view: the ashes and the oaks proudly framing the playing fields, the neat hedges cut into the top field and beyond the horizon, the dense woodlands. They scared her a little; she blamed the boys and their silly stories about the weirdo in the woods who they said lurked there. Nonetheless, they were beautiful woods all the same. In the quiet of the morning, the scene felt centuries old, and she was proud to be part of it. Before she had joined the school, she had been plain Linda Wallace, no one special. Whereas here, she was matron: a woman re-born.

Quiet never lasted long at the school, particularly first thing in the morning. Before seven am, the boarding house would start to come alive. Harry would be shaking the boys out of their beds and packing them off to breakfast. The rumble of feet from the floor below was a signal that she should join them.

Linda danced down the rickety stairs to the main dormitory floor, her heels tip-tapping on the wooden floor, telegraphing her arrival. With every step, she shed Linda and transformed into matron. It was as effortless as it was artless.

She moved quickly from room to room. The doors to dorms four and five were thrown open wide, the occupants had already departed for whatever concoction the kitchen was serving up for breakfast. Linda picked up a pair of discarded pyjamas and tossed them on to the nearest bed. There was no need to tackle the bedcovers and blankets; the boys had to make up their own rooms and pass her inspection before the start of school.

Walking through the bathroom she said good morning to the outside staff who were cleaning up after the boys, wiping down the basins and polishing the taps and mirrors. Passing through, she paused at the top of the stairs. The door to Harry's room was ajar. She knocked, calling out his name, half-expecting to find him recuperating after shooing the boys to breakfast. However, his room was empty and disgracefully untidy. From the ground floor she could already hear the rise of chatter and footsteps hurrying; day boys arriving for school. Linda retreated from the noise and walked briskly to the other end of the house, towards dorms three, two and one. She nosed into the first two, surveying the unmade beds, general mess and detritus, scarcely breaking stride. She did not want anything to stand in the way of getting to dorm one. It was her favourite dorm, where the youngest boys slept. They were the boys who needed her kindness the most. The beds had a just-made look about them. Wait until they have been here for a couple of weeks, she thought. Then they won't care about making a good impression.

A boy had left his teddy bear on the bed. She picked it up. The eyes were made of beads, blank and sightless. Linda tucked it under the covers, so its head rested on the pillow. The imprint of the boy's head was still visible. Without thinking, she leaned forward and pressed her face into the fabric. The smell was innocent and inviting. She wondered whose bed this was. Only five came into the dorm this year. Watson? She should know, but she couldn't remember. She would have to ask Harry, as he oversaw lights out.

By the time she had finished inspecting the dorms a few boys were already returning to make up their rooms and collect their books for school. She ruffled a few passing heads and told them to behave. From somewhere, out of sight, she could hear boys shouting. They sounded happy. She never had to worry about the loud ones. It was the quiet boys she had to keep an eye on. The boys who did not say much unless you asked and avoided meeting her eyes. There was something particularly cruel and British about sending boys away to board when they were so young. She wasn't supposed to think like that, and certainly never voice that, although she had said these things to Harry. How do you prepare them for it? What do you tell them? She would never do the same thing if she had a child. Not for all the money in the world.

The whole house now seemed to be on the move: boys rushed up the stairs in packs, pushing and shouting. She told them to slow down, as they thundered by. "Yes matron," chimed the older ones, laughing.

"You tell them," said a voice from dorm four.

"There you are," she said.

Harry emerged from the room, hands behind his back, wearing a satisfied expression on his face. Evidently, he was pleased with the way the boys had tidied up. They inspected the dorms together.

"Anthony's on edge," he said, as they completed the tour of the first floor.

"Perhaps he's had another difficult call with the trustees," she replied. In the last twelve months, things had been strained between the headmaster and the finance director. Anthony had briefed them at the staff meeting to expect a challenging year, hinting that there would be no pay rise on the horizon.

Harry hurried them out of the boarding house to assembly. Their colleagues were duly gathered for Anthony's inaugural speech of the term. A group of year fives stood by, waiting to bring the boys to the hall from their classrooms. Anthony caught Linda's eye. She smiled and walked over.

"Good morning, Linda, how are you this bright morning?" he asked.

"A little tired, but the new boys seem to be settling in and that's what matters."

"Good, good," he said, absently, with a far-away look in his eyes.

Linda touched his arm. "Are you ok, Anthony?" she asked.

"Sorry, I was miles away, thinking about the repair bills," he said, gesturing towards the general state of the playground. A flicker of concern briefly passed across his face. "Anyway, yes, I am fine. How was your summer? I don't feel like I have seen you since term started," he said, pointedly.

Linda looked down at the asphalt playground. There wasn't a uniform surface anywhere; it was a hotchpotch of repairs, a proverbial patchwork. No wonder Anthony was worried about upkeep. At that moment, she was standing on what looked like polished glass, which looked like it could crack open at any moment.

"Did you think of the place, or me, while you were galivanting around Italy?" he asked, awkwardly.

Linda felt her cheeks start to blush. Anthony touched her arm lightly. When she looked up, he was gazing at her. He had a forlorn look about him. She had hoped that the summer break had put some distance between what had gone on between them at the end of term summer party. It was after all, nothing more than a drunken fling. These things happened all the time. However, she was worried that he thought it might be something more.

"I thought of you all every second," she replied, with a forced laugh. "You know me, I live for all you boys!" she added, hoping it would deflect his question.

"I just thought…" he said, taking her hand.

"What?" she said, becoming defensive.

"Well, you know, after a long summer away from school, there's plenty of time for reflection," he said, looking embarrassed. "Things get put into perspective," he added, sounding strained.

Linda felt her muscles tighten and a rash start to spread from her chest to her neck. "If I'm honest, I was too busy enjoying the cheap wine to think about things," she said. The rash had reached full bloom. She touched her skin, wishing she could magic it away. "I really had a lovely summer break in Italy," she added, drawing in a deep breath. "I'll bring a few snaps along to the next House meeting, if you care to see them?"

"That would be nice," he replied, after a pregnant pause. "I'd imagine the staff would be pleased to see them. Harry has a soft spot for Italy, doesn't he?" he said. She could hear in his voice that he was keen to move the conversation on to a neutral topic. She felt relieved.

"I'll go and join the others if you don't mind," said Linda.

"As you wish or we could go together?" he said, offering her his arm. "Put on a united front and all that. Show the boys we mean business." It was such a ridiculous thing to say, yet so typical of Anthony. Linda folded her arm into his, wondering what on earth Harry would think. He despised Anthony and saw her as his only ally.

"Year five boys collect your charges!" bellowed Anthony, as they strode towards the assembly hall. The teaching staff broke off from their conversations and dutifully followed them into the building. Linda took a spare chair in the second row, while Anthony climbed to the podium. The boys continued to file in, noisily at first, and then they became quiet, stilled by the scowls of their form tutors.

Linda watched Anthony, as he surveyed the scene from the podium. This is what he *lives* for she thought, glancing around at the obedient, expectant faces. Anthony waited, luxuriating in the moment before finally commanding the body of the school to join in The Lord's Prayer.

Linda bent her head and closed her eyes.

She slowly recited the first sentence of the prayer: "Our Father, who art in heaven, hallowed be thy name; thy kingdom come; thy will be done; on earth as it is in heaven."

She let the prayer take hold, repeating the words in a loud, clear voice. "Give us this day our daily bread. And forgive us our trespasses, as we forgive those who trespass against us. And lead us not into temptation; but deliver us from evil."

She thought about Tuscany, Rome, the journey through the Mezzogiorno, to Sicily. Milazzo. "For thine is the kingdom, the power and the glory, for ever and ever." She intoned the words, her fingers knotted together around her womb, the veins on her hands bulging and blue. Her hands shook; Lord hear me now. She dabbed her eyes being careful not to smudge her eyeliner and wiped her emotions away.

Assembly finished at ten and the pupils remained seated until their form teachers were ready to escort them to their classrooms. The rest of their morning was given over to tedium: completing timetables, writing the lessons down from the blackboard, filling in the blank pages of copy books, trying not to make mistakes but making mistakes; rubbing out pencilled in words – music, games, English, etc. – and starting again. Then they were herded to lunch and then to the same stuffy classrooms. The afternoon drifted slowly by until it was time for the day boys to go home. It was a release for the boarders to go to their dorms and strip off their uniforms and get dressed into casual clothes.

Mr Scott gathered the new boys in the lobby: Giles and Hugh from dorm three, and the seven-year-olds from dorm one. He had arranged for their pilots to give them an extensive tour of the grounds. The weather was warm outside. Hepbridge looked nervous, uncomfortable to have been given the responsibility to pilot Giles and Hugh. The housemaster instructed them to stay out of the woods. The boys broke into a run as soon as he was out of sight.

The housemaster decided to join Harry in the staff room. Harry was half-asleep on the couch in the sun. David poured himself a tea and sat facing the playing fields. The afternoon sun cast long shadows over the cricket nets.

"What's the nickname the boys gave to Hepbridge?" David asked, sipping his tea. Harry appeared not to hear. David nudged him awake.

"Sweaty Heppy," he replied drowsily.

David laughed and said it was apt. "I gave him the job of showing Burton's boy and Ashworth around the school and the sweat literally started popping out of every pore." It was like he was some sort of anxiety attack. Harry felt sorry for Hepbridge. David pulled a face. "He's ten years old for goodness's sake," said David, setting down the teacup. His voice sounded particularly hoarse. "Think what you were like at that age."

Harry could remember exactly. He had been bullied rotten and it was not something that he cared to share. "Well, you know what the Jesuits would say?" he said changing the subject.

"Give me a child until he is seven and I will give you the man, or something along those lines," he said, in a slightly derisive tone.

"I take it you don't think there's much truth in that?"

David tutted. "A load of clap trap if you ask me," he said dismissively.

"Well, you can judge for yourself when there's a reunion in twenty years," replied Harry.

"Fat chance," said David. "I'll be happily retired."

"Claire would want to come," said Harry, easing himself off the couch to have some tea.

"Yes, probably," David replied. His wife was a stickler for things like that. If he was honest with himself, he knew that he would need little persuading. Curiosity would get the better of him. He'd relish the chance to see what had become of the boys.

"Have you seen the state of the crockery?" said Harry holding up a chipped cup.

By way of an answer, David swept his arm theatrically around the room, gesturing from the frayed curtains to the damaged bookshelves and the armchairs with their broken spines. "The whole place needs investment. God knows when the Trust last spent a penny on refurbishments."

"Well, where do you think all the money goes then?" asked Harry, who had settled into a window seat to catch the sun.

"Are you asking me what I think or what I *know*?" he replied.

"What you know, of course," said Harry, chuckling.

"The Trust is knee deep in debt. It's been like that for as long as I can remember, and I have been here for eight… no, nine years," continued David. He looked at Harry quizzically. "When did you come here, 1970?"

"1971," corrected Harry.

"Right, yes. Well, you must have noticed the changes then?" he replied, warming to the subject. Harry shrugged. "The collapse in boarder numbers, and our increasing reliance on people like the Ashworths," he said sniffily.

Harry understood. "They are the ones who can afford it I

suppose. Did you see the car he was driving?"

David snorted.

"Not any old Capri. Brand spanking new," said Harry. David was a snob. Harry thought the car was rather wonderful

"Well, it was a step up on what Burton was driving," muttered David. The old banger looked fit for the scrapheap. "You'll have to keep Hugh Burton on a short leash. Anthony asked me, so I am telling you," said David.

"You're worried that he will do another runner?"

"His father is a big cheese, despite the car he drives," replied David. "Hopefully the lad's put all that silliness behind him, but nothing like that can happen under *your* watch."

"*Our* watch, surely?" replied Harry, arms folded, with an air of defiance.

David waggled his finger in the air. "No, no, Harry. As a dorm three boy he is quite literally under your wing," said David. "I once slept where you now sleep, a wall apart from the little buggers. But now, I sleep in the cottage in the grounds. That's the way it works. Your time will come if you play your cards right," he said, in a patronising tone.

Talk about ramming the point home thought Harry. "Yes, of course," he replied, clearing his throat. "And what about Giles Ashworth? I got the impression from Anthony that he'd left his last school under something of a cloud?"

The boy had sailed through the exam said David. He'd sat in on that examination – and even though he had difficulty hearing some of the questions, something to do with having scar tissue on his eardrums said the dippy, dreamy mother – Giles had the making of a very good scholar. "And by Christ, we need more of them to compensate for some of the thickies we have from the military families," he said, laughing out loud.

"Ha, ha, very good," said Harry, appreciating David's wit. "But didn't Anthony raise a problem in the boy's background?"

David shrugged. Anthony had conducted the assessment interview and managed the application. In passing, he had mentioned that the headmistress of his junior school had made an oblique reference to his struggles in large friendship groups. "I got the impression that the boy can be a bit intense at times," said David.

"There's nothing like a boarding house to sort a boy out," said Harry.

"Indeed, kill or cure!" he said. The problem was Harry's. David poured himself another cup of tea and settled back into the easy chair and thought about his own children and what his wife Claire would be rustling up for dinner.

* * *

After the boys had sprinted away from the school they ran on until their hearts felt ready to burst. Hepbridge was dripping with perspiration. Giles put his hands on his hips, panting like a dog. Hugh plonked himself down on the grass, exhausted. Pausing until they had their breath back, Hugh asked, "Well, what now?"

Hepbridge pointed to the far field and the line of hedges.

"We're going over there." He had something important to show them.

"Not so fast though this time," said Hugh. Giles hauled him up and they set off at an easier pace.

The boys reached the hedgerow after what felt like an eternity, at least to Hugh. Hepbridge promised it would be worth it. They cut through a gap in the hedge and walked on for a couple of minutes until Hepbridge found the raised mound. It rose no more than a metre above the earth and only the entrance was visible, the concrete roof and structure long since covered over by grass. There were stone steps down to the entrance, the brickwork mossy but firm underfoot. "I bet you've no idea what this place is," said Hepbridge.

The three boys entered single file through a narrow doorway where once a reinforced steel door would have swung. Inside it was surprisingly cool and dark. Hepbridge asked them to close their eyes and count to ten, so that when they opened them again, they would find it easier to see in the dark. "It's an air raid shelter," said Giles. "No big deal." The pilot looked disappointed.

"It's cool," said Hugh, which instantly brightened Heppy's mood. Although Hugh had been inside lots of military buildings with his father, he had never been inside a real bunker. "How many people was it supposed to take?" he asked, looking around, staring into the inky depths. The air raid shelter was quite narrow, about the width of a goal post but lower in height. They could reach up and touch the ceiling. It was smooth and cold.

"It was built in the Blitz to shelter the boarding house. There were fewer boys at the school then because of the war," said Hepbridge, standing to one side so Hugh and Giles could inspect the space.

"It's a shame we don't have a torch," said Giles.

"We can still explore," said Hugh, starting to walk into the shelter.

"I don't think you should. No one is supposed to come here. It's out of bounds," declared the pilot.

"You're the one who brought us here. What was the point of that unless we could look around?" said Giles sniffily, following Hugh into the gloom. Despite his initial misgivings, he had to admit that the shelter was quite intriguing. It would make a great den. He touched the walls, tracing his hand along one side of the shelter. "It's strange being down here," he said, stepping further in. "How far does it actually go?"

"I don't know," said Hepbridge from the doorway. "This is as far as I ever go."

"Really? You are such a chicken," said Giles, making a clucking sound.

"I'm not coming," stated Hepbridge, backing away, as though being drawn to the light outside. "You go. I'll keep a watch in case anyone comes looking."

Hugh and Giles watched him go. "Well?" said Hugh. Giles shrugged. "Let's keep to one side, it'll be easier to trace our steps," said Hugh. He felt a little afraid now, but he was determined to go on. "You can put your hand on my shoulder if you want."

"Ok," said Giles without hesitation.

They said nothing as they edged their way along. Once they had grown used to the darkness, they lost their fear. Giles slipped his hand away. Further inside, the shelter widened out. "Hey, look at this," said Hugh. He had found a desk and chair. They looked like the ones from school. Giles opened the lid. Inside there were matches and cigarettes, and old newspapers. Giles lit the match. It flared and died. He struck another. This time it caught. Giles held the match for as long as he could, turning it this way and that to inspect the shelter before the stick burned down.

Hugh had an idea. "Let's use a newspaper to light our way," he said. Rolling one up, he held it out for Giles to light. Giles struck a fresh match and put it to the paper, which fizzed and crackled as the flame started to take. Hugh whistled at their success. "Quick, let's hurry further in while we can," said Hugh.

The paper was becoming alive with the flicker of small flames and starting to give off smoke. Hugh moved forward, nimbly stepping around some large boxes stacked further along the wall. They estimated that they had ventured some forty or fifty feet from the entrance into the shelter's depths. "Look at this," he called out.

Holding the torch aloft, being careful not to let the flames lick the ceiling, they could see that there was a door set into the wall. With the paper burning down, it was becoming harder to breathe in the confined space. "We'll have to go and come back another time," said Giles.

"Not before we see what's behind the door," said Hugh, trying the handle. He gave it one go after another, but it wouldn't budge.

"Let me try," said Giles, pushing Hugh to one side so he could take a crack at it. He twisted the old metal handle this way and that, but it remained steadfastly shut.

Suddenly Hugh yelped in pain, as the taper burned his fingers. He dropped it the ground, whereupon it flared brightly.

"Watch out," cried Giles, as the remnants of the taper caught on some debris. To their horror, a small fire began to take hold.

"Help"!" cried Hugh, panicking, stumbling backwards.

Giles glanced around and grabbed the nearest thing he could find, a heavy blanket. Frantically, he began to beat down on the fire. until the flames had been extinguished. Hugh coughed through the acrid smoke. "Come on," he said, grabbing Hugh by the hand and dragging him towards the entrance. Hugh retched as they darted through the shelter and up the mossy stairs. Coughing and wheezing, the boys drank in the fresh air.

"Did you definitely put out the fire?" wheezed Hugh. His face was blackened by the smoke.

"Yeah, no thanks to you," replied Giles angrily.

"I didn't mean to drop it. How was I to know what would happen?" said Hugh, gobbing up a huge ball of spit. He spat on the grass and wiped his hand across his mouth before launching into a coughing fit. "I think we should come back again and see what's in that locked room," he said, after he'd finished. "Who knows what's there."

"It's probably just a locked door to a boring room," said Giles, rubbing the soot from his eyes.

"But aren't you curious?" asked Hugh, sitting up.

"Yeah, I guess," he said, shrugging. "Where's Hepbridge?" he asked, suddenly noticing the boy's absence. "He was supposed to be on lookout." From the shelter's grassy roof, they could see a fair way, and yet Sweaty Heppy was nowhere to be seen.

Hugh shouted out his name, a few times. "Now, we are in trouble," he said, starting to cough again.

Giles swung a foot at Hugh. "Can't you finish coughing!" he said, irately. "Get it all out, because we've got to run back now."

Coughing some more, Hugh spat theatrically into the air. "Happy now?" he asked. Giles shrugged. "Just don't run too fast," he asked.

Jumping off the roof of the shelter, they broke into a trot. Very soon, they had crashed their way through the hedge and had begun jogging towards the open playfields. However, they had not gone far before Hugh had to stop; he had a stitch travelling into his ribs. "I don't think I can go on anymore," he stated, wheezing.

They were not even running hard, thought Giles. "Breathe in slowly and press your hands against the pain," he said, looking towards the school buildings, to where the brickwork was lit up by the sun.

Hugh held his side, and the pain eased a little. "Can you see Heppy?" he asked, wiping the sweat from his eyes. His orange Adidas t-shirt was soaked through.

Giles shook his head. "We've got to keep going," he said. Soon it would be dinner time and their absence would be noticed.

"Ok," replied Hugh, bending forward to ease the stitch out. "Is there another way he could have taken? He wouldn't have gone off in the wrong direction, would he?"

Giles screwed up his face, thinking. "How do I know?" he replied. "That's such a stupid question!" he snapped.

Hugh stared disconsolately at Giles, and thought about saying something rude, but then thought better of it – it was partly down to him that they were in this mess. After taking a breather, he said he was ready to run again. Once again, they set off, half-running, half-jogging. Giles quickened the pace, figuring they could enter the school through the locker room where he reckoned there would be less chance of anyone seeing them. Hugh tried to keep up, but he kept falling back. The pain was excruciating. Giles stopped and waited for him to catch up.

"I'm sorry. It hurts," said Hugh, crouching down and holding his stomach.

They were fast running out of time, "We'll get the slipper for this," said Giles.

"I'll say it is my fault," said Hugh.

"It *is* your fault," hissed Giles. "You're the one who insisted on exploring the shelter."

Hugh sat down on the grass and turned away. Overhead a pair of swallows crisscrossed the clouds, migrating south. He watched them swoop and soar until they disappeared. "You can carry on without me. I don't care what happens to me," he said, concealing his face with his hands.

Giles felt like shaking Hugh. However, he let the feeling pass and sat down next to him. Hugh had drawn his knees up to his chest, hoping to alleviate the stitch in his side. Pushing his sweat-drenched hair away from his face, Hugh gazed towards the school, recognizing the difficulty of their position, and how he had contributed to it. "You should go," he said, giving Giles a gentle shove. "There's no sense in us both getting it in the neck.

"If I go now, do you promise to follow me in a couple of minutes when you are feeling better?" Giles asked, apprehensively.

"Yes, I promise," said Hugh.

"What do I say if someone asks where you are?"

"Make something up," Hugh replied, shoving Giles with all his might even though the stitch hurt. Hugh lay back down on the grass and stared up at Giles.

"Ok," said Giles, looking down on Hugh before stepping away. Hugh turned his head in Giles's direction, watching as he broke into a sprint, running head down and hard towards the school. With any luck, things would turn out fine.

* * *

Jeffrey Ward stood with his hands on his hips, surveying the cottage garden. He had cultivated this small patch of ground for as many years as he could remember, through two headmasters and now a third. Now he was approaching retirement, he surmised that Anthony Richardson would be his last. He wondered what would become of the garden when his time was up. If he still had Jim working alongside him, he had no doubt that it would thrive. However, Jim was long gone. If his wife was still alive, Jeffrey knew what she would say: enjoy what you've got and accept when it's time to go.

He carefully inspected the beets, cabbage, and carrots. They would be ready to harvest soon. The cauliflower, leeks, onions, and spring onions were not far behind. After the summer they had had, there was a glut of tomatoes. He picked a handful from the vine and ate them slowly, one by one, savouring their ripe flesh and sweet taste.

He was watching the sun dip behind the high wall when he first noticed the boy. The boy was dancing on his tiptoes, as though he had been caught mid-flight and was anxious to pass through unnoticed. Jeffrey took the glasses from his shirt pocket to see more clearly. It was not a boy he recognised, and by and large he knew them all by name. Presumably, he was one of the new boys.

Jeffrey smiled kindly. "I don't think we've had the pleasure of meeting," he said, walking towards the pale-faced boy. He held out his hand to the child. The boy did not immediately reply, nor did he take up the invitation to shake Jeffrey's outstretched palm. The old gardener did not take offence. He figured that the boy was shy.

"Well, you must have a name," he asked, retrieving an upturned hoe that lay flat on the gravel pathway. He distinctly remembered putting it away the night before. Lately, he had become more forgetful. "Have you seen something you are interested in?" he enquired.

The boy looked at the old man thoughtfully, weighing up his words. "I used to grow potatoes at my old school," he replied.

The old man smiled. "Not as easy to grow as people think," said Jeffrey.

"I suppose," he replied, with a small shrug.

"Well, let me show you some of the veg and fruit we're growing for the school kitchen," he said, pointing to several plots in the garden, and drawing the boy's attention to the different produce he was cultivating vegetables, which were almost ready to harvest, and ripe, late-season blackberries, all purple and swollen.

"You can have one if you'd like," he said. The boy plucked a berry from the bush. It was soft and squishy, with a delicate taste. The boy took a couple more and ate them quickly. Jeffrey smiled, drawing pleasure from the boy's hearty response. "Hey steady on, don't bolt them down or you'll be sick," said Jeffrey, as the boy continued to wolf one down after another.

"I'm sorry sir," said the boy, wiping away the berry juice from around his mouth.

"There's no need to apologise," replied Jeffrey. "And you don't have to call me sir. I'm not a teacher. I just look after the cottage garden."

The boy looked like he could eat more. Jeffrey had a mind to ask him what the taste evoked, but he knew the thought would be wasted on one so young. It was only after you had lived a full enough life that the senses had the power to overwhelm you, and take you 'back', to wherever that was.

"I must go," the child said, somewhat abruptly, the tiptoe dance starting up again.

"I thought you would want to see the potato patch," said Jeffrey, surprised.

The boy scraped his heavy dark fringe to one side. Jeffrey did not understand why boys wanted to look like girls with long hair. "I can't be late for dinner. I hope you don't mind," he said, frowning.

"Of course not, off you go," replied Jeffrey.

"Thank you," said the boy, cutting up the pathway in the direction of the main school.

"Wait, boy, what's your name?" shouted Jeffrey. He wanted the boy to know that on Tuesdays and Wednesdays there was a gardening club after school and before dinner. However, the boy was already on his way.

After the boy had left, Jeffrey Ward took a handful of blackberries and sat down on a bench. They were perfectly ripe. The last time he had produced a crop as good was, when? He struggled to recall the year. His wife had not been diagnosed. The weather had been unseasonably warm, just like this one. Jim had just started in the garden, having satisfied Anthony's predecessor that he could be trusted to contribute more to the school than menial repair work. Jim had a nose for gardening, which was ironic given his nose was broken. He'd reluctantly told Jeffrey that he had spent some time in the ring. It was something to be proud about, he had said to Jim. But Jim didn't seem to think so. Jeffrey thought he was a good gardener, hands like hams but with surprisingly nimble fingers. It had been a travesty that Anthony had let him go. Jeffrey blamed himself. He plucked one last berry from the vine, almost ink black, as much to take his mind off the thought, as to enjoy the taste. He put it on his tongue and slowly rolled it around his mouth before biting into its sweet flesh, savouring the bitter-sweet taste. He felt as carefree as a child. He hoped the boy would return to the garden; he enjoyed the company.

* * *

Matron ordered him to stop right there, dead in his tracks. "Hepbridge," she said, "What on earth have you been up to?" she demanded, astounded by the sweat pouring off him. The pilot shifted uncomfortably and stared at his shoes. "Andrew?" she asked again.

"Just playing, matron," he replied, after a pause. "Going up and down the climbing frame, playing war…"

Linda took a step backwards to inspect the boy: his hair looked glued to his head, like he had stepped out of the shower.

"Playing war? Well, you look like you played and lost Andrew," she said, smiling at her own joke. Hepbridge looked nonplussed. "You need to clean up. A bath before bed would be a good idea?"

"But matron, it's not our bath time until Tuesday," he replied, sweat continuing to drip from his brow.

"Take a look in the mirror and tell me what you see? A clean boy or a boy who needs a good scrub?" she said, good-naturedly.

"Um."

"Um, indeed"

A commotion emanating from dorms four and five momentarily diverted Linda's attention away from Hepbridge. "Clean yourself up before dinner," she commanded, striding away in the direction of the noise.

Hepbridge was in two minds about whether to make an escape or do as matron had instructed. The boy decided to do as he was told. He let the tap run until the water was good and warm, and then closed his eyes, plunging his hair under the stream, letting the water swirl around until he felt clean. Instinctively, he reached around for a towel.

"Is this what you're looking for?" said Giles, turning off the tap. Hepbridge blinked up at him from the sink. Giles held it out. Hepbridge reached out. Giles pulled it away.

"Don't be silly," said Hepbridge, still bent over the basin. He did not want to move position, afraid he would be in matron's bad books for dripping water on the lino. "Please?" he said, holding out his hand.

Giles tossed the towel at Hepbridge. The boy grasped it quickly. Perching on the edge of one of the baths, Giles watched Hepbridge dry off. "Where did you shoot off to?" he asked, eventually.

"I got bored waiting," Hepbridge replied, with a faint smirk on his face. Giles knew he could push Hepbridge to the ground if he wanted and tell matron that Hepbridge had slipped in a puddle. It would be his word against Hepbridge's.

Giles quickly glanced in the direction where he had seen matron go. The commotion was continuing; some boy or other was pleading his case with matron. Giles jumped off the bath and tugged the towel out of Hepbridge's hands.

"I told you to wait," said Giles, flicking the towel in Hepbridge's face. The boy tried to step away, but he was penned in by the sink.

Hepbridge flapped his arms to stop Giles. "No, you didn't," he said, sounding upset. "I was keeping look-out. When you didn't come out, I, I…"

"I, I, what?" said Giles in a mocking tone.

"What's going on here?" said matron, from the doorway. Linda's antennae were finely tuned to trouble. She scrutinised both their faces.

"Nothing," said Giles, after a long pause. He glowered at Hepbridge, daring the pilot to contradict him.

"And what do you have to say Mr Hepbridge?" she said, eyebrows raised for effect.

Hepbridge looked first at Giles and then at matron, "Nothing, matron," he replied, fingering his top where the damp imprint left by the towel was starting to dry off.

Matron eyed them coolly. "Wring the towel out," she said sharply to Hepbridge. Giles watched on, maintaining a straight face, while Hepbridge attempted to squeeze water from the big, white towel. When it seemed a bit drier, he held it up. It looked like a flag of surrender. "In the basket," she said.

Hepbridge trudged across the bathroom and deposited it with

the rest of the dirty laundry. The basket was already overflowing. Linda made a mental note to call down to have it emptied out. Outside the bathroom, a few boys from Hepbridge's dorm had stopped on their way down to dinner, curious about the fuss. "Can I join my dorm?" asked Hepbridge.

"First show me your hands," she said. Hepbridge turned over his palms, holding them out for inspection. Satisfied they were clean, she said, "You're free to go."

"Thank you," he said, throwing a fierce look at Giles.

Hepbridge ducked out of the bathroom, his shoes clattering on the wooden stairs as he rushed to catch up with his dorm. "See you, Hepbridge," said Giles, smirking triumphantly.

Linda caught the smirk. "Weren't you and Burton with Hepbridge earlier?" she asked.

Giles paused before replying, playing with the scar above his top lip. "Yes, matron. Why do you ask?"

"I'm asking the questions" she replied, stiffly.

"Mr Scott sent us on a tour. We went for a walk over the fields," he said.

"I see," she said, instinctively feeling the boy was not telling her everything. "And where is Burton?"

Giles shrugged. "I think Hepbridge said something that upset him. He stormed off."

Linda suddenly felt alarmed. "In what way, where?"

Giles stopped fiddling with his scar and scratched his head. "I don't know," he said, finally.

"You must have some idea?" she asked, urgently.

Giles pretended to think hard, reading the agitation on her face. "Where were we?" he asked rhetorically. He donned a furrowed expression and scratched his head, like Columbo investigating a crime. Linda looked ready to explode. Giles wanted to laugh. "I don't know the school yet," he said, doing his best to sound apologetic. "On the main field," he unanswered, unhelpfully.

"The top field? Are you sure?" asked Linda.

Giles shrugged. "I think so," he replied slowly, "but then again, I might be mistaken. It's hard to tell, everything looks so much the same."

* * *

A rumour spread quickly that Hugh Burton was making a home run, and that he had been nabbed by matron. That quickly paled into insignificance among the boys: the first fight of the new term had erupted between the new boy Ashworth and Sweaty Heppy. Fight, fight, fight. Mr Rhys-Davis had coming running and pulled them apart. Now the dormitories were quiet after lights out, except for a few sniffles and coughs. Harry patrolled the corridors, torch in hand, switching off the dorm lights one by one, until it was time for him to retire to his room.

After Mr Rhys-Davis had pootled off, Hugh snuck out from the bed covers and plonked himself on the floor next to Giles, and gently prodded him. "Are you awake?" he asked, prodding him again. Giles shifted under the covers. "What happened with

Sweaty?" he whispered. Someone made a shushing sound. Hugh asked Giles again.

"Be quiet, will you!" exclaimed the voice in the dark. Douglas Rice.

Giles rolled over towards Hugh and inched his face out from below the covers. In the darkness, his face looked small and pale. Above his eye, he had a small bruise. Giles opened the bedclothes so Hugh could slip inside. Hugh climbed in. "Did Hepbridge do that?" asked Hugh.

Giles nodded. "It doesn't hurt," he said. Hugh touched the bruise; it was about the size of a five pence coin. Giles winced.

"Was it my fault?" asked Hugh. Giles shook his head.

Hugh had so many questions he wanted to ask, but he was scared about getting into yet more trouble by talking after lights out. He pressed his face up close to Giles and whispered in his ear, "I'm sorry about today."

"Did you want to run away like everyone's saying?" asked Giles.

"No, never. I was coming back to school like we agreed, but then I got spotted and nabbed by matron. She assumed I was doing a bunk," he whispered. The thought of running away hadn't crossed his mind.

Giles reached out, searching for Hugh's hand to hold. "I could imagine running away," he said. Earlier in the garden, when he had met the old man, Giles had thought about filling his pockets with fruit to keep him going. He'd hitch a lift like he had seen on TV. Instead of going straight home to The Close, he'd go to one of his dens and hide out. But even as he was enjoying the idea, another thought entered his head: he had no idea which way was home from the school. Finding Hugh's hand at last, he squeezed Hugh's fingers hard. "You wouldn't leave without me?" he asked in a serious voice.

"No. We'll stick together," whispered Hugh.

"Shut up will you, and get back into your bed," said Douglas loudly.

Hugh shook his hand free. Outside the dorm, heavy footsteps approached along the corridor, dull thuds growing nearer. The footsteps came to an abrupt halt outside the dormitory. Hugh could picture the blimp-like presence of Mr Rhys-Davis breathing hard behind the door. He slunk out of the bed and sat cross-legged on the floor. The lino was cold and unforgiving. The silence felt like it stretched on forever. Finally, the master thudded away. Hugh waited before finally climbing back into bed.

Under the blanket, Giles held his breath and waited for the dorm to settle. Tiredness would not come. He thought about all the television programmes he was no longer able to watch, thanks to the ridiculous early lights out. He wondered what his mother had cooked for dinner. None of these thoughts made him feel particularly sad.

Giles turned on his side, trying to get comfortable. From somewhere deep inside the building, he could pick out the occasional creak and the unmistakable noise of water running through pipes. The gurgling sound reminded him of the bubbles of the fish tank in the living room, back in The Close. Often, he liked to turn off all the house lights, leaving just the aquarium light on. The tank glowed green in the dark. Giles pictured the black guppy, gliding effortlessly through the water, its black tail fin cutting a swathe through the zebrafish and the tetras. It would often disappear into fronds of the octopus plant for hours upon end, content to bide its time alone. Giles understood that. After John had stopped calling round, it was how he felt: detached from everyone, watchful and wary.

Giles let his imagination wander: to the dens hidden in the recreational fields around The Close, to the emerald green of the aquarium and to the air raid shelter, that surprisingly quiet space with a locked door that promised to lead somewhere. Sleep was calling out to him. He turned to Hugh. Hugh had already drifted off. Giles listened to the sound of his gentle breathing and closed his eyes, letting the day give way to the embrace of the night.

4 – LIKE A FAMILY

Hector Burton was fond of saying it wouldn't be a bullet that would get him, but Summer reveille; too many years of too many early mornings of hastily eaten breakfasts and inspections. Today was no different. Boarding school had prepared him for these starts; Hugh would be ready to follow in his footsteps when the time came.

He studied the photograph on his desk. It showed the four of them on holiday in Greece in 1973. Veronica had her arms around the twins. They had just emerged from the sea, shivering. In their costumes, Hugh and Belinda looked like little sailors. They were almost identical in every way, from their hair and eye colour, dark like Veronica, to their sharp noses, high cheekbones, and cleft chins. Older by a minute, there was no doubt who was in charge. Even as a seven-year-old, Belinda knew her mind and what she wanted. The Greeks found it endlessly entertaining watching the girl boss her brother around. She was a drill sergeant in the making and her father's daughter.

Now they were nine, nearly ten, the physical similarities were still strong. Hector wondered what would happen when they both hit puberty. He did not plan to find out, that was what boarding schools and wives were for – in his case, an estranged wife.

"Veronica," he loved to say her name when they made love. There was something forceful and alluring about the way she pronounced the syllables, the emphasis on the Ve-ronika, which matched her personality. Her nickname among the men was the Pocket Rocket. When something needed to be done, the soldiers said don't ask the Colonel, ask his wife. She looked particularly gamine in the photograph. Hector placed the frame back on the desk and went to open the window and officially welcomed in the day.

From his barrack room office on the top floor of regiment headquarters he had an unrestricted view across the parade ground. Down below, the men were on fatigue duty. A six-man team raced one and other, jousting with mops and buckets. Cleaning toilets and washing down vehicles were not what new recruits had in mind when they joined up, but every soldier had to go through it. Hector felt like having a smoke. The doctor had told him to cut down, or better still, stop. He drank hot black coffee instead. On the far side of the parade ground men barked orders at other men. Some of those on the receiving end were no older than boys; boys trying to grow a tach and act like men.

Hector remained at the window fascinated and appalled by the drudgery. On mornings like this, it made him wonder how any soldier stuck at it; the endless repetition, the mind-numbing duties to perform for senior ranks, and having to deal with the petty jealousies, rivalries, and paranoias of one's fellow man. He decided to have that cigarette after all. Hector smoked it to the butt and tossed it out the window, one more chore for a squaddie to carry out.

By eleven a.m. Hector felt dog tired. Thank God for canteen food in an hour; he would be able to escape from the office and chat to the men, get a feeling for the mood, and take the temperature of the troops. Job cuts. How had it come to that?

They needed more soldiers, not less. The morning's newspaper headline made it clear the army was on the back foot in Belfast, the Provos on top. And yet the Prime Minister was demanding a cut in numbers, and it fell to Hector to draw up lists for the regiment. He wondered whether he should put his name at the top, there would be a decent severance package and pension. He could use the money to start a business. A pub would be nice, but too tempting. He would drink the profits away. Contracting was an option. There would be few blokes in Africa who could keep him busy, and the pay day would be spectacular. The pictures on his office wall told his story.

Aden 1967. Streetwalking: beret, shorts, and shirtsleeves. Veronica said he looked like a film star.

Lisbon Street, Belfast, 1972. Streetwalking: winter combat dress, gloved hand wrapped around an SLR, unsmiling, ever alert.

There were dead comrades in every photograph, but Hector kept marching on.

The ringing phone interrupted his thoughts. He snatched up the handset.

The telephonist asked if he would accept a collect call, "It's your wife and she says it is urgent. Hector was in two minds; Veronica's definition was always at odds with his own. "Put her through," he said, irritably. After a couple of seconds of electronic fuzz, Veronica came on the line.

"Hector. How are you?" she asked amiably. Hector was fine. What else do men ever say when they're asked?

"Good," she said, apologising for disturbing him and having to cut right to the chase. "The problem is Hugh. He was trying to run off again." Hector let out a heavy sigh. Veronica continued without skipping a beat, "To be precise, it seems like he was planning to and then he must have changed his mind."

The story did not make much sense. Hector asked for details.

"Matron got wind of things and nabbed him in the playing fields. I told you she was a sharp one, didn't I?" Hector thought she was too young for the post, but once again Veronica could claim to know better than he did.

"Mucky as a pup of course, like he had been rummaging around on the ground. Typical Hugh. Worse of all, he had absolutely no explanation to offer except to say it was no one's fault but his own."

With his free hand Hector twirled the pen on his desk, thinking. In the background, Veronica had started a conversation with someone. He assumed it was Gerald, the man who had supplanted him in her affection.

"Sorry," she said, "I had to tell the shop boy to take the groceries through." She was the only person he had ever met who had a home delivery.

"Go on," he said, clicking the pen off and on. "I'm still listening." He guessed there had to be more. There always was with Hugh.

She went through what had happened. "The poor pilot has got it in the neck because he was supposed to be responsible for Hugh and, somehow, they ended up going separate ways," she said, sounding exasperated. "It's all a mess and you need to talk to the headmaster, or the housemaster, or the matron. Whoever. You just need to sort it out. Because it's not on, is it?" she said, in a tone which left no room for doubt.

Hector put down the pen. He wished he had one of those new handsets, cordless, so that he could walk and talk and feel unencumbered. Behind the desk, he felt trapped and at her mercy. Hector dragged the cable to the window, until the cord threatened to snap. "What exactly does the school, or *you*, mean by running away?" asked Hector.

"Hold on will you, Hector," she said, breaking off again. He heard Veronica put down the receiver. He closed his eyes and imagined her darting around the house, *his* house, until she had kicked him out. The house she now shared with Gerald.

Hector reached across the desk and took a cigarette from the pack. By the time she had returned, he had smoked his way through it and was contemplating lighting another.

"Sorry, that was Gerry," she said. "Now, where were we?"

Hector felt the blood boil behind his eyes at the mention of the man's name; it was a name fit for a Cocker Spaniel. Addressing Hector like a child, Veronica went over things one more time. It still made no sense. As far he could tell, Hugh was not running away but returning later to school than he should. A storm in a teacup.

"So, what do you want me to do?" he said, feeling exhausted by the conversation as well as distracted by the commotion at the main gates to the barracks where a civilian van was waiting for admission, and the driver of the vehicle was loudly remonstrating with his men about being let through.

"I'm late for my next round," boomed the driver, so loud that surely the whole regiment could have heard. His protestations were a waste of time. Armed entries were posted either side of the gate with strict instructions on how to manage vehicles coming in and out of the barracks. Hector watched as one of his soldiers went through the same routine that he had put into practice at Frampton, inspecting every inch, paying close attention to the undercarriage, using a mirror to check for explosives. Veronica was still speaking, but he was only half-listening. Eventually, the sentries raised the gate and the van edged slowly forward.

"Hector, if you don't believe the school's interpretation of events then you should take it up with the headmaster," she said, in a testy voice.

Hector stepped back from the window and sat on the edge of his desk. "The headmaster shouldn't hold Hugh's record against him."

Veronica huffed down the phone. Hector craned his neck to look out of the window. The van driver had the rear door open. His men stood in a line handing grocery boxes to one another.

"You always want to see things your way, but that doesn't make it right," she said, frostily. "Try to remember he is our son, not one of your rank and file. He has a loving mother, but he also needs a father. One who is present and makes choices that are right for him!" she said emphatically. Veronica had him cornered. It had been his decision to send Hugh to Fleetwood, and now to Frampton.

The van was ready to depart. Hector stood up at the sound of the engine. The soldiers opened the gate. The van moved off.

He kept his eye trained on the vehicle until it had pulled out onto the road. "Look Veronica, I still don't think the school's got it right, but I will call Richardson," he said, conceding defeat.

"Thank you," she replied curtly.

"Is there anything else?" he asked.

"I hope you are taking care of yourself," she said, lowering her voice. He wondered if Gerald was listening in. It sounded like she had her hand cupped around the handset. Hector felt he could read the signs with any woman, especially Veronica. "Hector?" she said again.

"If you mean smoking, I'm doing fine." He lied and said he had not touched one in weeks.

"Good, the children worry," she said. "I must go, let me know if you have any problems." She put down the phone and the line went dead.

Hector held the handset until the telephonist came on the line. He set the phone down and returned to the window. Outside the men were all moving in one direction towards the mess. He thought about joining them. The sentries were sharing a joke. Perhaps he should go and find out what was so funny. He could tell them a thing or two about sentry duty that would wipe the smiles off their faces. But he did not feel inclined to throw his weight around. Hector felt his wife still had feelings for him. He could hear the concern in her voice. Hector would do as she asked and call Richardson straight away. He dialled down to reception and asked the telephonist to get the headmaster on the line.

* * *

The Burtons were a military family, and for a long time army life suited Veronica. As she unpacked the groceries that the village boy had delivered, she thought about Hector and the life she had left behind to be with Gerry.

When she had fallen in love with Hector, her London friends had been were amused and then aghast to discover how a fun-loving London girl could become captivated by the world of fighting men with their peculiar drills and rituals. She had truly loved Hector through all the difficult postings and the long periods of absence before the birth of the twins. She took on the role expected of an army officer's wife, and no ordinary officer. She was the wife of high-flying, devil-may-care, Hector Burton or HB, as he was affectionately known.

However, as Hector worked his way through the ranks, fast-tracked on an ever-upwards trajectory, the idiosyncratic officer who had wooed her away from the London crowd began to lose his wit and charm, as he became increasingly obsessed with his career and his men. One night, when they had too much to drink, she asked Hector how he could so easily conquer his doubts and fears under enemy fire yet struggle to do the same when they were together. He had promised to talk about his feelings and spend less time on the parade ground. What he imagined the role of a husband to be was modelled on his own experiences in a soldiering household. While for her part, Veronica was determined not to become a facsimile of his mother; nor did she wish to be married to a man like his father and bring up children in the same way.

After the birth of Hugh and Belinda, she expected Hector to

play a full and active role in their lives. Veronica gave it to him straight. But instead of seizing the chance to step out into their sunlight, Hector retreated further into his own shadowy world, to soldiering, routine and discipline, to hours on the parade ground, hours in the briefing room, then days, weeks, and months away on tours of duty. It got to become a relief when he went away. And then, she had met Gerry, which made it easier for her to leave that life behind. He made her feel important, appreciated, and desired. However, Gerry's presence in her new life complicated matters when it came to the twins.

As an older man with grown-up daughters, she knew Gerry wanted a quiet life. Having Hugh and Belinda boarding suited Gerry. After living for many years on his own between his divorce and meeting Veronica, she understood he had settled into his own ways; most people were unwilling to compromise as they grew older.

The twenty-three-year age difference presented itself in the usual generational ways: he often looked back to events when he was a young man – she had to remind him that she was not even a twinkle in her mother's eye at that point; she did the same thing – except he was more forgiving and seemed genuinely interested; and although he woke her up at night to visit the loo that was the only trouble down below, the sex they enjoyed was energetic and imaginative.

Many times, Gerry told Veronica that he was lucky to have another chance at his age. He had given up on that side of his life – love. Gerry's daughters were delighted when romance turned into a relationship, even the speed of it all did not faze them. His eldest encouraged him to tie the knot before Veronica changed her mind. However, until Hector agreed to a divorce that was out of the question. Sometimes he wondered if she really wanted that. When he felt at a low point – something he tried to disguise – he became convinced that Veronica would return to Hector. Of one thing he was certain however, he enjoyed the time he spent with Veronica without her children in tow. Hugh was too much of a tearaway. The idea of the boy living in his house was too difficult to imagine. As he wandered in from the garden and looked upon Veronica, he could see that she was troubled. "What's wrong?" he asked.

Veronica did her best to smile. "Nothing. I'm fine, really" she said. Gerry kissed her lightly on the lips, resting his hands on her hips. She tried hard not to think about whether he had dirt from the garden on his fingers. "You feel warm," she said, releasing herself and touching his forehead.

"You are changing the subject," he replied, resenting being fobbed off. "Tell me," he said, reaching out to take her hand.

"I am still smarting from the call with Hector," she answered. "He always makes everything more complicated, especially when it comes to Hugh."

"I thought you got your way on that?" he said.

"Eventually, yet part of me thinks I can't trust Hector to do it. Perhaps I should call Richardson myself?" she said resignedly.

"Don't do that. You'll undermine your own efforts," he said, shielding his eyes from the sunlight raking into the lounge. It was too bright, the migraine-inducing kind. Gerry pulled the venetian blinds shut.

"Hector did not believe Hugh was making a run for it. He

thinks the head has *his* head up his own arse," she said. Gerry smiled. Her barrack-room language was one of her many attractive qualities. "Frankly I don't know what to think any more. Hector will have to deal with it."

Gerry attempted to put his arm around her again, but Veronica was in no mood for affection, however well-meaning.

"There's something more to this though, isn't there?" said Gerry astutely.

Veronica had been wondering for some time about how he would really feel about being a second father to the twins. She'd gently teased him with the question after it had become evident that things were getting serious between them. They were still relatively early into their relationship, and at the time, he had given her an unequivocal 'yes'. She had no reason to disbelieve him; he had said it with conviction. But with Hugh and Belinda away at boarding school, it had been easy to say. Life, however, had a funny way of revealing its complexities in the simplest of things. Belinda had not long returned from prep school when she wanted to see Hector. Of course, with Hector being Hector, he could not accommodate his daughter at short notice. The earliest opportunity would be the following weekend.

Belinda had spent six days moping around the house, scarcely uttering a word, picking at her food, and snarling when Veronica asked her the most mundane of questions. The same week, Gerry had gone down with a bug and Veronica had confined him to the spare bedroom. She had made a chicken soup for Gerry, to help get his strength back. There was more than enough to go around, but by no fault of Gerry's he had consumed it all by the time Belinda decided that she was ready for a bowl. Having raised daughters, Gerry was well-versed in female hormones. However, neither she nor Gerry were equipped to deal with the vitriol that poured from Belinda on that day. Veronica understood her daughter was feeling angry and hurt. Whether it was due to her new relationship or because she and Hector were no longer together, she could only speculate. Perhaps it was both things or more besides.

A few days later, when Gerry was well, Veronica dropped Belinda to the barracks to spend time with Hector. She was excited to be with her father. However, after a tearful phone call, Belinda asked to come home. Her father, she said, had no time for her. Hector drove Belinda home. Veronica and Gerry met them on the doorstep. Belinda bolted past them both in a flood of tears, leaving Gerry speechless. She and Hector had had the most enormous argument. When she returned to the living room, Gerry was sitting quietly watching television. He didn't meet her eye. She guessed what he was thinking – she would always put her children first, at any time Belinda or Hugh could step between them – but she lacked the courage to say anything at the time. And now, she realised, was not the time to have a difficult conversation about Hugh. She would bide her time and see how things panned out at Frampton. As a soldier's wife, she had an instinct for these things.

* * *

If there was one thing Hector Burton and Frank Ashworth had in common apart from their sons attending the same school, it was the stubborn refusal to never give up when there was something worth fighting for. Frank was adamant *this* customer would not be leaving the showroom without buying the car.

Frank was a gifted salesman. He had been in the car game long enough to know when there was a chance to close a deal, and he was *close*. But his problem was not convincing the husband and the teenage children; clearly the boys were sold on the Cortina and desperate that their father did not miss out on the discounted price Frank was offering. The obstacle was the wife, inspecting every inch of the paintwork looking for what… a blemish, a defect, a reason not to buy the car. There was something about the wife that reminded him of a woman he had had a thing with just after Giles was born. Moira had been off sex at the time, immersed in Giles.

"Would you like a closer look again?" he asked the husband. The sickly-looking man slid behind the wheel for the nth time, the teenage sons spread out on the back seat. The older boy prattled on about how the car's fluted design was inspired by the Coke bottle, and how the new flatter dash and clocks were better for the driver. Best of all, in the boy's view, the 1.6 model had a punchier engine than its predecessor.

"The boy knows his stuff," said Frank to the mother. The woman ignored him and continued to examine the chassis. "The Mark III is one of the safest cars you can buy, much more substantial than anything else on the road," he said, moving nearer but being mindful not to crowd her out.

Like a cod psychologist, Frank knew that the longer the woman was left cocooned in her own thoughts the less chance the Mark III would be sold; and he had to clear the showroom glut before the new Model IV arrived at the end of the month. So, he thought, just how low could he go? What optional extras could he throw in to persuade the wife.

The woman glanced briefly at him, as she ran her hand along the Modena green bodywork.

"Safety is so important when there's about to be a new driver in the family," he continued, looking from the woman to the older boy, who was continuing to impress his father with information about the car… the faux walnut interiors, the shiny vinyl seats.

"I hear they get rusty around the doors and go rotten in the winter," said the woman, with a smirk, looking him squarely in the eye. She had a strong Essex accent, and an Essex way about her, no-nonsense and feisty, like she was gearing up for a row.

Frank cleared his throat and self-consciously adjusted his tie, a chocolate-brown patterned silk Pierre Cardin, which he had bought specially to go with the checked Bill Blass suit he was wearing. "May I show you something," he said, gesturing to the rear of the Cortina. Frank squatted down and pointed out the finishing around the door pillars and wheel arches to guard against the weather. "The Mark III is nothing like older versions. You know what they used to call them?" he said, giving her a winning smile.

"Dagenham dustbins," she replied, with a half-laugh. He knew she would know. A shared joke was all he needed. She was his.

Frank stood up and invited the woman to join her boys and inspect the interiors. Frank lightly touched her arm, smiling. "It's roomy inside," he said, with an impudent grin, before asking if she got to travel much.

"Well, you know," she replied, with a faint shrug. As she brushed past him, Frank took in her perfume, a distinctive floral peach-rose aroma. The smell of warm sunny outdoor days.

"Do you have any holiday plans?" he asked. He had the feeling that she would turn heads in a bikini.

"Maybe Spain. Mallorca, perhaps," she said, looking through him. "Depends on how much money we have to spend. Buying this car might put an end to that." She drummed her fingers lightly on the roof.

"How about we get you to Spain *and* drive away in a nice new car?" said Frank. He could work out a finance package if that would be of interest.

"Surprise me," she said, tilting back her chin, a furtive smile playing on her lips.

Frank disappeared into his office. He continued to watch her through the Perspex while he punched numbers into the calculator. He felt her eyes watching him. It was like a dance. He was certain she was enjoying the theatre of his performance. The boys whooped when she said let's buy it. Interest-free for two years; they would still have their week under the Spanish sun. Frank poured the husband and wife a glass of Babycham to celebrate. The whole showroom and the garage mechanics came out to see the family off. It was customary.

"You did well there, Frank. Keep this up and we'll clear all the old Mark IIIs," said Henderson after the Cortina had disappeared into the traffic. He patted Frank on the shoulder and returned to his office. Frank mentally totted up the commission: school fees paid for the next term, and enough for a couple of new suits and something nice for Moira.

Frank wandered across the showroom, just two remaining Mark IIIs on the floor. The woman's perfume still lingered in the showroom. He had slipped his business card into her hand as he had helped her into the passenger seat. She did not resist, in fact he felt that she had accepted it with almost indecent haste. "I'll be heading off in a minute," he shouted through to Henderson, knowing the boss could not very well begrudge Frank an early finish after making the sale.

Before driving home, he wanted to freshen up. In the bathroom, he slipped off his tie and rolled it away neatly inside his jacket, and splashed water over his face. Frank investigated the mirror. Keeping his hair longer, just clipped above the shoulders, and shaving off the moustache made him look younger. It was a sportier look and he liked what he saw.

Henderson walked in while Frank was combing his hair. The owner looked good for his age. Money. That's what it was. Money protected you from age, stopped the rot from setting in. Frank thought about the wheel arches on the Cortina. They will rust. They always did. Henderson unzipped and splashed loudly into the urinal. Frank shuddered at the sound and promptly left the bathroom. On the way through reception, Frank picked up on the song coming from the garage. It was one Moira liked. He hummed along all the way to the forecourt to where the Capri was parked up, washed, waxed, and polished. Keys in hand, the mechanic was waiting. Frank held out his hands. The mechanic tossed them to him and waited while Frank gave the car a once-over, steeling himself for whatever dirty spot he may have missed. Frank never failed to disappoint. "The alloys. Make more of an effort on those tomorrow," said Frank.

"Sure," replied the mechanic sullenly.

"Don't take it to heart. We all have to start somewhere," said

Frank, before slipping inside and accelerating away. He turned up the stereo. He felt good. He had sold another Mark III. The wife had made him hard. He wanted Moira to be ready for him, and why not? Giles was out of their hair and they had the house to themselves. He stiffened at the thought; in the lull of the traffic, he found it almost impossible to resist stroking his cock through his trousers. Her little red Escort was on the driveway; he bounded out of the Capri and trotted up to the house. "Moira, Moira," he called out, shutting the front door behind him. He checked himself in the hall mirror, while carefully putting his jacket on the clothes hanger that he insisted she kept by the front door along with his golf clubs.

The house was dark and quiet. From the hallway he could see through to the kitchen and beyond to the back garden and the unbroken line of Dutch Elms. He put his head around the door to the living room. Her cardigan was on the sofa, her handbag on the carpet. The fish tank bubbled away, the catfish prowling along the bottom. Little neon tetras burst in and out of the plastic castle Giles had bought with his pocket money. Instinctively he opened the aquarium lid and dropped a pinch of food into the water. The guppy glided out and took its fill, swallowing the food in greedy mouthfuls.

Frank called out her name again. "Are you up there?" he shouted, looking up at the ceiling, convinced he had heard Moira moving around in the bedroom. He jogged up the carpeted stairs.

"Moira," he said, softly, peeping into their bedroom. The cat was on the duvet. The tabby glowered at Frank. He hissed at the cat. She arched her back and jumped from the bed, disappearing to the sanctuary of the pine wardrobe.

Irritable now, Frank peered into the guest room, the bathroom and finally, into Giles' bedroom. The bed was freshly made as though she was expecting him home any moment. He had had to remind Moira that the boys spent the entire Michaelmas term at school. Giles would not be home until Christmas. She had started to cry again, and he had lost his temper and warned her that his patience was wearing thin.

The window was ajar. A warm breeze blew through the nets. Through the thin fabric, the brutish council towers where Giles went to play looked like Lego blocks. He hated this view. It spoke to his past and where he had come from. In the summer the elms saved him from the ignominy, but when winter came, there was no escape from it.

Frank sat down on the bed. He knew now Moira would be on one of her walks. She could be in any mood by the time she came home.

Frank could not fathom why Moira disagreed with what they were doing. One day he was sure she would thank him for the education and the opportunities that the school would provide to their son. Kicking off his shoes, he stretched out and put his head on the pillow. Staring absently at the ceiling, he remembered how Moira had called him a liar. It wasn't about a better education – it was about getting Giles away after the shame of what Giles had done and the assessment by the psychologist. Anger issues. What did that even mean? Everyone got upset from time to time. He was a child. The psychologist said Giles should explore these feelings. He knew Moira would come home when she was ready. Frank unzipped his fly and thought about the wife in the showroom. When he had cum, he expected to feel good, but he didn't, and he didn't know why.

* * *

Some days Moira had no energy. She curled up with the cat through the morning until hunger got the better of them. She poured biscuits into the bowl for the tabby and ate cereal herself. They watched each other eat.

"What shall we do?" she asked, following the cat into the lounge. The cat eyed the aquarium. Moira eyed the television. Daytime television was endlessly tedious. The lunch time news presented one horror after another. Bombings, shootings, earthquakes. Bagpuss was a poignant reminder of when Giles was a toddler. He liked the old cloth cat almost as much as he liked the tabby. When she inadvertently caught the children's programme on television, it reduced her to a flood of tears.

She slept again and then around three pm, she suddenly woke up and knew what she wanted to do. Hastily, Moira washed her face and dressed.

Downstairs, she put on a record while she did her make-up. The stereo looked dusty, yet she was sure that only yesterday she had run a cloth over the surface. Moira tilted her head and ran a finger over the plastic surface. Sure enough, she could see the flecks in the air. They floated away in her hands before dissolving.

Band on the Run was on the turntable. She picked up the record sleeve. Paul and Linda were caught in a prison searchlight. She hummed the title track and laughed out loud at the lyrics. If that was how they felt, she knew there was no hope for anyone.

Moira did her eyes. Her mother Mary wanted to know why she

did not get out more. Take the Escort for a spin. Nip into town for a bit of posh shopping. The matriarch of the family could not understand why Moira bothered having a flash little run around if the car remained rooted to the driveway. Moira wanted to yell out that she had nowhere she wanted to go. She only had the Escort because Frank insisted that they should be a two-car family.

Make-up done, Moira locked up and headed towards the recreational fields, hoping to avoid prying eyes. The Close was full of nosey people. How *is* Giles, they'd ask. On the rec, she felt free. When she was a girl the whole place had been a grassy field. She could walk from the town, over the river and lie back in the grass and no one would know she was there. She must have been a year or two younger than Giles. What were her parents thinking, letting her wander about like that?

There was one summer when the mercury hit 80F before noon. Dog days, literally, when even her boisterous dalmatian only wanted to lie in the shade; dog shit turned hard and white in the heat. She threw it at parked cars when she was bored. Tarmac melted in the street. She built an arena in the baked earth, collecting red and black ants, pitting them against each other. The black ants massacred the red ants. When it grew dark, it marked the time to return home. She would run hard and fast, head up, like she had shown Giles. No one would dare try to stop you. By the time she reached the garden gate, she would be slick with sweat, her dress stuck to her skin. Giant horseflies patrolled the patch of grass that Mary called a lawn, and the river stank as it turned a darker shade of green.

Lost in her memories, Moira did not realise she had walked much further than she had intended, to the edge of the playfield where the grass ended abruptly, and the concrete began. She looked up at the three high-rise towers. From Giles' bedroom they looked like small thumbprints on the horizon. Up close, they looked threatening. Moira started to count the number of floors. There had to be at least twenty. From up there you could see for miles.

She did not see them, she heard them – the bawling and cat-calling – and then she saw them. Moira wondered what all the fuss was about. She was shocked to find the fuss was over her. The men whistled louder once they saw they had her attention. The things they said were disgusting. They shouted louder, calling her over. Her face showed what she thought. At times like this she wished she was a man. She would smash their faces in, and laugh, but instead she had to run away.

Moira slowed her pace when they were out of earshot. The children's playground hoved into view. She decided to cut through. A couple of young mothers pushed their kids in the swings, smiling shyly at each other, neither looked inclined to say hello to the other. Moira would like to take the weight off her feet, but without a child in tow, the women gazed at her suspiciously. If she sat down on this bench, what would they do, report her for being one of those weirdos you read about in the paper? Part of her wanted to cry out and tell them to mind their own business; the other part of her wanted to reach out and tell them to hold their children tight and never let them go. Giles in a pushchair. Giles' first steps. Giles running to kiss her.

It was a short walk from the swings to the house. Ahead the high branches of the Elms swayed gently in the breeze. Their garden gate one of ten opening out onto the rec. Frank wanted to board it up and enclose the garden in higher fences. Moira fumbled with the key. The lock was sticky, but after a couple of attempts the key finally turned, and she pushed her way in. The bushes on either side of the little pathway already needed cutting back; the overgrown shoots bristled around her ankles. The veggie patch was dry. There would be no potatoes this year. Giles would be disappointed.

From the garden, the house looked small, shrunken. Perhaps it was the sun's reflection from the kitchen door or the way that the nets swayed lazily in the breeze in Giles's bedroom: a trick of the eye, an illusion. Moira felt like lingering for a while, picking at the dead heads of summer's bloom. There was a soothing quality to the warm breeze, and the gentle rustling of the elms. She could, she felt, fall asleep standing up like the cat. She closed her eyes, welcoming the chance to sleep, but as was so often the way the moment was stolen away; from the first-floor window, from Giles' bedroom, Frank bawled out her name, demanding that she come inside.

Usually, Frank never ventured inside his son's room; he never felt welcomed by Giles he said. Despite everything he did for their son Frank complained that he made time only for his mother. She had told him that he sounded like a petulant child. And now that Giles was away at school, Frank appeared to be at ease. The irony was not lost on her. Moira took another moment for herself and then went inside to find out what all the fuss was about.

* * *

Tom was a boy who lived for the moment. His mam worried all the time about the trouble he might get into. Everything fascinated him but nothing seemed to hold his attention. When his mam died, it fell to his brother Michael to take responsibility for the family. Michael smacked Tommy around along with the rest of his brothers and sisters. But Michael reserved the hardest treatment for Tommy. The older brother could see what no one else could see: Tommy was smart. Tommy had potential.

One day, when he was thirteen, Michael said he was bringing a friend to the house and they were all to make themselves scarce except for Tommy; and one more thing, he said, you are to call our brother Tom from now on.

Tom waited all afternoon and into the evening for Michael, but his brother never came home that day. Nor the next or the one after that.

It was a Friday when Sean came to the house. Michael had been arrested. His brother had sent him to make sure the family had everything they might need. Tom asked Sean if he was Michael's friend. He was but not in that way. Tom did not understand what Sean meant until later, and when he did, he assumed it was joke, although it was not at all funny. But then, humour was not Sean's gift. His gift was nurturing talent, and Tom had talent. Sean told the Council they had their man in Tom. The Council gave Sean their blessing; education, indoctrination, detonation. Like an eager apprentice, Tom lapped it up. Years ago.

Now: the journey out of west London was slow, traffic inching along; Brendan at the wheel, Tom riding shotgun. Roadworks everywhere. Workmen in orange jackets sweated in the sun. Orange. The colour of oppression.

Once they were clear of London, the traffic emptied out. They passed through tired-looking suburban towns and villages, out into the country. Two Irish lads going about their day. Sean had said, what do you say if you're pulled over? That we're off to kill some Brits. The quartermaster liked that one.

Brendan pulled the vehicle off the main road, into a quiet, leafy lane, all shady bowers and dappled light. Picture postcard stuff.

Tom was tetchy. The Land Rover up ahead spooked him. Brendan slowed down and they dropped back. Tom checked the mirrors. Nothing coming behind. Tom felt his pulse quickening. He had the revolver wrapped in cloth inside the glove compartment. Webley and Scott. All you needed to put a man down.

Farm roads, no street markings. Fence posts and barbed wire. Welcome to Suffolk. And still, the Land Rover. We should stop, said Brendan. Make like we need a piss. Hold your nerve, boys. That's what Sean would say. Steady as you go. Minutes dragged by. Finally, the Land Rover took a left turn into a private road. Brendan let out a sigh of relief. Tom wound down the window and sucked in the country air.

The farm was set back from the road, down a single grubby dirt track, like a scene from west Cork. Its surface was baked hard, bone dry; the car rattled and shook like a tin can.

Brendan knew the drill. He pulled up short of the house: Tom ducked out, head down, Webley tucked into his donkey jacket, while Brendan turned the vehicle around in preparation for a quick exit.

Tom watched Brendan. Tom watched the farm. Tom watched everything for anything. This wasn't London. They did not fit in here; fish out of water, collecting an arms cache from over the water.

He signalled Brendan to make his way to the rear of the farm. He would take the front. Tom crept passed the large shed: the fierce odour of chicken shit. The house was farmer functional. He stayed low past the windows, taking a sneak peek. Nothing untoward. Then, he fast walked the final twenty to the front door, thinking if he was to take one, it would be here.

Left hand slow, he tried the handle, staying way out of the line of fire. Auto readied. One, two, three. Go. The door gave out easily. Hallway empty. Sitting room empty. Dining room empty. Brendan whistled and came through the kitchen.

Tom pointed to the first floor. They took it as a team. Left, right, left. The three bedrooms were all made up. Pillows plumped, bedspreads soft and inviting, like the farmer was waiting for the three bears.

Brendan tapped Tom on the shoulder, the ladder to the loft lay on its side in the hallway. Careful now Brendan he said. Don't go getting your head shot off. Up Brendan climbed ready to push open the hatch. Tom trained the automatic on the ceiling and gave him the nod. The loft was clear of life and packed to the rafters with everything Sean had promised, and more.

It took them an hour to get the load down: automatics and semi-automatics, magazines, handguns, boxes of ammunition, material for pipe bombs, command wire to trigger explosives. How the fuck did Sean get this into the country? Tom broke into a grin, Brendan laughed. They wanted to break into song, but there was no time for any dilly-dally when they had to be on their way.

They worked as fast as they could: clock watching, passing the weaponry down. Brendan backed the car up to the front door.

They loaded it up, stashing the weapons under the back seat, in the vacant space where the spare wheel should be, into suitcases and holdalls. Jesus, fuck, what a haul. The car groaned under the destructive weight. Brendan took it slow down the rutted track, easing through the gears. The day was turning to night. Lights from cars on the motorway twinkled in the distance, the city was calling out to them.

Tom thought about the poem they had forced him to learn by rote: this blessed plot, this earth, this realm, this England. He asked Brendan if he knew it. As he spoke, he was aware that his voice sounded tired, his words slurred. The big Irishman did not, and he asked Tom why. "It's ours for the taking," said Tom in a whispered, sleepy voice. He slept through the journey to London.

They had lockups scattered across west London. Brendan and the boys wasted no time in ferrying their arsenal. While they went to work, so did Tom. Alone in the flat under the fierce, white light of the lamp, methodically. The devil's own work. Sean's words in his head be sure you can use your left hand to wipe your arse, just in case you blow your good hand off. Unintentional detonation. It was a risk that came with the job. Make sure there are no other fellas around while you are at it. Send them out to work. If there's no work to be done, send them to a pub. There's *always* work to be done in London town.

Tom glanced at his watch. He'd been at it for half an hour, the back of his neck felt wet with sweat. Sean said he should cut his hair, but Tom liked it long, liked the way it disguised his features. When he donned a suit and wore glasses, he blended into the university crowd that hung around South Kensington. An engineering graduate, a young lecturer in mechanics, an electronics specialist. He smiled to himself at the thought. He was all those things.

Tom reached across the table and felt for a screwdriver. Slow and painstaking. That was his way. He neatly bored the hole and threaded the fuse, then prepped the wrought steel pipe and packed in the gelignite and shrapnel. Almost done. He capped the pipe, worked the fuse in, tight, checking for balance and weight. Such a simple thing; all the bits from plumber and builders' merchants, save the newly acquired explosive material from their trip to the farm. Everything a gift from Sean for his boys; in a family it was how things ought to be.

5 - ADVERSARIES

Many months had passed since the birthday party at the driving range, and Moira still thought about Yvonne. As the youngest prospective mothers in the ante-natal class they had bonded quickly, and their friendship had blossomed after the birth of Giles and John, and then deepened as time went by. Inseparable with dreams of their own: opening a boutique in the town, or a hair salon or a nail bar – until then, until *that*. Their friendship died that day.

Yvonne stopped calling. She refused to take Moira's phone calls. The first time they met in the street, Yvonne blanked Moira. She thought it had to be a mistake. But it wasn't. John had poisoned the well and seemingly they all had to suffer. Moira learned to steel herself against the gossip until it all became too much.

Conceding to Frank's demand for Giles to try out for the boarding school seemed a simple enough thing; Moira did not expect Giles to pass the entrance exam. How wrong could she have been? Every time she entered her son's empty bedroom, she felt the weight of her culpability, as though she had a stone lodged in the pit of her stomach. She turned her anger on Frank. There was no one else to rail against, or so she thought.

A sharp tap on the glass.

Moira wound down the car window. The sun was in her face, blinding.

"I thought it was you," said Yvonne. "I recognised the car."

Silhouetted in the bright light, Yvonne radiated fragile beauty. Moira thought she would know what to say. She had the words rehearsed for just this moment. But instead, nothing. It was a strange feeling, being lost for words in the company of someone whom she knew so well.

Yvonne had her daughter in tow. She tugged on Yvonne's arm. Moira fixed her eyes on the fair-headed six-year-old. In just a few months the girl had shot up; she looked like John around the same age, not just the hair colour, but also the long legs and slender build. As Moira stared at the girl, she continued to pull on Yvonne. "She's turned into a right little live wire," Moira observed. She hated the pleasantry in her own voice.

"I blame the long summer holiday. She expects me to be at her beck and call. I can't wait to pack her off to Infants," replied Yvonne, grappling with the child. The girl was called Susan after Yvonne's mother, a kind and generous woman, far better than Moira's own mother. When Moira had gone down with the baby blues, the older Susan had rallied round. She brought Moira dinner and told her about her life during the war. She insisted on coming around to The Close until she was satisfied Moira was better. Yvonne's daughter seemed to have inherited the same determination, she kept on tugging.

"I'll have to belt her in a minute," said Yvonne, yanking the girl by the arm. The daughter yelped and started to press herself against the car, pulling faces in the glass. "How have you been?" asked Yvonne. The question seemed deliberately vague.

"Fine. Busy, I suppose," replied Moira. "How about you?"

"Dealing with this one mostly," she said, sighing. "You know what they are like at this age."

Moira forced herself to remember what Giles was like at six. Withdrawn was the first thought that came to mind. "And John?" she asked, her voice quivering. Moira could hardly bear to say the boy's name.

"The same as ever, always out playing football or some kind of silly game on the rec," said Yvonne.

Moira nodded. "What games does he like to play nowadays?"

Yvonne looked confused by the question. "I don't know," she said.

"Don't you ask him when he comes home? I used to always ask Giles." Yvonne seemed unsettled by the question. "Giles told me everything he did, right down to the tiniest detail. Everything. Now the best I can hope for is a letter once a week, and a home stay for Christmas." Moira could feel her anger rising. She stared hard at Yvonne.

Yvonne leaned forward, resting her hand on the open car window. "Mo…" she started to say, but Moira cut her off.

"Does John talk about Giles?" Moira blurted out, reaching through the window to grasp Yvonne's hand. She grabbed on tight to Yvonne's fingers. Yvonne flinched. They felt warm and soft like a child's.

"In what way?" Yvonne said nervously.

"Talk about him, mention him, you know, bring Giles up in conversations," Moira replied. She relaxed her grip, and Yvonne pulled her hand away and placed a protective arm around her daughter.

"You know what boys are like," said Yvonne, guardedly. "Impossible to get a peep out of them unless you threaten to do something they won't like. Not like my little angel," she said, attempting to change the subject. She played with her daughter's hair. The child stared up at her mother and asked if they were going home soon.

Her angel. My devil. Moira felt ready to explode. When John stopped coming to the house, Giles had cried on and off for days. She had comforted him, while Frank had disappeared to the showroom, acting as though nothing was wrong. "You've got to get her home," said Moira, feeling she was fighting a losing battle against her emotions. Yvonne seemed ready to go, but Moira sensed something was holding her back. "What is it? What do you want?" she exclaimed.

Fixing Moira with a steady star, she leaned forward again. "It was a terrible thing," said Yvonne in a hushed voice. "You can't blame John. It's not right." It was the worst thing she could have said. It was like uncorking a fizzy bottle, blind rage poured out.

"I know what's right. I know the truth, Yvonne," shrieked Moira. The little girl started to cry. Yvonne pulled the child away from the car. "I know who is to blame for my son going away. Your son. You. All of them!" Moira was hollering and she did not care who heard.

It was too much for Yvonne. She picked up her daughter and hastily walked away. The girl's dress fluttered like a butterfly's wing, red and white and black.

"*I* know and so do *you*," howled Moira with the unconditional belief in her son's innocence; her boy was not capable of doing *that* to another child. John was a liar; Yvonne was as complicit as her son. Moira had always felt Yvonne was responsible in her own way for what happened on that dreadful day. She grabbed the steering wheel and pounded it hard, again and again, until her rage had burned itself out.

* * *

The house football trials should have been a welcome distraction for Anthony Richardson after the difficult telephone conversation with Hector Burton. The gall of the man to blame the school. Why were some parents so bloody-minded when it came to their sons? Hector had torn a strip off him on the call, berating Anthony for jumping to conclusions. With the boy's track record why would he not think Hugh was absconding? As for Hepbridge, well, naturally he had to give him a stiff dressing down for messing up his duties as a pilot. It had been a simple task to show Ashworth and Burton around the school. Linda said there was more to it than that. Something fishy. However, he had been too tired to hear about things from the boys themselves – and, as he reminded himself, no harm had been done. Burton was where he should be, under their care.

"Make it yours," Anthony boomed out at the defender, but instead the boy mistimed the tackle and the attacker skipped over the challenge and thumped the ball past the goalkeeper. Three nil to David Scott's eleven before half time.

"Anthony, did you see that?" said David, striding along the touch line, perfectly on cue. "A rocket from Watson, eh!"

"The defender should have done better," he replied, sourly.

"We all know rugger is your thing Anthony," said David, slapping the headmaster on the arm. He jogged past, hugging the touch line, shouting out instructions.

After watching his team ship another two goals, Anthony had had enough and besides he had a mounting pile of paperwork to get through relating to the spiralling maintenance costs. But the thought of returning to his study to deal with it filled him with dread. He would, he decided, be better off reviewing some of the problems first-hand.

Parts of the old school were particularly run-down and requiring attention. At times like these, he regretted dispensing with Jim, the odd-job man. Anthony could read the expressions on some of the parents' faces when he was conducting school tours: they were investing in their sons' future and this was the sad, sorry, state of affairs. He was determined to make things right, starting with the classroom block. It was a relatively new build, but it was grossly unfit for purpose: baking hot in the summer, damp and cold in the winter. A disgrace. Going into the last meeting with the trustees in June he had been confident the works would be approved, enabling re-construction to take place unhindered through the summer holidays. And yet here they were, as they were a year ago with nothing decided. Anthony could, however, take some credit for having the swimming pool repaired. He decided to brighten his mood by checking it over.

"Six goals to nil, now," said David, as Anthony strode away from the pitch. He turned a blind eye and a deaf ear towards David's jibes. Preferring to take a short cut to the swimming pool, he cut across the pitch and entered the school via the lobby. There was a stillness about it today, as many of the boys were outside playing games. Two boys, however, were sitting together in the small lounge and Anthony was curious about what they were doing. "We're exempt from games because we are not well," said Arthurs, an impish boy from dorm two.

"We're playing cards instead, sir," chimed Patterson, a chubby boy whose father had recently joined the board of trustees.

"Not for money, I hope," replied Anthony, guffawing. The boys looked bemused and embarrassed. "It is a joke," he said. Patterson forced out a laugh and asked if they could continue to play. "Go ahead," replied Anthony. They resumed playing cards while he watched on. Soon they seemed quite oblivious to him, wrapped up in their game without a care in the world. Patterson thumped his winning hand down on the tabletop.

"You've played enough. Now, go and read a book," said Anthony, packing them off to their dorms. He then resumed his way through the ground floor room and into the boy's locker room, the last stop before exiting the building to reach the swimming pool. By force of habit Anthony paused to inspect the lockers. Every boy had a tuck box stored here. Once a week, on a Saturday, they were allowed in to open them up. It was Harry's job to watch over, making sure the boys did not attempt to take more sweets than they were allowed.

Anthony passed from one row to the next. He liked to play a game of his own, guessing the identity of the owner by the initials on the tuck box, or by the way it had been decorated. He felt it provided an insight into the child in his care. Logos of pop bands, lyrics from favourite songs, club colours and badges, pictures from Panini albums of football players, and so on, told him something about the boy.

He ran his eyes along the wall looking for dorm three, curious to find the ones belonging to the new boys. GA: the initials were etched into the varnished surface. That had to be Ashworth. Anthony lifted it out of the rack, holding it by the silver metal handles. The lettering shimmered like oil on water. The combination lock and clasps glinted under the light. It was exquisitely crafted and expensive. Apart from the initials, there was not a single word or picture on the tuck box. It spoke not of the boy, but of the father and the mother and their aspirations.

Burton's was adjacent to Ashworth's. Plastered all over were countless luggage labels – Delhi. Hong Kong, Lagos, Singapore, Sydney, and many more – official stamps of arrivals and departures. The owner of the tuck box was well travelled. No doubt it was a family piece, a hand-me down from father to son. He slotted it back into the rack, feeling he knew what he needed to know about Hugh. However, Giles Ashworth remained an enigma.

Anthony turned off the locker room light and opened the fire door, which led into the rear of the kitchen yard, a desolate spot where they stored rubbish and food waste. He pinched his nose and walked quickly towards the kitchen garden. Even as he crossed through it, Anthony heard the loud peals of laughter coming from behind the high wall that separated the garden from the swimming pool.

"Nudey. Nudey. Nudey." The year five boys were shouting as one. Six new boys from the first year were huddled together at the pool's edge, wet and trembling.

"Pull down his trunks," shouted a year five boy.

"Show us his willy," clamoured another.

The cold, cowering year one boys looked paralysed by fear and turned to one another, unsure what was expected of them.

A ghoulish looking year five made a dash for the younger ones. He attempted a tug on the waistband of the nearest boy's swimming speedos. The wet elastic ban thwacked back against the small boy's flesh. The child recoiled with yelp. The year five lunged forward to try again.

"Andrews. What. Are. You. Doing?" bellowed Anthony.

The older boy stopped in his tracks. The other year five boys did the same.

Anthony cupped his hand over his eyes. Where was Harry Rhys-Davis? He looked left and right and to his disbelief saw that Harry was dozing in the shade. Anthony swept around the pool and loomed over the teacher. "Mr Rhys-Davis," he shouted. The boys watched on, as Anthony shook Harry awake. The older boys giggled in the background. Anthony shot them a filthy look, which instantly silenced them. Harry opened his eyes, blearily for a second or two; and then quite abruptly he was wide-eyed and fearful. Harry pulled himself up out of the lounger, swaying on his feet. "Good god, you are drunk!" exclaimed Anthony.

Harry wobbled and steadied himself on Anthony's arm. "Headmaster if I may venture to explain?" said Harry, with a beseeching expression. Anthony grabbed Harry by the wrist and pulled him to one side so they could speak privately.

"Have you seen how terrified they are?" asked Anthony, glancing at the dorm one boys. Harry looked over the headmaster's shoulder. Andrews nudged his dorm mate and the boys covered their mouths to suppress their laughter. Harry started to speak, but Anthony hushed him; he could smell the whiskey on Harry's breath. Anthony did not trust what might come out of Harry's mouth or whether he might fall over. "Stay here," he demanded.

Herding the younger boys into the changing room to get out of their costumes, dry off and dress, Anthony then turned to the dorm five boys, singling out Andrews, in particular. "Well, what do you have to say?" he asked the boy. Andrews fidgeted and looked in Harry's direction. "Don't look at Mr Rhys-Davis for help," continued Anthony. Andrews looked down at the water pooling around his ankles. Taking the boy's silence as an admission of guilt, Anthony angrily tossed a towel at Andrews. "Dry up and stay put!" he barked.

His purpose had been to check the pool had reopened satisfactorily. However, an inspection would have to wait for another time. "Get a move on in there," he crowed from outside the changing room, growing impatient with the time that the dorm ones were taking. Eventually they emerged together, damp, and frightened with tousled hair.

"Sir?" enquired a small voice.

"Yes, what is it?" he replied, gruffly.

"I think that we might be late for dinner," said the boy.

The afternoon sun cast oblique shadows on the pool. Harry remained in the shade. Anthony eyed him suspiciously. "It's Walker isn't it? The boy nodded. "You can lead them back. Mr Rhys-Davis and I will bring up the rear." The dorm ones snaked around the swimming pool to join Andrews and his gang.

Walker whispered into Andrews's ear. The boys formed up behind Walker. "Lead on," said Anthony. The boys moved off, filing out in a single column. Gripping Harry by the wrist again, he said, a few final words. "Don't come down to supper!" and ordered Harry to stay in his room and sober up.

"Get off me," said Harry. Irrespective of the matter, he did not appreciate being treated like a naughty schoolboy by the headmaster.

Anthony let his hand drop. "Just do what I said," he replied, before shouting at the boys to speed up. Like an army in retreat, they walked to the school in silence.

* * *

Later that evening Anthony called David and Linda into his study. Before they made themselves comfortable, he started to fire out questions. How much did they know about Harry's drinking? Why did they not think to tell him? How did they think this would look if one of the parents, or one of the trustees for that matter, got to hear about it? Not to mention the consequences if something had happened to one of the boys who was in Harry's supposed charge.

David professed ignorance, while Linda said nothing. Anthony could hardly bear to look at them. They were supposed to be his eyes and ears. He knew David could not be trusted. However, he had thought better of Linda, particularly after what had passed between them. He realised he was mistaken. If they would not help him, then not only would Harry receive an official warning, but also there would be no more naked swims.

David was aghast, but not over Harry. "It's a tradition,

Anthony!" he said, angrily.

"It is sinister and unhealthy," retorted Anthony, describing in detail what he had witnessed at the swimming pool. "The dorm five boys were acting like little savages. It was like something out of Lord of the Flies!"

David stood up. "I think that's a little strong."

"You weren't there. The older boys' behaviour was vicious and cruel," he replied, fiercely. "Harry was asleep. Anything could have happened."

David turned to Linda, "What do you think?" he asked.

"For all we know, he may have been about to intercede," Linda replied. She felt it was the most valiant defence she could mount for Harry without sounding ridiculous. However, no one was fooled.

"Oh, come on Linda, you must see the risks?" said Anthony.

"What do you intend to do?" she said, after a long pause.

"Harry will receive a letter putting him on notice. One more misstep and he's out," stated Anthony neutrally. Linda looked disappointed. "As for tradition, I am not prepared to tolerate another scene like today," he said, turning to David "These swims are to be banned forthwith. In fact, it's probably not the only tradition we should dispense with."

Linda wondered where Anthony was going with this. However, David was already one step ahead. "You are not thinking about abolishing British Bulldog?" he asked.

Toying with the pen on his desk, Anthony shrugged. "It is an archaic game. If game is the right word," he replied, tersely. Every boarding school played the game. It was almost a rite of passage among the first years. But Anthony thought there was a feral element to it. Some boys revelled too much in the rough and tumble that ensued while playing the game. "You've seen what a mess it creates," said Anthony. "By the time it's over, you have to call in Sister to patch up cuts and bruises.

David decided to speak up. These were issues for the principal housemaster not the headmaster to decide. Anthony disagreed. "Well, then perhaps *you* should oversee all the other things I do out of hours for the benefit of the school for this term, and see how you like it," he said, standing up abruptly. Gripping the back of the chair, he stared at Anthony defiantly.

"Is there anything else you have to say?" asked Anthony, staring at the whites of David's knuckles. David looked for all the world like he would snap the chair into pieces.

"Not for now," he replied.

"Then, leave us," said Anthony, motioning for David to go and for Linda to stay. David thundered from the study, loudly slamming the door. Anthony raised his hand for silence. "Well, well, that was interesting" he said, after the noise of David's angry footsteps had faded away.

"Why don't you try and get on with David?" she asked, plaintively. "Things would be so much easier for everyone."

Anthony half-smiled, while he polished his glasses, turning them this way and that to check that he had removed every smear. "It's not that simple when the man is chasing my job," he said.

Linda sat back in the chair and heaved a heavy sigh. "Please don't involve me," she said.

Anthony tucked the cleaning cloth into the case and carefully set his glasses on his nose, "I don't intend to," he said. "But I do need your help with something else."

"Harry?" she asked.

"Precisely," he replied with a sardonic smile. "I know he will take the warning badly, as well he should. But I worry he will not actually stop drinking unless you get involved." He fished out the letter from his drawer and let her read it. Everyone knew Linda was closer to Harry than anyone on the staff.

"Are you asking for my help?" she said. Linda felt like Anthony was setting a trap and inviting her to fall head-first into it. Anthony removed his glasses and set them down, and let the room fill with silence until it was broken by the sound of stampeding feet coming down the main staircase. Supper beckoned.

Anthony took the letter from Linda and opened another drawer. Reaching inside, he brought out a yellow carrier bag, which he handed across his desk "This is what I found when I went back to the swimming hut. He must have hidden it there. Goodness knows how many more are stashed around the school."

Linda looked inside. "I'm surprised that it's Bells. Usually he drinks a single malt," she replied sarcastically.

"Make him stop," said Anthony, getting up. He was tired, hungry, and irritable. Linda read every emotion in his face. She regretted their silly fling, but fundamentally she thought Anthony was a decent person.

"I will talk to him, woman to man," she said.

Anthony smiled weakly, "Thank you," he said. He was relieved. Harry would listen to Linda, and come next September, Harry would be out of his hair; the trustees had agreed to Anthony's proposal to let him go. No one would know that he had had a hand in it. The chair of the trustees promised he would play the part of the judge, jury, and executioner. He just needed Harry to stay out of trouble for this year, so that it did not affect the smooth running of the school.

Anthony rose from his desk. "I must say that I am quite peckish. Have you eaten?" he asked.

"Not yet. I have to attend to something first," she said, frowning.

"Nothing serious I hope?" he replied.

"I doubt it," she said. "Douglas Rice claims someone stole his catapult from his bedside drawer."

The headmaster frowned. "I thought they were banned." Linda shrugged. "Do you believe him?" asked Anthony.

"I don't know. Douglas has a habit of stirring up trouble. One way or another I will get to the bottom of it."

"Good luck," said Anthony. He had every confidence that she would.

After she left, he poured himself a scotch from his drinks' cabinet. He didn't feel like a hypocrite. There was a fundamental difference between wanting a drink and needing a drink. He swirled the whiskey around the glass before taking a sip and savouring the taste as it scorched the back of his throat. Briefly, it made him feel better about the day.

* * *

Douglas foraged under his bed, huffing and puffing. He moved the bedside cabinet, then jumped up and pulled open the drawers. The whole dorm watched as he emptied out each drawer on the bedspread.

"It'll turn up eventually," said Declan optimistically.

"How the hell would you know?" replied Douglas, touchily, chucking books and pencils into the top drawer, comics and odds and sods into the next, and finally whatever detritus was left into the bottom drawer.

"Do you remember when you had it last?"

"Declan, for the last time, I had it here." Douglas glared fiercely at Giles and Hugh.

Hugh pulled the sheet around his shoulder and turned on his side so he could better read the book by the bedside lamp. Giles sat down next to Hugh and looked on.

"I know it was one of you who took it," said Douglas, nostrils flared. He pushed the hair out of his eyes and stared at the boys, challenging them to speak.

Giles stared back at Douglas. "Why are you blaming me?" His eyes were black and unblinking.

Douglas looked to Declan, Varun and Stephen Walker for

support. They glowered at Giles and Hugh. "Where were you yesterday, Burton?" demanded Douglas, ignoring Giles, and going on the offensive. Hugh put down his book.

"When yesterday?" asked Hugh, with an amused look on his face.

"After school?" replied Douglas aggressively.

Hugh scratched his head, making like he was thinking. "I don't know, Dougie. On the toilet, playing football. What does it matter? Where were you?"

The red-haired boy's face turned bright red.

"He was with me," said Giles neutrally.

"Is that right?" he said in an accusatory voice.

"Yeah." Giles stood up and perched on the metal frame of the bed, grinning at Hugh.

"You're lying," said Douglas, who had a nose for these things.

Sensing that Douglas was spoiling for a fight, Declan decided to throw his lot behind his friend. "Why don't we go through their stuff?" he suggested.

"You can't do that, only masters can do that," said Steven weakly.

"Shut up, worm," barked Douglas. "Open up!" he said, jabbing his finger at their bedside drawers. Giles shook his head. Hugh pulled himself out from beneath his bedclothes and sat on his drawer. It was like a red rag to a bull: Douglas charged.

Grabbing Hugh around the waist, Douglas tried to wrestle him to the ground. Hugh thrashed out and pushed Douglas away. Douglas came at Hugh again, but Hugh simply hopped over his bed, laughing. He had his back to the closed door.

"Coward!" shouted Douglas. Hugh laughed even louder, a comical high-pitched laugh that seemed designed to enrage Douglas.

Hugh put up his fists. "Queensbury rules?" he said, stepping forward into the wide space between the beds. He shuffled from foot to foot, keeping his fists up. Douglas looked all agog. Hugh punched him in the face before Douglas had a chance to raise his hands.

Then, everything suddenly moved fast: Declan jumped in quickly, throwing himself against Hugh. The three of them tussled together, tied in knots. Giles waited for the right moment and then kicked out against Declan. The boy released his grip on Hugh. Giles pushed him again, flattening Declan on the ground by his bed. The boy tried to pull himself up, but only succeeded in pulling his mattress and bedsheets to the floor.

"Something fell out!" squealed Varun, pointing towards the fallen bed clothes scattered across the lino floor.

Hugh found a way out of Douglas's headlock and started to laugh again. "Look what Declan's been hiding," he said. "Your precious catapult!"

Declan looked up at Douglas, with a bewildered expression on his face. Douglas scrambled around on the floor, throwing the bedding aside until he found his missing catapult. He glared from boy to boy, his freckles looked like livid red pinpricks on a crimson moon. "You did this," he said.

"Who?" said Giles, with a twisted smile on his face. He had only wanted the catapult as a trophy. It wasn't his plan to get Declan into trouble.

"You or you," he said, waving his hand wildly at Giles and Hugh.

Giles scoffed and walked back to his bed.

Hugh straightened his pyjamas. He had lost some buttons in the fight, but that was the extent of it. He pushed past Douglas, who responded with a half-hearted shove. The fight was over with no clear victor. Everyone knew that it was never going to end with just this, things were only just getting started.

***

An Austin Maxi, an anonymous dirt brown car. Nippy for a family. Stolen to order. Eddie was at the wheel, his ferret-like eyes ever alert. Brendan joined him up front, in Tom's usual shotgun seat. Brendan said stay at home, Tom. He was too important. The others were expendable. Harsh words. However, something in Tom's gut said go. Maybe because he had a bad feeling about this one. But he always had that. No, it was more than that. They were getting casual, the boys. The fear, the edge, the nervous energy you needed for a job, they were losing it. He was going. Brendan scowled. Was Brendan going to blab to Sean? Nah, of course not. Brendan was Tom's man first and last and always. He wanted that to be true. They were old friends, not just comrades at arms. Yet there was a glint in the big fella's eye, which spoke of ambition.

They cruised through Knightsbridge and peeled off at Green Park. From the back seat, Tom whispered instructions into Robbie's ear. Robbie was eager. Robbie was pumped. Into the square now. The office buildings were dormouse quiet. The pubs and restaurants were nice and busy. Taxis plied their trade, people jumped in and out, wealthy men with young wives and girlfriends on their arms. Booze hounds wandered aimlessly, sniffing out one more for the road. A bamboozled tramp had his face and his arms buried inside a bin, hunting for scraps.

Brendan hissed under his breath, copper on the right. The uniform was doing his rounds. They were doing theirs. Brendan readied. Tom quietened the boys down, like a horse whisperer. Eddie steered the Maxi past the bobby. The boys kept their heads down. Then Tom gave a quick heads up, giving the venue a once-over. Scott's. The hub of Mayfair in its day. Tonight, it was packed to the rafters.

Eddie knew the drill. He parked up on the side street. When he heard the bang, they would come running. Be ready.

Tom snagged the hold all. Brendan took point. Robbie walked in step, into Mount Street. This was what we promised: war on the mainland.

Fifty yards, near now.

Brendan tucked his hand into waistband, closed his fingers around the revolver. Tom unzipped the bag. The boys were perfectly in sync.

The light from inside the restaurant illuminated the pavement. Don't let anyone leave now.

Tom opened the bag. Robbie dipped in. He held it like the Olympic torch, awaiting the flame. Tom lit it. Robbie ran and threw it; the big glass window shattered. They were on their way towards Park Lane before the first ambulance came.

* * *

It's the worst scene that the bobby had seen. A restaurant for fuck's sake. Tell us about it again. Two am. He had given his statement. His head hurt. Now, he just wanted to go home. But Walters and Beresford, the men from Special Branch, demanded they heard it from him one more time.

Have another fag PC Sands, someone said. His hands were still shaking. Someone lit it for him. He sucked on it, took a deep drag, and came up for air coughing and wheezing like an old man.

This was how it went.

He was walking his beat, due off in an hour at ten pm. The streets were quiet. Nothing unusual there for a weeknight. He had stopped at The Footman for a chat with the landlord about some trouble he'd had the week previous. What time was that they asked. PC Sands read his notes. 8.20pm. The Special Branch men exchanged meaningful looks. Walters, the bearded of the two, told him to go on.

From there he had walked back down to Curzon Street and into Shepherds Market; the same route he has taken every night for months, once-around the cobbled streets looking into the doorways where the red lights wink away, checking the punters were playing nice. Did he see anything unusual? Not then, not there. So, when? The questioning was relentless.

"Do you want a glass of water, PC Sands?" asked his sergeant, visibly irked by the Special Branch officer's line of approach.

Sands shook his head.

"Take your time," said Beresford, the younger of the Special Branch officers, pen and paper in hand, diligently taking down notes. Sands wondered how you made it out of uniform that fast, rising through the ranks, special in every way.

Sands re-played the showreel in his head. How the brown Maxi slowed as it went up Mount Street from Berkeley Square. He noticed the car because the driver was taking it unnaturally slow even though there was light traffic, just a couple of vehicles, taxis dropping off and collecting.

"And it was a Maxi?"

Sands nodded.

Walter lit another cigarette, and pointedly asked the policeman about his location. PC Sands repeated exactly what he had said before: the beat took him along the Scotts' side of the street, heading back towards the square. The Maxi was coming up the street towards him on the opposite side of the road to the restaurant. Although he didn't get a good look at the driver, he could see there were several passengers in the car.

The younger officer referred to his notes and handed them to Walters. The older man ran his finger along the page. Checking. "How many were in the car? Think, because this is important," he said, giving Sands a searching look.

Sands ran his hands through his hair, feeling the prickliness of his scalp. "Two in the rear and one in the front next to the driver, maybe just one in the back."

Walters told him to take his time and cast his mind back. Visualise it.

After a while, Sands said firmly, "Four. Two in the front, two in the back." Beresford struck a line through what he had written on the page. The Special Branch men appeared satisfied. Sands looked knackered. His face was grey, the colour of his dust-coated uniform. His sergeant wanted the interview to end. "It's ok," said Sands. He would rather they continued. Beresford said they were almost done. He was also dog-tired, having been on his feet for hours.

An overflowing ashtray separated the policemen from Special Branch. "Now, again, for the record, where were you located when you saw the men?" asked Walters.

Sands opened his pocketbook and produced the map he had drawn. "Here," he said, indicating his position thirty yards past the restaurant. "And I was here when I heard the blast." He pointed to a mark in his pad denoting Berkeley Square.

"A five-minute walk away?" Beresford asked.

"About that. I started running back towards Scott's when I heard the sound…" said PC Sands, his voice trailing away.

"Did you guess that it was an explosion?"

Sands pictured the debris on the pavement. The shattered glass frontage, the smashed tables and chairs, the diners stumbling blind from the smoke-filled interior, some already sitting on the pavement outside, bleeding from the head, retching and crying.

"I knew it was something big, most likely a bomb." He stared through the Special Branch men. He had the blank, thousand-yard stare that Walters recognised from tours of duty in Aden when he was in the army.

Walters wanted to know what he saw, what he did, when the police and ambulances arrived. Beresford wrote it all down again on fresh sheets of paper and eventually PC Sands signed his name in ink pen. It had gone three am, way past the point of tiredness. The policeman asked if he could phone his wife. The sergeant told him not to worry, someone at the station had taken care of that. "What did you tell her?" he asked.

The big bald sergeant put his arm around the young bobby. "Nothing, son. Only that you had to pull a late one," he said.

The explanation struck Sands as being horribly out of kilter with what he had seen. The questions poured out of him. "The woman, how's she?" He had dug her out with his hands while the sirens wailed all around them. Her head was bashed in. Blood was running down her cheeks. Walters lied and said the woman was okay, and ushered Sands out. The sergeant would see him alright. He thanked Sands and let the sergeant lead the bobby to the canteen. Three of the night shift were there, their uniforms filthy like his from the glass and the debris. Sands took a seat among them. Veterans of the force. Years his senior. No one spoke. No words could fill the deafening silence left by the horror.

Downstairs the two men Special Branch officers remained in the interview room. "What do you make of Sands' testimony?" asked Beresford.

"I think we finally have something to go on," replied Walters, after a long pause. They had a clear description of the make, model, and colour of the car, and they knew that they were hunting for at least four men. "They've been hiding in plain sight. But they slipped up tonight. Forensics reckons they can lift something from the pipe bomb," he said, ruefully. He wanted to double the number of plainclothes men in the West End and put more uniform on the beat.

Beresford sat back in the chair. His legs were numb. He could do with a walk or a hot bath to loosen his limbs. "When did you hear the news about the woman, the one Sands dragged out?"

Walters took another cigarette from the open packet. He took a deep drag, blowing the smoke towards the ceiling, watching the blue vapour dissolve. "I didn't. I told him what he needed to hear," he answered, flatly.

Beresford nodded impassively. However, Walters could see the lie did not rest easily on the young man's conscience. He was still green. When Beresford had come to be in the job for as long as he had, he would understand the truth was not always what people needed to hear. It was better for PC Sands to go home feeling he had achieved something than to learn that the medic gave the woman only a fifty-fifty chance of making it through the next twenty-four hours.

Walters stubbed out the Rothmans and added it to the pile. He could not fathom the change in tactics, from planting a bomb to using a thrown device where the risks to the bomber were much higher – not just unintentional detonation – but also visibility. He asked Beresford what he thought.

"They want us to know what it's like in Belfast," said Beresford. "The feeling that you are never safe, no matter who you are, where you are or what you are doing." There was something else: "They don't give a fuck about being caught."

Walters was old enough to remember the declaration, how young men who he had sworn to protect from loyalists had turned their back on the ballot box and taken up the gun.

"Even when we nab them, there'll be others ready to fill their shoes," said Beresford.

Walters pushed back his chair and rose to his feet. The day would be long, but this is what he had signed up for. "This is a war without end," he said grimly.

6 – BAD VIBES

Within minutes of waking, the nausea hit Linda hard and fast. She sat down on the bed and tried to let it pass. Her skin felt clammy and cold. Laying down made her feel worse: the room span. She could not go down to breakfast feeling like this or inspect the dorms. The water rose in her throat. Linda searched for anything into which she could be sick. Bending forward sent the room spinning. She burp-vomited into a wastepaper bin, but nothing came up. Linda pondered over what she had eaten last night. If she had food poisoning, then half the house would have it too. Ten nauseating minutes passed before she felt able to leave her bedroom and make her way to the first floor. At the sight of Isaccs loitering in the bathroom, her spirits sank; the dorm two boy had clearly been crying and wanted her attention. Linda summoned up her motherly instincts, such a sensitive boy could not be denied. She willed herself to bring out the matron.

Isaccs had wet the bed. Despite feeling wobbly, she went to dorm two. The boy's wet sheets were hanging from the metal frame. Linda covered her nose and mouth. She pushed past the boy and dashed to the main bathroom, throwing up a sickly yellow bile. Linda washed her face and rinsed her mouth until she felt something like herself again.

Isaccs was still waiting for her outside the dorm, awaiting her instructions. He sat timidly on a chair, looking younger than his eight years. His cornflower blue eyes were full of tears. "Come on," she said, taking his hand, and walking him to the laundry room. "There's nothing to worry about, it's just a phase you are going through." She forced a comforting smile.

Linda took a new set of sheets and a wool blanket, which almost matched his irises, from the freshly laundered stack. The boy put them in a basket. "After you've made up the bed, take the soiled sheets to the utility room." Isaccs looked up at her shyly. "What is it?" she asked.

"The other boys…" he stammered shyly.

"What about them?"

The boy blushed and bowed his head to the floor. "All of them were singing wet-a-bed, wet-a-bed, stupid little wet-a-bed. They sang it all the way down the corridor. Everyone will know." Isaccs put the basket on the floor and shielded his face. Linda pulled the boy towards her and hugged him "You know what we're going to do, John? We are going to make up the bed together and then you're going to run along to class, ok?" She made him promise to speak to her if the boys teased him again.

By the time they had made up the bed and opened the windows Linda felt like the worst of the nausea had passed. The boy looked brighter too. She handed him the basket of wet bedding. "You know where to go?"

"Yes matron."

"I will not permit any name calling. Remember what I said?

His cornflower blues shone. "I promise," he said, darting away.

The day had not yet started but already it had the feeling of being a long one. Linda decided she might as well get the conversation with Harry out of the way before he took morning school. She knocked hesitantly on his study door. "It's me Harry," she said. Linda heard his shallow cough, followed by the scrape of the chair on the floor and the sound of Harry fumbling to turn the handle and open the door.

"Linda, how nice. I've been expecting you, although not as early as this," he said. Linda pushed her way past a tower of books and searched for somewhere to sit. The room was as fusty as ever. Books piled on the floor; blinds drawn down. The day kept at bay. She thought he looked rheumy-eyed.

"Pull up a chair," he said, gesturing to the two battered lounge chairs almost hidden by yet more books and a pile of clothes. Linda cleared the nearer of the two and pulled it across the carpet. She sat opposite Harry, their knees almost touching.

"So, you know why I'm here, then?" she asked rhetorically.

"I had rather hoped Anthony would have given me the day before sending in the shock troops," Harry replied, theatrically. He was wound up tighter than a clock.

"I am not Anthony's lackey, Harry," she said, smoothing her skirt. She noticed there was an unpleasant stain on the hem from changing Isaccs' bedding. "I am here as your friend rather than at Anthony's behest."

Harry scoffed, sat back in his chair, and played with some papers on his desk. After a pause, he looked up at her wearily. "I slipped up," he said with a shrug.

It was a typical Harry understatement. She almost laughed. However, she judged from his hang-dog expression that he seemed in a contrite mood. He had had a quick nip from the bottle before taking the boys to the pool, he explained, and then took another while the boys were swimming. "You should have seen them splashing around, they were having such fun," he said, smiling wistfully. "I just got carried away in the moment."

It was at times like these that Harry reminded her of her father. Remorseful, apologetic, the morning after a night of heavy drinking. She wondered how many bottles he had stashed away in his room or concealed around the school. It had taken Linda ten years to put her father's alcoholism behind her, a whole decade had flashed by since he had passed away, and now, she thought, I am back in familiar territory having to cover up for a drunk. "Whatever you do, don't wait around for Anthony. Get to him first," she advised.

"What do you suggest I do, fall on my knees, and prostrate myself at the altar of Saint Anthony?" Harry replied, sarcastically.

Linda half-smiled. "Well, you could do that I suppose, but I think an apology will suffice." She knew Harry hated the idea of giving ground to Anthony, but there was no other way out of the present dilemma.

"Fine," he huffed.

"Good. I couldn't imagine things here without you," she replied, leaning forward, and squeezing his knee affectionately.

"You are just saying that!" he said with camp coyness, knowing that it was true. He always felt Linda had his best interests at heart.

"Yes, you are right, you are nothing but a nuisance," Linda replied, laughing now. "Give me a hug," she said, standing up. Under his shirt, she could feel the stiff awkwardness of Harry's frame relax a little. "You can hug me back, you know," she added. Harry guffawed and gave her a polite hug. He was so English like that. It was only when he was under the influence that he relaxed and loosened up. "There's one more thing, though. Anthony's decided there will be no more of *those* swims. He thinks they are unhealthy."

Harry let his arms drop to his sides and sighed heavily. "Is that another nail in my coffin?" he asked, studying her face.

Linda shrugged, "I don't think it's anything more than what it is," she said, although with Anthony she felt you could never tell.

Harry shook his head slowly, "The boys enjoy them so much," he said.

"You can't let on that I've told you," Linda said, giving him a maternal pat on his broad shoulders.

"Is that it or do you have any more good news to share?" Harry asked, ironically.

Linda gave Harry a look as if to say, 'give me a break'. "I better run along," she said, "I've already had to change one boy's wet bed this morning and I feel a bit sick."

"Do you think you've got a virus?" said Harry, concerned.

"I'm sure it's just a passing thing. But I might just take a few minutes," she replied, although, in truth, she was starting to feel quite queasy once again. Harry shushed her away. He was a complete germaphobe.

Back in her room, Linda changed her skirt and waited for the nausea to pass. Outside the sun was shining. Another beautiful September morning. She pulled open the window and breathed in the fresh air. Hearing the distinctive honking of geese, she craned her neck to look outside. A skein of geese was flying in formation, carving a V into the blue. She leaned out of the window to follow their flight. They were migrating and although they were beautiful to watch, she suddenly felt sad. Before she knew it, she was crying, not softly like in assembly, but big, loud sobs. She cried herself out, and then just as inexplicably she began to laugh. "What's got into you Linda Wallace?" she asked herself out loud. She didn't have a clue.

* * *

After the poolside shenanigans of the previous day, Harry elected to keep a wary eye on the year five boys for signs of trouble. However, they kept mostly quiet and to themselves, worried about incurring Anthony's wrath. Harry feared that too but knew what he had to do: apologise. Anthony was strangely absent at lunch time. Harry had to bide his time until the school day was nearly over to make his grovelling apology to the headmaster. He had the distinct feeling Anthony was not listening. However, he had got in there first, as Linda had advised, and he felt better for it. He dropped in on Linda at the end of school and said that the deed was done. "Well done," she said, looking relieved. Later, he joined Linda as she made the rounds.

"Don't forget, we are running clubs soon," he said. Linda was fussing over the youngest boys, who were changing out of school clothes and into casuals.

"I'll see you in a while," she said, as she helped the boys fold their things away. Harry decided that he would take the opportunity to have a lie down in his study before the madness of clubs began.

A few doors along from Harry's study, Hugh and Giles were already making preparations of their own. Their dorm had been allotted to the kitchen club. Hugh perched on Giles's bed, watching Giles change out of his uniform. Hugh was already dressed in faded jeans and an orange Adidas top. Giles pulled on a long-sleeve cord shirt over jeans. The boys were wearing identical Gazelles.

"I like your top," said Hugh.

Giles picked at the logo. "Thanks," he replied, tucking his shirt into his jeans. "I wish you wouldn't sit on my bed all the time," he said, tetchily.

Hugh rolled his eyes. "Sor-ree," he said, sliding off. Giles straightened the sheets and plumped up his pillow. Giles had been grumpy all day. "Are you still fed up about the rumpus over the catapult?" asked Hugh, now sitting on Singh's bed, kicking his heels together.

Giles was still busy making up his bed. "Yes," he said without turning around.

"Because it was found in Declan's stuff and you wanted to keep it?"

Giles shrugged.

"Did you want to get Declan in trouble?" asked Hugh, persisting with questions. Giles continued to ignore him while he tended his bed. Giles smoothed down the blanket, looking satisfied with the results.

"We need to do yours," said Giles.

Hugh got up and helped Giles with the bottom sheet. "Why did you take it?" asked Hugh. He was determined to get an answer. The catapult was nothing special in his opinion; nothing worth getting into a fight over or facing the slipper. At least that had been avoided by Douglas telling matron he had found his missing catapult. He was surprised about that. He had expected Douglas to lay the blame on him or Giles. No doubt, Douglas would find a way of getting retribution.

"I took it without thinking," said Giles, eventually. "Don't you collect things?" he asked Hugh.

"Like what?"

"Things. You know… pens, watches, coins, things like that." Giles looked at Hugh with an air of expectation.

There had been a boy in Hugh's dorm at Fleetwood who collected stamps. He was an oddball. No one liked him. Giles didn't seem like a weirdo – although the idea of collecting things seemed like an unusual thing to do – but it obviously meant something important to him. "Yeah, I suppose," Hugh replied, saying what he thought Giles wanted to hear.

"Like what?" asked Giles, looking instantly interested.

Hugh had to think quickly, "Marbles." He wondered if Giles could see from his expression that he was making this up.

"Me too!" replied Giles, his mood brightening. "I'll show you mine. They're in my tuck box."

Hugh frowned. "We can't go now, though. We'll be late for clubs."

"Of course not, silly! We'll have to wait until Saturday. I bet you've got loads of ones that I don't. We can play swaps," he replied, excitedly.

Hugh thought on his feet, "Mine are at home," he said. "They were confiscated after I got expelled from Fleetwood." This was a lie and a good one, it could not be questioned. Hugh felt rather pleased with himself.

Giles looked disappointed by Hugh's answer. "Never mind," he said. "You can start a collection here. There's a boy in dorm two who collects marbles. Arthurs. We can take some from him."

Hugh started to laugh, but Giles looked perfectly serious. "He won't miss them, he's got lots," Giles said. "Come on, let's go to clubs, and we can help ourselves to Arthurs' collection when his dorm is empty. The stupid boy keeps them in a jar on his bedside." Giles had it all thought out. Hugh was glad that they had clubs to go to, otherwise he feared that Giles might want to act on his idea.

By the time Hugh and Giles arrived at the kitchen the rest of their dorm was already there, gathered around the big food preparation island. Douglas and Declan looked as thick as thieves. The pock-marked chef was going through the safety rules. He rambled on before setting the boys a challenge of making a pasta sauce. They would work in pairs. An unsmiling woman in chef's whites whispered something in his ear. Short and stout, she wore her hair knotted in a bun. Her blue, unblinking eyes were set unnaturally wide apart. She reminded Giles of a fish. The woman did not notice that he was looking at her. She was far too busy staring at Douglas for that: she glowered at him.

"Fran will be on hand to help," said the chef, referring to the whispering woman. "But let's be clear boys, she is not going to be doing the cooking for you. Ok?" he said, raising his voice above their chatter.

The boys formed into pairs. Hugh and Giles stood together, as did Douglas and Declan. Varun Singh and Steven Walker assumed they would work together.

The chef and Fran exchanged looks. "Not so fast," said the chef. "You two swap pairs." He pointed at Declan and Hugh. Declan looked horrified by the idea of being forced to pair up with someone other than Douglas. Hugh was also less than enthused by the idea, but they did as they were told. All six boys spread out around the island.

"Are you boys keen cooks?" Fran asked, with a blank expression. No one replied. "Do you cook at home?" The boys looked at Fran like she was an alien. "This will be interesting," she muttered to herself.

Fran had set up a demonstration area on the island: a jar of salt, a small bowl of sugar, knife and chopping board and a can opener, plus cooking various ingredients – a garlic bulb, dried chilli flakes, two tins of peeled plum tomatoes and a packet of spaghetti, which she picked up and handed around. "Do you know where noodles come from?" she asked. No one proffered an answer. "No? They come from China. Marco Polo brought them to Venice, and that's how Italy gave us spaghetti." It was a well-rehearsed speech, which she had given at least a dozen times to boys of the same age over the years, to varying reactions.

"That's what I was going to say," said Douglas sourly.

"Is that right?" replied Fran with a faint sneer. She had had problems with the boy before; he was a proper nuisance in her opinion. It had been her suggestion to the chef to prise Douglas and Declan apart. Together, they spelled double trouble. Divide and rule was her motto.

Fran showed the boys how to use the ingredients, carefully peeling the garlic and separating out four or five cloves on a chopping board. "This is the fun bit," she said, raising her clenched fist and bringing it down hard on one clove. It popped open. She asked each boy to give it a go until the cloves were unpeeled. Next, she heated a little olive oil in a saucepan before tossing in the garlic and a little chilli. She stirred away gently until the cloves were light brown. Fran then removed the bowl from the heat and spooned in the plum tomatoes, before adding two tablespoons of salt and her special ingredient, two teaspoons of sugar. She smiled at her own handiwork.

"This stays on the hob with a low flame," she said, stepping back so they could judge the heat for themselves. "Just give the sauce a stir every so often, then after half an hour it'll be done."

"What's it supposed to taste like?" asked Giles.

"Good question," she said.

Fran opened a cupboard in the island and pulled out a jar, handing it to Giles, together with a spoon. He scooped up a generous amount and put it in his mouth. The sauce was sweet and slightly spicy. She dished out spoons to the others and they passed the jar around taking generous mouthfuls until they had taken their fill and it was empty

"Are you ready to give it a go, then?" she said. A few nodding heads was a good sign. Douglas still looked disinterested, but if he didn't play up, she would be happy.

Fran sent the boys off to cook. Each pair had their own working area. "Mind them hot taps," she said, pointing at the sinks.

Before long, the boys were cooking away, the kitchen alive with the sound of chatter. Fran walked from pair to pair. Hugh was vigorously stirring the sauce. Fran dipped her finger in. "Not bad, " she said, sprinkling in a little bit of salt. Hugh gave it another stir.

The chef had laid out three large bowls on the island, in readiness for a blind taste test. Fran called time and asked each pair to ladle their sauce into a bowl. The chef kept his back turned, rhythmically tapping a wooden spoon against his thigh.

"Let's judge the sauces," said the chef with a theatrical wave of the spoon. The boys gazed at him with lurid interest, as he dipped his spoon into the first bowl. He made no comment, he didn't even crack a smile. On to the next he went. This time he raised his eyebrows and pulled a puzzled face. He raised his spoon over the last bowl like he was casting a spell and plunged in, greedily. The boys giggled at his theatrics. Fran stood alongside the chef like a little drill sergeant. "In third place, the blue bowl." Declan looked disappointed. "Less chilli next time," said the chef. Giles didn't seem bothered by the result. He tapped the green bowl and then the yellow bowl, toying with the boys. "The winner is this one," he said.

"That's mine," said Hugh.

"Mine more like," snapped Douglas. "I did all the hard work." He shoulder-barged Hugh.

Fran sighed heavily, prodding the chef to do something. "Boys, boys," said the chef, raising his voice. "That's enough. Stop before I change my mind."

Hugh rubbed his shoulder and stepped away from Douglas. The red-haired boy glanced over at Declan, who gave him a sly grin. Giles caught it all.

Fran bottled up the sauces; they would serve them for dinner on another night. The chef formed the boys into pairs again. It was time to wash up. One boy to wash, the other to rinse and stack.

"Scrub-a-dub-dub," said the chef. "There are more than enough sinks to go around. Use the deep one to wash and the smaller one to rinse," he continued. The chef said he expected everything to be cleaned properly by the time he returned. He winked at Fran and sauntered away towards the fire exit. She guessed he was nipping outside for a quick smoke and to check the rubbish; the chef had convinced himself that someone was sneaking into the school and pilfering leftovers from the bins.

"Boys who are washing up must use gloves," said Fran, waving a large pair of yellow rubber gloves in the air to make a point.

There was a pile of dirty dishes and pans, and cutlery to wash.

Declan scowled at Giles. "I don't want to do the washing," he said.

Giles shrugged and pulled on the rubber gloves. "You aren't so smart without Dougie around," said Giles, concentrating on filling the larger of the sinks with hot water. Declan looked momentarily stung.

"Give me that," said Giles, pointing to the Fairy Liquid. Declan slid the plastic bottle along the work top. Giles tossed a drying up cloth at Declan.

Fran was busying away at the back of the kitchen. The boys seemed to be beavering away nicely. There was no sign of any ill feeling between Hugh and Douglas.

Giles squirted Fairy Liquid under the hot running tap. As the sink filled with water, he loaded in the dirty saucepans and utensils so they could soak a bit, while he scrubbed away at the chopping board and the cutlery. "Here, rinse this," Giles said, jabbing Declan in the ribs with the chopping board.

"What did you do that for?" said Declan, pulling it out of Giles' hands. Declan put it under the cold tap in the smaller sink and set it aside on the draining board to dry off.

Giles thrust a soapy saucepan at Declan. The smaller boy backed away slightly. Giles glanced furtively over his shoulder, while Declan rinsed the suds away. Giles could see Fran was occupied with something or other. The other four boys were getting on with the task set by the chef. No one was interested in what they were doing. He quickly scrubbed the rest of the utensils and the cutlery and dropped them and the knife into the small sink.

"Don't do that! You nearly got my hands," snapped Declan, annoyed.

"We've only got this last one left and then we are done," said Giles, heaving the big cooking pot which they had used to make the sauce from the soapy depths of the sink. It was so big and heavy he needed two hands to hold it. "It's slippery," said Giles.

"Watch out, you'll drop it," said Declan, alarmed by the way Giles was shaking, the pot wobbling in his fingers. Giles pretended to struggle with it. He up-ended it into the small sink.

"Quick, grab it," said Giles urgently

Declan lunged forward to catch the pot. As he did so, Giles gave the hot tap a sharp twist: boiling water gushed down. He let it run for a nano-second – just enough – and then, he shut it off. The chef heard the high-pitched scream from outside the kitchen and came running. He could see that Fran was struggling to restrain Declan. It looked like they were fighting. She had his arm in the sink. "He's scalded," she shouted, while attempting to keep his injured hand and arm under flowing cold water.

"You keep away," shouted the chef, gesturing wildly, but the boys ignored him. Fran told someone to run for matron. Douglas said he would go.

"What happened?" she asked, wild-eyed, looking from Declan to Giles, and then to Burton, Singh, and Walker for answers.

"It was my fault," said Giles. "The saucepan was wet and soapy. I tried my best to hold on to it." Giles tried to make himself cry, but the tears would not come. He wondered if Hugh would see through him or realise that he had done it for a good reason. Declan had had it coming since he had sided with Douglas over the catapult.

"Ok, ok, it doesn't matter right now," said Fran. She was only concerned for Declan. He had given up trying to struggle against the cold water and he let Fran hold his arm under the steady flow. He was shaking now, going into shock. Fran hoped matron would come quickly. Declan started to cry. For some reason, she thought it might be a good sign.

Linda arrived breathless having dashed across from the main school. Douglas, followed by Harry, entered the kitchen soon after. She could see the burns were bad. She looked first to the chef and then to Fran for an explanation. Neither had a satisfactory one to give. Giles answered for them through a veil of crocodile tears.

"It's not your fault," she said, tending to Declan's wounds. Accidents happened all the time. Giles dried his almost dry eyes and looked at Douglas; the red-haired boy was bawling for real.

* * *

The new public golf course was a step down from what Frank had been used to. He heaved the clubs from the boot of the Capri and skirted around the Club House and paid for his round. His tee off time was on the hour and by the time he was ready to play both the first and second holes were clear of players. In the distance, a couple of golfers were on the back nine. The fairways were his to enjoy; this was his precious time.

Frank drove poorly at the first hole, thrashed away at the second and third, before finding his eye and settling into a rhythm. A lovely long second shot on the seventh set him up for a simple putt, which brought his score for the round up to a decent level. He filled in the scorecard and smiled with satisfaction at his improvement. From the eighth hole on, his play was calm and composed. He completed the course five-over-par and felt good.

Frank dropped his bag outside the Club House. The lounge bar was quiet, just a couple of old codgers were seated enjoying a pint. He nodded politely at the unfamiliar faces, keen to be on friendly terms with the members, before sauntering through to the saloon, hoping that the atmosphere might be livelier.

The saloon was a riot of colour: mauve wallpaper and a garish orange and chocolate brown patterned carpet. In a pleasing way it reminded Frank of the estate pub where he occasionally went for a drink after work, a proper dive and a notorious local pick-up joint where the mantra among the mechanics was pull a pint and pull a bird. Frank eyed the room and caught the barman's eye, who beckoned him over. Frank ordered a pint of Double Diamond and pulled up a stool. Five minutes on and he had drained the pint. Before he had time to think about whether he wanted another one, the barman had set him up and passed down a bowl of peanuts. "On the house," he said.

"Thanks," replied Frank.

The kid's name was Eric, and he was working at the Club House while looking for a permanent job. He had a university degree in engineering, but there was nothing going, at least not around here, so he said.

"Why don't you move, go to the Midlands or up north?" asked Frank. That was where all the manufacturing and car making work was to be found.

"What's the point? At some point all the work will go overseas or be carried out by robots. Just you see," he said, while making himself busy by rearranging the bottles on the spirits shelf. "So, why bother, eh?"

Frank looked questionably at Eric as he took a long thirsty drink. He was surprised to find he had almost finished the second pint. "There's no way the government will let people lose their livelihoods to foreigners, never mind machines," Frank said dismissively. "Voters would never forgive them." If this was the kind of nonsense being taught at university, Frank thought Eric would never make it out from behind the bar.

Eric however, disagreed: politics was personal. He launched into an impassioned monologue about how and why British jobs were under threat from cheap, international labour and automation. Frank stopped listening. He could not be bothered to get into a debate on the subject. When Eric finally drew breath, Frank ordered another beer, made his excuses, and then wandered off to play the slots. After feeding the machine with change and receiving nothing in return, Frank decided to venture back into the main bar, which was starting to fill up fast.

Finding a space between drinkers at the bar, Frank pointed to his empty glass. The barmaid asked him if he wanted the same again. Simply having a woman serve drinks made things more interesting. "A Double Diamond works wonders," he said, quoting the advert for the lager, which was plastered on posters in every pub in the country. The barmaid did not blink or smile. She had seen and dealt with his sort a thousand times. "What's your name?" he said, smiling.

"Karen," she said, handing him the pint. Before he could say anything clever, she had turned away to serve another customer.

"Charming," said Frank under his breath, looking around to find a table. He suddenly felt a little bit drunk. Eyeing up a free chair, he swayed across the bar and asked the two golfers at the table if they minded him taking a seat.

"Sure," said one, the older of the two.

"Frank Ashworth," he said, extending his free hand.

"Tim," said the one who had invited Frank to the table.

"Bob," said the other.

The three men shook hands.

"Cheers," said Frank, with a boozy smile. They clinked glasses.

After another pint, Frank felt like they had been pals forever. Tim and Bob ran a builders' merchants. Work was slow, but they did not seem to care. "The Club House is our office," joked Bob, boasting that they managed to get in at least two rounds of golf every week. Frank agreed they were lucky.

"The perks of being the boss," said Tim. Frank guessed he was of a similar age, but he was already turning to fat.

The golfers wanted to know about his line of work. Five pints in, Frank was delighted to give them chapter and verse. They tucked into their pints, while Frank held court. "If you love your cars, I'm your man," he said, slurring his words.

"You should take Paula in to show her the Cortina," said Tim.

"To get back in her good books?" replied Bob, chuckling. "My wife's sick of being a golf widow," he added.

Frank said he had just the car in mind if Bob was serious. He was thinking about the Mark IIIs. Frank decided another round of drinks might help sweeten a deal. "Same again?" he said.

"Why not," they replied.

Karen loaded the tray with three brimming glasses. The bar was busy now. Frank had to manoeuvre his way through a group of flush-faced septuagenarians, boring each other to death about their scores.

"It is Frank, isn't it?" said one of the men, as Frank edged past.

Frank paused, tray wobbling. The older man did seem familiar to him.

"I bought a car from you last year," said the man. Frank's thoughts inevitably turned to problems, to what would require fixing.

"Ah-ha," said Frank, doing his best to keep moving, but the man seemed intent on having a conversation. He stepped away from his group and blocked Frank's path.

"It's running fine if that's what you are worried about," the man said, correctly guessing what was going through Frank's mind.

"That's good to hear." Frank was relieved, the last thing he needed was a disgruntled customer putting the spanners in the works when there was a potential sale on the cards. Frank glanced over at the table; Tim and Bob were engrossed in conversation. He could indulge the man in brief conversation.

"I wanted to inquire after the little boy. Marcus?" said the older man.

Marcus. The name landed like a blow. "I didn't catch your name?" said Frank, uneasily.

"Gerald Jones," he said. "But everyone calls me Gerry." Gerry had thick, wavy hair, silver grey. His face was etched with life's lines and liver spots.

Frank looked at Gerry nonplussed. The tray felt leaden in his trembling hands. The pints wobbled. He splashed some lager in the tray.

"I tended to the boy before the ambulance arrived…"

Suddenly Frank felt the tray go. There was nothing he could do about it. It crashed to the floor. People stepped away. Someone whooped and laughed.

"You should sit down," said Gerry, taking Frank by the arm. Frank steadied himself, clutching Gerry's shoulder. Gerry shushed his friends away, but the old men continued to stare. Frank stole a glance towards Tim and Bob. The golfers gazed back, perplexed.

Frank let Gerry lead. Gerry sat Frank at a quiet table in the saloon bar, and asked Eric for water. The young barman came over with a jug and two glasses. He hovered by the table, snooping. Gerry waved him away. "Drink slowly," he said, handing Frank a glass. Frank's face had an ashen hue about it. He took a sip the water. "The colour is returning to your cheeks," said Gerry, with a concerned look. "I didn't mean to give you a fright."

Frank breathed slowly, collecting his thoughts. "I think I have had one too many drinks," he said, setting down the empty glass. "I should know better at my age." Frank was aware of the hush in the room. He could sense everyone watching and listening.

"We've all been there," said Gerry amiably.

"This is awkward isn't it?" said Frank. Gerry shrugged. "I remember you now and how you helped," said Frank, looking into space. He pictured the golf club lying next to the fallen boy. Marcus was on his back, blood pooling in a single eye socket. Gerry was hunched over the child, trying to staunch the flow and keep Marcus calm, while instructing people to get back and call for an ambulance.

Giles and John were standing side by side. They were so quiet and still. Where was Moira? He could not remember. A crowd formed around Marcus, blocking the narrow passageway. Frank stood among them. He did not know what had happened; he had no idea what he was supposed to do. All the while, Gerry was whispering words of comfort into the boy's ear, holding his hand until the paramedics pushed their way through.

"Are you feeling better?" asked Gerry, as he refilled Frank's water glass.

"My wife and I weren't there when the accident happened," said Frank, his voice breaking. "We had only stepped away for a moment..." Frank felt it was important Gerry knew this. Gerry nodded. Frank had turned a shade of yellow.

"Can I call your wife and let her know that you are under the weather?" Gerry chose his words carefully.

"Not Moira," said Frank. "You can't ask her to come to a golf club and be reminded about all that…" He couldn't find the words he wanted to say.

Gerry understood: "A taxi then?"

Frank straightened up in the chair, doing his best to pull himself together. "I'll be fine," he said, taking another sip of water. "I'll just sit it out here for a bit."

A man walked past the table and tutted loudly. Eric stood behind the counter, gawping. "Stay here for a moment," said Gerry. He rose and went to the bar. "Are there many in there?" he asked, gesturing towards the lounge bar.

"It's full, sir," said Eric, looking over Gerry's shoulder at Frank. Gerry asked if the fire exit could be opened to spare Frank from walking through the lounge bar. Gerry waited impatiently while Eric disappeared to ask Karen. "It's not possible," said the barman when he had returned.

Eventually, Gerry walked back to the table, feeling he ought to stay with Frank. "You have been kind. In ten minutes or so I'll be as right as rain," said Frank. He waved his hand drunkenly in the direction of the lounge bar. "You should re-join your friends," he slurred.

Reluctantly, Gerry decided to go. "I'll be through there, if you need anything," he said.

Gerry discovered the number in his group had swollen during the time he had spent with Frank. He could hear what they were saying as he approached. Is he the father of the boy? Which boy? *That* boy? We don't want to be tarred by that brush at our club. Gerry guessed word had gone around about Frank. It was a small town: everyone knew everyone else's business.

"You have been with him for ages. Spill the beans?" said one of the extended golf party, a thin-faced man with a nose like a stork.

"About what, exactly?" asked Gerry, indignantly. He hated being put on the spot and, in truth, he had learned nothing at all. And even if he had, he was not the sort of man to gossip. He batted away their questions, closing his ears to the general chorus of disapproval. Gradually, the conversation returned to who had the bragging rights for the day's play, and the room gradually thinned out, as people left for home.

"Is he still in there?" asked Karen within Gerry's earshot. He swivelled around in her direction, assuming that she was addressing him. Instead, he discovered that she was engaged in conversation with a burly-looking golfer, not one of the regulars at the club. "I wonder what he is doing on his own in there?" she said in a disparaging tone.

"Who knows with people like that," grunted the golfer. "Anyway, I want you to meet Bob, not only a friend of mine, but also my business partner," he said proudly.

Gerry moved closer to earwig, as Bob joined them at the bar. "To think I was looking to buy a car off him for Paula," said Bob.

"Think again, right?" said Tim, knocking back a scotch.

"What exactly went on anyway with Frank thingy?" asked Karen.

Bob leaned across the bar conspiratorially. "He was booted out of where he used to play and told to find a new club after a nasty incident involving his son and another boy…"

Tim cut in quickly and loudly, "Nasty incident! That's putting it mildly," he exclaimed. "His son smacked another lad in the face with a golf club." He made it sound as though it was an attempted murder. Karen gasped. "By the time the ambulance men came, Frank and his missus had shot off home and left the poor kid alone with the medics."

"I don't believe you!" screeched Karen in indignation. "No parent would do that!" she said, shaking her head in contempt.

Out of the corner of his eye, Gerry watched the stork-nosed golfer push his way to the bar. The man tottered over. He too had clearly consumed a lot of alcohol. Gerry recognised him now from Round Table. He was a regular on the local golf club circuit around the county. It explained why he looked familiar.

"You're talking about Frank Ashworth's son, aren't you?" said the man. His face was gleaming, like he had been inside a steam room. "I was there when it *happened*," he said smugly.

Gerry strained to hear what the man was saying above the noise, feeling his pulse quicken.

"There were three boys playing. I was in the next booth along." They were making an almighty racket. Putting him off his own game. Something must have happened to turn things nasty. The man put his arm around Bob and drunkenly leaned into him and said loudly, so the whole bar could hear, "It was no accident, he did it on purpose, he did."

The drunk golfer gazed around at the faces staring at him. "I overhead the blonde boy, John, I think his name was, telling the medics. I heard him tell 'em it was deliberate." He grinned at his captive audience.

"Never," said the barmaid, looking aghast.

Gerry put his hand on the counter, feeling he needed to hold on tight; he felt suddenly like the wind had been knocked out of his sails. He gazed incredulously at the man with the big nose and then in the direction of the saloon, not sure who nor what to believe. He must have looked shaky because one of his golfing buddies suddenly appeared by his side. "Are you alright Gerry?", he asked, with a worried frown.

Gerry caught his breath and steadied himself on the bar. "It's nothing, I'm fine, thanks," he said.

"Are you sure?" asked his friend, still looking concerned. "Because you look for all the world like you've just seen a ghost."

* * *

Tom's adult life was also littered with ghosts. The dead always seemed to be in his thoughts and dreams. Sean said it was a good thing. You should never let them go. They would keep him strong.

Wars are fought with money, and the coffers were running low. The Council handed down fresh orders. Kidnap, ransom, kill. The initial targets were high ranking military men. The modus operandi would be familiar to Tom. Sean wanted a reprise of the snatch of the industrialist. Tom remembered how they had taken the Dutch man just like it was yesterday. They'd held him for a month in a box room until the company paid up. The order would come tomorrow. The wheels had been set in motion. Sean said stand down for the day. Watch the TV news. Something big was 'on'.

Hector was in his office when the van pulled up at the main gate. Where's Paul, the usual fella the sentries wanted to know. Off sick said the new driver. He had gone down with some bug or other.

You got ID? The driver had ID. The sentries walked slowly around the van. You don't mind opening up, do you? He did not mind. One soldier opened the rear while the other stepped inside. Pallets of fresh fruit and veg and assorted sundries. The driver kept his hands on the steering wheel with the ignition off as instructed while they completed the search. The soldier bounced out of the back and closed the door.

The sentries let him through the gates into the holding area. The driver had the sweats. The Provos held his family. Take me, he had pleaded. The IRA man had laughed. It wasn't up to collaborators to decide their fate. *They* determined the price to pay. Keeping his wife and children safe from harm, that was to be his redemption.

The barriers swung shut behind the van. No going back now. The driver slowed the vehicle and came to halt inside the parade ground. Wait until they tell you to turn the engine off. Wait until they tell you to get out of the van. Wait until…you'll know when.

Up on the ridge, the two IRA men trained their eyes on the van, coats hauled over their heads, shielding their binoculars.

Three soldiers circled the stopped van.

A young lad in his late teens had the task of inspecting the undercarriage, screening for explosives. He crouched down, carefully extending the rod with the welded-on mirror beneath the vehicle. The soldier was methodical, taking his time. The IRA men held their breath, willing the soldier to give the driver the green light and drive on, into the heart of the barracks towards the soldiers' mess.

The driver drummed his fingers on the wheel, nervously. A soldier approached the cabin. The driver wiped his brow. The urge to run was powerful. The Provos had warned him against it; picture your kids, picture what we will have to do if you don't come through for them.

The teenage soldier rubbed his eyes and did a double take: the device was strapped tight around the exhaust pipe, neat and tidy, almost invisible to an untrained eye. But he was *sure*. The unit on the hill watched him roll back, read his signs – the panicked waving arms – there was not a second to lose: they triggered the bomb with the remote control.

The soldier would never forget the sound of the loud pop and the smoke billowing out from under the van. Up on the third floor, in his office, Hector also heard the unmistakable noise and dived for cover, shielding his face from the glass of his office window. He expected it to rain down from the blast. However, the glass did not shatter; the bomb had failed to detonate. An eerie silence followed – momentary, mere seconds – then a sharp burst of automatic fire, as all hell broke loose on the parade ground.

The three soldiers kept their weapons trained on the van,

blinking through the small cloud of white phosphorus, trying not to rub their eyes. Slumped over the wheel, the driver appeared locked in an embrace.

By the time Hector arrived on the scene, more soldiers arrived, pointing SLRs at the cabin. Someone shouted that the vehicle was clear. A grizzled veteran opened the door and dragged the man out. Lifeless. The sentries had riddled the van with rounds. He was shot through. The back of his head was gone.

Hector commanded the van to be sealed off and the driver covered up, and the barracks to be locked down. The siren started up, a vicious wail. No patrol order had been issued to hunt down the bombers. Hector waved his arms in fury. Soldiers fanned out following his instruction, but Hector knew it would be too late, the unit would have already slipped away.

The young soldier took off his helmet and sat with his head in his hands. "What's your name?" Hector asked.

The private stared at the commanding office blankly. Hector repeated the question.

"Private Dowd, sir," he replied, trembling. The boy's face was ashen. Hector asked him to explain what happened. Dowd tried his best, but he could not get his words out. Eventually, Hector said stop, and called for a medic to look after the private.

The driver lay by the vehicle. Hector knelt and pulled back the sheet. The driver stared dead-eyed back at Hector, his face creased and dirty, hair matted with blood. Later, Special Branch identified him as Eric Hughes, a married, Belfast-born father of three. And then, months later at the inquest, Private D would read a testimony written by Colonel Hector Burton exonerating his men of the unlawful killing of the unarmed driver. Asked to recount events by the defence, Private D will speak with an eloquence that eluded him on that day when his CO had put the same questions to him. The newspaper will praise the soldier for his heroism. Dowd will remember the day differently: he will know he got lucky – others there among them would not be so fortunate.

Tom watched the news coverage of the failed attack on the barracks with a sense of disbelief. Sean had promised a spectacular. This was a fucking disaster. Target missed and something worse: The Brits had enough material from the device for a field day at forensics; it was evidence sufficient to identify the bomber maker, to trace it back to his hands.

As the night wore on the TV news went from bad to worse; the SAS boys had tracked down one of the unit. Liam McQuinn was dead. Some bastard from Special Branch said the net was tightening around the location of the second member of the gang; Freddie Mac was still on the run.

Tom's boys were jumpy. They wanted to change safe houses. Tom needed quiet and time to think. Robbie could not stop babbling. Jesus. Brendan poured large scotches into coffee mugs. Curtains drawn, they sat around the TV set and drank.

Tom turned the volume up and stared into the screen. The grainy black and white footage showed Liam's shapeless corpse under a tarpaulin. The stolen car was upended in a ditch. Berets patrolled the country lane. The cameraman panned to an Army chopper wheeling overhead. It looked like Bandit Country South Armagh rather than a sleepy English shire. The editor cut back to the barracks. Colonel Hector Burton was strutting his stuff, posturing for the news crew. Every word that came out of his mouth seemed designed to provoke. "Turn that man off," said Tom.

Between them they had finished the whiskey and smoked through two packets of ciggies. Every passing car outside the curtained window threatened an arrest. Brendan eyeballed Tom. A long hour passed, and then another. Tom knew Brendan was growing leery and expected him to tell them what to do. "We just wait out the night," Tom said, finally. Come the morning he felt his head would be clear, then he would decide about what to do next; they had weapons and volunteers enough to wage a war on the mainland, indefinitely.

They took it in turns to keep watch and sleep. No one slept. At first light, Brendan made a brew: strong, sweet tea which they drank from whiskey-soured mugs. Tom tuned in to the World Service. He usually found the Shipping Forecast a comfort, but not today, he craved to hear the latest news. There was none. Freddie had continued to evade capture.

"Do we telephone in?" asked Brendan, resting his huge hands on his scuffed jeans. His eyes were like black coins, cruel and hard. Tom patted his old friend on the shoulder and helped him to his feet.

The walk to the phone box gave Tom the willies. The streets were too quiet. Only the corner shop was open. Brendan nipped in and bought the newspaper and more cigarettes. Tom hovered outside and had a smoke, and then they walked on. The little red box stuck out like a sore thumb on the junction. Brendan crossed over the road, while Tom continued along the deserted pavement. As he neared, Brendan started to whistle a song:

Tom was clear to proceed.

The telephone box stank. The little panes were smeared in some sort of crap that could be crap. Tom kept the door ajar with his foot to let out the fetid smell. Brendan looked on from the corner. If he tapped his wrist, it was an instruction to abort. The big Irishman leaned back against the wall and whistled away, while Tom dialled. Sean answered on the third ring.

Freddie had made a home run. "You're the only one in play now," he said. Sean wheezed heavily. He sounded breathless.

"You got the newspaper with you? The Mirror, right?"

"Yeah." Did he recognise the man? Of course, he did. The man was front page news.

Sean coughed and spluttered. "The fish is a prize catch. You need to reel it in, alive if possible. We want it done immediately." They were to move out of the flat. Now. "You remember the farm? Make it your new home," wheezed Sean. He laid out the plan. Tom memorised every word. "The recons in place. When you get the green light, you go in." Tom felt the hairs on his arms stand up. Tom was buzzing. Tom was ecstatic. He had a spring in his step the whole walk back.

At the flat, Brendan unfurled the map on the kitchen table. The boys gathered around, pleased as punch to have been handed this one. Tom wondered if they had what it took. Robbie was raw. Eddie worried him. He drove okay the other night, but this was way different. A snatch would be difficult in daylight. It was all about the planning and the driver really had to show his mettle. You had to trust the driver. Tom ringed the target. He tossed Eddie the keys. Eddie beamed. Brendan and Robbie, and

Sean's recon man would be in the vehicle. He'd run the show along with another of Sean's new recruits, another local lad. Two cars. Six men. One target.

Back to the map. Tom traced his finger along the routes, evaluating the options, looking for pinch points.

"You think he will travel out?" asked Robbie. Tom knew the type: cautious but cocky. The target should expect to be on their watch list, but he was arrogant – that much was clear to Tom – and that would be Colonel Hector Burton's undoing.

7 - INQURIES

"You took your time this morning," said Veronica, glancing up from a steaming mug of coffee and a plate of toast. The kitchen was warm and inviting, the sun streaming in through the blinds. Gerry bent down to kiss her, feeling every bit his sixty-six years.

Veronica had the paper open in front of her. "What does The Daily Mail have to say about the attack on the barracks?" he asked, resting his hands lightly on her shoulders. Veronica lifted her head to his and sighed.

"You can imagine," she replied with a frown. "There's a quote from Hector." She pointed to the paragraph.

"A straight lift from the TV interview last night," said Gerry, scanning the front-page article. "Have they caught the other member of the gang?"

"It doesn't say. I guess not," Veronica said. She smiled weakly at Gerry.

"You are worried about the effect on the children?" It was not so much a question from Gerry as a statement.

She nodded. "A little." Veronica offered Gerry a slice of toast.

"No, thanks," he replied. He no longer had much of an appetite in the morning. A bowl of cereal seemed enough. No doubt it was another sign of getting old. "What else does the newspaper say?" he asked, propping himself up on a stool at the breakfast bar, letting the warmth of the morning sun wash over him from the conservatory windows.

"Here, you take it. I've read enough," she said, passing the paper to him. She looked upset, although more composed than she had been last night watching Richard Baker present the television news.

Gerry read the piece over cereal, while Veronica tidied up around him. "Imagine that, being forced to drive a bomb knowing that if you don't your family will be murdered." He shook his head in disgust.

"Really, Gerry, do we have to," said Veronica, drying off the plates at the sink. She recalled Hector telling her about a similar incident in Belfast. How a husband had been taken at gunpoint from the family home in front of his wife and children, bundled away into a car by men in balaclavas. For three days the family had been held hostage in their own home, waiting for news. The abducted man drove a car packed with explosives into a police station. The gang promised to return for the eldest boy if they breathed a word to the RUC.

Gerry set the paper down, "I'm sorry," he said, realising he should know better. "I imagine that you thought you'd escaped all this stuff once you came to live with me."

"Perhaps I did," she said with a shrug. "We should care about these things. I just wish it would end," said Veronica. She folded the tea towel and pulled up a stool next to Gerry. "Why don't you tell me about the thing at the club yesterday? With all this damn IRA business, I never gave you a chance to tell me. It was about the Ashworth family, correct?"

Gerry tried to keep the story short and stick to what he knew, explaining how he had started up the conversation with Frank by inquiring about Marcus.

"You shouldn't have done that," she said. "Some things are best left in the past."

"I disagree," replied Gerry. "Anyway, that's by the by. Do you want to hear or not?"

"Yes, of course!" she said, and moved the stool closer to him. Veronica listened intently, as Gerry outlined everything that had passed between him and Frank, and what he had heard at the bar. By the time he had finished, Veronica's face had clouded over. "People should know better than to go bandying about, making comments about things they have no idea about," she exclaimed.

Although Gerry was used to Veronica's contrarian views, he was surprised by her reaction. "So, you don't think there is any truth that the Ashworth boy clubbed the child on purpose?" he asked, eyebrows raised.

"No, absolutely not." Veronica said with conviction. "I'm amazed *you* do. You were there!"

Gerry looked at her carefully: "In all the years I practised medicine, I learned a lot about people," he said, taking time to choose the right words. "In all that time, I have come to realise people are full of surprises. Even the most innocent looking can do the most awful things to others. Believe me, I've treated more victims of violence than I cared to remember and dealt with the perpetrators."

Veronica scowled. "Even children?"

"Especially children, their behaviour is often primal, rooted in the most basic urges." Gerry reached out to take her hand in his, but she brushed him away.

Veronica was thinking back to the occasion when she had been introduced to the Ashworths, and now she remembered. It was New Year's Eve. They seemed perfectly pleasant and quite normal. "Surely you remember them?" she asked.

Gerry tried casting his mind back to the party, but he drew a blank. As far as he was concerned, the first and only time that he had dealt with the Ashworth family – the parents and their son – was at the driving range, when he had come to tend to the injured boy. All his efforts that day had gone into staunching the bleeding and keeping Marcus calm. The son and his friend were little more than blurred memories.

Veronica nudged him, "Well, do you recall meeting them at the party?" she asked, again.

"No, I'm sorry but I don't," he said, irritated by her question. "What's your point?"

She did not want to make Gerry feel old and forgetful, but she felt unable to let it drop. "Darling, we met them together, at the Rotary Club New Year's Eve party. 1972," she said, sympathetically. Veronica could imagine the little cogs whirring away in his brain. "I wore a yellow sparkly dress." She knew he would remember the dress, it showed off her finest pert assets; Gerry could hardly control himself on the taxi ride home.

"Ah, that dress. Now, I remember!" he said, his mouth

widening into a smile.

"I thought you might," she said, with a teasing grin. Gerry reached out and this time she was happy to entwine her fingers in his. "I liked Moira," said Veronica. "She was young and fun, if a little ditsy, but better than all those old spinsters." They had danced together and shared lipstick in the ladies. Moira had shown Veronica a picture of her son. He had a pageboy haircut like Hugh. "We even joked that they looked a-like.".

Gerry could start to picture Moira now. She was a petite, willowy blonde. "I never spoke to her, but I think I know who you mean," he said.

"Good. So, before we trust the words of a drunken idiot let's give the Ashworths some credit for being decent people."

"Ok, ok. Case rested?" said Gerry, with a half-smile. Nevertheless, he remained unconvinced. However, he was growing weary of the conversation and he knew that Veronica wanted to contact the children and reassure them about Hector's safety. Although their respective headmasters had promised not to let the news leak out, she was convinced that it would. Someone would tell Hugh or Belinda and they'd be worried. Gerry hoped for the best. The idea of Hugh in particular, becoming unsettled at the new school set off alarm bells in his head. No one wanted another repeat of Fleetwood, with the boy doing a bunk. It was imperative Hugh settled in the new school.

"What are you thinking about?" she asked.

"Nothing," he said.

"Liar. I can tell that something's up," she said. "Are you annoyed with me for going on about the Ashworths? It's fine to be forgetful at your age," she said, and gave him a gentle nudge. Gerry pulled a face. "Oh, don't be like that. Why don't you give me a hug?" she said, lifting herself off the stool. Gerry rose to meet her and squeezed her against him. He twitched through his trousers. Veronica laughed. "Is that what I think it is?" she asked, kneading him.

"Quite possibly," he said with a wolfish grin. "How about we kiss and make up on the couch?" he suggested, taking her hand, and leading her towards the three-seater.

"Like teenagers?" said Veronica, giggling. She wrapped her arms around his neck, gently caressing his cheek and running her hands through his grey hair. Veronica arched an eyebrow. "Really?" she said, feeling him fully stir against her.

"I know it's early…" he said, his voice thickening.

Veronica glanced at the kitchen clock. She would expect the headmasters to be available for a call. She felt momentarily torn. "Ok, but let's be quick," she said, letting him pull her down on to the sofa. Veronica kissed him hard with an urgency that demanded his attention. Naked and laughing, he responded with an uncharacteristically aggressive thrust, which took them both pleasantly by surprise.

* * *

Giles and Hugh joined the breakfast queue. Instead of the chef and his usual team an unfriendly man and woman stood in their place serving a choice of sausages, eggs and baked beans, or fish cakes and baked beans. "You can have one or the other, but not both," said the po-faced woman.

"Fishcakes," said Giles, holding out his plate.

"The same please," said Hugh. The woman slapped three fishcakes on each plate and poured beans on top.

They took their trays and sat with matron, who wanted to hear again what had happened in the kitchen on the previous day. For once, with nothing to say, Hugh ate silently, while Giles re-imagined the slippery pot and the boiling tap. He winced as he recalled the chilling cry that Declan had made. "How is he?" he asked, wearing a look that people wear when they are supposedly concerned. Out of the corner of his eyes, he could sense that the headmaster was watching on from his seat on the raised dais.

"You can take the afternoon off school to see Declan in the sanatorium. It'll cheer him up," replied Linda, studying Giles's face. "Finish your breakfasts and get to what classes you have," she said.

"Do you think Declan will be pleased to see us?" asked Hugh when they had left the dinner hall. Giles shrugged. He was preoccupied by the way the headmaster had stared in his direction throughout breakfast.

Linda had also noticed Anthony peering over towards their table. "May I join you?" she asked Anthony when the boys had emptied out of the room. She waved a pot of black coffee in one hand and an egg and bacon roll in the other.

"I didn't see that on the menu?" he said, looking at Linda, wearily.

"I've got friends in the kitchen," she replied, with a nod towards the temporary chef. It had fallen to Linda to organise the replacement staff after Anthony had abruptly sacked the chef and Fran over Declan's accident.

"Thanks," he said, accepting the roll. She watched him eat while fiddling with a napkin, folding it into squares, trying to work out when was the right time to ask. Finally, she summoned up the courage. "Did you speak to Declan's parents?" she asked.

Anthony set the sandwich down and wiped his mouth. "Not yet, I'm going to try again shortly," he replied, following the dance of her fingers.

Linda placed the napkin to one side: "Sister says Declan is already on the mend. I'll be going across to the san later to see for myself." It was possible Declan might be back in the dorm within a day, but Linda did not want to raise expectations. It was not unrealistic: she had seen plenty of scalds heal remarkably quickly. Fortunately, Declan had only sustained second-degree burns. It was better than first feared. "Without Fran's quick thinking Declan's injuries would have been much worse…"

"That's irrelevant," he snapped. He had called the Sister in for an audience in his office that morning; the boy could have long-lasting blistering to contend with. "How on earth could they let this happen?" he muttered, darkly. "There's no excuse for any of it."

Anthony was thinking not only about the difficult conversation with the parents, but also the trustees. He wondered if he should have already telephoned the chair. David Scott had been noticeably absent from proceedings; Anthony knew he was close to the chair.

"If you can hear me out for a moment Anthony," she said, taken aback by her own belligerence. "Accidents occur all the time, especially in a kitchen. I'm not sure that I would have had the speed of thought to react like Fran..."

"I will take that into consideration," he replied flatly. Anthony thought no one could see the big picture like he could. "Coming on the back of Harry's antics, this is not the start to the new school year that any of us needed," he said.

"I didn't think about that," Linda replied, recognising that he had a point.

He shrugged. "I have to report these things to the trustees," he replied in a resigned tone.

"I suppose it's necessary?"

Anthony nodded his head slowly.

"Are you including Harry in the same report?" she asked, with a worried look.

"Goodness, no," said Anthony. Linda sighed with relief. He had thought about it. However, he figured that reporting two serious incidents in the first week of term would undermine his own position as much as anything else. Hugh Burton's antics would have made a third, and thankfully, nothing had come of that. "I do need you to do one more thing for me with regard to Harry," he said, inclining his head towards her in a conspiratorial manner.

"Of course," said Linda, uneasily.

"Tell him that you'll be taking on lights out, forthwith," he said, in a hushed voice. Linda sat back and looked around the room. She was taken aback. Lights out was the housemaster's duty. It was how authority was expressed to the boys. Taking that away from Harry would send a message to the older boys that his position was greatly diminished. She assumed that this was Anthony's game plan: inevitably, it would force Harry to tender his position. "I understand this will make things difficult between you, but it has to happen," said Anthony, emphatically.

"You know what you are asking me to do?" she asked, by which she meant not only his dirty work, but also to force Harry's hand.

Anthony beckoned her to move closer, but Linda refused to give any ground and stayed at the same spot, the table separating them. Her message was clear enough. "There are no more important things than the health and safety of the boys. Mr Rhys-Davis clearly needs a lesson on that subject," he said, stiffly, pushing the plate away.

"When do you want me to talk to Harry?" she asked.

"No time like the present," Anthony replied curtly.

"Seriously?" she asked, uttering the word with every ounce of disdain she felt. She could not recall him being so callous. It seemed like he had changed into someone she did not know. "I'll do it as soon as there is an opportunity," she said, refusing to look at Anthony.

"Good, that's settled then," he said, rising to his feet, scraping the chair loudly on the parquet dais surface. "I need to telephone the Morris's and explain things away," he said, as he brushed past. Usually, he would offer to take her chair and walk with her. Instead, he walked away, without so much as wishing her a pleasant day. Her mother always said she had a lousy taste in men. At least, it meant nothing, she thought. She pushed Anthony right out of her thoughts and drank the rest of her coffee, while the cleaners wiped down tables.

"Are you finished, luv?" asked a large, buxom woman who was part of the temporary staff.

Linda handed her the plate with the half-eaten sandwich. "Is anyone in the kitchen?" she asked.

"Search me," replied the woman, unhelpfully, snatching the plate from her hand.

"Thanks for your help," said Linda, sarcastically, but the woman had already turned away to clean another table. The woman looked up as Linda left the table. Their eyes met over the empty plate. The cleaner shrugged and carried on chewing.

"No sense in letting good food go to waste," she said cheerfully.

"I suppose not," said Linda, weaving her way through the tables towards the kitchen. She wanted to inspect the taps again. Something was not quite right.

Only the janitor was in the kitchen. He grinned a toothy grin when he saw Linda. "The headmaster's in a right old strop," he shouted. He was deaf in one ear and tended to bellow. The man had been at the school for as long as anyone could remember, even longer than Jeffrey Ward, the gardener. "What are you looking at?" he yelled. Linda was studying the sinks and turned on the taps. The mains hot tap was taller than the standard hot and cold taps, turning the tap was no easy matter in any of the sinks. The one where Declan and Giles had washed up was no different.

Linda asked the janitor to come over. He shuffled across and stood by her side like a soldier on parade. At full height he only reached her shoulders. She had never noticed. Linda twisted the taps on and off, while she explained to the janitor what had occurred the previous evening during the kitchen club. "I still don't understand how the accident occurred. The tap is a good six inches taller than the other two, and it's not even that easy to turn on," she said, twisting it and then standing back to release boiling water.

"Tell me about it," said a voice Linda recognised.

"Hello Fran," boomed the janitor. She had been summoned by Anthony to empty her locker.

"I said the same thing to the chef. God knows we should have been right there with them boys," she said, staring at the offending tap. "Honestly matron, we kept telling them both to mind the tap. It beats me. It's almost like someone willed it to happen," she said, shaking her head, remorsefully.

* * *

It was a pleasant walk from the boarding house to the sanatorium, up along the private road that ran through the school, passed the new gym block and the old almshouses, which had been converted into art studios. They had hours to do what they wanted. Play a board game matron had suggested; just do something nice to take Declan's mind off things. He'd asked apprehensively if Douglas would be there. She wanted to know why. Because they're friends, he'd replied. She had asked Harry if it was a mistake to let Giles and Hugh pop over to the san. Harry told her to relax: their visit would cheer Declan up.

"What are you going to say to Declan?" asked Hugh as they approached the san.

"I dunno, sorry I suppose. I haven't thought about it," said Giles, speeding up. He seemed intent on getting there quickly.

Hugh grabbed on to Giles's jumper. "Are you?" he said, searchingly.

Giles paused mid-step, "You don't have to come along," he said, shoving Hugh's away.

"I know," said Hugh, huffily. "Matron thought it would be nice if I did."

"Ok, then," said Giles.

The sanatorium turned out to be a drab little building at the end of the road. It looked like it had been thrown together as an afterthought. Sister was waiting for them outside the concrete shell, arms folded. She wore a starched marine blue uniform and had a face like thunder. "Ashworth and Burton?" she asked, stiffly. The boys nodded. "Which one is which, you all look the same?" The boys pointed at one and other.

"I'm Ashworth," said Hugh.

"And I'm Burton," said Giles, stifling a giggle.

"You better come in, then," she said, ushering them into a cramped ante room. "First, sign the Visitors Book," she said.

Hugh winked at Giles and signed as Giles, making an exuberant signature on the page – a giant G and a swoosh below the surname. Giles broke into a smile when he saw Hugh's handiwork, and attempted to out-do him with an enormous H and B.

The walls were festooned with public health information and posters advertising vaccinations. Sister exuded a sharp smell of TCP. "You are not to touch his bandages," she said, opening a red door into the main dormitory. Declan was propped up in bed, the solitary inhabitant among ten freshly made beds. "You've got visitors," she announced.

When he saw Giles, Declan visibly retreated beneath the bedding.

Sister bustled passed Giles and Hugh, waving her hands. "Wait until winter, this place will be full to the rafters," she said, without any warmth or kindness. "Measles, chicken pox, mumps," she mumbled loudly to herself. They waited patiently while she blathered on. After what felt like an eternity, she ceased the monologue and went about her chores, leaving the boys alone with the patient.

"Hello, Declan," said Hugh, brightly, sitting on the adjacent bed. "We came to see how you are feeling?"

Giles plonked himself down next to Hugh. "Budge up," he said.

Hugh shuffled along the bed. Now, Sister had gone, they could take a good look around. In some ways it was like their dorm with the same type of metal-framed beds and bedside tables. However, the paintings on the walls gave it a cosier feel, and the shelves were lined with books, comics and boardgames. Hugh decided the place was not as bad as it looked from the outside.

Declan had his right arm folded across his chest. The hand and lower arm were bandaged, preventing the blistered skin from getting infected.

"Does it hurt?" asked Hugh.

Declan gave Hugh a sceptical look. "Yes, a lot," he replied.

"We brought you some fruit," said Giles, waving a plastic bag of oranges. Declan shrank away. "Don't you like them?" inquired Giles.

"I didn't know you were coming," said Declan.

"Do you want an orange?" persisted Giles. "I can peel it for you." Smiling, he broke the flesh and started to peel it away in strips, which he let drop to the floor.

Hugh helped himself to an orange. The boys ate in silence.

"Why are you here?" asked Declan, suspiciously.

"Don't you want us to stay?" asked Giles, deflecting the question like a seasoned politician.

"No, I feel tired," said Declan and turned away on his good side to face the wall. Giles and Hugh exchanged looks and decided they might as well leave. Giles opened the plastic bag, which was laying on the floor and reached down under the bed. Fishing up the comics while Declan was not looking, he stuffed them quickly into the bag. There was no point in hanging around any further. He gestured to Hugh that they should leave. "Get well soon," he said and headed towards the door.

"See you then," said Hugh, slinking out of the room after Giles. Outside, Giles flashed the comics at Hugh as they walked away. "Why did you take those?" asked Hugh, in a shocked voice.

"Because!" he replied, tersely, with a typical shrug of the shoulders.

"Give me that one," said Hugh, trying to snatch it from the bag.

"That's mine," laughed Giles. "You can read it when I'm done with it." Hugh made another grab for it. "Here, take it if you want," he said, handing it over.

The little road was deserted. It was like they had the school to themselves. "What shall we do now?" asked Giles. Excused from lessons, they could do what they fancied.

"Let's go and explore the air raid shelter again," suggested Hugh. They could play war. Although Giles thought the idea would be fun, he wanted to save the air raid shelter for another time. They'd yet to explore the school, and he wanted to check out the modelmaking room.

"Sure," replied Hugh. It was as good an idea as any, and preferable to be sitting in a stuffy classroom learning Latin

The modelmaking room was situated on the top floor of the boarding house, on the opposite wing of the building to where matron slept. It was the only room on that floor which was accessible to the boys. The other rooms were used for storage and kept locked. However, much to the boys' disappointment, so too was the door to the modelmaking room. They would have to come up with something else. "We should have gone to the shelter like I suggested," said Hugh.

"Stop moaning, Hugh," said Giles. "Why don't we see what's up there instead," he said, pointing to the ceiling hatch at the end of the corridor.

"It's the attic, where they store our trunks," said Hugh. He had heard about it from Hepbridge. A ladder was attached to the wall for access. The padlock swung free, invitingly. Quietly and carefully, they took the ladder down and set it up below the hatch.

Giles climbed up first. Supporting himself with his left hand, he pushed open the hatch and eased himself inside. "Are you coming?" he asked. Hugh nodded and started to climb, taking each rung carefully. Giles stuck out a hand to help Hugh up and then moved to one side once he was up, so they could sit together and take in the vast, cavernous space. A cord for the overhead lighting dangled from a ceiling beam. "Let's turn it on after we close the hatch, just in case someone sees us," said Giles, lifting it and placing it back into position. He left space for his finger so they would not get stuck inside. The attic was momentarily thrown into semi-darkness. "Boo!" said Giles. Hugh jumped, and then laughed at himself.

Striplights fastened to the old beams of the house slowly juddered into life, casting a pale, yellow wash over stacks of boxes, huge pots of paint, various lights, beds, desks, and other assorted paraphernalia. "It's like a school within a school, don't you think?" said Hugh.

Giles could see what he meant. However, he felt it was more reminiscent of the flea market he had visited with his mother when they had holidayed in York. The idea of discovering something interesting or forbidden captivated his imagination.

He started immediately rummaging away while Hugh set off to explore the space. Opening one packing crate after the other, he discovered books and more books. It was like a car boot sale full of hardbacks, and softbacks, which all gave off the same musty, unpleasant smell. Finally, he found one that he liked, Jack London's White Fang. It was a handsome hardback edition with an illustration of the wolfhound on the cover, teeth bared, howling at the moon. Pasted inside was a label listing the names of every boy who had borrowed the book from the school library. The last entry was dated 1952. Giles' grandmother had a Coronation tea set from the same year. "Have you read this?" he asked.

"What is it?" replied Hugh, clambering over boxes.

"I think you'll enjoy it. I did." Giles passed Hugh the book. "Keep hold of it," he said.

Although the attic was not that creepy, it felt strange to go digging about and taking things, thought Hugh. They would be in a lot of trouble if they were discovered. But now they were here, they might as well have some fun.

Giles saw the light coming up from the floorboards and skipped lightly across the room to see where it was coming from. Kneeling down, he peered into the gap between the boards and spotted Heppy lying on his back in dorm four.

Giles put his fingers to his lips and beckoned for Hugh to join him. Hugh tiptoed across. "It's Hepbridge," whispered Hugh. Hepbridge lay on his back reading. They watched him mouth the words from the book. He reminded Giles of the catfish which swam open-mouthed along the bottom of the tank, hoovering up surplus food "Wouldn't it be funny to drop something on him?" said Giles, glancing at Hugh.

"Don't you like him?" asked Hugh, earnestly.

"It'll be funny, and after he whacked me in the face, he deserves it," said Giles, pointing to the faint bruise on his forehead.

"Oh yeah," said Hugh, digging around in his pockets. "How about this?" he said, handing Giles a fifty pence piece.

They both lay flat staring through the narrow gap at the boy below. Giles waited until Hepbridge was lying comfortably on his bed and then dropped it quickly. The sharp edges of the coin struck the wooden floor at the foot of the bed. Hepbridge sprung from the mattress.

"Who's there?" he cried.

Giles and Hugh ducked out of sight, tittering. Giles wished they had something else. Hepbridge called out again and then they heard a door slam. The boys held their breath, listening before Hugh inched forward to steal a look.

"Wait, a moment, just in case it's a trick," said Giles, grabbing Hugh by the collar. Five, ten seconds passed, and then they snuck forward together and spied below. The book was flung open on the mattress, the bed was empty: Hepbridge had legged it.

"Do you think he's gone to tell a master?" asked Hugh nervously.

"What would he say?"

"That he heard something fishy," replied Hugh, sitting up.

"I bet he thinks it's the school ghost," said Giles, grinning. "We should scare him again!" he exclaimed, yanking Hugh up so they could continue to explore the space.

"We better get going soon," said Hugh. However, Giles wanted to inspect their trunks.

"We still have some time," replied Giles, glancing at his watch. He straddled the huge old beam that separated one side of the attic rooms from the other, casually surveying the scene. Although it was gloomy, the dark shapes of the trunks were silhouetted against the rafters. "Let's find ours," he said, scampering over the beam.

The trunks were arranged by the dorm. Hugh needed both hands to pull out his. The trunk belonged to his father. Hugh flicked open the catches and the lid sprang open. HEB was stencilled inside the box in large gold letters.

"What does that initial stand for?" asked Giles, fingering the letter E.

"Ernest after Shackleton," said Hugh, crawling inside the trunk. It was the perfect name for an explorer such as himself. "I could play dead, and no one would find me," he added, curling up and pulling the lid down. Without a moment's hesitation, Giles slammed down the lid and sat on top of the trunk and started to bang his feet on the side. "Hey, that's not funny," shouted Hugh with a muffled cry. Giles pretended not to hear. "Oi!" bawled Hugh. Giles slid off and opened the lid.

"What's it like playing dead?"

Hugh jumped out quickly: "Horrible! Warn me next time," he

said, trying not to look concerned even though his heart felt like it was about to come out of his mouth.

"Where's the fun in that," replied Giles, running his hands over the shiny leather surface of his own trunk.

"Show me inside yours, then?" asked Hugh.

"Why? There's nothing in it," he said, playing with the clasps.

"It's really nice," said Hugh, inspecting it carefully. "I bet it's got loads of fancy drawers and stuff like that inside it." Hugh began to fiddle with the lock.

"No, don't," said Giles, fiercely, pushing him back. Giles looked suddenly teary.

"Does it make you feel homesick?" asked Hugh. He got like that sometimes when he came across something special, which had belonged to his father, or if he turned up something his mother had given him as a surprise. He knew just the trick to distract Giles. "Help me pull out Douglas' trunk," he asked Giles. "Come on." He nudged Giles to shake him out of whatever it was that had upset him.

Douglas's trunk looked like it had taken a beating: the tartan cloth exterior was worn and ripped in patches, so the wood showed through. The lock was rusty and fiddly, and it took some effort to prize it open. The inside was as pathetically grubby as the outside; the fabric lining had peeled away, the pockets for underwear and socks were long gone. "Watch and listen," said Hugh, perching on the lid with his bottom inside the trunk. Hugh strained, his eyes bulging and then he let out an enormous fart and jumped off. "Quick, close the lid," he said.

They slammed it down together and sat back on the trunk, laughing.

"How do you manage to do that?" asked Giles, still laughing.

"It's just something I can do," he replied. "I bet there's loads of things you can do that I can't do."

Giles looked suddenly serious. "I am good at golf, but I'm not allowed to play anymore."

"Why not?" asked Hugh.

"My father put a stop to it and took my clubs away," he said, with a low grunt.

"Don't worry, you can play with me during the holidays," said Hugh, enthusiastically. "We've got loads of spare clubs. You can have Belinda's. She *hates* golf."

"Who is Belinda?" asked Giles quizzically.

"My twin. Didn't I tell you that I had twin?" Hugh was sure that he had mentioned his sister to Giles.

"You have a *twin*, a *twin sister*?" asked Giles. He looked slightly repulsed by the idea. "Isn't that really weird? Do you look a-like?"

How can you describe someone who looks a lot like you, but isn't like you because she is a girl? Hugh had never had to explain this before, and he struggled to find the right words. In the end, he gave up. "I'll show you a photo sometime, she's pretty. You'll like her, everyone does," he said. As Hugh pictured Belinda, he saw something which had been there all along, the passing likeness between Belinda and Giles. He suddenly felt uncomfortable. "Do you have brothers or sisters?" he asked quickly.

"I am an only child," answered Giles. His mother had sometimes mentioned in passing if he would like a brother or a sister, while his father had made no bones about the fact that he'd like a daughter. One of each, an heir and a spare. Giles wandered over to Hugh's trunk and played with the catches. "My father said boarding school would be fun, like being part of a big family. Do you agree?" he said, gazing at Hugh.

"I don't know."

"You ran away from your last school, didn't you?" he asked, opening, and closing the lock.

"Yeah, so?" asked Hugh, puzzled.

"Was that because you wanted to be with your family, your real family, not a fake school family?" he asked, flicking the lid open and tracing his finger over the large H.

"It wasn't anything like that," said Hugh. "I don't want to talk about it now. I'll tell you another time," he said, feeling awkward and tongue-tied

"Tell me now ..."

"No!" said Hugh, loudly.

Giles slammed the lid down on the trunk, "Would you take me with you if you ran away?" he said, intently.

"There's no need to run away. It's okay here," replied Hugh, lowering his voice.

"Is it?" said Giles moodily.

"I think so," replied Hugh, as neutrally as possible, sensing the Giles getting het up.

"What if *I* ran away?" said Giles. "What would you do?" Hugh fell silent. "Would you come if I asked you?" said Giles, turning and walking away.

Hugh followed Giles, "Where would you run to?" he asked, clambering over the beam, and then picking his way through the storage boxes.

"We could go anywhere we wanted," said Giles, glancing over his shoulder. Hugh knew this was nonsensical; you had to have a plan, you had to have somewhere to go. "We could go to the barracks," said Giles, preposterously.

"My father would send me back," answered Hugh in a flash.

"What about the air raid shelter?" said Giles, sounding agitated. "Or here?" he continued, waving his arms around, animatedly. "No one would think to look here." Hugh wondered what on earth had got into Giles. "Boys need to watch out for one and other," uttered Giles, reaching the hatch. He lifted it gently and pushed it to one side.

Hugh nodded. "Yeah, I guess." For a moment, he thought about leaving the copy of White Fang where it was, except he didn't want to rile Giles any further – and he figured, who would notice one less? The book had been boxed up with the others for years, gathering dust.

"There's nothing I wouldn't do for my brother Hugh," said Giles, dropping through the hatch and descending into the void.

Hugh heard the thud of Giles's feet on the landing. "I turned on the tap on Declan for you," said Giles from below. Hugh felt his stomach lurch. "Did you hear me?" called out Giles.

Hugh stepped across to the hatch and looked down. Giles was staring up at him with a feverish glint in his eyes. "Everyone knows it was a silly accident," said Hugh. "Why are you saying that?" He was aware that his voice sounded shrill, like Belinda's when she was upset or angry.

Giles gazed up: "I thought you'd be pleased," he replied, sounding hurt. "You are, aren't you?" Giles held his eyes. He looked solemn now.

"What do you mean?" asked Hugh weakly, lowering himself through the hatch. The drop from the attic to the corridor looked much higher from above, and the ladder felt wobbly under his feet and quite precarious with White Fang in his hand. "Here, catch this," he said, dangling the book in his hand.

Giles stepped beneath the ladder and held out his hands; Hugh let it drop. The book slipped through Giles's fingers and landed with a heavy thud on the stripped wooden floorboards. The baying wolf pictured on the book jacket grinned up Hugh.

"Get a move on," said Giles, with irritation in his voice. He shook the ladder to hurry Hugh along.

"Don't!" hissed Hugh, busying himself with closing the hatch. Giles did it again. "It's not funny," he said, looking down.

"It's not that high," said Giles, dismissively, stepping away so Hugh could descend.

Safely down, Hugh shoved Giles. "Next time, I will do it to

you," he said. Giles returned the shove. "What you said about Declan, is it true?"

"Shush, later!" said Giles, pointing to the modelmaking room. The door was ajar, and light poured into the corridor. Quickly they put the ladder back.

"We'll have to sneak past," said Hugh.

However, Giles was intent on looking inside and edged nearer. He crept up to the door and peeked in. On one side, there were a variety of models neatly arranged in rows – aircraft, warships, tall ships, artillery, tanks, and painted miniature soldiers – on the other, every type of paint brush, paint pots and glues. Gingerly, Giles stepped inside. A small boy sat alone under the far window, head bowed, immersed in painting a model aircraft. He looked up and put down the tiny brush, which he was using to decorate the wings. Picking up a finished German Stuka, he grinned at Giles and pretended to open fire upon him. "Rat-a-tat!" he exclaimed, through gap teeth.

"Where is everyone else?" asked Giles, ignoring his childish play.

The boy held out the plane to Giles, the paint was still fresh and wet on the wings. "They're coming later," said the boy. Giles didn't want to encounter whoever was coming and answer any questions about what he and Hugh had been up to. "I've got to go," he said.

"Stay a bit, you can help me make the other plane," said the boy, plaintively, gesturing towards the Lancaster B.111 bomber. The Airfix model was still boxed up, wrapped in cellophane, untouched. Giles had a B.II in his tuck box; the boy had the special Dambusters set. It was just what he had always wanted.

"Maybe another time," replied Giles.

The boy went back to painting his plane.

"Who were you talking to?" asked Hugh as they hurried away.

"Some little boy," said Giles glibly.

"Do you think he noticed the ladder and the hatch?" said Hugh, looking anxious.

Giles shrugged. He didn't care. He had his eye on the boy's Lancaster, and at some point, whenever he could, he'd come back for it and add it to his collection.

* * *

Frank Ashworth awoke with a monumental hangover. He blinked slowly, growing accustomed to the light and the familiar yet unfamiliar surroundings – the board games, Airfix models, Meccano sets, Lego toys and the many glass jars brimming with pebbles, coins, crystals, and ephemera; he must have passed out in Giles's bedroom. Frank had no idea what time he had come in, nor any recollection of whether he had seen or spoken to Moira. Frank looked at his watch: he was late for work.

Showering quickly, he was grateful to discover his wife was not at home. Neither, however, was the Capri. Snapshots of the journey home from the golf club came to Frank: stumbling into the taxi, falling asleep, thrusting money into the driver's hands, the cabbie swearing and speeding off. Drunk and incapable of driving, he had been forced to abandon the Capri at the golf club – no matter, he thought, he'd collect the car after work. He shaved and dressed and then phoned for a minicab to drive him to the dealership. He had the driver drop him off by the entrance to the workshop.

"What's wrong with you mate?" asked the mechanic with a surly smile. "It's unlike you to skulk in through here. Have you been a naughty boy?" Frank gave the mechanic the cold shoulder and stormed past. "You sure you're alright?" chirped the mechanic, bouncing a tyre from a battered Cortina across the workshop towards a stack of old rubber tyres.

"Fuck off," said Frank marching through. The mechanic laughed. Their loathing was mutual. The receptionist was behind the front desk, filing her nails. "Where's the boss?" Frank asked. She thumbed in the direction of the office and started on her cuticles without looking up.

Henderson's door was half-open. Reclining in his new expensive leather office chair, the owner looked deep in thought.

"Morning," said Frank.

"Morning. Pull up a chair," replied Henderson without any of the usual chumminess. Frank was happy to sit. His head was pounding. Henderson offered him a cigarette.

"No thanks," said Frank. He'd smoked too many the previous evening and his throat hurt.

Henderson raised his eyebrows. "First time for everything, I suppose," he said, lighting one for himself. "Rough night was it?" Ah, so that's why Henderson was acting off, thought Frank. "I heard you had a skinful at the golf club?" Henderson said through a cloud of smoke. Frank speculated about who had been sounding off.

"Probably not the word I'd use, but I did have one or two more than usual," Frank replied, sensing something else was up.

Henderson finished the cigarette. "Not what I heard. You know what it's like in a small town, people talk."

Frank shifted uncomfortably in the chair. "Do they?" he said, a blunt edge to his voice.

"They do, I am afraid," said Henderson, scratching his stubble. "While you've been my top salesman, I've always had your back." Frank guessed there was a 'but' coming. "Thing is, I heard you blew a sale, and then you got into a fight in the car park?" he said, studying Frank for a reaction.

Frank thought hard. He remembered the barman pushing him out of the bar. Eric, that was him. He had ordered a taxi to take him home. Gerry something-or-other had insisted. Then, what? "Do I look like I have been in a scrap?" Frank said, turning his face to the light, jutting out his chin.

Henderson laughed a hollow laugh. Everyone knew Frank was useful with his fists; they had seen him in action at the local when things had gotten out of hand. Despite wearing expensive suits and having the kind of hair that would make any woman proud, Frank was the classic get in first, ask questions later type of bloke. "I had a complaint from the club and from the bloke you were pitching the car at." He picked up his notepad and squinted at his own handwriting. "Bob Wade. I gather he's a bit messed up. I am sure you remember him now?"

Bob and Tim. How could he forget? Bob thought he could say what he wanted. Tim egged Bob on. Bob thought he could take advantage. Bob should have kept his mouth shut. "What is this all about?" said Frank, feeling weary. He found his attention drifting to a dirty spot on the wall, a foot, or so above Henderson's head. It was the only mark on an otherwise pristine white wall. If he sat where Henderson sat, he'd have it cleaned. Things like that annoyed him. From the repair shop came the whine of cutting tools, the mechanical grind of bodywork. Henderson spoke. His jowly features wobbled, animatedly in time with his lips, but the words made no sense.

"I'm sorry, with all the noise, can you repeat what you said?" Frank asked. The light in the room was too much, couldn't Henderson dial it down, turn off the lights or pull down the blinds. His head throbbed. His eyes felt like they were popping out on stalks.

Henderson poured Frank a glass of water, "I've got no choice, mate. I will have to let you go."

"What?"

"Mandy has got your things together…"

"What?" Frank said again, incomprehension turning to something far worse, a feeling of plummeting, free-falling, the ground coming up too fast.

On cue, the receptionist Mandy tapped lightly on the office door and entered. "Thanks Mandy, just put the box there." Mandy's mood was perma-sunny. Today she was positively beaming. Henderson shooed her away, mouthing 'thanks'.

"I don't understand," said Frank slowly.

Henderson rubbed his chin and pushed the folder across his desk, "Take a read."

Frank flicked through the information. Every page seemed to hang him out to dry: a mis-selling case against the dealership from 1974. Pages of paperwork. High-pressure selling tactics scrawled in red felt tip pen. Henderson had settled out of court with the customer. Another wad of A4 sheets. Improper conduct with a female member of staff.

"Come on, this is ridiculous. Half the garage put their dipsticks into her at some point in time," said Frank. Henderson sat back, poker-faced. The last sheet documented Frank's sale of the Mark III to the gormless-looking husband with the good-looking wife and teenage boys. "Oh, really?" questioned Frank. "You brought out the cheap bubbly as a reward for shifting the rust bucket before the new Mark IVs came in." Frank chucked papers across the desk. "This is a load of bollocks."

"That's before I had the latest complaint come in," exclaimed Henderson, turning angry. The booze-hound veins on his bulbous nose looked set to explode.

"About what exactly?" asked Frank, fighting to push the hangover away and get a grip on the conversation. He did not like the direction that it was taking.

"What do you think?" Henderson waved his arms dismissively.

"I don't know, that's why I am asking," said Frank, looking perplexed.

"The wife! You stepped over the line when you went after the wife. You shouldn't have gone there," said Henderson, becoming increasingly agitated and aggressive. The owner got up and pulled down the blinds. About time, Frank thought. The room was hot. Henderson stepped around the desk and opened the office door. "Take your stuff Frank," he said pointing at the box.

"Seriously?" Frank replied, incredulously, feeling oddly out of body. Through the open door he could hear in the silence that the whole dealership was listening. "So, what, that's it? I don't get a chance to give you my side of the story?" he said, thinking about his mortgage and the new school fees and the skiing holiday he had planned for January.

Henderson bent over and picked up the box. He plonked it on Frank's lap. "Listen, I never cared what you got up to outside of work until it got in the way of work, ok?" he said, leaning in so close Frank could feel the heat of his breath on his cheeks.

"But I didn't… I haven't done anything."

"Come on," said Henderson, tucking his hand underneath Frank's arm, hoisting him out of the chair. "Anyone who is anyone in this town knows everyone's business, Frank. You can't go around hitting on customers' wives and thumping someone who rubs you up the wrong way." Henderson eased Frank towards the exit.

"You don't have to man-handle me. I know the way out." Henderson let Frank pass. The reception was empty, only the faint sound of the radio emanated from the workshop. Frank understood Henderson had cleared the decks, envisaging some sort of scene. No doubt all the staff were all gathered in the kitchenette gossiping about him. I'll show them, he thought.

Keeping his chin up, he strode through the prestige cars in the showroom and walked out into the forecourt. Henderson trailed him, like an old sniffer dog.

"Your keys, Frank," said the owner. Frank set the cardboard box on the bonnet of one of the two remaining Mark IIIs and retrieved the office keys.

"All yours," he said.

"Frank, I need the keys to the Capri from you too?" Henderson stared through Frank towards the main road and the passing cars. "There's a taxi coming to pick you up. It'll be here in a moment," he said.

In the heat of the moment, Frank had quite forgotten that the Capri came with the job. The sound of the engine was a visceral roar. He could feel it in his chest the moment he turned on the ignition. It was almost heart-breaking to let her go. He handed Henderson the key.

Henderson wrapped his fingers around the fob and tucked it away inside his jacket pocket. "Thanks. No hard feelings, ok?"

Frank turned away. The taxi had pulled into the forecourt. "It's your loss not mine," he replied, belligerently. "The car is at the golf club. You better send one of your lackeys to fetch it." The golf club was miles away and the journey there was a pig due to roadworks.

"Don't worry about that, all taken care of," replied Henderson with a mocking smile, which remained stuck on his face until the taxi had cleared the forecourt and entered the stream of traffic heading into town.

"Where to?" asked the driver from behind the plexiglass panel.

Frank gave the cabbie his home address, but then abruptly changed his mind. The old pick-up joint was just the place to plot his next move. He asked the driver if he knew the place.

"What's the occasion, hair of the dog or something else?" asked the cabbie with a conspiratorial smile.

"Something like that," replied Frank. The driver did a sharp U turn and brought the taxi back around to take the slip road towards the railway station. Frank let slip the cardboard box containing his belongings. It careened across the back seat, jettisoning his fountain pen, money clip and notebooks. Just reaching forward made him feel sick.

"You ok, mate?" squawked the driver.

"Yeah," said Frank, struggling to open a window and get some fresh air. The taxi came to a stop in the traffic opposite the dealership. Mandy was outside with the mechanic. He had his arms around her, looking smug. The cars were sparkling in the sun. The mechanic reached down and picked up a banner, which he proceeded to drape over the car on the podium.

"The fucker," shouted Frank, at the sight of his car.

The cabbie caught Frank's eye in the rear-view mirror. "What's that?" he said, suddenly turning hard eyed and looking like he was ready for anything.

"Nothing, I wasn't addressing you!" replied Frank, as the taxi jolted forward, and the driver accelerated away. Frank had a foul taste in his mouth, like metal. "Slow down, please," he called out. He wanted to read what was printed on the banner. The mechanic and the receptionist unfurled the banner across the Capri's windscreen. They were giggling like teenage lovers. It read Used. Like New. Priced to Sell. Frank asked the driver to pull over: he threw up kerbside.

* * *

"How long has it been John? Ten, eleven years?" said Hector holding out his arms to give his old friend a bear hug.

"Eleven," said the Special Branch officer, returning the hug.

"It's hard to believe it has been that long. You look well. And this must be your number two?" he said, looking Beresford up and down.

The younger officer stepped forward and offered his hand to Hector, "Simon Beresford, sir."

"Please, come sit," gestured Hector in the direction of the long briefing table, which had been set up for their meeting. "You can leave us," he said to his assembled staff, taking a seat at the head of the table. "Terrible times," he said when they had the briefing room to themselves.

"The worst of times," replied Walters, scowling. "Worse than Belfast. Ruthless. That's why we're here."

"The attack on the barracks?"

"Yes, and a specific line of inquiry we're developing," said Walters. It had taken some doing for them to obtain permission to leave the investigation in London. They were short of men on the ground to hunt for the bombers, but he had convinced the powers-that-be that Hector could help.

"I'll do what I can," said Hector, although he admitted that he was more than curious about how they thought he could.

"Beresford will explain," said Walters, happy to defer to his younger colleague's intimate knowledge of the forensics.

Beresford set out what they knew about the IRA gang and its modus operandi. Hector listened patiently. "The pipe bomb is a crude but effective weapon. However, this one was exceptionally well assembled to maximise impact. Whoever designed it, knows their stuff," said Beresford. He didn't need to refer to his notes, although he had a briefcase full of information available should Hector want to familiarise himself with the details. "Usually, there is nothing for forensics to go on. But with the Scott's attack, we got a break." Beresford cleared his throat and placed the evidence bag on the table. "We found a partial material match to the unexploded device driven into your barracks," he said with a look of grim satisfaction.

Hector reached across the table. The metal fragment was scorched, no more than a fingernail in size. Hector held the bag up to the light. "This is fantastic news, incredible work."

"Thank you, sir," replied Beresford. Turning up the fragment casing had been the result of a methodical, painstaking search. Beresford was pleased with their efforts. More than that, he felt for the first time that they were no longer on the back foot.

On the journey from London to the barracks, Walters had shared some of his experiences in the police and recollections of the time he had spent in the army in Aden with HB. Beresford would have been too young to have known about the history of the times. Nasser had stoked the fire of Arab nationalism, and the British army had been called in when terrorists narrowly failed to assassinate the British High Commissioner in a grenade attack. After that, said Walters, it all kicked off. Units were called in from all over the place to restore order. A two-year living hell. Eventually, they were shipped out. HB went to West Germany, while he saw out his commission and joined the Police, and then transferred into Special Branch. Now, they were up against another terrorist threat, one that was far more deadly and efficient than they had faced.

"There's more though isn't there? That is why you are here," said Hector.

"Yes, sir," said Beresford. "Walters explained that you had served in Aden, and that you'd seen plenty of action in Belfast. The level of sophistication that the Provos have brought to the mainland is something that we've never faced before. And there's at least two active service units in play, perhaps more," said Beresford, looking at Hector squarely in the eyes.

Hector looked grave, "Two or more?"

A look passed between Walters and Beresford.

"Yes, heavily-armed and very well-trained," said Walters. "We are convinced that a four-man outfit is operating in the capital based on a confirmed visual ID from a police officer, and one or more outside London."

"McQuinn's gang?" asked Hector.

Walters nodded, "That's our hypothesis."

"Usually, the units do not come into contact with each other to prevent infiltration or giving up information under interrogation, but here we have two groups using the same high-quality explosives and parts," said Beresford.

"Go on, tell the CO what you think?" urged Walters.

"May we? I'll need to use the full table."

"Be my guest," replied Hector, sweeping up his paperwork.

Beresford laid out two maps: the first, a detailed map of central London showing Park Lane, Mayfair, and Green Park; the second, covering the entirety of London, from Ilford to Edgware, Enfield to Croydon. "The red dots indicate where attacks have taken place since the start of their campaign," said Beresford. "You can see, sir, that some of the attacks have been carried out in proximity to one and other. But what we hadn't figured out until the Scott's attack was that many have occurred not just in proximity, but within days of each other…"

"They have even attacked several places more than once," said Walters, cutting in.

Hector glanced up from the map, feeling a tightness in his chest like the air was being squeezed out of his lungs. An old sensation borne out of fear. He's felt it on patrol in Londonderry, and in the old Arab quarter of Crater in Aden as a young major with Walters at his side.

"I want to show you something else," said Beresford, shuffling the maps along the table, so that he could spread out a map of London and the Home Counties. "We are here," he said, pointing out the barracks, and then indicating when and where other attacks had been carried out within the vicinity. "You can see that the other attacks are more dispersed reflecting the wider geography, but there is a clear pattern," said Beresford looking up, checking that Hector was keeping up with his analysis.

Hector leaned in and examined the map closely, running his finger from his barracks to the nearest dot: the market town explosion, fifty miles away. Then, to the next, just ten miles further from there, to the shooting outside the pub where two soldiers were wounded. He continued to the next, and the next, and the next. Seventeen attacks in four distinct clusters. "When did these take place?" asked Hector, looking visibly shaken.

Beresford cleared his throat again. "Over twelve days."

Hector ran his hands through his hair, "Jesus, and no one made a connection?" he said in disbelief.

"Different police forces each focused on the individual case," said Beresford, looking uncomfortable.

"I know it looks obvious, but it wasn't until we had the forensics from the pipe bomb-making material that the pattern became clear," said Walters, with a heavy sigh.

"Who knows about this?" asked Hector, staring intently at Walters.

"A handful of senior people and just us."

"Does the PM know?" asked Hector.

"Yes," said Walters, emphatically. "He's keen that we exploit the intelligence, quickly and effectively. That's why we are here." Walters reached for the open packet of Rothmans and lit a cigarette.

"I get it," said Hector, still studying the map. "You think they will have another go here, or if not the barracks then somewhere nearby," he said, taking a cigarette himself. Walters tossed him the zippo.

"It's a strong possibility. The barracks, or somewhere that you and your men go to unwind, like a pub or club. Perhaps one that they've even targeted before," said Walters, through a veil of blue cigarette smoke.

"So, what are you doing about things?" asked Hector, taking another drag, before launching into a coughing fit. "I keep meaning to quit," he added, with a touch of gallows humour.

"We're flooding the streets in London with plain clothes, concentrating our efforts around Mayfair where they struck last," explained Beresford. The plan involved police, army and security services working together in an unprecedented way. "It's been signed off by Number 10," he said. "But we don't have the numbers or the coordination in place to replicate the same approach in the regions," gesturing to the large map of the regions. Five different police forces were acting independently in the immediate area around the barracks.

Walters interrupted his junior colleague, "Part of our job is to get them to work as one, and collect all the data into one place, so we might be with you for a few days yet..."

"Presumably that's why you are here, to see where I can help?" asked Hector.

Beresford pulled out a thick brown envelope from the briefcase and passed it across the table.

"It's all in there. A lot to digest, signed off by the Number 10," said Walters. The envelope was marked confidential and sealed with a government stamp.

"Do you want me to read it now?" asked Hector, weighing up the envelope in his hands.

Walters nodded, "Your diary has been cleared for you," he said.

"I see," said Hector, looking surprised. He was not used to anyone other than himself having access to his diary. This was a first. Hector started to break open the seal, but Walters stopped him.

"We will step outside and let you read it alone. That's how I look to do things," he said. Another first. Walters gestured to Beresford to collect up the maps and his briefcase. "We'll be back in two hours and answer your questions then," he added.

"You are staying the night with us, I hope?" asked Hector.

"We've lodgings in the Officers' quarters," replied Walters.

"Good, then we can enjoy a dinner together," said Hector, toying with the envelope. He always thought Walters would go far, but he did not imagine that he would go to the very top. Hector wondered what Veronica would think, she always had a soft spot for him. Once this was over, Hector decided Hugh should meet his old friend. He had the feeling Walters' influence would have a positive effect on his son.

* * *

While Hector's thoughts turned to his son, Hugh's returned to what Giles had said about getting back at Declan. However, every time he tried to quiz Giles about it, he had shrugged him away, and now that the headmaster had decided there would be an impromptu game of British Bulldog between dinner and lights out, Giles was in no mood to discuss anything else. He was not alone. The whole boarding house had been thrown into a mood of excitement at the prospect. David and Harry were far less enamoured by the idea. David, in particular, could not fathom Anthony's sudden volte-face. Yesterday, Bulldog looked as though it was to be confined to history along with nudey swims, and yet, less than twenty-four hours later, Anthony thought a game of Bulldog was just what the boys needed. "It'll be terrific for house morale," said Anthony over dinner with the staff. When he stood up and made the announcement, the raucous response from the boys seemed to indicate that he had made a good call.

Seated with David and Linda, Harry looked peevish. "I thought Anthony was against all this stuff?" he whispered.

"He's full of surprises," said David, arching his eyebrows. It was an extraordinary reversal by the headmaster.

Meanwhile, Linda surveyed the dinner hall, looking from table to table. She wasn't quite sure who or what she was looking for, but she felt unsettled by Anthony's decision to let the boys loose – his words – after a fraught start to the term. He had, he said, a plan to energise the boarding house and get the boys livened up for the gruelling rugby and athletics seasons. "David doesn't know it yet, but he will be helping get cross-country running started in the next day or so, and then we will have a screening of a new BFI film in the assembly hall as a reward for the boys."

Linda could see Anthony had expected her to be more excited. However, perhaps it was the gnawing sickness that continued to grip her when she least expected it that prevented her from being excited about his idea, or the uneasy feeling that there was trouble brewing in dorm three. She was not sure which it was. Finally, her eyes came to rest on Giles and Hugh. Seated together, they had been joined by Andrews. Linda had watched the boy grow from a shy boy into a boisterous, burly eleven-year-old, who was always making mischief. If she had been a fly-on-the-wall in their conversation, her fears would have been well-founded.

"Rice is angry with you," said Andrews, munching his way through a plate of sausages.

"This is Andrews, from dorm five," said Hugh to Giles.

Andrews scooped bullet peas into his mouth and chomped into a burned sausage with relish, "Alright?" he said, glancing up at Giles. He ate open-mouthed, meat and greens revolving around, like washing in a drum. "Are you not eating yours?" Andrews asked, prodding his fork at the untouched sausages on Hugh's plate. Hugh shook his head. Andrews speared one and then the other.

"How do you know each other?" asked Giles guardedly.

Andrews sliced into the sausage and started in on it, "Dunno, just around," he said.

"Yeah, I guess," added Hugh.

Giles had a put-out expression on his face.

"I suppose Douglas is cross about his ruddy catapult?" asked Hugh, looking around.

Andrews wiped the back of his hand across his mouth, and then reached across the table for an empty water glass. Hugh passed Andrews the jug. The thick-set boy poured half in the glass and spilled the rest on the table and laughed. "Sorry," he said, realising he had splashed Giles. "Something like that, but with Rice you never know, he's such a prat," he added.

Hugh laughed, but Giles looked serious. "Have you heard what he's planning to do?" he asked.

Andrews inclined his head in the direction of the kitchen, to the long table where Douglas was seated. The red-headed boy was ensconced in deep conversation with Hepbridge and the dorm fours. "Are you playing Bulldog?" asked Andrews.

"Yes, of course," replied Giles, while keeping a furtive eye on the proceedings on the dorm four table.

Andrews finished the plate and tossed his cutlery to one side. "Watch out for Rice, he'll be after you both," he replied. The boy took another swig from the glass and swung his legs out from under the table. His socks were rolled down to his ankles. Hugh noticed he had bruises running up one leg. They were purple and blue, each one the size of a thumb.

"How did you get those?" asked Hugh.

Andrews laughed, "In the swimming pool. We were larking around, and I slipped off the diving board." Andrews bent down, leaning into Hugh. Giles had to crane his neck to hear what Andrews was saying, but the boy whispered quietly and spoke quickly and the only distinct words he heard were nudey and Mr Rhys-Davis. Hugh started chuckling and beckoned Giles to draw near so he could tell him, but Andrews prodded

Hugh hard. "Not here," he said, glancing towards the teacher's seating area.

"Maybe we shouldn't play Bulldog," said Hugh, once the two of them were alone again. "We don't have to play. We could just as easily go back to the modelmaking room." Ordinarily, Giles would have liked that, and he did have his eye on the Lancaster. However, he was keen to play; he was good at it, and unlike Hugh he understood that things were heating up with Rice, and matters were better off being settled sooner rather than later. "This thing with Rice, it's not just about his catapult. This is because he is Declan's best friend. Do you think he knows what you did?" asked Hugh.

Giles shrugged.

"Don't always do that, say something!" said Hugh loudly.

"Shh," said Giles, looking quickly around the hall. Part of him wished he had kept what he had done to himself. Except Hugh had to know, that was the whole point, that's what bound them together like brothers, that's how things had been with John.

The noise in the dinner hall was growing louder by the minute as the boys finished dinner and started to eagerly head outside to the playground. Douglas joined the stream of boys, leading a small gang of dorm fours, as well as Varun Singh and Steven Walker. Douglas seemed to have numbers on his side. The hall was emptying out, very soon, they would be among the last to leave and that would not do, thought Giles. He had made up his mind about Douglas the first time they had met. Their loathing was mutual. Giles pushed back the bench and got to his feet. "Come on brother Hugh, let's get to Bulldog and show everyone who are the top dogs!" he exclaimed.

Hugh looked up nervously, thinking about his father and the words of wisdom which he had given to him when he had first gone away to board at Fleetwood. His father had said there would be times when Hugh would be tested; those times were part of the experience to be gained from boarding school. How Hugh responded to those challenges would help him through adult life. His father had bent down and kissed him, and then when his mother was out of earshot, he had pulled him close so he could whisper in his ear: "My father – your grandfather – only gave me one decent bit of advice, he said when it comes to a fight, make sure you get in first." Hugh realised the time had come to put those words to the test.

***

Tradition had it that the winner of the previous game of Bulldog started the new game. However, that boy had moved on to senior school. Anthony could picture him clearly – wiry, all legs, with the graceful movement and speed of a gazelle – but for the life of him he could not recall the lad's name. Never mind, he thought, casting his eyes around the assembled group of boys looking for inspiration.

Back when he was a boy, around the same age as his charges, his prep school headmaster liked to select a weedy-looking child. The man was something of a sadist: he claimed that it toughened a boy up. Such things were not Anthony's style, instead, he looked to choose one of the finest athletes in the boarding house. Age was immaterial.

The boys lined up at the far end of the playground awaiting Anthony's decision. There was an almost feverish sense of anticipation in the air. With the floodlights on, the asphalt surface looked particularly ugly and brutal.

"Are you sure this is a good idea, what if someone trips and falls?" asked David. When he organised the game, it was always out on the football field, which made for a softer landing.

"It's tag only," replied Anthony. "And besides who would dare do anything silly while we are watching?" Craning his neck to survey the boys one more time, he said, "How about we make Furnival the Bulldog? He's got good stamina, don't you think?"

Harry gazed at the pack of boys, the older ones jockeying for position, among them Andrews, Mountjoy and Furnival, his face a shock of acne. "I'd go with Mountjoy," urged Harry, "He's a pleasant enough boy. Spotty has a nasty streak."

"What about Douglas Rice? He's been down in the dumps since Morris went to the san," said Anthony. With hindsight, it was one of those occasions when Anthony would have benefitted from Linda's counsel; she had had an inkling of trouble brewing, but she was attending to something else in the boarding house, something trivial. It was just bad timing.

Anthony strode across the playground, calling for Douglas to step forward. The boys understood the head had made his choice. Hepbridge glanced around looking for Ashworth. Giles was in the packed middle. Where was Burton? Hepbridge frowned: he could not locate Hugh in the crowd.

"Sir?" said Douglas, standing tall and proud, with a look of expectation on his face.

"You know the rules, Mr Rice. No pushing or shoving," said Anthony, reminding the boy that he and the housemasters would be present throughout, gesturing towards David and Harry.

"Yes, sir," replied Douglas, turning around to face the boys, grinning. He could not believe his good luck.

"Go and take your position," said Anthony, pointing to a spot on the playground. "Shout out when you're ready," he added, stepping to one side.

Giles had played Bulldog more times than he cared to remember in the rec near the house with John and boys from the estate. Hugh had only played once or twice. They had agreed to watch out for Rice and any of his cronies. Neither of them had foreseen Douglas being made Bulldog; he would be sure to go after them from the off. It had been Giles's idea for them to split up and make things difficult.

"Are you scared?" asked Giles, as they had trooped out of the dinner hall.

"Not really," said Hugh. However, now that he was standing towards the back of the pack, he had the butterflies.

Giles had told Hugh to run without thinking. "Sprint as hard as you can. The slower boys and little ones always get picked off first."

They had stood together at first and then gradually separated once the boys had started to jostle for position. When the head called Douglas forward, Giles made his way to the front. He caught the smirking look from Hepbridge and readied himself.

"Settle down, boys," bellowed the headmaster from the side lines. David and Harry stood well back in the shadows of the high wall.

Crouching down on his haunches, Douglas looked left to right across the front row, narrowing his sights. At the san, he had sat with Declan while the sister had changed the bandages. Declan's skin was burned in patches, livid and red. He was convinced Giles had done it on purpose. Declan had made him promise to get Giles. He'd not expected the opportunity to have arisen so soon. The headmaster had inadvertently handed it to him on a plate. It was time for a reckoning. "Bulldog!" he screamed at the top of his voice.

Like a scrum, the boys charged forward; Douglas rushed out to meet the pack, picking out Giles as he ran. However, in the frenzied charge, Giles had passed him before he knew it. Douglas tagged three boys, but his quarry had eluded him. How? He almost had Giles, but another boy had got in his way.

"Spread out, you lot," said Douglas. The three boys joined him in a line. He shouted, "One, two, three, Bulldog."

The boys came running again. In a flash, they had tagged six or seven, among them Hepbridge, who had slowed down, letting himself be caught. Sweat dripped off the boy.

"Well?" said Hepworth, looking around. Ashworth, and Burton, were still in the game.

From the sides, Anthony watched on. With the rugby season in mind, he was making a mental note of which boys could try out for the first XI.

"Let's go after Ashworth together," said Douglas. "Bulldog!"

Hepbridge sprinted towards Giles. Hugh saw Heppy make the

move and came bounding towards hitting him hard in the ribs. The dorm four boy crumpled and fell backwards.

"Foul play!" shouted Douglas, as Giles and Hugh sprung passed. Furiously waving his arms, he beseeched the headmaster or the housemasters to act. David expected Anthony to intercede, but the headmaster bellowed, "Play on," and told Douglas to stop making such a fuss.

The Bulldogs and runners were now almost equally matched, twenty or so boys facing off against one another. Giles ran across to Hugh and whispered in his ear. They stood together now. Douglas Rice yelled "Bulldog!" and now the two boys ran *at* Douglas. Giles and Hugh had closed on him before he had time to think about what to do. At the last moment, they feigned left and right. Douglas lashed out. Hugh and Giles hurtled past, laughing. Anthony applauded their efforts, clapping enthusiastically from the side lines; they had the making of good players, and he had to admit, they had taken him by his surprise with their speed and guile.

Red-faced and panting, Douglas instructed the Bulldogs to spread out in close formation. "Close up," he shouted to the smaller boys. The odds were now weighted in his favour.

Giles and Hugh once again stood together. Alongside them, were just three remaining boys. "Shall we do the same again?" asked Hugh, with nervous excitement in his voice.

"No, let the three charge forward, and hold back, then run for a gap when the Bulldogs break for the runners," replied Giles, staring intently ahead.

"Bulldog!" howled Douglas.

The five remaining runners broke into two groups; three dashed ahead, while Hugh and Giles jogged forward. The Bulldogs split up to tag the runners. "Now," shouted Giles, spotting a space in the line. They ran for it together. This time, Douglas was sure he was ready. Commanding Hepbridge and his dorm mates to hunt them down, he came hurtling across the playground, oblivious to the field of play, the rules of the game tossed aside.

Swinging out at Giles, Douglas landed a glancing blow, which although was sufficient to knock him off his stride, was insufficient to knock him down. Giles glanced around, looking for Hugh. A dorm four boy had his arms wrapped around Hugh's waist and seemed intent on dragging him to the ground. Hepbridge grabbed Giles by his T-shirt. Giles jabbed him in the face and ran over to help Hugh. "Bulldog!" he shouted as he landed on the back of the dorm four boy.

Hugh untangled himself from the boy and yelled, "Bulldog!" at the top of his voice.

Giles grabbed Hugh by the hand, and they stood together as one, raising their hands in a victory salute. "Bulldog!" they yelled, as Douglas and what seemed like the whole of the boarding house came running at them.

"Jesus Christ," said Harry, at the sight of the melee.

"Well, don't just stand there," shouted the headmaster, striding across the playground, boys scattering away. David waded in, while Harry continued to dawdle. More boys broke and ran for cover as Anthony and David rounded on them. Harry finally joined them.

"Let go!" bellowed Anthony at the tight knot of boys who

continued to grapple with each other, ignoring the masters. David pulled Hepbridge up and away by the armpits, legs thrashing wildly. With that, his dorm mates abruptly stopped fighting.

"They're cheats!" exclaimed Douglas, flushed and furious, pointing wildly at Giles and Hugh. Giles grinned at Douglas. Although he and Hugh were dirty and bedraggled, they had come through unscathed, without any cuts or bruises.

"What's the meaning of this?" said Anthony Richardson, glowering at the two groups of boys. He did not know who to blame.

Douglas repeated his accusation, "They shouted Bulldog, sir, even though we caught them."

The entirety of the boarding house was ringed around the scene, listening intently, wondering what the head would say or do next. "Did any of the other runners make it through? Do we have a winner?" asked Anthony. The boys' attention turned to Mr Scott, who they quite rightly feared.

The principal housemaster glared at Rice, Hepbridge and the rest of their gang, and then at Furnival, Giles and Hugh who stood either side of Douglas. After a lengthy pause, he pointed to Furnival. "Today's winner!" The boy whooped with excitement.

"Every dog has its day," said Hugh loudly, setting off ripples of laughter among those in earshot.

"That kind of quip will land you in hot water," cautioned the headmaster.

"Not as much as Declan," murmured Giles to Douglas, calculating his words would achieve the desired effect.

"I heard that!" shouted Douglas, lunging at Giles.

Mr Scott attempted to jump between them. "Enough!" he shouted. However, Douglas was all fired up and it required every ounce of the housemaster's strength to make him stop. The whole house watched transfixed by the spectacle of Douglas being frogmarched to the main school building. It was the most exciting thing that had happened since the start of term.

Eventually, Harry clapped his hands and shouted that the show was over and that it was time for lights out.

"Linda will help join you for lights out, tonight," said Anthony. "Emotions are running high in the house and you'll need another pair of hands."

"I can manage…" he replied, but Anthony waved his protests away.

An hour after the game had ended, Harry and Linda succeeded in quietening down the chatter in the dorms. She had seen through Anthony's plan. However, she had no intention of following through with it: if he wanted to demote Harry from lights out, he would have to tell Harry himself. Her friendship mattered more.

"Are you sure you don't want Douglas to sleep in my room tonight?" asked Harry, as they patrolled the corridors.

Linda shook her head: "No, he's best off in the room next to mine," she replied.

"Can you lock the bedroom door?" asked Harry, casually, pausing outside dorm three.

Linda stopped dead in her tracks. "Why would I do that?" she asked, a look of horror spreading across her face.

"In case he tries to slip out, of course," replied Harry, nonchalantly. "Better to be safe than sorry."

"This isn't a prison, Harry!" she exclaimed. Separating Douglas from the dorm seemed the sensible thing to do, but the idea that a nine-year old boy should be locked up for the night was positively barbaric. Words failed her.

"If you say so," he replied, pushing open the door to dorm three. The four boys had their faces in comics. "Lights out, boys," he said, going from bed to bed, taking away the comics from Varun, Steven, Giles, and Hugh in turn. Harry put them on the bedside table adjacent to Douglas's empty bed.

"Where is Douglas sleeping, sir?" asked Giles, pulling the sheet up to his chin.

Linda poked her head into the dorm and answered for Harry, "Upstairs, with me. Why do you ask?"

"I was just curious," he said, with a smile. "And how is Declan?"

"He's a lot better. Now go to sleep, it's a busy day tomorrow," she said, in a hostile tone. She glowered at Giles and then nodded at Harry, indicating that time was up.

"You were a bit sharp," said Harry, after they had turned out the lights and retreated to his study to watch television together.

"It's been a long day. Can we talk about something else other than school? I'd just like to sit quietly and watch whatever's on," said Linda, switching the TV on. The BBC was showing a repeat of the period drama, The Onedin Line, which charted the ups and downs of a shipping family. Her thoughts returned to the offer to join the cruise ship. Harry settled in alongside Linda. Within ten minutes, she was sleeping.

In dorm three, no one was sleeping.

"Is it true that they put Douglas in the attic?" asked Steven.

Hugh slipped out from the covers and wandered across to Douglas's bed. "I might sleep here tonight," he said.

Giles pulled the torch out from beneath his pillow and shone the beam on Hugh. Hugh pulled faces until his muscles ached.

"Someone said he's been sent home," said Varun. Giles trained the light on him. The boy covered his eyes and disappeared under the blanket. Giles flicked it off and on, again and again.

Hugh shuffled across the room. "Why don't you make your funny face with the torch?" he said.

In the gloom, Giles concentrated his effort on contorting his mouth and features into the most hideous shape he could imagine.

"Come on, you can do better than that!" said Hugh impatiently.

Giles placed the torch below his chin and turned on the light.

Steven had to stifle a shriek, "You look like a gargoyle," he said.

Giles held the pose, feeling his jaw stiffen and his eyes bulge.

"A monster more like!" said Varun, peeping out from the covers.

"I know what you are" exclaimed Hugh, excitedly. "A Bulldog!" and he got on to all fours and started to growl.

Giles flicked off the torch and relaxed his jaw, and then under the cover of darkness, he too started to make a growling sound, quietly at first and then louder, like his grandmother's terrier when it was roused.

He recalled playing with the dog at her house on the day his father announced that he had been accepted into the boarding school. The terrier had kept fighting to keep hold of the plaything, resisting his attempts to prize it away. Giles understood the feeling, and now he embraced it, releasing a howl like White Fang. He expected an angry response from matron or Mr Rhys-Davis, but his howl was met with silence from outside the dorm. Emboldened, he did it again and then a third time, at which point he and Hugh were joined by Steven and Varun: dorm three had a new pack leader.

8 - INCURSION

Once all the woodland had belonged to the school. But gradually over the years when the trustees needed to raise funds, parcels of land had been sold off to housing developers until some fifty or so acres remained; more than enough the trustees felt to uphold the school's traditions and values as an academic yet outdoorsy environment for boys.

Before Anthony Richardson joined the school, the previous headmaster had employed local people for odd jobs. It was a point of principle he felt to create jobs in the area; the school advertised in the local job centre and word soon got around the town when there were vacancies. Occasionally, people would try their luck and knock on the headmaster's door looking for work, having heard about opportunities for casual labour. That was how Jim had come to find employment at the school.

After four years in the army, Jim had drifted from one construction site to another until the work started to dry up. He had even toyed with trying his hand on the continent; he had an ex-squaddie mate in West Germany who had mentioned work, but nothing came of it, so he stayed put doing labouring in London. However, when the last tower block went up in Stratford, he decided it was time to move on and he took the train east for Southend and the seaside.

Jim took board and lodgings on the seafront. By night, he worked as a door man. His hands were still quick even though he had not stepped inside a ring since he had left the army. The disco owner said he should go pro and put the cash on the table. Take it, he said and pay me what you owe with some interest from the winning purse. Jim had never seen money laid out like that. He scooped it up and went back to the bedroom near the pier and got drunk. Jim lasted four fights as a pro. He paid back what he owed and left town.

Nineteen seventy-one drifted into 1972 and Jim went back to nightclub door work and then to building sites. Eventually, exhausted, and almost broke, he found his way back to where he had grown up.

Jim remembered the boarding school from his wilder days before he had enlisted; he had picked fights with the so-called posh boys; they had learned to give him a wide berth if they came across him in town. Now here he was, a decade on, outside the school gates wearing second-hand clothes and a homemade haircut seeking work.

With his lank hair and lopsided fringe, the headmaster thought Jim looked like he had stepped out of a Brueghel peasant scene. There was an everyman quality about him, which Anthony's predecessor found reassuring. The headmaster set Jim to carrying out maintenance work on fixed schedules. It was his way of keeping tabs on new contract staff. The work was monotonous, but Jim stuck to the timetable and earned the headmaster's trust. When an able-bodied man was needed to help Jeffrey clear a plot of overgrown land and extend the kitchen garden, Jim got the job.

The old gardener was kind and generous. He had always been drawn to vulnerable types, and there was something in Jim that reminded Jeffrey of his younger brother. Of the three brothers who went to war, Sidney, the youngest, was the one who did not come home after 1945. After the show was over and he was back in civvies, Jeffrey had met up with Sid's old pals to reminisce. He was a simple, softly spoken sort they said. It was intended as a compliment. Jeffrey could say the same about the ex-soldier with the big fists: whatever he asked of Jim, Jim would do without question or complaint.

As they worked together, clearing the site, preparing the soil, and then planting the vegetables and the fruit trees, Jeffrey felt increasingly attached to his quiet, capable handyman. He invited Jim home for supper with the promise of home-cooked food prepared by his wife. But Jim always had a reason why he could not accept the offer. The old gardener didn't take the refusal as an insult; there was a big age gap between them, and it was normal, of course, that Jim would want to spend his free time with people of his own age. However, on that subject, Jim never had much to tell.

By the end of the year, the garden had come on leaps and bounds. However, while the work was progressing to schedule, Jim started to slip up: occasional late arrivals became increasingly regular and he often took to turning up in the previous day's clothing, looking unwashed and unkempt. The boys called him names. Stinko was the one that stuck.

Jeffrey asked what was wrong. It was nothing, Jim said. The gardener warned him to be careful. Anthony's arrival as the new headmaster could not have come at a worse time. Keen to stamp his authority, eagle-eyed and alert to any issues concerning contract staff, Anthony sent Jim back to repairs: fixing gutters, clearing blocked drains, and cleaning the outside toilets. Jim's gardening days were behind him.

Over the winter months of 1974, Jeffrey saw Jim less and less. When he tried to engage him in conversation, the handyman appeared anxious, avoiding eye-contact. Jim cut a ragged sight. Knowing Jeffrey had a soft spot for him, Anthony called him into his study and instructed the gardener to get Jim to clean up his act, literally and metaphorically. He would give Jim a week, or he would be letting the handyman go. Jeffrey was appalled. And so, wasting no time, he decided to take Jim to one side. Jeffrey's wife made a packed lunch for two. Don't be too tough on Jim, she said: have a father-son conversation. And so, over ham and cheese sandwiches, he did just that, laying out the headmaster's concerns. It was to be the last lunch they shared together; the morning after Jim did not show up for work, not then, not ever. Jeffrey thought about it often, wondering what he could have said differently.

However, unbeknown to Jeffrey, Jim had already made up his mind to move on. His landlady had been badgering him about the filthy state of his room and his dishevelled appearance; he was also behind on his rent. The old crow claimed he was putting off guests. She made it sound like she was running a holiday-let, rather than a pokey Victorian house divided into measly flats, with one shared bathroom between eight.

While they ate that day – Jeffrey doing all the talking – an idea started to form, which Jim felt answered the problem in hand. Once the school day was over, he returned to the lodgings, bundled up the few possessions he owned into plastic bags, and then re-traced his steps across town to the school. Waiting until nightfall and sidestepping the floodlit entrances, he climbed the low wall, edged around the school buildings, and walked silently through the grounds and out into the woods. His plan was simple: he would lay low, hidden away in the woods, until he was back on his feet. It was, he felt, an elegant solution.

Knowing the school and its routines was advantageous, of course. He washed in the outside toilets after the boys had gone to dinner and scavenged for leftover food from the refuse bins behind the kitchen. Once or twice, he had come within a whisker of being discovered by the chef on one of his frequent cigarette breaks.

Scavenging the school grounds and buildings for timber and materials, Jim found what he needed to build a lean-to inside the wood. His handymen skills and his soldiering were useful. Anything that was surplus or could be repaired, he would take and make a use of. With old pallets and tarpaulins, the lean-to was perfectly sufficient during dry weather. Deep in the woods, buried inside the bracken and thickets, he remained out of sight. Only animals disturbed him. Foxes were a menace. Weeks passed; then, one day, he discovered something of a lifesaver: the wartime air raid shelter.

At first, he took to going there only by night, worried the boys might stray there during the day. But after a while he realised the shelter must be off limits because no one ever dared venture beyond the hedgerow in the top field; for all intents and purposes, it was abandoned.

When the boys left school for summer, Jim felt confident enough to make the shelter his own. Gradually he began to clear away the debris inside. There were old ammo boxes a-plenty, long since emptied out. He broke these down for firewood. The entire rear wall was covered from floor to ceiling by packing crates. By torchlight, he took them down one by one and set them aside, while he decided what to do next. That was how he came to discover the other room. Hidden away behind boxes, the key was still languishing in the lock, as though waiting for its owner to return.

The room was wide and at least as deep as the first, the air damp, but surprisingly fresh. Jim lit a match and held it aloft. Following the flickering flame, he found the source of the air, three narrow air vents that opened out onto the field outside. Perching on a crate, he could reach out and touch the grassy bank, which covered the entirety of the shelter's exterior and take in a lungful of clean air.

In the days following, Jim sifted through the crates, unpacking gas masks, flares, smoke grenades, oxygen cylinders, bottled water, canned food, all with long shelf lives dating from 1941 onwards. And improbably, stashed below a bunk bed, he laid his hands upon dozens of bottles of wine and beer. He figured that the room had served as barracks for the teaching staff and Home Guard. Jim sat on a crate and felt at peace; it could be made perfectly habitable, he could stay warm and dry, and safe.

Through the summer of 1974 Jim enjoyed a pastoral existence. The weather was warm and fine. The school was deserted save for contract staff who fixed things up, doing the grunt work which the headmaster had once set him to do. Occasionally, he would catch a glimpse of Jeffrey taking a late walk through the fields. At moments like this, he yearned for human contact. When it became too much, he tidied himself up and ventured into town. People steered around him, giving up the pavement in return for avoiding trouble. Jim wondered if any among them were the self-same boys with whom he had fought when he was young and reckless.

The school shaped the pattern of his life. When the kitchen fired back up at the start of a new term, he ate well from the scraps. In the garden, he helped himself to what he fancied, enjoying the fruits of his labour. However, the boys' return from holidays also put Jim on his guard; he had to be more vigilant and attentive, as the playfields teemed with sporting activities and cross-country running began in earnest. Older boys liked to explore the woods, even though Jim understood the area was out of bounds, but as he knew better than anyone, boys will be boys. And ever since, he had taken to the woods and the shelter, Jim knew that chance encounters were inevitable.

On the very first occasion, he had been relieving himself in the woods. Sensing a presence, he finished as fast as he could, but the boy had seen everything and fled in terror. Jim expected a search of the woods would follow, or worse, an exploration of the shelter. However, nothing came of it, *then*.

After that, sporadic meetings occurred, without unduly concerning Jim. Boys might catch a glimpse of a long-haired man at the edge of the wood, or imagine, while playing in the assault course, a little deeper into the trees, that they had caught sight of him retreating into the bushes. Jim was unaware that the boys talked about these sightings among themselves. The older ones scaring the youngsters with stories about what would happen if they fell into the clutches of the weirdo-in-the-woods. If the stories made it to Anthony Richardson, he must have decided it was just stuff and nonsense, no different to the silly stories the boys shared about the school being haunted.

September 1975 and the Michaelmas term brought with it the usual influx of new blood into the boarding house. Jim was fascinated by the circus of the first week: the tearful farewells of some, contrasting with the eagerness of other boys to return to the boarding house, as though the school was a lifeline. Jim looked on from a spot deep in the undergrowth close to the school; so near, in fact, his body shook with the tremors produced by the cars driving in and out the gravelled driveway. Everything about what he saw made him question why people went to the effort of having children only to then send them away; and to wonder why some boys were seemingly pleased to leave their families behind.

The new term was only days old – perhaps the second or third day, time played no active part in dictating his life – when he had caught sight of the three boys advancing up the playfield, walking purposefully like little men on a mission. Peering through the trees, he had seen them coming from a long way off. He watched them with growing anxiety, realising they were heading for the gap in the hedgerow. Were they seeking out the shelter, *his* shelter? In horror, he looked on as their little heads disappeared.

By the time Jim had reached the tall grasses from where he could spy on the shelter, only one boy was standing alone outside, the other two had ventured inside. The boy, his face slick with sweat, hopped anxiously up and down calling out their names. He shouted out for them out one final time and then bolted away like a frightened rabbit.

Jim slunk out of the grasses and crossed over to the shelter, ducking down on the far side. Fearing that he might come face to face with the boys, he lurked in the lee of the shelter, biding his time. He counted the minutes. Attuned to everything around him, he caught the smell of smoke emanating from the shelter.

Inching forward towards the vents, he breathed in and was hit by the fumes. Then, he heard the retching noise. Scampering around the far side of the shelter, he saw two sooty-faced boys come tumbling outside, one still coughing and wheezing, the other shouting angrily.

"He's legged it. Now, we're in trouble," he heard one say, before launching into a coughing fit. The other boy's face was a picture of cold fury. He dragged his friend to his feet, cajoling him to get going. Jim wished they would; he was desperate to see what had occurred inside. Finally, the smaller of the two said he was feeling okay, and they left. As they reached the gap, Jim darted inside the shelter. Reaching up above the doorway, his fingers closed around the torch he kept for emergencies. Panning from side to side, the beam revealed the scorched remains of burned newspapers. Above the doorway to the second room, the ceiling was black and charred. They had discovered its existence. Instinctively, he pawed the key, which he kept tied around his neck for safekeeping. Squeezing it hard, feeling the metal dig into his palm, it was a sharp reminder of what he held dear, and everything he stood to lose if the prying boys returned.

* * *

Hector needed little reminding of what was precious to him; every tour of duty required writing a letter to those he loved. He fashioned a brief note to Veronica and the children, which he entrusted to Walters.

Hector had read the plan alone the previous evening, as Walters and Beresford had instructed. The dossier contained within it revealed that nothing in his life was secret. His relationship with

Marianne was months-old, no more than that, but inside the envelope were photographs of them together, dates and times when Hector had surreptitiously slipped out of the barracks without an escort to meet Marianne. To lure the gang out, the plan involved staging a car journey to Marianne's cottage. Assuming the unit took the bait, SAS and Special Branch would be laying in-wait and arrest them as soon as they made their move.

The file contained two other sets of photographs, which made for chilling viewing. In one batch of grainy black-and-white pictures, a tractor had pulled across the road feigning a breakdown. The IRA hit squad had been hiding in the ditch. The driver of the vehicle was a sitting duck. They had pumped round after round into the car.

In the other set of photographs, two cars had collided. One had rammed the other at a crossroads. The gang had snatched the target, a wealthy industrialist, and sped away in another vehicle. Hector had a dim recollection of the ransom demand. He had asked Walters why they would make a move on him. He was the highest-ranking officer, and he also enjoyed a high profile in the media and government circles, Walters had replied, over whiskies in the officer's mess. However, they were also evaluating other options based on the gang's MO and preparing for them, including the likelihood of another attack on the barracks, on pubs and bars frequented by the soldiers in the market town. They were all on the table.

Alone in his quarters that night, Hector studied the map again while they went through the journey, mile by mile. No escort. No tail. No visible support on the ground. Nothing untoward to spook the gang. The Land Rover was wired up for communication. Back-up could be called in at any time. Hector picked up the photographs of the industrialist's smashed car and the bullet-ridden vehicle with the dead man slumped in the seat. Neither of these men had been expecting the attacks, whereas he knew what was coming. Hector had retired for the night convinced of the plan's success.

Now, in the light of the new day, he prepared himself for what might lie ahead, dressing casually in civvies as he always would for a visit to Marianne. He tucked his St Christopher under his shirt, hoping that he would not need the saint's protection and made his way out of the building toward the parade ground, and crossed it with practised nonchalance, then sat behind the wheel of the Land Rover. Modified for British forces with a strengthened-frame, bullet-proof glass, and a souped-up engine, it was bomb resistant but not bomb proof.

All eyes, all thoughts, all actions were focused on Hector: the sentries at the gates, raising the bars and saluting the CO as he passed through; Walter and Beresford watching on from behind the barrack's opaque windows; Special Branch and SAS teams arranged in deep cover, positioned in the lane and at Marianne's cottage, ready to make their move. And the IRA gang, plotting moves of their own to take Burton alive, if they could – one Brit CO in exchange for one hundred special category status men. No civilian casualties. Powerful friends in America had made their displeasure clear to the Council over the Scott's bombing: it was bad news for fundraising. Bring in Burton and force the Brits to release their prisoners from Long Kesh. However, if the kidnap failed, Sean had authorised Tom to take Burton out.

Tom was meticulous in the planning. Two dry runs had shown the plan was viable. Brendan disagreed. The big Irishman had said his piece the previous night, laying out how he thought they should take Burton. Tom had heard him out, saying he would sleep on it and decide in the morning.

Tom had slept fitfully. He dreamt of his brother and awoke with a headache and bloodshot eyes. Brendan sat hunched over the kitchen table where Tom had left him the night before, wearing a scowl. Robbie and Eddie kept their heads down. They were joined by two reconnaissance lads drafted in by Sean for the operation: Conor and Roy. They had no surnames. They looked scared and sheepish. "Come and stretch your legs outside," said Tom, staring straight at Brendan. "We are going with the plan today," he said, curtly. "You, Eddie, Robbie and Roy in one car. Me and Conor in the other, just as yesterday."

Brendan shook his head slowly. He had hoped a night's sleep would have cleared Tom's thoughts.

"Do I need to remind you that I run the group? Because it feels like I'm having to pull rank," Tom said.

Brendan glared at the ground. "Of course not, you know that well enough," he replied. Of all people, surely Tom knew he was the one who would do what was right by the cause. "You can stop with all the hard man stares, it's not necessary," he added, with a half-smile.

"Are we good, then?" asked Tom.

"Do you even have to ask?" replied Brendan.

Tom clapped Brendan on the shoulders. He was built like an ox. The big man walked inside. Tom heard Brendan rallying the boys around. Tom lit a cigarette and leaned back against the brown Datsun and waited, going through the operation in his head. "Ready, lads?" he asked, as they filed out of the farm.

"As ready as we'll ever be," replied Brendan, banging his fist on the roof of the blue Ford to hurry the men along. Robbie and Roy slid into the rear, while he settled into the passenger seat alongside Eddie.

Tom walked around the car, giving it a final once over, checking that the new plates were in order and that there was nothing untoward like a broken lamp, which might give the police cause to stop the vehicle. Brendan wound down the window. "You're acting like a mother hen, Tom. Relax. We're just four farm lads on our way to work," he said, holding out his hand for the walkie-talkie. Tom handed him the re-wired banana phone. "It's pre-set to the right frequency, so don't go fiddling with it," said Tom.

"Aye-aye, captain.," said Brendan, turning the device over in his giant palms. "I can see why the thing got its name, it looks more like your prick," he said, waving it in Robbie's face.

Robbie laughed, "So, you were peeping then when I had a shower?" he countered, always ready with a quick answer.

Brendan gave him a theatrical wink, "In your dreams," he said, tucking the walkie-talkie into his jacket.

"If you boys have quite finished…" said Tom, bristling.

"Oh, come on man, let us have a joke," said Brendan, leaning out of the car window. "We know what's expected. We won't let you down."

"I know, it's just me getting jumpy. Be careful, ok?" he said, and he rapped his knuckles on the roof of the car signalling for them to head out. Conor joined Tom by the gate to see them off. Brendan gave them a thumbs-up as they went. It would fall to Brendan to capture Burton. Tom suddenly wished he was alongside him in the Ford, rather than overseeing operations. They'd carried out every mission together. Brendan had earned the right to lead this one. He'd be feted by Sean and The Council. His role as the planner would be forgotten in the excitement. Momentarily, he felt envious towards his comrade. Tom pushed the thought away, reminding himself that all that mattered was the outcome. He lit another cigarette, one final smoke to calm his nerves before they went on their way.

Their viewpoint over the barracks had everything, an unrestricted field of view across the parade ground and near-perfect concealment. Tom and Conor hunkered down, training their binoculars on the barracks. Under the cover of the foliage, they stayed out of the sun. Sean's mole said Burton was a man of precise habits.

"There he is," whispered Conor.

Twizzling the focus ring, Tom zoomed in on the tall figure striding purposefully out of the main building. Without doubt, they had found their man. Tom panned left and right, from Burton to the sentries, across the parade ground to the featureless buildings, looking for any movements, tells, anything that might seem out of place. "We're on," said Tom, unable to control the excitement in his voice. "Call Brendan."

Conor ducked out from their position and slid down the bank to pick up the strongest signal. "The cargo is heading your way," he whispered into the mouthpiece.

"One piece or more?" answered Brendan over the clear, static-free line.

"One, repeat, one," he replied.

"Got it," said Brendan. "We're on our away. See you on the other side."

Hector took the left turn from the barracks, as instructed. He had Walters plugged into his ear. Keep a steady pace. Don't deviate from your usual driving style. Avoid doing anything that arouses suspicion. However well-meaning, Hector could have skipped the pep talk, and yet, despite all his years of experience in the field, he was struggling to maintain the veneer of normalcy at being used as a target. He'd driven these roads many times in the last month alone. So why didn't he remember seeing the skid risk sign, or the low wall in Cotswold stone and the driveway to the country hotel? Everything seemed strangely unfamiliar.

Hector glanced in the mirrors. If an attack came it could come from any direction, from a tailing vehicle or from advancing traffic. But Walters thought they'd make their move in the quiet country lanes near to Marianne's property. How far until he reached the turning to hers? Ten minutes, he estimated.

As Hector approached the hidden dip in the road, the traffic was slowing. He decelerated, dropping the speed from forty mph to thirty to twenty. His heartbeat went the other way: 85, 95, 120…

In the belly of the valley, vehicles were at a standstill. Temporary roadworks. This is it; they'll make their move here. It made sense. Hector decided to break radio silence, "I've come to a stop in Avery Valley," he said. Static. Hector repeated the message. The line crackled, then dead. He'd lost the signal in the valley bottom.

There was a small queue ahead backed up behind a stationary flatbed truck. One lane closed for repair. Road workers were shovelling steaming asphalt on to the verge for rolling flat and packing down. A bored youth in a hard hat held aloft a Stop sign.

Hector pulled up half-a-car behind a mid-size Peugeot. A woman sat behind the wheel, loud music blaring from the car stereo. She began to sing along to the radio. It was a song he recognised, one that Belinda liked. The driver caught his eye in her rear-view and smiled warmly. To Hector, it looked fake and forced. He loosened the safety belt so he could reach for the service revolver tucked into his belt, while counting the number of cars between him and the truck. Five. Hector drummed his fingers anxiously on the steering wheel.

Time seemed to crawl.

Eventually, on-coming traffic hoved into view. The first car passed on his right, coming from Marianne's direction: an old man on his own, hands gripped to the wheel, eyes glued to the road. Two more cars followed. Hector tracked them in the mirror. As he watched the cars disappear, a dark coloured vehicle approached from his rear. Hector squinted into the mirror trying to make out the people inside. Walters expected at least a two-person team. Hector released the hand brake, letting the Land Rover gently roll back, increasing the distance to the Peugeot in case he needed more room to manoeuvre.

The brown hatchback slowed to a stop: two men sat in the

front seats, long haired fellas in denims. As he watched, two more vehicles came into view. Without adjusting his position, Hector felt for the Heckler. One of Walters' men had ripped out the plastic gubbins on the inside of the doorframe and strapped the semi-automatic into place. All he needed to do was give the velcro a sharp tug to pull the Heckler free. Hector wrapped his fingers around the butt. It felt reassuringly cold.

The shrill blast of the horn startled Hector. The Peugeot had already moved off and was starting to round the truck. The driver of the hatchback honked the horn again, gesticulating for Hector to get a move on. Hector fumbled over the gear change and almost stalled the vehicle. Stamping his foot down on the accelerator pedal, the Land Rover abruptly shot forward. As Hector steered the car around the truck, the bored youth stepped into the road and stopped the traffic. The hatchback juddered to a stop, the driver waved his hand out of the window and gave Hector the finger.

The earpiece snapped back into life. Walters. "Sorry about the roadworks," he said, in hushed tones. "Are you ok?"

Hector swallowed hard, "You could have warned me."

"All rather unexpected I'm afraid," replied Walter in a quiet, brisk voice.

"Do you think it's on?" asked Hector in the same hushed tones, carefully clocking the surroundings while he passed the line of queuing traffic on the south bound stretch. The earpiece emitted a whining, popping noise. Walters continued to speak but the words came out garbled. His voice sounded robotic. "What?" shouted Hector. Did he hear Walters say it was on? The earpiece spluttered and died. Hector shook it hard, but it seemed dead. Sweat ran in a rivulet down his neck. Checking his rearview mirror again, he breathed a sigh of relief at the sight of the empty road. If the unit had been on his tail, then the roadworks would have dented their plans. However, if they lay ahead of him, the game was still in play. "Come on, bring it on," he said, out loud, going through the gears and climbing out of the valley and into flat open country.

The left-hand turn to the lane was coming up in half a mile. At that point, he would leave the main road behind. Two minutes to get there, then three minutes up the lane to Marianne's.

Hector rounded a wide bend. The Peugeot was parked up on the side of the road just before the turning, approximately three hundred yards ahead. The carriageway was clear, just his Land Rover and the Peugeot.

Two hundred yards. He felt his pulse quicken. Where was the woman? He couldn't see her. The crackle scared him half to death. "Pull in behind the Peugeot," said Walters with urgency in his voice.

One hundred yards and closing.

Breathing hard, Hector shouted Walters' name into the receiver.

Fifty yards.

"Walters!" he bellowed again.

Walters screamed back, "Pull in, pull in. Harding is one of ours. Do exactly what she says. Trust me, HB!"

Hector swung the Land Rover onto the verge. The woman – Harding – was visible now, crouching behind the Peugeot, glancing left and right, concentrating on the southbound carriageway. "Come over here," she shouted, gesturing for him to join her by the vehicle. Hector tore the velcro away and grabbed the Heckler, jumping out of the Land Rover.

"Give me the gun and take this," she said snatching the weapon and thrusting a car jack into his hand. "Get up and stand by the offside. You've changed a tyre, right?" she barked.

Hector felt strangely out of body. "Yes, of course," he replied, sounding dazed.

Harding looked to her left. "They're coming for you. Four men in a blue Ford, advancing towards us, down the hill on the southbound stretch." Hector gazed in the same direction. It was a pretty part of the county. Usually, the only incidents that occurred involved an occasional drunk driver veering off the road.

"How do you know?" asked Hector.

"Intel. It doesn't matter now. Just do as I say and make yourself look like an easy target by playing the part of a chivalrous man helping a woman driver," she snapped. "You can do that, right?"

Walters had it all figured out: he knew the gang was coming and he had set a trap, and he had not trusted Hector with the information in case he blew it. "He should have told me!" bellowed Hector, angrily.

"You know how it works," hissed Harding. "We couldn't afford you to fuck up." The happy-go-lucky woman who had been singing along to the car stereo just minutes before had cold, calculating eyes. "Are you following me?" she said, fiercely.

Hector nodded. "What do you want me to do?" he asked.

"Stand tall, where they can see you," she said, "Over there," she pointed, while checking the rounds in her automatic. "We've got this covered. When they come for you, get inside the Land Rover. Then, stay down until the shooting stops, that's an order!"

Harding's handset bleeped loudly. Ducking down, she quickly spoke into it. "Get in position, now," she said, walking casually to the Peugeot's supposed blown tyre. She turned her back to the southbound road. "Tell me what you can see?"

Hector strained his eyes. Over the crest of the hill, a dark coloured car was approaching. "A blue saloon is heading this way," he replied.

"Step into the road, make yourself big. Show them your face," she ordered.

Hector took a couple of steps into the carriageway. "It's the Ford," he said, quickly. "Two men in the front, closing fast. I think they've seen me." Harding shouted for him to step back towards the Peugeot.

300 yards. 200 yards, 100 yards.

"Jesus, that's Burton, right there.!" yelled Eddie. The sun was streaming through the trees. Brendan narrowed his eyes: the man had the right height and build. The face matched. The boys in the back bounced forward in their seats so they could see for themselves.

Brendan hesitated.

"What do I do, what do I do?" Eddie screamed in Brendan's ears.

Brendan looked around quickly. The coast was clear. "Go, go, go," roared the big Irishman.

Hector had never left a man in the field before, never mind a woman; nor had he run from a firefight, only to it. Never had he been instructed to take shelter; he had always given shelter to others. He saw himself as a protector, never requiring protection.

As the Ford skidded and hurtled to a violent stop and the doors sprang open, Harding barged Hector aside, out of the line of fire. Brendan and Eddie were out of the car fast, running towards the Peugeot, weapons drawn, screaming at Burton to stand still.

"Take him alive," Brendan hollered.

Harding brute-forced Hector towards the open passenger door of the Land Rover. Brendan sussed it and aimed at them. Eddie panicked and let off a round, the bullet ricocheting off the vehicle's toughened exterior.

Behind Brendan and Eddie, Robbie and Roy were clambering out of the Ford. Robbie blinked in Hector's direction and drew his weapon. Instinctively, Hector pulled out his service revolver. Harding pushed against Hector, keeping her body between him and the gang. Neither inside nor outside the Land Rover, they were vulnerable. Brendan closed in, shooting indiscriminately. Harding pumped several rounds into the big Irishman. Brendan staggered forward.

Eddie stared at Brendan. The ox had a quizzical look on his face, as though he had an important question to ask. The answer came from the SAS men hidden by the roadside. Flanking the gang, they opened up with automatic weapons. They gave no quarter.

* * *

The road out of town was chock-a-block with stationary traffic: OAPs, housewives, skivvying kids, dossers, all loaded into cars, trucks, and buses. They were all out for Market Day.

Conor looked shit-scared. Directly in front of their stolen car, a lorry edged forward. Conor tailgated. A thousand thoughts rushed through Tom's head, but only one question: why could he not get through to Brendan on the comms? "Take your foot off the pedal," he said, quietly. It seemed like they would be held up in traffic for a while.

A sharp tap on the window had Tom and Conor jumping out of their skins. A traffic cop. Instinctively, Tom stretched his hand out towards the glove compartment and his piece, but the fresh-faced policeman already had his face to the glass, peering inside. Tom withdrew his hand and sat back. "Wind down the window," said the uniform.

Conor looked side-long at Tom, questioningly. "Do it," said Tom under his breath, trying to calculate how they could make their way out of the traffic jam should the copper prove to be a nuisance.

Window opened, the policeman bent down and leant in, taking

his time to look them over. "There's been an accident up ahead," he said, in a sing-song voice. He was a couple of years older than Conor, maybe twenty-three or twenty-four years old at a push. The young ones were the worst, always having a point to prove. "We're going to hold you here for a minute or so while my colleague clears the other carriageway," he added, continuing to nose around.

Another uniformed traffic cop was directing the vehicles, signalling to the drivers to wait, while they got to grips with the situation. With the lorry in front and cars behind, their vehicle was hemmed in. Tom knew they would have no choice but to dump the car in the traffic and make a run for it if the copper caused a problem.

"Are you in town for work?" the policeman asked Conor. Tom wished he was behind the wheel. He would have had no issues in shooting the breeze with the cop, whereas Conor could hardly bring himself to look at the policeman and open his mouth. Sweat popped on Conor's brow. Tom willed the boy to say something.

After what seemed an age, Conor spoke. "I work in the Tavern up in town," he said, the colour rising in his cheeks. The policeman nodded pensively and stepped away from the vehicle. He's going to run the number plate, thought Tom.

"Call him back, ask the copper if he knows the pub," hissed Tom, following the uniform's every move.

Conor dragged the words out, raising his voice. "We serve a decent pint of Wadworth up at The Tavern," he said, trying to sound chummy and relaxed. His body language told another story.

The policeman edged back into view. "Can you switch off the engine please?" he said, firmly. Conor looked side-long again at Tom, spooked. And then suddenly, the policeman's radio sprung into life. "Hang on," he said, gesturing for them to wait, giving them his back. He then walked briskly away towards his colleague.

Reaching inside the glove compartment, Tom pulled out the bag containing the two handguns, handing Conor the snub nose. "What do I do with that?" Conor asked, a confused look on his teenage face. Nineteen. Old enough to drive, old enough for action, Sean had said. I'll show him action, thought Tom, pressing his piece into Conor's ribs.

"Use it on the cop if I tell you to," he whispered. Conor looked petrified. Tom tucked the Wesson revolver inside his jean jacket.

The uniforms were still gathered together, talking. Up ahead, traffic appeared to be starting to move. Filthy exhaust fumes belched from the lorry, as the driver gunned the engine. Things were looking up. However, the traffic cop shouted at the lorry to stay put; Tom caught a look of fear on the cop's face as he hollered the instruction.

"Follow my lead," said Tom, resting his hand paternally on Conor's arm. Everyone Tom had ever served alongside had faced moments like this; this would make or break Conor. Tom kept his eye on the policeman. He had spent a lifetime watching uniforms. Eventually, the cop broke off the conversation, looking squarely in their direction. Here he comes. Feeling inside his jacket, Tom released the safety catch.

"Move on!" The copper barked at the lorry driver, and then, in turn to them, and to the vehicles queued up behind them. He walked hurriedly along the side of the road, repeating the order to ensure everyone had heard. "Come on, what are you waiting for?" he said, as he passed their vehicle. He looked inside but looked right through them. A look that meant nothing. The police radio continued to gabble away. Tom pricked up his ears. Garbled phrases. Snippets of conversation. Incoherent shouts. Tom recognised the sound of panicked voices when he heard them.

"We can't go back to the farm, something's gone down," said Tom, as they started to move off.

"Do you think something's happened to Brendan?" asked Conor, in a panicked, jittery voice.

"Shush, boy and drive," instructed Tom, fearing the worst. Slowly, they edged forward and passed the scene of a tractor laying on its side. Conor drove on, keeping to the speed limit before gradually accelerating as they cleared the area.

"Shall I drive us back to London?" asked Conor, nervously, glancing at Tom.

As they approached the outskirts of the town, they heard a wail of sirens approaching in the distance, growing louder until several ambulances hoved into view, followed by patrol cars and a police van with all the windows blacked out.

Tom pulled down the sun visor and turned his head away. Conor slunk down in the driver's seat and focused on the road as the emergency vehicles flashed past. They were heading in the direction of the barracks and open country.

"The London road is coming up," said Conor.

Tom glanced in the mirror, the road behind was clear. "Drive to the safe house," he said.

"You said the farm was out," said Conor, glancing over.

"Don't you understand nothing!" shouted Tom, striking the dashboard with his fist. "Take me to the place where Sean's mole is holed up, so I can find out what the fuck is going on!" he screamed.

"Ok, ok, sorry," replied Conor, stunned by Tom's outburst. He pulled the car to the side of road and promptly did a U-turn. Before they reached the section where the tractor had come off the road, he took a sharp left. Feeling Tom's eyes on him, Conor stole a glance. "I'm doing what you want," he said, nervously, fearing what Tom might do next.

After they had driven for a couple of miles in silence, Tom wound down the window, trying to compose his thoughts. "Do you smoke?" he asked. Conor shook his head. "You should try it, it'll calm your nerves," he said, lighting a cigarette. He waved the packet at Conor. The boy hesitantly accepted the offer and coughed his way through his first cigarette. "There's a good lad," said Tom.

Conor took the second exit at the roundabout and headed west towards the lonely council estate that fringed the town.

"How far?" asked Tom, after a while.

"Two minutes," he said, still coughing. "She won't be there yet."

"Good, we'll make ourselves at home," said Tom, trusting his instincts that he'd get the answers he needed one way or another.

* * *

A heavily moustachioed soldier is charging towards the camera, angrily waving at the news crew to stop filming. There's a brief scuffle as the young TV presenter attempts to block the soldier before the report is cut short. Momentarily, the programme is blacked out. Then, the broadcast resumes from the studio, news anchor Richard Baker speaking in sombre tones: at least two men dead and three persons seriously wounded. In the corner of the screen, the BBC showed bodies lying beneath blankets.

Gerry stared into the screen, reading the caption: Avery Valley, Oakbury. Hector's town, Hector's barracks. Standing by the roadside some distance away from several cordoned off vehicles, the presenter described the scene. A suspected attack on military personnel. Overhead, an Army helicopter wheeled, hugging the hedges. "Vero," shouted Gerry. From upstairs, he heard Veronica moving around the bedroom. "Veronica!" he boomed from the bottom of the stairs. "Something's happened at Oakbury."

Veronica came running.

"What's he saying?" she asked Gerry, panicked. Gerry turned up the volume, but the reporter's words were being drowned by the noise of the helicopter's rotating blades. Shaking footage showed wrecked vehicles and Army personnel blocking the road. Veronica's eyes widened at the sight of the military Land Rover. It was exactly the type of model that only senior officers like Hector would be given access to. "Oh, God, no," she murmured, swaying on her feet. "I need to get hold of Hector," she said, reaching into thin air for the house phone.

"Sit back down, I'll bring the phone to you," he said, helping her into an armchair. Veronica punched in the numbers, "My mind's gone blank. I can't remember his number." She looked up at Gerry like a frightened child, desperate for help. Gerry took the phone and dialled for Veronica. There was no answer. He tried again. "Maybe it's the wrong number?" she said, feeling increasingly certain that something dreadful had occurred.

Gerry fetched her handbag, rummaging through it until he retrieved her address book. He dialled again. No reply.

"Call his flat at the barracks," Veronica said. The call went to the answering machine. Gerry ran his finger down the page until he found the main switchboard number. After three rings, the operator answered. He passed the handset to Veronica.

Gerry watched intently, while Veronica gave answers to the person on the other end of the phone. "What do you mean?" she said, sounding exasperated and frightened. "I am his wife, Veronica Burton," she said, clutching the phone, and then after a longish pause Veronica said, Curry and Chips, the code words used to identify next of kin.

"What's going on?" mouthed Gerry.

Veronica shook her head slowly. "The operator asked me to hold. I can't wait like this," she said, holding the handset away from her ear. Then, finally, after what felt like minutes, a male voice came on the line. She recognised the voice on the other end, instantly. "John, it's you, isn't it?" she asked, in alarm.

"Yes, it's me," he replied, briskly.

"I've seen the news and I can't reach Hector," she said tearfully.

"Sit down Vero," he said in a calm voice. "Hector is unharmed, but we are keeping him out of the media for operational reasons. Best to take a seat while I explain why."

* * *

At the school, David Scott heard the news flash on the radio. The identity of the dead had still not been confirmed, although the media speculated that at least one serving British Army officer and several members of the Provisional IRA were among them.

David picked up the house phone and dialled Anthony. No answer. Then, he dialled Harry. Harry answered immediately. "Have you heard the news about Oakbury?" asked David hurriedly. Harry was watching news coverage unfold on television. "Do you think Burton's father might have been caught up in it?" he asked.

"He could have been the target. For all we know, he might be one of the dead," said David, "I tried Anthony in the study, but he wasn't picking up."

"Surely he would have heard something if Burton was involved?" asked Harry

"I'd imagine so. In the meantime, we need to take care of Hugh Burton," said David, emphatically. The boys would be in and out of lessons. Radios were always on in the kitchens or gardens, or they could easily pick up the information from gossiping cleaners and groundsmen. "Let's convene with Linda at Anthony's study. We need to agree on an approach, quickly.".

By the time the three of them had gathered outside his study, they could hear the headmaster talking loudly from outside the door. David rapped once, twice, and then a third time before barging in. Anthony looked up startled and angrily shushed David away, but the housemaster refused to budge. "I'll call you back," said Anthony, slamming down the phone. "If this intrusion is related to the news, you can calm down. I have matters in hand."

"So, Hector Burton is caught up in things?" asked David.

"What are you talking about, man," replied Anthony, incredulously. "If you must know that was the chair of the trustees on the line informing me to say and do nothing until this Oakbury mess has been cleared up."

"That's a curious choice of words," said Linda.

"They were *his*, not mine," replied Anthony tersely.

"Have you tried to reach Hector Burton or his wife?" asked Linda.

"No. Why would I do that?" Anthony replied, looking surprised.

"The press is speculating that a serving officer is involved, dead …" she said.

"That's all the media does – speculate," he said waving his hand derisively. "What would you have me do? Jump to conclusions and assume the worst? Don't be ridiculous!" he said, thumping his hand on the desk. Linda jumped and stepped back. She had never seen Anthony lose his temper so suddenly.

"Steady on, Anthony!" said David, rallying around Linda. Anthony glowered at David, and then sat back in his chair. The two men continued to stare hard at each other, neither seeming prepared to back down. "This will get us nowhere," said David, at last, shaking his head. "We came to discuss how we should handle Hugh."

"And, as I've said, we must not jump to conclusions," he stated, sighing heavily.

"So, we carry on as normal?" said Linda, after a pregnant pause.

"Where is he now?" asked Anthony, with an exasperated expression.

"He's at running practice in preparation for the house cross country run," said Harry. "For another hour or so," he added, glancing up at the clock on the study wall.

"Well, that settles it, then," said Anthony, crossing his arms.

"In what way?" asked David, perplexed by Anthony's cryptic reply. He turned to Harry and Linda to see if they had understood what David meant. But from their non-plussed expressions, he could see that they were none the wiser. "Can you enlighten us further?" he asked, sarcastically.

Anthony shook his head slowly. "If you need me to explain, then you are clearly not the housemaster I thought you to be," he replied, in a tone dripping with disdain.

For a moment, Linda thought David was about to step forward

and strike Anthony. Instead, David let out a hollow laugh. "You are playing a dangerous waiting game by banking on saying nothing." said David. "You better hope and pray that Hugh Burton doesn't hear the news from someone and react by doing something silly

"I've heard enough from you," said Anthony.

"Are we being dismissed?" retorted David.

"I have calls to make," he replied, without looking up from his desk.

"Calls to make," repeated David sarcastically. "Well, if I was in your shoes, I'd be making one of those to his father or mother. But you know best, Anthony!" he said before storming out of the study. It was becoming a regular occurrence observed Linda.

"Well, that was awkward," said Harry, after they had tramped out in the wake of David's hasty exit. Linda tutted and put her finger to her lips, and leaned into the study door, pressing her head to the wooden panel. "What are you doing?" whispered Harry.

Linda kept her finger pressed to her lips while she eavesdropped on the conversation. Anthony was barking into the telephone; an ugly argument was taking place with whoever was on the line. Listening intently, she picked out Hugh's name. Anthony raised his voice again, and then repeatedly shouted no, until she heard him bang down the phone. Linda backed away from the door, and shooshed Harry along.

"Well, what was all that about?" asked Harry, eyes sparkling. He had an almost devilish look about him.

"Something to do with Hugh, of that I have no doubt," she said, anxiously.

"It must be bad news."

"May be. Who knows?" said Linda. All she had understood was that Anthony had had the all-mightiest argument with someone, which did not appear to go in his favour.

Harry wandered to the lobby and stepped outside on to the driveway. In the distance, the sound of boys' shrill voices could be heard carried by the wind. "It's a lovely day for a practice run," he said to himself, looking up at the sky.

"Not quite so good for tomorrow," said Linda, joining him outside. Rain was due. It had not rained in weeks.

"Just think the poor boy is out there now, and his father might be dead," said Harry.

Linda squeezed his arm. "Try not to think about it," she said. "Things might turn out for the best."

Harry grunted in reply.

"Who's overseeing the practice today?" asked Linda.

"Jeffrey," replied Harry. The old gardener had been an amateur distance runner, right up into his fifties, before his knees started to give way. But once a year, he delighted in ignoring medical advice so that he could participate in the run. "Jeffrey's formed quite an attachment to Giles Ashworth, hasn't he?" remarked Harry.

"Has he?" asked Linda, surprised.

"Oh yes, seems that Giles has got the gardening bug." Harry had spotted them beavering away, laying new beds. "Giles was beaming about something."

Linda found it difficult to reconcile the version of the boy described by Harry with the slightly taciturn and aloof boy she recognised. "Where was Hugh while this was going on". Not that she felt she needed to ask.

"Digging away with a spade alongside Giles," he replied, without a moment's hesitation. "Those two really are as thick as thieves."

* * *

Can we meet? Three words. Such a simple note. Moira picked up the card from the mat and opened the front door. Not a soul was within sight, whoever had pushed it through the letterbox had hurried away, quickly. On the card's reverse, a date, time, and location were written in neat handwriting. Moira held the card up to the light and studied the green ink. She brought the card to her nostrils and breathed in a faint scent of perfume. As she had already suspected from the carefully written words, the cologne confirmed the identity of the sender: such melodrama was typical of Yvonne.

Lyon Park was as Moira remembered from when she and Frank were courting, pretty in an understated way. Stopping by the pond, needing to kill time, Moira gazed at the bloated goldfish swimming lazily through the water. They reminded her of the Japanese prints on the walls of her mother Mary's bedroom. They had been passed down from Moira's grandfather to Mary.

Stationed in the Far East during the war, he had returned with hundreds of prints. Periodically, he would sell a bunch at the local antiques market or trade them for something else that took his fancy. His penchant for taxidermy was well-known among hawkers. After he died, she had helped her grandmother gather up a small flock of stuffed birds and the carefully preserved cat. They didn't fetch much money, but the house felt brighter and no less sinister without beady eyes peering out from various nooks and crannies.

Their clearance had also rubbed off on her grandmother. With her grandfather dead, her gloom lifted. She became warmer and kind. Within a year she had remarried – a childhood sweetheart, who was also recently widowed. Her grandmother sold the house and settled by the sea.

Moira spent five of the happiest years of her childhood with her grandmother and her second husband by the seaside: carefree days playing in the Chines and on the long sandy beach, falling in and out of friendships. She had her first period in the beach hut. However, Moira's journey into young womanhood coincided with the start of her grandmother's decline. The speed of the old woman's deterioration was fast and unforgiving. Moira became strangely fascinated and horrified in equal measures by her transformation, particularly in the way in which her grandmother turned into another woman in front of her eyes: the old woman's body shrank to the size of a small child, while her pale skin acquired a terrible fragility. The paper-like texture of the flesh around her grandmother's mouth was particularly startling to touch. Kissing her grandmother was almost unbearable, almost worse than the stench of stale urine, which permeated the care home and her grandmother's nightie.

She took to visiting less frequently and staying for shorter periods. Finally, Moira reached the conclusion that a total metamorphosis had occurred: her beloved grandmother had become an alien form, in every way. Moira said her goodbyes there and then. She didn't expect to see her grandmother again. Within a month the old lady had gone.

Moira's own mother had not seemed fazed in the slightest, if anything her mood was brighter, just as her grandmother's had been when her grandfather had died. Perhaps, she wondered, as she circled the pond that was how things were meant to be. She certainly would not mourn Mary – their relationship had always been fractious. But Giles, surely, would feel her loss, wouldn't he?

The bowling green hoved into view. It was a peculiar choice for a meeting. Moira wondered if it held any significance for Yvonne, like it had once held for her and Frank. Up close, the green was still as manicured as she remembered. Benches were arranged thoughtfully for the elderly to sit and follow the field of play. Sitting alone on one of these benches, Yvonne had her back turned, hair tied back exposing the nape of her swan-like neck and shoulders. She was wearing a canary yellow dress. Yvonne jumped when Moira said hello. "I nearly didn't come," said Moira, taking a seat.

"But you did, thank you," replied Yvonne, nervously tapping her feet.

"The colour suits you," said Moira, after a long pause. She would love to have the confidence to wear bright colours, but she hated the attention they brought.

Yvonne glanced quickly at Moira, "You know what the advert

says, a bright way for a bright day!"

Moira shrugged in reply.

For a few minutes they allowed themselves to settle into the peaceful setting of the park; neither woman appeared willing to speak first and express what was on their minds. After months of avoiding contact, Yvonne had initiated the conversation at the car and then pushed the cryptic note through her letter box, so quite naturally Moira expected Yvonne to go first. Finally, Yvonne spoke. "I'm sorry I avoided your calls," she said, playing with her hands. She had long, slender fingers. Moira noticed that the cuticles were perfectly shaped. "I've been trying to summon up the courage for ages," said Yvonne, stuttering slightly. "It wasn't the first time I went out looking for you. Mind you, it was the first time I had dragged Mandy out with me. I guess she's a lucky charm!"

Moira thought back to their recent encounter. Their brief conversation had brought up all the emotions associated with the unhappy birthday, but that wasn't all. The presence of the child, Mandy, the way she demanded Yvonne's attention, tugging at her mother's sleeve, had unsettled Moira. The daughter had refused to yield, even though she was making Yvonne cross; it was the normalcy of the bond between them, that cut Moira to the quick. In the car, while she pummelled away at the steering wheel, Moira had understood something about herself, which perhaps she had always known but had been afraid to admit – she had been pleased to let Giles go away to board. A new start for Giles was a convenient excuse: she had felt ashamed of being his mother. When Frank had painted a picture of Giles' future at the new school, it was one where she could temporarily forget the past, and the pain he had caused. Frank may have dreamed up the idea, but she was just as culpable. Moira felt bitter tears well up in her eyes.

However, Yvonne mistook them for something else: she figured Moira *knew*, and she too started to cry. In no time at all, her carefully applied mascara was smudged. She looked bruised, but still beautiful and Moira found her hard feelings fleetingly soften toward her oldest friend. "When I saw you the other day, I was just having one of my days," Moira said, lying. "I should have known you had something important to tell me," she added, looking into her lap, aware that she sounded flustered and nervous.

For a moment, their attention was drawn to the bowling green by a ripple of applause from the spectators. A match had ended. Two elderly women shook hands, laughing like schoolgirls. The scoreboard displayed 2-3. "Maybe we'll be like them when we are old," said Moira. Suddenly, Yvonne looked agitated. "You don't see us like that?" Moira asked, with a concerned frown. Yvonne sat quietly. "What is it?" said Moira.

"I do. It's not that. I came to say sorry," said Yvonne, unable to look Moira in the eye.

Moira felt her muscles starting to tense, "For cutting me off all these months or something else?" she asked.

Yvonne nodded, "Both," she said, softly, fiddling with her hair band.

Moira sat up bolt upright. "Has John said something? she asked, sounding excitable.

"I didn't bring you here to talk about *that*," she replied, unkindly.

"Then, what?" Moira asked ferociously. "What's more important than the truth!" she said, getting to her feet.

"No, don't think about leaving!" exclaimed Yvonne, grabbing Moira by the wrist. "It's about Frank," she said, holding on tightly to Moira's hand. Moira tried to pull away, but Yvonne refused to let her go. "It was just the once. John and Giles had gone to play at the rec. Frank came by to collect Giles, and it just *happened*. I'm sorry Mo. It's why I couldn't face seeing you."

Moira struggled and finally pulled her hand away. "I thought you had something important to tell me!" she yelled. Her words came out as a high-pitched shriek. Old-aged pensioners turned away from the green and stared. Yvonne tried to cover up her tears.

Moira studied Yvonne, sizing her up. Frank had always had a thing for her sylph-like beauty. Moira knew Frank had had flings. "Do you think you are the first?" she asked, with a calculated sneer, aware of how callous she sounded and wanting to revel in it. Yvonne let out a loud sob. "Here, let me help you," Moira said, helping herself to a packet of Kleenex from Yvonne's bag and planting them in her hands. Yvonne sniffled and blew her nose. "Spit it out then," continued Moira. "You brought me all the way out here to confess your sins, so you might as well get on with it." She wanted every word and action to hurt, although it took all the strength she could muster; her emotions were making her feel light-headed, nauseous. Fearing her legs might give way, she sat back down on the park bench. The air felt heavy like a storm was brewing.

Hesitantly, slowly, Yvonne told her truth: Frank had telephoned her from the dealership. Work was slow he said, and Henderson was giving them the rest of the afternoon off. If it wasn't an imposition he asked if he could collect Giles a little earlier than usual. He was passing their door on the way home. Frank had arrived at the doorstep with a bunch of flowers. It was his way of saying thank you. We talked about this and that, and then he kissed me. Yvonne stopped talking.

"You make it sound so romantic," said Moira, mockingly. She could picture Frank brandishing a bouquet. However, never did she imagine that Yvonne, the one person in whom she had confided about Frank's infidelities, was so gullible and naïve as to succumb to her husband's shallow charms. She felt disgusted. "And then, what?"

"John saw us together as we were coming out of the bedroom," she whispered. He'd run ahead of Giles and had come hurtling up the stairs. "I was buttoning up my top. He knew we were doing something wrong. I could see it in his eyes." She started to weep uncontrollably.

The sound that filled Moira's ears had no name. It was a cacophony of noise, which only she could hear. Jumping up, she yelled into Yvonne's face showering her with spittle, blinding Yvonne with her rage. "He was damn well right, wasn't he!" exclaimed Moira. Yvonne vainly attempted to put her arms around her, but Moira feared what she might do if Yvonne laid her hands upon her. "Don't," said Moira, stonily. "We sent Giles away to that school because of John's lies"

"You never said?" replied Yvonne, breaking into loud sobs.

"How could I? You refused to take my calls. You went out of your way to avoid me, to avoid us all!" she shouted. Spectators had stopped to stare. On the green, the match had come to a halt. The men had their hands cupped over their eyes, watching the spectacle taking place.

"I came to say I was sorry. I am, truly," said Yvonne, oblivious to the old people who gawped on. "I might be a useless friend, but my boy is not a liar. He saw what he saw. Giles clubbed Marcus on purpose. He tried to brain him!"

Moira gasped and lunged at Yvonne. In that split-second, she realised she was capable of extraordinary violence. But then, as quickly as a surge of anger had exploded within her, it died away. Instead, she swiped the air. The look of fear on Yvonne's face was satisfaction enough.

She had responded to Yvonne's invitation to meet in Lyon Park because she knew that there had to be something of vital importance, and she had been right to come: John had witnessed his mother together with another man, not a stranger, but the father of his best friend. A terrible betrayal, a terrible burden for a child to carry. John would have tried to banish the image away, only to discover it was something he could not forget. It would have gnawed away. So, when the moment came, when his emotions were running high, when he felt excluded by Giles and replaced by Marcus, wasn't it natural to lash out? Who was to say that *he* had not taken the club to Marcus? It was the sort of thing any angry child would do; at the same age, she could easily envisage herself reacting in the same way.

* * *

Moira drove away from Lyon Park feeling initially euphoric. However, with every passing mile, her mood started to dampen, her sense of certainty replaced by feelings of doubt. By the time she had arrived at The Close, she felt anxious and in need of time and space to compose herself, and there would be time enough with Frank at work for the day. She had, however, barely stepped foot into the hallway for Frank to make his presence known: from the living room came the booming sound of the television. Moira found him on the sofa, engrossed by the news.

"Have you been following this?" he asked, without so much as looking up from the screen. "They're talking about an IRA attack near the base where Colonel Burton is based. The fella we met at the school."

"I see," she said, absently, wondering why Frank was at home. She had craved time to be alone, to think about what to do next, and yet, here he was hogging the living room, invading her space. Moira noticed Frank was wearing the same T-shirt and scruffy jeans he had pulled on after getting out of bed in the morning. The lounge smelt stale. "Have you not been to work?" she asked, opening the front window that looked out onto the street.

"I called in sick," Frank replied quickly.

"Where's your car?" Moira asked inquisitively.

Frank looked up, "I left it at the showroom. It was playing up." He launched into a convoluted explanation about a problem with the clutch. It affected only specific models. Whenever he babbled on, she knew he was covering something up.

Moira opened the aquarium lid and fed the fish. The black guppy swam up to meet her pinched fingers, greedily sucking up the flakes. "You're lying about something, as per usual," she said, closing the lid. Frank appeared not to hear.

She studied his unshaven face, which hovered ghost-like in the reflection of the TV screen. His head looked like it had become detached from his torso. "What's happened to the Capri, Frank?" she asked. Frank was absorbed by the image of the Land Rover and the upturned vehicle, and the army foot patrols milling around the scene. Eventually, her patience snapped, "Can you turn the damn thing off!" she said, irascibly.

Frank hit the remote and the set went to sleep. "Happy now" he said, wondering what was troubling her. Had the news got around about his run-in with Henderson? It looked that way. She had no reason to worry, plenty of dealerships would be delighted to have him. He would be back on his feet in no time at all. In fact, he should use the opportunity to take a bit of time off before starting a new job. "What's wrong?" he asked.

Moira could smell the alcohol on his breath. "You've been drunk every night," she said. Frank attempted to give her a cuddle, but she squirmed away.

"I just went for a couple of drinks, that's all," he said, pulling a sad face.

She turned away from him and went to the window that faced on to The Close. Her little red car on the driveway gleamed in the sun. Every day continued to feel like summer. Today, the temperature was energy sapping. Autumn could not come soon enough. Moira steeled herself. "I saw Yvonne, earlier today," she said.

"John's mother?" he replied in a questioning tone that implied he knew more than one, when they both knew there was only one Yvonne. "Why on earth would you do that?" he asked, looking baffled.

"She wanted to meet," she said, opening the window to waft away the stale smell. "We met in the park. Lyon Park, actually." Moira expected a reaction, at the very least a comment about it being the place where they used to go together. But there was not even the faintest flicker of recognition in Frank's eyes. Evidently, the importance of Lyon Park was lost on him.

A light breeze filled the lounge through the window. Moira lent back against the windowsill and looked up at the sky. It was clear and blue and featureless like a blank canvas. "Don't you want to know what we discussed?" she asked, feeling slightly dizzy, unsure whether that came from tilting her head back or whether it was a symptomatic of her barely controlled emotional state. Her giddiness provided an oddly satisfying sensation.

"We agreed to put all that business at the golf club behind us," Frank said, his facial features finally starting to change and rearrange. She recognised the expression of defensiveness, the muscles tightening around his jaw, eyes narrowing, lips turning in on themselves.

Moira straightened her dress. "We did get on to that, eventually, after Yvonne told me about what the two of you had got up to." She had expected to feel angry. Instead, she felt hollowed out. She remembered what her mother had said when they had announced their engagement: marrying a man like Frank meant things would inevitably end in tears. Except, today, Moira had no intention of shedding any. She was content to bide her time, knowing that whatever he said would make no difference at all in her feelings toward him. Frank gazed forlornly at her, like a child hoping to hear that all was to be forgiven. Moira stared at the fish tank and watched the bubbles climb up the gurgling pipe.

"It really meant nothing. You have to believe me," Frank said, slowly and quietly, starting to rock back and forth, hands clenched around his knees.

Moira sneered at his theatrics, "Nothing? You can do better than that! Did you think I'd missed all those stolen glances you've given to Yvonne over the years?" She asked if he needed some details to help jog his memory. Yvonne had been quite specific. He tried to ignore her sarcasm. However, he had underestimated her fury and misunderstood what Moira wanted from him. She was, she said, not remotely interested in what he had got up to with Yvonne: she wanted to know what John had seen. "Let me spell it out for you," she said, jabbing her fingers in his face. "When John came home and caught you coming out of the bedroom, how did he react? What did he do, Frank?"

Frank gestured for Moira to close the window. "You're worried about the neighbours?" she asked. Moira began to laugh. "After going with my best friend, you think the neighbours are a problem?"

"Mo, please," he said. "Don't". He sounded just like Yvonne. Moira realised she was finished with the pair of them, but she wanted an answer.

"Don't wring your hands," she said. "Just tell me the truth for once."

"Will you give me a chance if I do?" he asked.

Moira sighed heavily and forced herself to give Frank a reassuring smile. "I'll try," she replied.

In his truth, Yvonne had thrown herself at him. He had resisted. Then, somehow, they had kissed, and then… It was a mistake. He knew that instantly. The boy had mysteriously appeared in the hallways. "We were fully clothed!" he exclaimed. "He's a kid, he wouldn't have understood a thing."

"And where was Giles when all this was happening? On the landing, in the hallway? Where, Frank?" she demanded, aggressively. Frank did not know. "You don't seem to know much," Moira said, disdainfully.

"Can't we stop all this?" said Frank tiredly. "You know I am sorry."

"No," she said, building up a head of steam, firing more questions at Frank. With every question, he failed to give an adequate answer. "I'll ask you one more, after that we're finished. Ok?"

Frank nodded obediently in reply, offering up a weak smile and a plaintive expression, which no doubt he thought would lead to a closure, a reconciliation, time to kiss and make-up. She could read him like a book. "Do you believe that anyone other than son hurt Marcus?" she asked, pressing her face up against his

"What sort of question is that?" he asked, backing away, shocked by her aggressive behaviour.

Hands on hips, Moira repeated the question.

"Have you lost your mind?" he said.

Moira strode towards Frank. "Who was responsible for Marcus's injury? Who hurt him, Giles or John?"

"This is madness," said Frank. "You know who."

"What if Giles was protecting John by taking the blame? Never had something felt so true. Her hands began to shake. "Who is to say you knew and said nothing to save Yvonne from the shame." she said, her voice reaching a loud shriek, her fiction metastasising, becoming a cogent reality.

Frank began to laugh in her face. "So, you're going to ignore the other occasions, the other things he has done, like throwing stones at kids, hurting that poor woman's cat?" he said, circling Moira. "Why can you not be honest with yourself when it comes to Giles?" he shouted. "Why are you so blinkered about the boy?" he asked, crowding around her.

"Don't come anywhere near me," she howled. "You're the one who refused to support Giles."

"That's not true," he snapped.

"You are the one who sent him off to that quack doctor."

"We both thought that was the right thing to do," he screamed back.

Moira wished she had the psychologist's letter in her hand, to thrust into his face. However, Frank knew every line in it, just as well as she did. However, unlike Frank, she had stupidly read it again and again, until she had convinced herself that the words on the page were true: Giles will benefit from a new start, the specialist had written, and she had gone along with that. "Whose idea was it to pack him off to boarding school?" Moira boomed. If she looked crazy, her thoughts had never been so lucid.

Frank stared at Moira and to the open window, and the street outside, to the homes where their friends and neighbours lived. "Please close the window," he said, in a composed voice.

Moira laughed hysterically. Ignoring his wishes, she opened the window wider and then rushed to the left-hand pane and flung that open too. Her eyes were blazing. "The Close can know what kind of man you are."

Frank gazed at Moira intently. "What kind of people *we* are. You couldn't bear to have him around you. You are as much to blame as me!" he hissed.

It was too much. He'd gone too far. The wailing sound was unbearable. Moira clasped her hands to her ears and begged it to stop. But the orchestra in her head refused: Moira ran towards him, boiling with rage.

Pivoting backwards, rocking on his heels, Frank's first thought was to defend himself. He tried to pick her up, but instead they collided awkwardly. As a child Moira had loved dance and ballet. In that moment, she and Frank pirouetted on the carpet: his hands around her waist, lifting her skywards, her hands flailing, then seeking out his throat, his eyes, and ears with her nails. Anyone looking in from the street outside might have mistaken them for over-eager dancers strutting their stuff, or drunks lurching from one corner of the living room to the other. No one would have imagined that they were locked in an almost deadly embrace as they careened into the aquarium.

Frank fell hard against the heavy tank. It tottered on the spindly metal frame, legs starting to buckle. The crystalline water slopped from one side to the other, pushing against the flimsy lid until a tipping point had been reached – and then, the whole thing gave way, toppling as they wrestled, collapsing as they collapsed on to the carpeted floor, the water pouring down on their writhing bodies. And on they wrestled, as the plants, rocks, reeds and fish, dozens of beautiful coloured fish, flapped around them. And then, finally the glass, great chunks of glass and small dagger-like shards rained down upon them until their struggling ceased. They lay there in silence. Eventually – slowly and carefully – Frank turned on his side towards Moira. Blood oozed from a gash on his forehead. She lay facing away, perfectly still in a patch of glass.

"Are you hurt, Moira?" he asked, shaking her lightly by the shoulders.

"Let me go," she replied flatly.

Frank leaned across Moira to read her expression. Her green-brown eyes were no less striking than they had always been, but they no longer radiated warmth – rather they had an icy, callous look about them, which made him shudder inside.

Moira slowly got to her knees, brushing away the wet fronds and silt from her hair. "He loved that fish," she said quietly to herself, crawling towards the black guppy, which lay on the sandy, waterless bottom of the broken tank. She edged forward impervious to injury or pain, and picked up the fish, spreading him out on her open palm. Gently she caressed the guppy, shushing him quietly like she used to do with Giles when he was a baby and unable to sleep. She stroked him along the dorsal fin, looking into his tiny eye. The guppy raised its tailfin, flapping with all its strength, and then it flipped over on her hand for a final time. Moira gently closed her fingers around the fish and stood up.

"Mo? Where are you going?" he asked.

She had already blotted him out; without so much as a backward glance, Moira walked calmly to the lounge door and up the stairs to the bathroom and deposited the fish into the toilet bowl and flushed it away. She then went to the bedroom, which she had shared with Frank since they had been married and packed his bag. She flung it into the hallway, imagining the look of shock on Frank's face. And then finally, she opened the door to Giles's bedroom. Her eyes danced around the room, taking in his things. She grabbed the pillow from his bed and squeezed it to her chest. Her mind was made up: she wanted the house for just the two of them – he was coming home.

* * *

Having made himself at home in the house rented by the mole, Tom had spent hours in front of the television set, hoping to understand how events had unfolded. The latest bulletin confirmed two dead and three persons injured, potentially life-threatening. No details about the identities. The army had imposed a news blackout.

Conor sat at the upstairs window, watching the road, waiting for the woman to return from her shift at the barracks. She was late, *hours late.*

Between watching TV news and listening to radio announcements repeating the same useless report about

Oakbury, Tom rifled through every drawer and cupboard, box, bag, and suitcase in the house, looking for any scrap of information about the occupant that might be useful.

"She's a pretty thing," said Conor, picking up the photograph of the woman on the beach, which Tom had found inside a book by the woman's bedside. Inscribed in faint pencil on the reverse: Cala Mellor 1973. A holiday snap used as a bookmark.

Tom held out his hand for the photograph, "Give it here," he said. There was something about the auburn-haired woman that was familiar. He tucked it into his pocket and sent Conor back to watch the street from the bedroom window.

Just when Tom was beginning to think that the woman had decided not to return home from the barracks, Conor called out. A car had approached and slowed, coming to a stop some twenty or so feet up the street. Tom darted upstairs to join him in the bedroom, gun in hand.

The woman seemed to hesitate on the front step. Tom put his finger to his lips. Hush now. A turn of the key, the careful opening and closing of the door. Then, the sound of silence. He imagined her head cocked to one side, listening, sensing something was off. Slow footsteps from below, as she moved around the house: the pokey living room, kitchenette, the downstairs cupboard and bathroom, toilet flushing. Footsteps padding along the hallway, climbing the stairs. Into her bedroom, at the rear. Minutes passed. She would be getting undressed. Water gushing from a running bath. Then, her dulled footsteps on the carpeted hallway outside their room. Conor stood way back. Don't spook her. Tom stood to the right of the door, in the recess, revolver aimed at head height. In she stepped; he put the muzzle to her temple.

"Don't shoot," said Carrie, tossing her gun to the floor. Raising her hands above her head, she turned her face to the wall, knowing what came next. Quickly, Conor patted her down before Tom kicked her legs out from under her. Dropping to the floor, Carrie guarded her face, expecting another blow. Tom levelled the gun at her face. "Was that necessary, Tom?" she asked, calmly.

"Sweet Jesus, Searlait Culligan. I could have blown your head off," he said, putting the weapon down.

Her green eyes twinkled, "You've been away too long. No one calls me Searlait. Too Irish and too difficult for the Brits to pronounce. Here, I'm plain old Carrie," she replied casually.

He reached down and helped Carrie to her feet. "You can go," said Tom to the boy. Conor hovered on the landing, apprehensive. Carrie caught his eye.

"Make us a tea, will you? I'm sure you know where to find everything by now," she said, with a wry smile. "What about you Tommy?" she asked, her smile widening. No one had called him that name since he was a boy.

Conor made tea, then supper, while the two of them talked alone about the operation. The Brits had locked down the base immediately after news of the ambush had come through. No one knew if Burton was alive or dead. And Brendan, Robbie, Eddie, and Roy? She shook her head. The Brits were now combing the area around the barracks and Avery Hill. Roadblocks were everywhere. It's why she had taken forever to get back to the safe house. "I'm worried one of the boys will talk?" she said.

"Brendan would never talk," Tom replied with certainty.

She was surprised he felt that way. "Everyone will spill their guts when things get bad," she said. Every friendship had its own price to pay. The Brits would torture the information out of them if that's what it took.

They watched the news, hoping, praying to learn something, but the media was providing no further updates.

Conor went to bed. They stayed up talking. Tom wanted to know about Michael. There wasn't much to tell about his brother that he didn't already know, except that her aunt still visited him when she could, when the bastard Brits let her. So, *she* was the woman he recognised in the photograph "She still holds a candle out for your brother, you know," she said. Her aunt would have to wait a long time.

"But how is he, in his head?" he asked. There were so many stories about prisoners going mad inside Long Kesh, the conditions were appalling.

She said he was thinner, but he had not lost his head, neither his marbles nor his unruly shock of black hair. Tom smiled. He could picture himself and his older brother playing together as young boys. The other lads took the piss. Michael Moptop – that became his brother's nickname.

"Why did you volunteer?" he asked, eventually. It wasn't something he would usually ask, but he needed to know.

"Derry," she said quietly. She had joined the march in protest against the internments. Thousands had taken to the streets.

"People were howling while they beat on us." She knew one of the boys killed. Her aunt made the introduction to Sean.

She knew his story, but she asked him all the same. "You've got talent in those fingers," she said, taking his hand in hers, threading them together one by one. She leant forward and kissed him softly on the lips.

"What about the news?" he asked.

"It can wait," she said.

"I don't know what to do, Carrie," said Tom bleakly.

"You will, come morning, just stay here with me for a bit," she said, gently pulling him towards her.

"You're beautiful, Searlait Culligan," he said. "I guess you hear that a lot?" He traced his hands over her hips and along the outline of her breast to her shoulders, her throat and to the nape of her neck. Carrie tilted back her head and let him run his hand through her hair. She laughed for a moment.

"What's so funny?" he said, pausing.

"This. Me and you, after all these years," She reached down and undid his belt, and eased him out of his trousers. "Look at you," she said, smiling, running her fingers over his cock. Tom closed his eyes and let her work him. They tugged off their clothes and he lay on his back so she could play some more. Carrie worked him into a sweat until he ached to cum.

"Not yet, it's my turn," she said, gently rubbing herself against him. He begged to enter her. She shook her hair free. Her long auburn tresses framed her breasts. Tom raised his head to kiss her nipples. "No," she said, firmly, pushing him back down, moving inexorably forward, inch by inch until she was over him.

"Kiss me here," she said, tugging at his hair, opening herself for his tongue, and then his fingers as they swapped positions, so she could take him in her mouth. When she was ready, she told him to prepare himself for the shag of his life. Laughing as she said it, she pushed him on to his back and straddled his cock, fucking him hard until the pleasure flowed.

After they had made love, Carrie studied the livid scars on his chest and back. Tom had a story for each one. That one – the nasty big bastard – he got that with his brother. It hurt like hell. She had a brother and a sister. He remembered them.

"They don't understand this thing of ours", she said, touching each scar in turn, then tracing a line from one scar to another, making intricate patterns that only made sense to her, until he finally drifted off to sleep.

She lay in the darkness, wondering whether she had done the right thing; Sean had prepared her for this eventuality. They needed a leader they could trust. We need *you* to be ready to fill those shoes when then the time comes, Sean had said. If that was their decision, so be it; nevertheless, she hoped that day would not come too soon.

Tom murmured in his sleep, the faintest of frowns crossing his lips like a passing cloud. She curled up next to him. Come morning, she would return to the barracks and see what information she could glean from being on the inside.

9 - PROMISES

In the subterranean briefing room located deep within the Oakbury barracks photographs of the gang members had been pinned to the wall together with images showing the weapons used and rounds discharged, the vehicles involved and the maps and drawings showing how the attack had played out and the chalked-out locations where the dead had fallen.

It had been an exhausting twenty-four hours and he should be ready for sleep, but the adrenalin won't let him. Hector had yet to receive an adequate explanation from Walters about how Special Branch had known about the unit's plan, and why he had been kept in the dark about it. Rather cryptically, Walters had countered Hector's questions with the same answer: Hector would come to learn all in the fullness of time.

"What do we know about them?" inquired Hector, walking slowly from one photograph of the gang to the next. Their faces had acquired a peculiar familiarity, yet they still knew so little about the individuals who stared lifelessly back.

"We believe this is Brendan Mullins," he said. "Fingerprints match a file for someone with that name. We're waiting for confirmation from Garda that they match the face."

"What's on his file?" asked Hector, looking carefully at the man's face, recalling the instant that the big Irishman had got his shot off.

Walters lit up, coughing. "Minor convictions as a youth in County Tyrone, and a year at Her Majesty's pleasure in Belfast for falsifying documents."

Hector helped himself to a cigarette from the open packet and cadged a light. "He doesn't sound like your normal hardened Provo," he said. Walters shrugged. "What about this one?" Hector said, pointing to the man they had identified as the driver of the stolen Ford.

"We're still in the dark about him and the other two," interjected Beresford. "Although once we confirm Mullin's identity and establish his recent whereabouts, the pieces ought to fall into place." They had sent copies of the photographs to Mayfair, hoping PC Sands might finger the gang for the Scotts' blast.

"You really think they're the same ones behind the Scott's attack?" asked Hector. The youngest member of the gang had an innocent look about him.

"There's a very strong probability," said Beresford. They had solid forensic matches from the failed truck bomb and the restaurant blast, and PC Sands was certain a four-man outfit had been involved." Beresford poked his fingers towards the pictures on the wall. "One, two, three… and four," he said with grim satisfaction.

Hector stared at the image of the ambush scene. "Four to our one," he said, looking at the photograph of Harding's blanket-covered corpse. "Has the family been informed?" He caught Walters and Beresford exchanging glances. "What's going on, what aren't you telling me?" he asked.

"Let's get some air," said Walters. "Somewhere quiet where we can talk."

They went to the private garden reserved for senior ranks. It was a good place to escape the hubbub. Veronica had planted roses several years ago, which flowered abundantly in vibrant shades of crimson and red in the early summer.

"I'll cut to the chase," said Walters once they were alone. "We're 99% certain Harding died from friendly fire. I still can't bring myself to call her next of kin." Forensics had matched a round in her vest to the same calibre used by the SAS unit.

Hector was taken aback. During the brief firefight, Harding had pressed her body against his, refusing to buckle or yield even as he had felt the dull thwack of rounds pumping into her chest. She had been wearing a bullet-proof vest. Then, suddenly, he had tasted blood, her blood. A head shot, a round to the lower jaw, which had propelled her backwards into Hector. She had fallen against him, and he had thrashed away beneath her, trying to push her body off. Eventually, she had rolled onto her side, a sickening, gurgling sound emanating from her throat. Hector had tried to pull her tongue free, oblivious to the small arms fire crackling all around him. However, by the time the gunfire had ceased, and he had cleared her airways, Harding lay dead in his arms. She had drowned in her own blood and mucus. Walters lent back against the wall, "I planned the flanking manoeuvre. It's my fault," he said, quietly.

Hector studied the rose bushes, their petals long since fallen. "Do you remember the ambush in Airport Street?" he asked. They had been coming to the end of their Aden tour. Pinned down by rebels, they had been forced to wait out for the arrival of reinforcements. Hours had passed until heavy armour came, flushing the rebels into the street. Sandwiched between Hector's patrol and the advancing British support, the rebels found themselves outfoxed and outgunned. "How many did we lose that afternoon?"

"One," replied Walters. "McConnell."

"Correct. Andy Mac. I can picture him like it was yesterday," said Hector, bending down to admire Veronica's handiwork. She had planted well. Every bush flowered on time, year in, year out. He pulled away a couple of damaged leaves, being careful not to touch the deadheads. Tiredness was finally coming for him. "You and I were together when he got hit," he said, straightening up and trying to shake off the exhaustion.

They had been standing to McConnell's left when the shell hit their position. It was a miracle they had only lost one of their patrol. "I remember well enough," said Walters, beginning to understand where the discussion was heading.

"So, you'll recall how Andy Mac died – in friendly fire?" he asked, rhetorically looking at Walters squarely in the eye. "A ridiculous expression, by the way," said Hector, "and then we went to see his widow together. Do you remember what I said to her when she asked how he died?" Walters said nothing for a moment. "John?" Hector asked, again.

"I don't recall the precise words," he replied.

However, Hector could tell that Walters had grasped the gist of it. "No one wants to hear they lost someone they love to one of their own, in a terrible accident," said Hector. "Susan Harding and everyone involved in thwarting this attack and, god knows how many others, are *heroes*. That's what her family and the public expect to hear, and that's what you should tell them," he added, emphatically.

"So, I should ignore forensics?" asked Walters.

"It's your operation, John," said Hector in a matter-of-fact tone. "How you write it up is up to you. Stop blaming yourself and focus on the outcome, the gang's been destroyed. Harding would want that!"

The morning sun had finally broken through the clouds. Moments like this were a reminder of the sanctity of life. Hector felt for the cigarettes in his breast pocket and remembered he had smoked his way through the packet.

"Here," said Walters, proffering a Rothmans.

"Thanks," said Hector.

They smoked in silence, each man lost in his own thoughts.

"You spoke to Veronica, I hear," said Hector, furrowing his brow. "Was she worried?"

Walters thought back to dinners at the Burtons in Germany. She was the life and soul. The army wife others aspired to be, and she knew exactly how to handle Hector. If they were unhappy back then, it didn't show. He wondered when things had started to go wrong between them. "She knew the drill," replied Walters, underplaying the conversation.

"I hope she didn't say anything silly to the twins," said Hector. Hugh would be impressed and excited about the whole thing, but Belinda would be distressed.

Walters crunched the cigarette butt into the gravel pathway. "I asked her not to call the schools because of the news blackout. We'll be lifting that later. My office can take care of the schools if you'd like," he said.

My office – how grandiose of Walters, thought Hector. It was another reminder of how far Walters had come and the influence he had in government circles. "Thank you, that would be helpful," he replied. "I suppose a telephone call from me to Hugh and Belinda wouldn't go amiss at some point. Reassure the twins about their dear papa, and all that!" said Hector.

"I'm sure they would like that," said Walters, glancing at his watch. If he was going to tidy up the report, he ought to do it now. "Shall we?" he said, gesturing toward the exit.

"You go," said Hector. "I'm going to take a chair and soak up the sun before I clear my office papers and go to bed."

Walters nodded. "Ok, sleep well," he said. Hector had his eyes closed; he looked ready to sleep standing up.

"I'm sure you'll do the right thing by Harding," replied Hector drowsily, falling into sleep.

He awoke blinking into the sun, feeling hot and anxious, his heart was racing like he had run a sprint.

What he needed was a hot shower and clean sheets, but first he had to deal with some important paperwork in his office. The short walk through the barracks felt draining, made worse by the lack of air inside the building. Inside his office, the heat was unbearable. Just standing by his desk made him feel like a fly trapped in a glass jar. He couldn't think. Where were his notes?

Hector pawed at one stack of papers, and then another. Surely, he hadn't filed them away.

"Can I help you with something?" a female voice asked from the doorway.

"How long have you been there?" he asked, confused.

"Not so long," she replied casually.

"It's fine, you can carry on," he said, dismissively, turning his attention back to the mountain of papers and the search for the blue personnel file containing the names of the mid-ranking which had been identified as potential redundancies. He tugged the file free and inadvertently knocked the photograph of Veronica and the twins to the floor, the frame snapped in two.

"Here you are," said the woman, who seemed to have magicked her way to his side to clear up the breakage. "Lovely looking kids," she said, politely, handing Hector the photograph.

"Thanks," he said, laying the photograph on his desk, before scooping up the paperwork and taking what he needed and locking the rest away.

The woman continued to stand there, looking at the photograph. "I'm a twin," she said without looking up. "Do they get on?" she asked.

Hector looked the woman up and down. As exhausted as he felt, he could still appreciate a beautiful woman when he saw one. The woman had searching blue eyes. Her red curls were almost Pre-Raphaelite. "Most of the time," he replied.

"I'm older than my brother by a minute, so he has to do what I tell him," she said, her mouth widening into a shy smile.

Hector gazed at his children, as though seeing them for the first time. "My daughter too, she's the boss." He wanted to say like his wife, his *ex*-wife.

The woman finished dusting around the desk and started on the windowsills, moving quickly from one to the other as though she was up against the clock. There was a performance-like quality to the way she moved. She caught his roving eye. "They will be looking forward to seeing their daddy," she said.

"I don't know about that," he replied. They are away at boarding school."

The woman frowned. "I'm sorry, that must be difficult. Do they board far away?"

"My daughter's school is a fair old drive, but my son is not that far. He's at Frampton," he said, in a slightly pompous tone. Realising he sounded self-important, he felt foolish and clumsy.

She smiled at his embarrassment. "You're worried I'm offended that I don't know the name of some fancy sounding school?"

Hector coughed and cleared his throat. "Forgive my manners, I'm exhausted. It's been a hellish couple of days. I just need to get some sleep," he said, apologetically.

"Yeah, I know how that feels," said the woman, a wry smile continuing to play on her lips. "I can lock up," she added, twizzling a key in her hand.

"You've got a security pass to go with that, I suppose?" asked Hector, collecting his coat and briefcase.

The woman reached into her back pocket and pulled out a green ID card. "Here," she said, inviting Hector to read the information.

"It's nice to meet you, Carrie Culligan," said Hector.

"You too, whoever you are," she replied with a throaty laugh.

"I do apologise, I should have introduced myself," he said, offering his hand. "Colonel Hector Burton."

"Oh, right, the big boss!" she said with an ironic curtsy.

Hector burst out laughing. "That's very good, very drole," he replied. "You strike me as being too smart for a job like this if you don't mind me saying."

"That's good of you to say," she said, holding his gaze until Hector looked away. "Have a good day," she said, as he reached his office doorway.

Hector turned around and smiled warmly. "Thank you, have a pleasant day yourself, Carrie," he said, with a polite tilt of his head.

As he descended in the lift toward the basement, his thoughts drifted to the children. The conversation with Carrie had reminded him about what was important. A surprise visit would be so much better than a telephone call. Hector made a promise to himself that he would clear his diary and take matters into his hands. He'd buy a present for each of the twins. They'd be over the moon and he'd get back into Veronica's good books.

* * *

"Our target is very much alive and kicking," declared Carrie, describing how she had managed to work her way into a conversation with Hector Burton. Tom hated the sound of his name. "We already know, the news blackout's been lifted. The bastard got out, while all our boys are dead," he replied angrily, jabbing his finger at the television.

Four faces filled the screen. The presenter read out their names: Robbie Duggan, Eddie Young, Roy O'Neal, and Brendan Mullins, reputed to be the master bomber. The report went on to list their so-called string of atrocities – the Hilton Hotel, Scott's of Mayfair, Harrow School, a whole list of London addresses and the recent attacks on Oakbury – the failed truck bomb and botched kidnap. The reel then switched to a sombre photograph of a woman in uniform, named as Captain Susan Harding, a long-serving member of the SAS, and a photo of Hector taken in West Germany.

"The intended target was a high-ranking British Army officer," said the news reader. The screen showed the aftermath of the ambush. "The PM paid a personal visit to Captain Harding's family, earlier today. She is expected to receive a posthumous award for bravery," concluded the presenter with great levity. No details were given about how the Army had intercepted the unit.

"They got Brendan all wrong," said Conor in a derisory tone.

Tom shot him a fierce look, "Like that matters!"

"It does, Tom," interrupted Carrie. "The Brits believe the master bomber is dead and the gang's finished. Instead, we've got a massive arsenal at our disposal, and we've got you!" she said, with fierce pride.

"It still doesn't change things," he said. "No disrespect but what am I going to do with two novices?" They'd have to join up with another unit. Until then, they would have to lay low. Once Special Branch had cleared out of the area, he wanted to move on. They'd be okay in London. He'd rent another flat near the lockups. In the city, they blended in. Conor was all for it.

"Burton's a womaniser, that's his flaw," said Carrie.

"Tell me something that's new," said Tom dismissively. Burton's occasional trips to his woman had been key to their plan.

"Burton was flirting with me in his office. I could have knifed him there and then," she said, chuckling at the thought.

"Why didn't you?" replied Tom with a cynical smile. "I might have had a different view about you if you had?" Carrie went to answer, but he cut her off. "Even if you had it in you, Sean wouldn't let you get your hands dirty. It's not women's work!" he said curtly, reaching for the cigarettes and ashtray. Carrie snatched them away.

"I'll have one, first," she said, sparking up. She blew smoke into his eyes and leaned in towards him. "You don't think I've killed people?" she asked.

"Fill us in, the floor is all yours," stated Tom condescendingly.

Her first was an off-duty policeman in Derry. Two shots to the head. Body dumped by the roadside. Two squaddies next. Car bomb, Derry. Then, she relocated to the mainland and joined Liam. She had planned the market town blast, which took out the pub party. Four dead soldiers. Fourteen injured. Conor looked incredulous.

"Stop staring at me, boy!" she snapped.

"So, you've been a busy girl?" said Tom. Carrie looked at him stone-faced. "Ok, you should have said. I would have treated you with more respect."

"Is that right?" she asked, raising her eyebrows questioningly.

"Yeah, it is," said Tom truthfully. "So, why don't we rewind and start the conversation about Burton?"

Carrie tossed him the cigarettes: "We'll get to him through his kids," she said, and then she pitched her plan: two recon teams, one per school. She had gleaned the names of the schools and their locations from Burton. The schools were small. Keeping tabs on the boy and the girl would be straightforward.

"We don't kill kids," he replied.

"You've misunderstood," she said, patiently. Should Burton pay a visit – and she was sure he would – there would be options aplenty.

"Like what?" he asked.

"You're no stranger to kidnapping, Tommy," she said, as though reminding him about the industrialist was necessary. "Burton would give up his own life for one of his own. You would, wouldn't you?"

Of course he would, she knew that. "Is that the grand plan, then?" he said.

"Jesus, go easy on a girl will you. It's one option, isn't it?" she said, cadging a cigarette. She had seen the look on his face when she had handed him the photograph of his kids. She saw the look of longing in his eyes, "He's going to want to see them soon, and we need to be ready."

Nevertheless, Tom remained sceptical. It relied too much on intuition and left their people exposed. However, since losing Brendan, he hankered after completing the mission. "Let me talk to Sean," he said.

Carrie shook her head, "It's not safe for you or Conor to venture out. You look like outsiders, and you admitted that the traffic cop was suspicious."

"Sean will need to hear this from me. You don't have the authority," he said, with an air of superiority.

"I'm sorry Tommy, but he's already taken it out of your hands," she replied. He looked momentarily confused, and then he understood.

"You're taking over from Liam?"

"Yeah, and he's instructed me to fold this operation into my command." There, she had said it. She hadn't wanted to, but he had left her no choice.

"Hats off to you," he said, trying not to look shell-shocked.

"It changes nothing," she replied, but the look of hurt in his eyes told its own story, and she thought better of saying anything more, knowing that it was better for the news to sink in and for Tommy to come to terms with it in his own way.

* * *

Linda's day began with a shock of her own, with the discovery that she was pregnant. After recovering from the sudden surprise – having checked and re-checked that the thin blue line was not a figment of her imagination and she really *was* with child – she kicked her foot against the bed and burst out laughing, wondering why she had not put two and two together.

A child. She had longed for this moment, except when she had imagined being a mother, she had expected the father to be by her side. What would people think? A single mother, and a good church-going woman at that. Linda realised that she didn't care. She would have to see a doctor of course, but she knew well enough when it must have happened: Italy.

Linda sat back on the bed and opened her diary. Flicking back through the pages, she stopped at the entry about Milazzo, mid-August. Gio, the student-cum-waiter with the wandering hands and wolfish smile. Like Linda, he had been taking a long summer holiday, travelling his country, taking in the sights before returning to Rome to complete his degree. However, Gio had fallen in love with the aquamarine water and slower pace of Sicilian life. So he had taken a part-time job at a trattoria to fund his sojourn. Unlike the owner, Gio could put his flawless English to use and beguile the tourists, encouraging them to venture inside the seafront restaurant with a promise of traditional arancini, homemade pasta and local wines. Linda had only intended to be in Milazzo for a day until she took a ferry out to the Aeolian islands. Gio had tempted Linda inside the restaurant, and then into his bed, and convinced her to stay in the port town for a few extra days.

"The islands will still be there next week. The volcano will still be smouldering away, whereas I am active here and now," he had said in a teasing voice, pulling back the linen top sheet to show her he was ready. It was clichéd, but so what? She enjoyed making love and instinctively he seemed to know what she liked. He was the first man she had been with who did.

Linda held the pregnancy test to the light, letting the memories come flooding back – the carefree rides along the coastal roads on the back of his Vespa, splashing around in the sea like lovesick teenagers, and ardently making love whenever the mood took them. When the time had come to say goodbye, he'd walked her to the ferry where they had kissed longingly without a care in the world. She had stayed port side waving, until the solitary white-shirted figure on the quayside had faded into the distance.

Unexpectedly, however, the sea crossing had cheered her spirits; strung out like beads on a necklace, the seven islands had an enchanted, other-worldly appearance to her English eyes. As the islands grew near, she gazed with fascination at the plumes of smoke rising gently from the conical tip of Vulcano. As she breathed in, she caught the distinct smell of sulphur and momentarily gagged. An elderly man standing beside her said it was something you never got used to, but which you learned to love. The smell of homecoming, a gift from the gods.

She smiled to herself now, in her little attic bedroom at the school, thinking about what the old man had said. Regarding herself in the mirror, flattening her hands on her belly where the baby was growing, his words felt prescient; while with the benefit of hindsight, even her morning sickness felt like a continuum of the sulphuric journey across the narrow water, something to cherish and forever hold dear. She simply *had* to share her news with Harry.

"You look excitable," he said. "Feeling better, I take it?"

Linda took his arm and marched him outside the building. "Don't worry, there's nothing wrong. Quite the opposite," she said, reading the concerned expression on his face. Linda's thoughts were already racing ahead, to a new life away from the school. She loved the boys, but now she was having a child of her own, her priorities would have to change.

Linda dragged Harry to a quiet spot in the playground and clutched him tightly by the hands. "You'll never guess, but it looks like I am pregnant," she said, barely able to contain her grin. "Say something," she said, still beaming.

Harry looked taken aback, briefly lost for words.

"You seem very happy about it?" Times had changed. Single mothers were no longer personae non gratae, but he wondered how Linda would reconcile it with Jesus and her ghastly, overbearing mother.

"You are the only person I have told," she said, continuing to hold his hands.

"Thank you," he said, still wracking his brains for the right words to say. "Congratulations," he added at last.

"Isn't it wonderful?" she said, still beaming.

"When did you find out?" he asked.

"Literally just now, with one of those new, fangled test kits."

Harry arranged his face to disguise his surprise at her haste to share the good news. "Shouldn't you get a second opinion?" he asked.

"Of course," she said, "But I know, I can feel it. Everything makes sense now, the morning sickness and my mood swings."

He hadn't noticed any change in her mood, he had been too preoccupied with himself ever since Anthony's attitude had hardened towards him after the swimming pool debacle.

"How far along are you if you don't mind me asking?" he said.

Linda counted the weeks on her hand. Seven or eight, more or less. His eyes flickered in the direction of her belly and back to her face.

"You're trying to guess the identity of the baby's father?" she asked.

Harry's thoughts went back to the end of term party and how Linda and Anthony had been ensconced together for most of the night. They had disappeared together for a while, during the evening. Only Harry alone, or so he thought, had been alert to their brief disappearance from the marquee and their flush-faced return. In his milieu, a casual glance returned in full by another could very quickly turn into something more. He shuddered inside at the idea of Anthony Richardson fathering a baby with his best friend.

"Of course, I'm curious, more than curious if truth be told," Harry replied, earnestly.

What she said rather took him aback. "It was while back-packing around Italy, with a man I met at a bar."

"Good God, that's deplorable, I thought only men like me did things like that!" he exclaimed, looking wide-eyed in disbelief.

Linda laughed, not so much about what Harry said, but by the look on his face; his eyes seemed like they were popping out on stalks. "We did take precautions," she said.

"Well, clearly not enough," retorted Harry. Linda shrugged. "And you're sure this man, this waiter, is the father?" he asked.

Linda frowned, picking up the note of condescension in his tone. "Would you like his CV?" she asked defensively. "Gio is studying medicine. When he graduates, he will be a qualified specialist."

"An eminent enough qualification for a sperm donor," replied Harry ironically.

"You still don't look convinced?" she said, irritated by his attitude. "What is it, the fact that he's Italian or something else? She could guess what he was thinking, "You think he's not the father."

"It's none of my business," said Harry, avoiding her eyes.

Harry had pressed her for an answer about the summer party on several occasions, convinced as he was that there could be no innocent explanation for sneaking away with Anthony. It was a spur of the moment thing, the result of drinking too much white wine. Anthony had sworn her to secrecy – no one can ever know, he had said, almost the moment they were done – and she had kept her promise. Sharing *this* news with Harry would be tantamount to professional suicide. The only person who would lose out by exposing a summer party fling was herself, and she had no intention of ruining her prospects, nor Anthony's marriage.

"I want to make it your business," she said. "I'll need someone to help me through the next six or seven months, and I can't imagine a better surrogate than you," she said.

The school bell had started to ring, calling the house to order. The day had been precisely arranged around the cross country run and a film screening later in the day. Harry glanced in the direction of the ringing bell, waiting until it eventually fell silent. "I am really pleased for you," he said, extricating his hands from hers and pulling Linda close, hugging her tightly.

"Go easy on the big hugs," she replied, half-jokingly.

"Sorry! I'll need to be gentler when you start to show," he said, letting go quickly.

"Don't worry, I won't let you forget," she said, smiling.

"This is what you want, isn't it?" Harry asked, quietly, still holding her close. Linda nodded. "It's not too late if you had second thoughts," he said gently.

Linda looked up at Harry, appalled. The stupidity of men was astounding. "I'd never do that," she said, touching the silver cross on the necklace. "You know how much I want a baby, and I don't care what people say. It's His will."

Harry gazed at the crucifix. He had never understood religion. Linda had faith, whereas he did not. "I'm sorry," he said, earnestly.

"Promise you won't breathe a word," Linda said, as they made their way back towards the main school building.

"Who would I tell?" he asked. She reminded Harry that he was a notorious gossip. Laughing gently, Harry conceded there was some truth in that, but on this matter he would be the soul of discretion.

They hovered outside the staff room. "Are you coming in for the pre-race briefing?" he asked. Anthony expected them all to be there, having tasked David with managing the race. It was either an olive branch or another test of will. Harry wasn't sure which.

"No, I'll see you out there," Linda said. She wanted to lie down – it was a white lie; she wanted to bypass a visit to the doctor in town and call in on the sanatorium where Sister could confirm the results of her pregnancy test.

Harry entered the staff room to find David skimming the newspapers and bemoaning the fact he had to give up his Saturday – first, to organise sporting activities in the morning, and then, to give over the rest of the day to a film screening in the assembly hall. Jeffrey listened patiently.

"Ah, there you are," said David. "No, Linda?" Harry ducked the question and said she would join them at the starting line. David grunted an affirmative reply; he was becoming increasingly preoccupied by the weather. After weeks of sunshine, autumn was in the air. Looking out across the playfields, the sky had turned a headache-inducing shade of grey, cloudless in a way that seemed unique to Britain, the threat of rain ever-present.

"Not what you had in mind for cross-country?" said Harry, gazing outside. Days like this made him regret choosing teaching. However, there was not a chance of the race being postponed. The first cross-country meeting of the new school year was a time-honoured tradition, pitting boys against each other, as well as the masters.

"I trust you've got your running kit washed and pressed, so you'll be ready as first marshal," said David with the hint of a smile. It was a thankless task reserved for the least able-bodied athletes among the teaching staff. Another poison pill that Anthony had served up for Harry to take.

"Raring to go," he replied mordantly, picking up a copy of The Times from the pile of newspapers on the coffee table. Every front page led with Oakbury. The coverage was starting to shift to the nature of the SAS response.

"Read that," said David, gesturing to The Guardian. The leader alluded to a shoot-to-kill operation. "If it's unlawful killing, it will be the greatest own goal imaginable." A picture of Hector dominated the page.

"What are we going to do with Hugh today?" asked Jeffrey. David had almost forgotten the gardener was in the room.

David shrugged. "Keep him close, I suppose. How does he seem, Harry?"

The re-introduction of Douglas into dorm three had weighed heavily on Harry's mind. He was prepared for another altercation; Douglas was also just the sort of boy who might try to taunt Hugh about the events surrounding his father. But outwardly, Hugh looked as cheerful as ever. "To be honest, he seems as right as rain," replied Harry, eventually.

"Well, let's hope it stays that way. It seems like Anthony got away with his decision to say nothing to the boy" said David gruffly. "And what's your verdict on the dorm three situation, then?"

Harry did not expect things to go smoothly. "Douglas Rice is still smarting. I doubt that'll be the end of matters."

"Best you keep an eye on that," said David.

"How many pairs of eyes do you think I have?" he retorted. Harry felt as though he was being set up to fail.

David told him to calm down. "I have your interests at heart," he said, "and your health. Have you knocked the booze on the head, like you promised?"

Harry set down the paper, theatrically. He hadn't had a drop, he said with an uncomfortable expression. David didn't look as though he believed him. "Do you want to search my study?" asked Harry in a belligerent tone.

"Don't be like that," said David, distracted by the sound of rain falling on the windowpane. "Isn't it typical," he muttered.

The race was set for 11am, three miles through the fields and woods. No staggered start. They had tried that last year and it had been a disaster, impossible to marshal. This time, the event reverted to an established format; the boys lining up together and sprinting off as one, followed by the teachers and staff. The whole scenario conjured up the images of the First World War, with young lads going over the top at the command of an officer's whistle.

"Do we have any parents attending?" asked Harry. In the past, they had invited a select few to watch on from the side-lines. It helped create an atmosphere. However, Anthony preferred things like that to be reserved for the end of the year, for celebratory moments like Sports Day.

"No, why?" asked David.

"I was thinking about the Burtons. After everything that's gone on, I thought the sight of Hugh enjoying things might be good PR."

David conceded it was not a bad idea, but it was too late in the day to do anything about it. "Moira Ashworth would have been another good candidate to invite if we'd have had the time. Apparently, she has misgivings about Giles' boarding."

Harry raised his eyebrows in surprise, "Why?"

David lowered his voice. He was not privy to the details. However, it was something along the lines of a parental dispute over the boy's education. "Anthony only mentioned it in passing at breakfast, something along the lines of taking him out of school. But he did not care to be pressed on the subject," he said, rolling his eyes.

"Goodness knows what effect that would have on Hugh. They are like two peas in a pod, inseparable," said Harry.

"I can vouch for that," interjected Jeffrey, whose presence in the room they had again forgotten. Harry and David both turned in his direction at the same time. "They make a good little team," he said, recounting how they had helped him clear the beds and prepare the ground for seeding.

David screwed up his nose. "I'm sure Burton would cope, but the timing would be a bit off," he admitted.

"That's an understatement," said Harry.

"Anyway, who knows where it'll lead, probably nowhere," said David. In his view, it wasn't uncommon for parents to get cold feet about having their children away at school, particularly mothers, and the Ashworth woman struck him as being a little highly strung. If he was in Anthony's position, he would focus his efforts on the positives. "Boys like Ashworth never used to get a chance to attend a school like ours. She should thank her lucky stars," he said dismissively.

Jeffrey had heard enough and didn't want his mood ruined by any of David's pompous remarks. "Unless you need me, I'll be making my way outside," he said. His old legs needed time to warm up, especially in weather like this, he added, peering at the darkening clouds.

"I didn't know about the gardening business," said David, somewhat tersely, after Jeffrey had departed.

"It sounds like a good thing," Harry replied nonchalantly. He knew David hated not being kept informed about every detail of the boys' activities, especially as Anthony had charged the staff with keeping a particular eye out for Burton. Harry glanced side-long at David. His expression was hard to read, but Harry sensed underlying irritation.

"Is there anything else to discuss?" asked Harry hesitantly, feeling a little like how he imagined one of their young charges felt when called in front of the class.

David, as always, picked up on the note of anxiety in Harry's voice. However, he was not inclined to exploit his advantage. He could do with Harry's help on the choice of the film for the screening.

"Anthony wants me to choose a subject that sets an appropriate tone, and I'm stumped," said David. The trustees had purchased a whole batch of films from a defunct cinema chain. "Choose one, will you?" he asked, pointing to a box on the shelf. Harry lifted it down and started to sift through. "You can take the box with you," said David.

Traipsing back to his study with the sagging box, Harry emptied the contents onto his desk. A dozen or so films. Perennial favourites of Anthony's were westerns. He loved a hero, like Shane. However, even Anthony had come to realise the boys needed to be inspired by more contemporary subjects. Judging by the condition of these cases, the films had passed through many hands. He arranged them into categories – comedies, westerns, war, drama and miscellaneous. Engrossed by both the familiar and unfamiliar movie titles, Harry didn't hear the soft knock on his door.

"Are you dressed?" asked Linda, poking her head inside. She was dressed in a tracksuit for the cross-country race.

"You're not running, are you? Not in your condition," Harry asked, looking worried.

"You haven't said anything to anyone? You gave me your word." Her eyes searched his face looking for clues.

"Of course not," he replied, irritated that she needed to ask. "Anyway, that's not the point. You need to be careful." Linda looked touched by his concern

"What on earth are you doing with that lot?" she asked, approaching the desk. "Some of these are positively ancient," she said, picking up a copy of This Sporting Life. "You must know the story?"". It was a classic. Harry remembered something about it. Linda read the synopsis on the cover. The story of an ordinary working lad who escapes 1960s working life through playing sport.

Harry laughed. "I don't think Anthony would approve. He's far too much of a snob."

"How about this?" She flashed the cover of Davy in his face. It purported to be a comedy about an entertainer torn between going solo or remaining with the family's music hall act.

"Good God, it sounds dreadful," said Harry. "Is that the best on offer?"

Linda picked up one more. "I like the sound of this. Tom Sawyer, a *musical adaptation*," she cooed. The book was on the syllabus and Anthony, she observed, was rather fond of describing boarding school as a boyhood adventure.

"How bombastic," said Harry, looking at the illustration on the front of the box, which depicted Huckleberry Finn dressed in a wide brim hat and a ginger-haired Tom sitting astride a tree. It looked a bit twee.

Linda looked up at the wall-mounted clock; there was less than an hour before the race. "We better dash," she said.

Harry took another look at Tom Sawyer. "Ok, let's go with a rousing Mark Twain sing-along. What could possibly go wrong with a film like that?"

* * *

The old gardener limbered up, going through the same, time-honoured stretch routines as when he had been a force to be reckoned with in national amateur running circles. "At least the rain is coming from behind us," he said, turning towards Harry. "There's nothing worse than wet weather in your face."

"How about wet weather, full stop?" replied Harry, with a deadpan expression, holding aloft a golf umbrella. A group of first year boys huddled around him. The gardener kept a cap pulled down tight over his wisps of hair.

"Where's David?" Jeffrey asked, looking along the line. "The boys will catch a death at this rate."

Harry peered out from beneath the umbrella. The sky had darkened, turning to slate-grey rain clouds. The conditions were deteriorating. Finally, Harry saw David come bounding across the playing field towards the start line.

With the housemaster's arrival, the boys quietened down, but even Harry could sense the tension in the air: the rivalry among the older boys was fierce – usually the race was won by a dorm five boy – with experience, age, and stamina, all playing their part. "You'll need to put that away," balled out David. Grudgingly, Harry collapsed the brolly.

"Never mind, boys. It'll all be over soon," said Harry sardonically. They were hardly words of encouragement; Jeffrey gave him a disapproving look.

The boys started to spread out along the starting line. "Budge up there, Baxter. You boys too," shouted the housemaster, motioning towards a group of ten- and eleven-year-old boys. Pressed up against each other, they were like dogs straining on a leash using their elbows to gain more space and get off to a good start.

Standing away from the crowded middle, Giles and Hugh surveyed the scene; Hugh with his hands on his hips, Giles with a hand cupped over his eyes to shield his vision from the rain. He was studying the first stretch of the course: the wide, open playing fields and beyond them the woods. Hugh had asked him if planned to take the race seriously; Giles had confidently replied he would win.

Mr Scott stepped out in front of the racers, giving the boys a long, appraising look while he reminded them all about the route and the need to watch their step in the woods, especially now that the hard ground had had some rain on it. Anyone requiring First Aid should look to Sister and Mr Rhys-Davis, he added.

"Mr Rhys-Davis will be running at the back of the pack to look after any stragglers," bellowed Anthony, with a mocking smile. Harry returned the compliment by giving the headmaster a mock salute.

Finally, Mr Scott brought the whistle to his lips, "On my whistle, three, two, one, go!" he bellowed and blew loudly into it. The pack began to sprint away.

Giles got his head down, running as hard as he could, knowing his best chance was to be towards the front well before they neared the woods. Hugh also sprinted off, but after a 100 yards or so, he had slipped back from the leading group. "Good luck Giles," he yelled, before settling into a rain-soaked jog. Cross country, he decided, was a waste of time and energy.

Out of nowhere, Mr Richardson came alongside him. Without

his glasses, the head looked weird. "Come on Burton, you made a good start. You can do better," he commanded, arms pumping.

"Oh, hello sir," replied Hugh, wheezing slightly. "A nice day for it," he said looking up at the dark clouds and wiping the rain from his face.

The headmaster let out a brittle laugh. "Most amusing, young man," he said. And then in a typically cajoling manner, he urged Hugh to pick up the pace.

Reluctantly, Hugh tried to put more effort in. The rain was falling at its heaviest, the grass turning slick. A couple of young boys slid and fell. The headmaster sprinted across. "No harm done," he called out to no one in particular, while the boys picked themselves up and set off again. It was a sufficient distraction to enable Hugh to slope off from the headmaster and disguise himself in a bunch of runners. Glancing left and right there were familiar faces from every year group, hair plastered to their heads, thick cotton running tops stuck to their backs, faces wearing varying expressions of exhaustion. A few boys gave up, deciding to trudge the rest of the race.

Up ahead though, the race was being run in earnest. Hugh thought he could make out Giles cresting the hill, leaving the open playing fields behind for the woods. There must have been a group of five or six boys, with the masters in pursuit.

Giles had been among this leading pack since the start of the race. Now, with the tree line approaching, he knew that he had to keep up with the two strongest runners, Furnival and Mountjoy. The dorm five boys were ten or so yards ahead of him and he would have to find the energy to move clear of the chasing group, which included Douglas Rice, panting, and looking grim-faced.

Furnival and Mountjoy slipped inside the trees, disappearing quickly from view as though they had been swallowed up by the sagging weight of wet leaves and branches. Giles followed in their wake, crashing through the gap, almost losing his footing on the loose ground. Inside the wood, several pathways cut left and right around tall trees and broken stumps. The wood smelt earthy and damp, but at least the rain couldn't penetrate the thick canopy. Afraid he might make the wrong choice and end up in a dead end, he continued to follow where they went. Nimbly running and skipping over fallen branches, he could see now that the route opened into a clearing where the remnants of a battered assault course had long since fallen into disrepair. Dancing their way across the broken ground, the boys negotiated broken pieces of timber and overgrown bracken. The pathway then soon began to narrow. Giles concentrated on keeping up, feeling confident there was plenty of running left in his lungs and legs.

Which boy saw the weirdo-in-the-woods first would become much debated long after the race had ended. Mountjoy claimed it was him. Furnival called Mountjoy a liar. However, the two eventual winners of the race agreed on one point: the weirdo had sprung out of the undergrowth, arms waving, determined to drag them away into his lair inside the forest.

Narrating the story for the third or fourth time to an excited group of younger boarders, Furnival described how the weirdo had been lurking behind a tree. "He was filthy dirty with scaly, outstretched fingers like this!" he exclaimed, reaching out to grab hold of the nearest boy. Each time he told the story, he remembered something even more terrifying than before. The weirdo's teeth were yellow and jagged. His hands were pitch black and he stank of dung. And worst of all, he had blood-red eyes that looked into your soul.

"He must be the devil," exclaimed Isaccs.

"He is *the* devil!" whistled Hepbridge, grabbing hold of the boy by his arms. "Feeding on the bones of the dead from the graveyard by night!" he said, trying not to laugh when he caught Furnival's eye.

"Let me go," screeched Isaccs, squirming. He felt certain that he was going to have nightmares, or worse, to pee his bed.

How they escaped the weirdo's clutches was a little short of miraculous, said Mountjoy. "It was thanks to me that the weirdo ran off into the bushes," he said, puffing out his chest.

"I saw him off, not you!" said Furnival, and they broke into yet another squabble.

Running close behind Furnival and Mountjoy during the race, Giles had a quite different perspective on events to theirs: the stranger had seemed startled, almost scared by their presence, even though he was a grown man and they were boys. The man had shielded his face with the crook of his arm as though he was ashamed and had stumbled away into the bracken. He must have hurt himself because Giles distinctly heard the man cry out in pain. However, no one seemed interested in what he had seen; the only topic that could compete with the story about the weirdo-in-the-woods was his fight with Douglas.

"How come you didn't see Dougie coming?" Hugh asked, when

they were finally alone after the whole sad sorry cross-country race was over.

With the man darting away into the forest, Giles had quite forgotten about the runners coming up behind him. Then he heard Douglas rudely shouting, yelling at him to get out of the way. When he didn't budge, the boy pushed him to the ground and stamped on his hand.

"He pushed me from behind like a coward. There was nothing I could do," said Giles. It wasn't a fair fight; it wasn't a fight at all, even though Douglas was now waltzing around the boarding house saying he had won. "Which is nonsense!" declared Giles. "If Mr Scott hadn't separated us, I'd have clobbered him."

Giles looked around quickly to check that there was no one near who could overhear things. They had the playground almost exclusively to themselves. Everyone else had gone to get changed before the film or they were still at lunch.

"There's sure to be a search for the weirdo after what happened," said Hugh.

"Maybe," said Giles, "but they'll never find him, he's far too clever for that," he added, wiping his eyes with his rain-sodden top.

"What makes you say that?"

Giles shrugged; he just did.

Hugh knew what happened next from other boys: how Mr Scott had marched Giles and Douglas back to school. While they were heading one way, Mr Rhys-Davis had been heading in the other. "You should have seen his face when he heard about the weirdo. He shrieked like a girl!" said Giles, throwing his hands up in the air to imitate the master's reaction.

"That's so mean," Hugh replied, laughing hard.

"You only say that because he likes you," said Giles, with a smirk.

There was some truth to that, thought Hugh. Ever since the news had broken about the attempts on his father, Mr Rhys-Davis had been particularly attentive. The headmaster too had had a *quiet word* with him about the incidents at Oakbury. He was safe here cooed the headmaster in a reassuring tone. Hugh wanted to speak to his father, but Mr Richardson said he would have to wait a few more days until things had calmed down. However, he would be allowed to have some extra tuck at the film.

With no one still around, Giles continued with his impersonation of Mr Rhys-Davis. Cocking his head to one side and resting one hand on his hip, he pretended to smoke a cigarette. Putting on a high-pitched voice, he turned to Hugh and said, "Goodness, do you think there is a strange man living in the woods, Mr Scott? Do you think he would like to go for a nudey swim?"

Hugh laughed loudly and did his best to reply with a stentorian voice like Mr Scott, but unlike Giles he had no gift for mimicry. "You need to stand up straight and strut around like a peacock. I hate him!" he said vehemently.

Scott's punishment was particularly unfair: double detention, and worse of all, he'd have to sit it in the same classroom as Douglas. "That's so mean! Douglas started it," said Hugh, indignantly.

"I hate him too. He's got it coming," he replied darkly. He shot Hugh a fierce look, which stayed on his face for a moment before his lips softened into something reminiscent of a smile. "Come on, let's go and watch the film, and eat some of your extra tuck," he said, dragging Hugh by the arm towards the assembly hall.

Every boy in the boarding house, along with all the teaching staff and casual workers, were gathered inside to watch the film. Harry and Linda closed the heavy velvet drapes to keep out the daylight, while David worked the winch by the side of the stage; slowly, the large screen descended from the ceiling and came to rest on the wooden stage.

Anthony had asked David to say a few words about the film. Reflect on Tom Sawyer's theme of friendship and adventure; the purpose of the screenings was not simply to provide entertainment, but also to embed the school's values of integrity, learning and endeavour among all the boys.

The lights in the hall dimmed down and the projector crackled into a life, temporarily blinding the housemaster, and casting his shadow against the blank screen. He looked like a spectral figure from a Victorian stage show. "Boys, hush, please," he said, clearing his throat.

Linda put her finger to her lips and shushed for silence.

Having taught the book, David required no notes. "Many of you will have read Mark Twain's 'The Adventures of Tom Sawyer' in my class," he said, somewhat stiffly. "It's a wonderful adventure story written almost a century ago, yet it still has the power to enchant readers." David stared out into the hall. The audience was a homogeneous mass of heads, each one bowed, concentrating on the bag of sweets in their laps and soft drinks in their hands. Although the boys had no interest in what he had to say, he droned on "Friendship, adventure, courage, that's what makes Tom Sawyer everyone's favourite childhood story." Five minutes passed, and still he showed no signs of coming to an end. Linda nudged Harry to do something. Sliding out from his seat, Harry slunk away in the darkness, edging towards the back of the hall, and instructed Jeffrey to start the film the moment David paused for breath. Jeffrey needed no further invitation: he flicked the switch and the opening credits roared into life. Harry briskly returned to his seat.

"Thank God," said Linda, "I thought he would never stop."

"We should take it as a compliment. It means David likes our choice," replied Harry, settling once more into a padded chair. He'd purloined one for Linda and one for himself. Having had a nip of scotch before the film, he felt a little sleepy.

Linda prodded him in the ribs again. "Don't even think about nodding off," she whispered over the strings of the opening title song. On the big screen, Tom Sawyer had ditched his pack and was making a dash for the Mississippi river to watch the paddleboats steam by.

"I never had Tom pegged as a ginger-nut," Harry whispered, gesturing to the child actor. Linda giggled. "I'm sure Douglas would approve," he added, looking around to see where the red-haired boy was seated.

Douglas had taken up a seat towards the rear of the hall with Declan. They were no different to Ashworth and Burton, always together in cahoots. Like most of the boys, the film was merely a pleasant backdrop to filling their faces.

After twenty or so minutes had passed, Hugh turned to Giles. "If you had to be Tom or Huck who would you choose?" he asked. One the big screen Tom and Huck were milling around the gold, which they had discovered under a big rock in the cave.

"That's easy," said Giles, imitating a lazy mid-western drawl. "Human beings can be awful cruel to one another," he said, and lightly punched Hugh on the arm.

"You sound just like Huck!" said Hugh, although his eyes remained fixed on the big screen.

"Some people are cruel," muttered Giles, but Hugh was now miles away, mouthing along to the words of a song.

Looking around, Harry could see that the younger boys were growing restless and fidgety. However, by contrast, the usually troublesome dorm five boys appeared to be rapt in the plot. Having demolished their sweets and cola, they were following Tom and Huck as the pair snuck through the haunted house. Harry stole a glance at Anthony. The headmaster had an inscrutable expression on his face. However, by the time the end credits rolled across the screen, he broke out into applause and led the clapping. David swivelled in his seat to acknowledge the boys' gentle applause and winked at Harry and Linda.

"After that success I think we can all rest easy," said Harry to Linda, as they started to file out of the hall. Well, at least I can," he added. He had plans for the evening, which would take him away to spend the night in London. "

"Lucky you!" Linda hoped for a quiet evening. However, there remained a buzz of excitement in the air from the incidents at the race, which she found unsettling.

It was still light outside, with time to kill before dinner and lights out. Giles looked fed up. "Are you thinking about detention?" Hugh asked.

"I told you before, I don't care," he replied tetchily.

"You must do, surely?"

"I don't," said Giles, pushing the door through to the playground. "Come on," he added, walking away from the hall in the direction of the skateboard area. Together they found a dry spot to sit away from everyone else. A weak afternoon sun pricked the sky, too late in the day to force its way through the low clouds. Evening would soon be setting in. Giles rummaged in his shorts, retrieving some sweets. He handed Hugh a hot and sweaty Chewit. For a while, they sucked on sweets in silence.

"Did you like the film?" asked Giles eventually.

"It was okay for a musical."

"Did it seem real though, the running away bit?"

"I suppose," said Hugh.

"Did people think you were dead when you went missing?" Hugh scowled. The idea had never occurred to him. "Where were you running to?" asked Giles.

"To home, well, to my grandpa's," Hugh replied.

When Hugh thought about it, none of it seemed real. It seemed such a long time ago. "Do you want to hear?" he asked.

"Yes!" said Giles.

He didn't have to jump over a school wall or do anything dramatic like in Tom Sawyer, he had simply walked out the front gate and kept going until he reached the railway station. Waiting for a train had been scary, as he expected someone, an adult, would stop him. Once he was on board, he had read a book. When he reached his destination, he left the station and waited for a bus. "Except the bus didn't come and an old woman did, and she thought it was strange that I was alone," he said, kicking his feet together. "And then the police came, and then my father, and because I'd already run away, I had to change school, which is why he had come here." He realised he was gabbing away.

"I'm sorry you got caught," said Giles. "If it wasn't for the nosy woman you would have made it home."

"Maybe," said Hugh, eating another Chewit. "Do you want to go and play?" Hugh asked after a while. Giles shrugged in reply. The playground clock struck five. Boys ran in and out of doors, hollering and playing. Hugh got to his feet. "I'm bored," he said. "I think I might go back to the dorm for a bit." He felt a little cold and his legs were numb from sitting cross-legged.

Giles looked sullen again. "How about a game of hide and seek?" he asked, not wanting to be left alone.

"In or out, you decide," replied Hugh, warming to the idea.

"In, where there are more places to hide," he responded

immediately. "Let's flip a coin to decide who hides first?" However, neither of them had any loose change in their pockets. "Let's use something else instead," he said, looking around for something suitable. Breaking a stick in two different lengths, Giles put them behind his back and asked Hugh to choose. "The shorter length wins." Hugh guessed incorrectly. "I'll hide," said Giles excitedly. "Shut your eyes and count to twenty. No cheating. Swear?"

Closing his eyes tightly Hugh promised not to peep, making a three-fingered salute like a cub scout to show he was serious about keeping his word.

"Spin round, while you count," said Giles, his voice trailing away.

Hugh spun around until he reached twenty. When he opened his eyes, he felt giddy. The playground was deserted, "Coming ready or not," he hollered.

Hugh tried to put himself in Giles' shoes. Where would he go and hide? Dashing inside the building, he decided to focus on the ground floor. Quickly he skirted through five or six rooms, and then an idea came to him like a flash: the piano room. Giles purported to love the piano, although he had yet to play anything for Hugh. Rushing through the lobby and the small lounges rooms, he raced inside and dived on to the tatty floral sofa expecting Giles to be lurking behind it. However, he'd guessed incorrectly, and Giles was neither there, nor in the nearby locker room, which also offered loads of places to hide.

With the ground floor chalked off, Hugh headed upstairs. Halfway up, he chanced upon Isaccs coming in the opposite direction, taking the stairs two at a time in a tearing hurry. Hugh blocked his path. "Have you seen Ashworth?" he demanded.

The boy stared at Hugh, his blue eyes shining brightly. He looked permanently startled. "Not since the film," said the small boy.

"Are you telling the truth?" asked Hugh, sceptically.

Isaccs glanced nervously over his shoulder, as though he was expecting someone to be there or listening in. "No. Yes. I mean," he stammered.

"Which is it, yes or no?" asked Hugh, impatiently.

"Yes, but he said not to tell, or else," said the boy, his face reddening.

"We're playing hide and seek. Tell me where he is!" said Hugh, grasping the boy by the shoulders.

"Don't say it was me."

"No, I won't. Where was he?"

Isaccs sniffed loudly, "In your dorm."

It was so obvious; Hugh felt like an idiot for not thinking about their dorm. Barging Issacs to one side, he charged up the stairs, along the corridor, and hurled himself into dorm three. He flung one the largest cupboard with a loud hurrah. Parting the curtain of winter coats, he felt around for his friend: empty. He quickly tried the other two: the same. Hugh threw himself on to his bed.

The game was losing its appeal and he was tempted to wait for lights out to be called, and for Giles to come out. However, then he would never hear the end of it. With herculean effort he dragged himself up and started to search the rest of the first floor. Marching from room to room, he asked one boy or after another the same question as he'd asked Isaacs, and was met with a raft of unhelpful replies: Why? No. Who cares? Piss off!

Perching on the edge of one of the bathtubs, he wondered what to do next. Varun looked up from washing his face. "Giles went that way," he said, pointing towards dorms four and five. Hugh didn't fancy the thought of running into Heppy and his crew whilst he was on his own. However, he thought what his father would say, and he decided to press on.

"I suppose you are looking for Ashworth?" asked the thick-set boy, standing at the doorway to dorm five. "Cat got your tongue?" he said, giving Hugh the once-over, much in the same way the school tailor had done when fitting Hugh for a blazer and pairs of trousers before the start of term. Hugh had the same uncomfortable feeling as he did then that he didn't quite measure up. The secret, he knew, was to hold your nerve and bluff it out.

"Hello Furnival," said Hugh, as casually as possible.

"Are you after your bum chum or something else?" asked Furnival, with an expression that was a cross between a smirk and a grimace.

Hugh had a vague idea what this meant; it was not complimentary. "Mr Rhys-Davis sent me to find Giles," said Hugh, thinking on his feet.

"You should find yourself another friend," said Furnival. "You can come and play chess with me if you want?" It was less of an invitation, more of a threat.

"Mr Rhys-Davis told me to hurry," said Hugh, backing away.

"He was heading upstairs to the modelmaking room," said Furnival, motioning to the second floor. "And don't forget what I said about coming to see me, Burton," he added, and with that, he stepped inside his dorm and slammed the door.

Feeling emboldened by not only keeping his nose out of trouble, but also by discovering where Giles was hiding from the unlikeliest of sources, Hugh made his way quickly but quietly up the rickety stairs that led to the second floor. Pressing himself against the corridor wall, he edged forward cautiously, trying to avoid making any noise that might alert Giles to his presence. He planned to scare Giles with a wolfish howl when he found him. Light glowed from beneath the door. Carefully, Hugh turned the handle and stepped inside, making ready to howl, but the sight of Giles standing alone in a scene of devastation stunned him into silence. Hugh stared at Giles open-mouthed.

Scattered all over the floor were broken pieces of every type of model, from aircraft, artillery, and tanks, to ships and submarines. Whole armies of miniature soldiers lay crushed on the parquet floor. Weeks of work had been destroyed. Only one or two pieces had escaped intact, and Giles held one of these in hand, a replica Dambuster. "Isn't it lovely?" he murmured, dreamily, holding it up to the light. "Here, take a look," he said, handing it to Hugh.

The bomber felt as light as air in Hugh's hands. Surveying the scene, he started to feel the same, as though the air was being sucked out of his lungs. "What happened here?" he asked. Giles looked around the room, as though the answer lay there and shrugged casually. "Don't shrug, stop shrugging," said Hugh, angrily.

Giles snatched the Lancaster from Hugh's hands. "It was like this when I got here," he declared in a sullen tone.

"We need to tell someone, matron or one of the masters," said Hugh, starting to shake. "If we get caught here, they'll blame us. They need to find out who did this." Hugh stepped back and trod accidently on what remained of a Sherman. The tank made a popping sound like a final shot of defiance. Hugh kicked away the piece. "I'm going to find someone," he said.

"Don't do that," said Giles, reaching out to grab Hugh's arm. The Lancaster slipped from his hand and took a nose-dive and broke in two. Giles looked crestfallen.

"We'll have to, there's no choice. Isaccs and Furnival, and plenty of others know that I was looking for you. They will think all of this is down to us," replied Hugh, gesturing to the mess.

"Please don't, brother Hugh. I swear it wasn't me," he said, making the sign of the Honest Injun.

"This isn't Tom Sawyer, Giles. This is real life!" exclaimed Hugh. "Boys get expelled for doing stuff like this. Promise me it wasn't you!".

Giles picked up the broken wing of the Dambuster and threw it against the wall. "I said it wasn't me!" I thought *you* of all people would believe me?" Kicking the remains of the fuselage against the wall, he stomped across the room to the window. It was still light outside. In the town, families would be settling down to watch television after supper. Giles opened the window. "I always get the blame for everything. It's not fair," he said. Hugh watched in horror as Giles scooped up half a dozen broken models, and then tossed them out of the window.

"Stop it Giles!" he remonstrated.

"Why, what's the point? If you think I smashed everything up I might as well as get the blame for something I actually did!" he replied aggressively. He grabbed a damaged Hurricane and two Messerschmitts. "Look, they're having a dogfight," he said, imitating the sound of machine gun fire. "One German's been hit, and the other one is on fire. They're going to crash," he cried, hurling the Messerschmitts away.

"Giles, please!" beseeched Hugh.

"Don't you want to play?" asked Giles, tossing the Hurricane at Hugh. It broke apart in Hugh's hands. "Never mind, there's more where that came from," said Giles, rushing over to the work bench where replica Heinkels were grounded, ready to be painted. "I think they're ready for take-off," he said out loud.

Hugh dashed over and pushed Giles out of the way. Giles shoved Hugh back, sending him toppling forwards into the workbench where pots of paint and brushes were kept. The scuffle sent everything tumbling to the floor, along with Hugh. "I'm sorry, I didn't mean to do that," he said, retreating to the open window.

"We're in for it now," said Hugh, edging away from Giles toward the corridor, deciding that this was the moment to fetch help.

Giles appeared lost in his own world, gazing once again outside. "You told me you came to Frampton for a new start. So, did I," said Giles. "But I never said why, and you never asked," he said, gripping the window frame. He pictured Marcus falling in slow motion, a look of shock on his face, the blood blooming, pooling in the shattered orbit, and then the hideous scream. He didn't know a boy could make a sound as loud and hideous and fearful as that. "They said I bashed up a boy, and I said it wasn't me! You believe me don't you, brother Hugh?" Giles swivelled around quickly, desperate to see how Hugh would react, but Hugh had gone.

At the foot of the stairs, Hugh heard Giles cry out. He paused, pricking up his ears, wondering whether he should call out or go back. And then he heard the baying sound, which grew suddenly into a desperate howl, and he felt scared, and so he ran.

Having invented a story about Mr Rhys-Davis sending him to seek out Giles, Hugh now found he needed his help. He banged furiously on his door. When he received no answer, he wondered if it was a sign. However, just as he was on the point of giving up, a stern voice called out for him to stop. "Mr Rhys-Davis has the evening off," said matron, walking hurriedly towards Harry's study. "Can I help?" she asked, reading the agitation on Hugh's face.

Hugh plunged his hands into the pockets of his shorts and glanced away nervously.

"Hugh, what is it?" she asked. Ever since the Oakbury incidents, she had been on tenterhooks about the wellbeing of the Colonel's son. Linda crouched down and gently lifted his face. Up close, she noticed he had the faintest trace of mole to the left of his ear. "Well?"

"Someone has smashed up the modelmaking room," he said. "I thought someone should know."

Linda took a deep breath and straightened up. "That sounds serious," she said. "You better show me."

They hurried along in silence. All the while, Hugh's thoughts returned to Giles. At the stairs, she asked Hugh to let her pass. As he trailed in her footsteps, each step nearer to the room started to make him feel sick. A horrible feeling of dread overcame him. Giles had looked so angry and frightening, unrecognisable from the boy he counted as his bestfriend. Giles had worn the same expression on his face when he had told him about scalding Declan, and then all the destruction, and the hideous howl. Why? And then he suddenly understood what it meant: Giles had been calling out to him. He clutched his hands to his head, realising that he should have gone back to Giles there and then. Hugh stopped abruptly on the stairs, knowing that he made a colossal mistake in fetching matron. However, it was too late to undo what he had started.

Hugh caught up with matron outside the modelling room. She seemed hesitant about what to do next. Hugh could hardly bear the suspense. Finally, she seized the handle and pushed open the door. A warm breeze passed through the room. Even before she had turned on the overhead light, the wreckage was plain to see. "Oh, my goodness," she said, covering her mouth in shock. "Who did this?" she asked, looking angry and flush-faced.

"I don't know," he said, sheepishly, eyes darting around

everywhere.

"Stop lying and tell me," she said, telegraphing his every movement.

"Giles was here, but it wasn't him," he blurted out. "I swear he had nothing to do with it."

She had already guessed as much. The boy was a bad penny. She could feel it in her water. "Then, who did?" she said, "And don't so much as a skip a detail. This is a very serious matter."

Hugh told her his truth: they had been playing hide and seek, and when he had found Giles, the models were already smashed up. "Giles loves modelmaking, so he'd never, ever…" he said, his voice trailing off. He could see in her eyes that she did not believe him. She had the same look as his mother when she thought he was making things up. He decided not to tell matron about Giles throwing the rest of the models out of the window. That would seal his fate.

"Where will I find Giles?" she demanded. Offering up a Giles-like shrug, Hugh guessed Giles had to be getting ready for bed. Linda's exasperation got the better of her. "I'd have expected you to know, Burton," she said, with a raised voice. "After all, he's *your* friend and you were here together just now."

Inside dorm three, Varun lay in bed reading Warlord. He was collecting coupons and nearly had enough to exchange for a replica Bronze Star. Douglas was lounging on Declan's bed. He stiffened up on matron's arrival, instantly alert to trouble. "Where is Ashworth?" she asked.

Douglas glanced at Hugh. "Burton should know. They go

everywhere together, even to the loo," he said with a smirk. "Ashworth's probably in there causing a stink."

"Cut it out," she snapped.

Douglas continued to smirk at Hugh as he followed matron out of the dorm. From the corridor, he heard the three boys burst into laughter.

Irritable and anxious, she strode to the bathroom with Hugh in tow. Wary eyes met hers, but none belonged to Giles Ashworth. Next, she rapped on the stalls. A frightened voice confirmed the identity of a dorm one boy, while another told her to bugger off. "It's Matron and I won't have words like you used towards me or anyone else," she barked.

"Sorry matron, I thought it was one of my dorm," replied Andrews from behind the closed door.

The situation was making Linda feel increasingly exasperated. What had gone through Giles' head, or Hugh's, to wantonly destroy everything like that? One or both had to be responsible; and for as long as the question about Ashworth's whereabouts remained unanswered, the more convinced she was about his guilt. "While we're here, you might as well get ready," she said to Hugh. "Go back to the dorm when you are done and tell Ashworth to come to my room as soon as you see him." Linda figured the boy was busy making up an excuse. She would find him soon enough. She had been down this road before.

Washed and teeth brushed, Hugh traipsed back to the dorm. "Cheer up, Burton," said Douglas with a sarcastic smile. "I'm sure Ashworth's around here somewhere unless the weirdo's got his hands on him," he said, snatching at thin air. The others laughed along; in Giles's absence, Douglas's primacy had been restored. "Anyway, what's going on?" Spill the beans!" he pronounced, with a threatening expression.

"Nothing," said Hugh, pulling on his pyjamas. He hung up his Adidas top on a hanger next to Giles's one.

"That's nice, do you and Ashworth always put your things side by side like girls," teased Douglas. Hugh slammed shut the cabinet door and wheeled around angrily.

"Enough," barked Mr Scott standing in the open doorway. He had an unerring knack of appearing when trouble was getting started. The boys exchanged brief glances. Unfinished business would have to wait. "Come with me, Burton, and get to bed Douglas," said the housemaster. "Lights out in five."

David strode down the corridor towards the main stairs, leaving Hugh struggling to keep pace. Hugh guessed correctly that their destination was the headmaster's study. Anthony Richardson spun around the moment they entered. "Are you or Ashworth responsible for the destruction of the models belonging to boys of this school and to school property?" he demanded.

"No, sir," said Hugh timidly, cowered by the headmaster's words and the look of cold fury carved into his face.

"What did you say? Speak up," said Anthony, eyes narrowing behind his glasses

Hugh looked down at his slippers, his gaze drawn to a white splodge of toothpaste, "No, sir," he said again, glancing up.

"I'll ask you one more time, and I will know if you are not telling the truth," said the headmaster, looming over Hugh.

Again, Hugh repeated 'no'. "In which case, why is Giles Ashworth missing?" said Anthony.

"Missing?" said Hugh slowly.

"Yes, that's also why you are here, to tell us what you know about that," said Mr Scott, tersely.

"Did you hear what Mr Scott said?" shouted the headmaster.

Giles would not, could not be missing. Everything they did, they did together. They were bulldogs. Brothers. Theirs was a bond like Huck and Tom. Except he, Hugh, had broken that, by going to the masters.

"Speak boy!" said Mr Scott savagely.

Hugh was lost for words. They had frightened him into silence. The study door banged open. "Have you taken leave of your senses?" asked Linda of Anthony and David. "I could hear you from upstairs," she said.

Crossing the study floor, she wrapped her arms around Hugh's shoulders "Can you help us find him?" she asked Hugh. Linda felt his chest start to heave. "Don't get upset," she said. "It'll be ok."

Hugh gazed up, blinking through his tears, still unable to find the right words.

"Let's start from when you went to play hide and seek," she said, softly, and Hugh began the story all over again.

* * *

All hands had been called in to the search for Giles Ashworth.

Only Harry was absent: he had taken his evening off in London and was not due back until the following morning. However, between David and his wife Claire, they had mustered fifteen or so members of staff. Armed with torches they were searching the school buildings and the grounds.

David felt lousy about the way he had treated Hugh and wondered if he had mishandled the altercation between Giles and Douglas at the race, and if that had contributed to Giles' disappearance. Claire reassured him that they'd find Ashworth soon, and that he was being unnecessarily hard on himself. She blamed Harry for choosing a film about runaways. David had not made the connection.

"Who's helping Linda in the house with Harry being away?" Claire had asked over coffee in the staff room. In truth, he had not given Linda a second thought. "Doesn't she already have enough on her plate?" his wife asked.

Now that Claire mentioned it, he recognised that Linda could use an extra pair of hands. "Could you help muck in?" he asked.

Claire finished her coffee and kissed him lightly on the cheek. "You know where to find me," she said.

Linda was grateful to receive more support. None of the boys were ready to sleep, the dorms were full of whispering. Claire shepherded the younger ones upstairs to the room adjoining Linda's and read bedtime stories until they were sleepy. They spread out over the bed like kittens, one on top of the other. Apart from the help, Linda was pleased to have some adult company to take her mind away from fretting over Giles.

In the darkness of dorm three, Hugh could feel the boys' eyes on him.

"You sneak," hissed Douglas. Hugh tossed and turned beneath his sheets and gazed at Giles' empty bed. "Sneak, sneak, sneak," repeated Douglas, again and again until the others had started to join in. Hugh wrapped the pillow around his head to block out their words. "Sneak, sneak, sneak," they chorused loudly.

Hugh threw the covers on the floor, "I'm no sneak!" he yelled and ran out of the room.

Linda had to chase Hugh to catch him. He blurted out what Douglas and the others had said and buried his face in her chest. "You will find Giles, won't you?" he asked with a tremulous voice.

Linda ruffled his hair, "Of course we will. He won't have gone far. By the morning, everything will be ok. You'll see," she said, involuntarily caressing the cross around her neck. While Hugh held her tight, she brought it to her lips. She kissed the crucified Jesus and asked Him to forgive the way she felt about Giles and to ask Him to bring the boy safely home to school.

She decided to settle Hugh into her bed and sit in with Claire. The seven-year-old boys were sound asleep. They had lost all track of time. Hours had drifted by. "Has there been any news?" Linda asked. Claire shook her head. "Why don't you keep David company for a while?" She could take things from here. The older boys would not dare play up or there would be hell to pay.

"Only if you're sure," replied Claire, softly closing the bedroom door behind her. David was still sitting where Claire had left him, gazing out into the darkness of the grounds from the study window.

"I hate not being out there, helping," he said.

"Someone has to hold the fort," Claire replied, cuddling up to David.

"You mean do Anthony's job for him?"

She knew that most people only saw his tough exterior. However, beneath it, there was a kind and generous man who cared about the boys in his charge. "And where is our illustrious headmaster? she said, ironically.

"With the police."

Claire looked shocked, "I didn't think they'd need to be brought in, not so soon." Claire pressed her face up against the glass panes. "How awful, what if he's in danger?"

David had had the same thought, "Let's go outside for a moment. It wouldn't hurt to get some fresh air.

She understood that he craved to be involved and felt powerless marooned in the study, awaiting instructions from Anthony and the police. He wasn't the passive sort: he was at his best when he could get stuck in.

Standing together on the gravel driveway, Claire had often imagined being in the position of the wife of the headmaster, welcoming parents and boys to the school. Anthony kept his wife Fay away from things, hogging the limelight. David was a different man altogether. He welcomed having her by his side, just as things were now. They would find the boy – she was convinced about that - and when they did, and once the trustees assessed things again, it would be obvious that time should be called on Anthony's tenure as headmaster. There was only one credible candidate to replace him. She squeezed his hand, but David was focused only on the search. "How much longer will they be out there?" she asked, folding her body into his.

"Another hour, more or less," he replied, looking at his watch, "and then they will resume again at first light." He pulled Claire in close, thinking about how much he loved and their own two children. "There, look, it's the search party!" he exclaimed, glimpsing flashes of torchlight, as the phalanx of staff members fanned out, combing the grounds. A flash of a hi-vis top, the crimson red of a field jacket; they suddenly reminded Claire about the man she had seen parked up in the little lane near their cottage. In all the fuss, it had slipped her mind and now she felt it was important.

"There was a red car parked up in the lane. A man was dozing inside," she said. "He nearly jumped out of his skin when I walked by."

David was only half-listening. "Sorry, what was that?" he asked. Claire repeated what she had said. "You didn't think there was anything fishy about that?" he said, eyes narrowing.

He was dressed in smart country clothes, so she'd assumed that he was probably from the local country estate. Their staff occasionally used the lane to park up and walk their dogs. The man had a kind smile too, she remembered, and he'd waved at her in passing. When she glanced over her shoulder, he was already pulling off. "He drove away slowly, showing far more consideration than some of the parents who hare along the lane," said Claire.

"All the same, I think I'll mention it to the police," replied David, looking back in the direction of the search party. The torchlights were becoming faint. The party would be heading into the woods for one last time. "Furnival said he saw that long-haired man again," he said, frowning.

"The one the boys call the weirdo-in-the-woods?"

"I assume so, although I'm not sure whether I believe him," he said distractedly, his voice sounding as distant and detached as the lights from the search party. "Nevertheless, I told Anthony that he should inform the police."

"Why would Furnival make something like that up?"

"Who knows," he replied, squinting into the darkness. "You know what boys are like at this age. They say and do the most ridiculous things. No doubt Ashworth's out there right now having a good laugh at our expense."

"Let's hope so," she said, hugging David hard. She didn't have Linda's blind faith, but she had something else, a gut feeling, and more often than not, it was right.

10 – FAULT LINES

The headlights swept across the study window. David looked at the study clock. Four fifteen am. Slipping into his shoes, he stepped lightly from the building to greet Harry. "Thank you for coming back so soon. We need all the help we can, and I knew you would want to help."

"What's the latest??" asked Harry, softly closing the door of the Triumph Stag.

"Nothing, yet" said David, "They will resume the search at dawn."

Feeling fragile from the journey, Harry rested his hand on the bonnet, letting the engine warm his fingers, which were stiff and aching from the drive. "Where have they searched?" he asked.

"The school grounds and far fields, and part of the woods. Jeffrey's been coordinating efforts on the ground, while Anthony's been dealing with the police," replied David flatly.

Under the yellow wash of the outside lights, Harry thought that David's skin had acquired a sickly hue. Feeling the engine start to cool, he asked if there was any breakfast going. He needed a coffee to wake himself up and to pop some headache tablets to stave off a hangover. Tony was pouring another dram when the call came to get himself back to school. Reluctantly, Harry had had to say goodbye to his friend. Tony said he understood, but he looked offended.

Harry and David took coffee in the main school kitchen, which had been transformed into the meeting point for the search. Some twenty or so people were having breakfast or catching up on sleep. Jeffrey and someone Harry recognised from the ground staff were seated together, looking sombre. Harry nodded in their direction. While David fetched steaming mugs of coffee, Harry dived into his overnight bag for a couple of pills, swallowing them hurriedly before David returned.

The coffee was bitter and strong, just what he needed. "How is Linda faring?" Harry asked, worried about how the stress might be affecting the baby.

"Fine, why?" asked David, with a suspicious expression.

"It's a lot to take on fifty boys without you and me," Harry replied, staring into the coffee mug.

"Yes, quite right," said David. "I had the same thought and asked Claire to get stuck in."

Harry felt relieved.

"I've also been doing a bit of digging into the pupil records while I was lodged in Anthony's study," he said furtively.

"Snooping?" said Harry with a wry smile.

For once, David ignored the comment. While the search was on, he had read the entire pupil record for Ashworth, looking for any clues into the boy's character and motivations. Within the paperwork he had come across an oblique comment about his character from the headmistress of his previous school, which troubled him. "She inferred that he has a problem controlling his emotions. A bit highly strung. I should have brought the document with me," he said, knowing that there was more to it than that. "Ah, that was it," he said remembering, "She wrote that he tends to fixate on someone or something and becomes quite difficult to deal with if he doesn't get his way with things."

Harry smiled to himself, thinking about Tony.

"I rather got the impression that there was something a bit sinister or unhealthy. It made me think of Ashworth's friendship with Burton," said David "It is rather intense, isn't it?"

"Surely no more so than Douglas and Declan's, or others," said Harry stifling a yawn. "What does Hugh have to say about Giles?"

"I think he feels that he's to blame for Giles going missing, that it's his fault for dobbing him in, even though it was the right thing to do. Anthony's reaction hasn't helped matters," he said, describing how he had taken a heavy-handed approach, treating Hugh like a criminal. "He bullied Hugh into going over the story more than once or twice, pressing him for answers, which the boy didn't have. It was relentless, like an interrogation. God knows what the parents will have to say about it when they hear about it."

"Maybe it won't come to that. If Giles turns up soon, the whole thing will be over quickly, like it never happened and no one will be any of the wiser," stated Harry, trying to strike a more hopeful and optimistic note.

David leaned in, giving Harry a conspiratorial look. "It's too late for that," he said, "The chair of the trustees has asked me to prepare a written report into Anthony's management of the situation."

"That's a bit underhand. I thought they were great pals," said Harry, flicking a quick glance over the room. "It'll bring a heap of trouble for Anthony," he said, keeping his voice down. "Or is that what you want?"

"I think it's what we all want, isn't it," said David. Everyone on the staff recognised the rivalry between the two, and that David saw himself as a more suitable headmaster. Although Harry was stunned by the chair's move against Anthony, he surmised that he might benefit from a regime change. "The chair has quite a dossier on Anthony, including a dalliance with a certain member of staff at the summer party!"

Harry's face fell. "Oh, don't look so horrified, Harry," David said, in response to his stunned expression. "They were hardly subtle about it, were they?"

Harry thought only he had been wise to Linda and Anthony's fling. "Shouldn't we be focusing on Giles Ashworth?" he said, trying to deflect the conversation away from the topic.

"There's no reason to alarm Linda. The chair sees Anthony as the predator," he said, "and to answer your question – yes, we need to apply ourselves to Giles." David took a large gulp of coffee and turned in his seat toward Jeffrey. "I need your help, yours and Jeffrey's," he said, waving an arm in the air to attract the old gardener's attention.

Catching David's eye, Jeffrey left his table and joined them. "Gentlemen, how can I be of assistance?" he asked, taking a seat.

At first light, David said he wanted three search parties organised so they could cover more ground quickly. One led by Harry, another by Jeffrey, while he would lead the third.

"Where will Anthony be while all this is taking place?" asked Jeffrey.

"Coordinating efforts, here, with the police and working up the courage to call Ashworth's parents." David felt that he should have been given that responsibility. Anthony had had little dealings with the Ashworths, whereas he had given the mother and father a tour of the school, making them feel at ease and welcoming their son to the house. "I feel like I have failed the boy," he said with an air of finality.

"No one is to blame," said Harry.

"Or if they are, we all are," said Jeffrey, sitting back. "There's no point in dwelling on the whys and wherefores. Let's focus on finding him, eh?" he said, before tailing off; Anthony had entered the dinner hall via the kitchen and was hurriedly making his way towards them.

"We've had a breakthrough," said Anthony, with a glint in his eye. "Someone's been helping themselves to waste food from the bins behind the kitchens. Ashworth must have been stocking up." Anthony looked from David to Harry, and then to Jeffrey, for a response. He expected a positive reaction.

There was a pregnant pause during which the three men looked at one another quizzically. "Forgive me, Anthony, but what does it change?" asked David, eventually.

"What does it change?" he answered, rhetorically, lifting an eyebrow. "Everything, of course! The boy is as cunning as a fox, stealing school food so he doesn't have to go into shops. He must be planning quite a journey. We'll need to widen the search area," he said, his voice growing louder.

"But why would he bother? His family lives only an hour or so's drive away," said David.

"Who is to say that is where the boy is heading?" retorted Anthony. "We should thank Haggerty for being alert. Good thing I got rid of the other chappie." Anthony gave the new chef a thumbs-up. "It's a solid lead for the police to work with, so stand ready to help them when they arrive," he said, rubbing his hands together.

"We don't need to wait. We're ready to go out at first light," said David firmly. "I'd planned to break us into three smaller groups and get going…"

"What?" cut in Anthony, "No," he said, looking irritated. "The boy is *long gone*. There's no sense expending energy on a fruitless effort. The police are the experts, they'll take the lead and tell us what to do." David went to speak. However, Anthony shushed him away with a curt raised hand. "Don't say another word. You might have been at the school for a long time, but I make the decisions."

"Surely, it's better to keep looking?" said Jeffrey in a patient manner.

Harry looked up at the main clock. "It's been ten hours and there is not the slightest trace of Ashworth," he said.

Anthony glowered at Harry. "I appreciate you coming back to

help, but the best thing you can do is to freshen up, and no doubt sober up, so you are ready *if* you're called upon," spat Anthony venomously.

"That was uncalled for," said Harry.

Jeffrey and David shook their heads in surprise at Anthony's cruel and callous comments. However, Anthony seemed not to care. And, after a long silence, Harry decided to leave the table.

"I'm glad we all understand each other," said Anthony, as Harry walked away.

"We don't," replied Harry defiantly.

Anthony appeared to be in two minds about how to react to Harry's comment. "Goodbye Mr Rhys-Davis," he muttered through a tight-lipped smile before turning in the opposite direction towards the kitchen, cutting a swathe through the tables where volunteers were eating breakfast.

David and Jeffrey watched on, aghast at Anthony's behaviour. "Unbelievable," said Jeffrey, under his breath, after Anthony had bounded out. "What do we do now?"

David had a thunderous expression on his face. "Let me think," he said.

"Well, I've seen enough. After this is over, I'm going to retire!" said Jeffrey, unable to control himself.

"That's a bit excessive, isn't it?" said David. "There's no point getting hot under the collar and doing something rash. Who knows how long Anthony will be here? You've outlasted every headmaster. You'll outlast him."

"I don't care to," said Jeffrey, "I have had enough of the way he treats people. The way he spoke to Harry, and how he dismissed Fran. I've seen it all before, I have too many bitter memories."

David had never seen Jeffrey so upset and angry. "Like what?" he asked.

"Jim. Remember him?" answered Jeffrey, with a question of own. David looked at him quizzically. "The young chap who used to help me in the garden and carry out repairs and maintenance. Longish hair?"

"Vaguely," said David. "Why?"

"Anthony made me fire him! I should have resigned there and then," he said, relating the events that had led up to Jim's abrupt disappearance.

"Where was I when that was going on?" asked David, wracking his brain.

"You were on the staff at the time, but that's not the point," he said, recounting how Anthony had taken against Jim – first, pulling him out of gardening, which he loved – and then, sending Jim back to the most menial and degrading maintenance tasks. "It's the same pattern all over again. It's his way or the highway!" he exclaimed, attracting curious looks.

Jeffrey lowered his voice. "I tried to reason with Anthony, but he wouldn't listen. He was thuggish towards me for weeks after that, all because I challenged his views," he said, staring intensely at David. "The garden was never the same after Jim left, I couldn't keep up with it on my own. I should have more principles and tried to find him," he said, with a heavy sigh.

"I wish I had known about this, perhaps I could have done something to help," replied David.

"It wouldn't have changed one iota," said Jeffrey, unable to control his emotions. "Look around," he said, pointing from one table to the next. Tired faces looked up, wondering why the usually placid old gardener was angry and upset. Jeffrey was beyond caring. "We're all sitting here when we could be out there looking for a missing boy! God only knows what's going through Anthony's brain, he seems to have lost the plot." Jeffrey's hands were shaking with rage and frustration.

David reached across the table and placed his hand over Jeffrey's. "Change is coming," he said, glancing sidelong in his direction, "and when it does, we can all breathe a sigh of relief."

"You obviously know something I don't," replied Jeffrey with a faint smile, but then his eyes darkened, as he looked around the dinner hall, taking in the threadbare furniture, the cracked ceiling paint and rusty pipework. "One thing's for sure, if change is coming, then this place is crying out for someone like Jim. Remember that, David, when your time comes!"

* * *

The new chef Haggerty had been erroneous in his assumption about who had been raiding the kitchen bins. While the search party had been sweeping the far fields, Jim had snuck in under the cover of darkness and helped himself to damaged fruit, wonky vegetables, and a half dozen of over-cooked sausages. He'd taken as much as he could, fearing it might be some time before he could forage safely again; ever since the start of term when the boys had descended on the shelter and poked their noses around, he had been on edge, dreading the discovery of the home he had fashioned inside. Then, having stumbled into the cross-country race and come face-to-face with the runners, he feared that he had made matters worse for himself. He assumed, quite mistakenly, that the search party was out looking for him. And then there was the unsettling presence of the occupants of the red car.

Keeping to the shadows of the trees, Jim could see that a man and a woman were seated together in the back seats. At first, he thought they were making out; it wouldn't be the first time that a courting couple had used the quiet little spot for such things. However, as he drew near, it was plain that they were not engaged in anything of the sort; a heated row was taking place, which culminated in the man striking the woman across the face.

Instinctively, Jim dropped to his knees and slunk into the foliage where he bided his time. Eventually, he heard a soft click of the car door and the man and woman emerged. He shifted position in the undergrowth to look at the couple. Moon-faced, with a sallow complexion, except for a livid mark on one cheek from where she had been slapped, the woman was dressed for the country in a Barbour jacket and cords. She reached into the boot and handed the man a holdall. While the man unzipped it, the woman pulled a hat over her peroxide bob, tucking the bleached curls behind her ears.

"Are you set?" said the man. Jim recognised the accent: the hard, brittle sound of Belfast.

The woman grunted. "What if the police come and run the

plates, Eamonn?" she asked. Like the man, she shared the same Belfast accent.

"I thought we'd settled that business," he said, jabbing his finger in her face. "Don't make me do it twice, Eva!" he snarled. "Remember why we're here, for the boy," he said, tapping his breast pocket where he kept the photograph, which Carrie had filched from Burton's desk.

In Northern Ireland, on his first and only tour of duty, Jim had had to stop and search men like this man on a routine basis. You had to be careful about how you handled things: a word out of place could be enough to start a brawl or lead to something much worse. There was no good reason for the man and the woman to be venturing into the school grounds unless they were up to no good, and despite their country jackets, the man's flared jeans gave the game away.

Eamonn led the way from the vehicle. Jim watched them carefully as they slipped down the lane, the man swinging the holdall in his left hand, while the woman stayed close behind him. When they had disappeared, Jim scuttled across to the car and rattled the handles. Nothing gave. In the rear, an Ordnance Survey map of the area lay partially open on the back seat with the town ringed in marker pen. Jim glanced in the direction that they had taken, feeling tempted to follow them. However, the sound of voices coming from the woods put paid to the idea. The torchlight procession that he had tracked through the night was drawing near, returning to the school. After the misjudgement that he made which had led him coming face to face with the schoolboy runners, he had no intention of getting caught out again. Jim craned his neck and looked around. Satisfied that the coast was clear, he headed home to the shelter to formulate a plan.

Back inside the shelter, his army training kicked in. First, he prepared a go-bag: warm clothes, food, water, torches, ropes and knives, and a coin wallet, with all the money he owned, barely twenty pounds. Setting the bag to one side, he unfurled the tarpaulin and ground sheet and checked they were ship-shape. They'd served him well in the past when he had needed to build a lean-to in the woods. If the shelter was at risk of being discovered, he'd have the basics to get by, and to stay reasonably warm and dry.

Jim took a good look around the two rooms, peering into the dark corners in case there was anything else of use. When he had first discovered the second room, he had decided to retain all the military paraphernalia. An ugly gas mask grinned at him from an open packing case. Along with the mask, it contained a few gas canisters and emergency flares. He stuffed a canister into the mask and hid it under an old blanket.

Despite feeling nervous, he was hungry. He took a couple of the sausages and went outside to eat. The night air was damp. Sitting cross-legged on the grassy roof, he ate the sandwich slowly, savouring each bite. The school was his breadbasket, the shelter his sanctuary. He hated the thought of having to leave it all behind. Where would he go? He had no idea. It felt like his luck was running out and he was powerless to do anything about it.

* * *

At the sound of approaching footsteps on the landing, Linda opened her bedroom door, heart in her mouth, wondering if there had been some news about Giles. Instead, a belligerent dorm two boy stood there, hands on hips with a disgusted look on his face. "Isaccs has wet his bed, and he refuses to clear up his mess," he announced.

Hugh awoke, startled by the voices. Linda told the boy to hush but he blathered on. By the time he said his piece, Hugh was wide awake and changing out of his pyjamas and into his casual clothes. "You don't have to get up yet," said Linda, "It's still early."

Hugh, however, was as eager for news as she was. "Have you got news about Giles?" he asked Baxter.

"It's something else, Hugh," she said kindly. "Why don't you go and help Mr Scott's wife get the little ones ready?" she added, pointing to the room next door. "It'll be breakfast soon and everyone will be hungry."

Hugh shook his head. "I'd rather not," he said.

"Then, you'll have to help me," she said.

Baxter raced ahead, clattering down the stairs. When Linda and Hugh caught up with him, he was standing outside the dorm with his fingers pinched over his nostrils. Arthurs, Hubert, and Smith were hovering outside with their hands over their noses and mouths. Isaccs was sitting on the linoleum floor, swathed in sheets

"Wet-a-bed, wet-a-bed, Isaccs is a wet-a-bed," Hubert started to sing, the others joining in. Isaccs stared at the trio and said something inaudible, and then lifted a wet towel heavy with urine and tossed it at them. The boys jumped back, squealing.

"Look there," shouted Arthurs, pointing at Isaccs' sheets.

"What's all the blue stuff mixed in with his pee. Ugh!" he said, the glasses on his sharp nose steaming up.

Linda leaned over Isaacs. "What's this, John?" she asked, touching the blue paint stains on the soaking sheet. The little boy looked beyond Linda towards Hugh. The paint matched the colour of the flotilla of hand-painted ships, which had been stamped into smithereens in the modelmaking room.

"Is that what I think it is?" asked Linda. Hugh had never heard matron sound so cross, nor look so disappointed. Isaccs stared up at Linda and then recoiled, pulling the sheets around him even though they were wet and dirty. Linda repeated the question and gave the boy a shake. Hugh looked around. The corridor was swarming with boys, eager to discover what was going on.

Eventually, Isaccs sat up and whispered to matron. Hugh pressed in behind her. "I'm sorry," Hugh heard the boy say.

"But why did you do it?" asked Linda.

The boy sniffled and withdrew from her touch. "They won't stop teasing me," he said, after a long pause. Baxter and the other three boys looked away. She would deal with them another time.

"Are you telling me that *you* vandalised the models, destroying everyone's things?" she asked, trying to keep her voice calm, and measured.

Baxter poked Hugh in the ribs, "So it wasn't Ashworth, then," he said, loudly enough for the word to quickly spread along the corridor. Hugh glanced over his shoulder to dorm three. Varun and Steven looked shamefaced. Douglas and Declan were nowhere to be seen. Hugh remembered that he'd met Isaccs on the stairway while playing hide and seek. The boy had sent him on a wild goose chase. He'd been trying to cover his tracks. He felt a momentary spark of anger.

Sensing that Isaccs' admission was in danger of turning into a sideshow, which was an unhelpful distraction from the search for Giles, Linda called for the boys to disperse. Gradually, the corridor cleared as boys returned to their dorms. "Not you four," she said. "You'll help me by clearing these wet sheets and bringing clean ones from the laundry room." Arthurs and Baxter tutted, looking disgusted.

Hugh looked down at Isaccs. He no longer felt any anger towards him for all the trouble that he had heaped on Giles. Instead, he felt pity for the scared and sheepish-looking boy; Isaccs would be in for a pasting from his dorm mates for having to clean his bed

"Move along unless you plan to help with things here," said matron.

"No fear," muttered Hugh, sidling off.

He was not particularly hungry, and he had no one to go to breakfast with. Nevertheless, he had to eat. An army marches on its stomach was one of his father's favourite expressions. On his way to breakfast, he thought about Huck faking his own death to escape his drunken father and start a new life. Huck had spied on the townsfolk, laughing at them while they searched in vain for his dead body to wash up from the river.

During the film, Giles had nudged him, finding it funny. "You could have done that instead of running away. There's countless places to build a den here," he had said to Hugh with a sly grin.

Hugh stopped dead in his tracks outside the breakfast hall, remembering what Giles had said, and how he talked about building camps and dens and hidey-holes in the rec behind his house before he had come to the school. Hugh experienced a sudden rush of blood; Giles hadn't run away, he was here. Hugh could feel it in his bones, and he knew exactly where to look.

* * *

Douglas had branded him a sneak, and true to those words, he was sneaking out. If things were not so desperate, he might have laughed ironically at the thought. However, with the police mustering the search parties in the driveway, he was anxious to get out of the school and find Giles. Heading off in the opposite direction to where the volunteers were gathering, he bolted quickly through the main school and snuck through the locker room. Outside, the sky was waterless and white. A weak sun was hidden behind the clouds attempting to break through, and the air felt heavy and humid. He started to break sweat almost the moment he broke into a run.

Hugh figured that by now Giles had been missing almost as long as when he had run away from Fleetwood. No doubt his mother and father had been informed. Hugh supposed they would be worried. Giles had shown him a Polaroid photograph of himself standing together with his parents by their car on the day he had come to school. Hugh had fallen in love with the car. The army provided a courtesy car to senior officers, but they were ugly and decrepit, whereas the Capri was a thing of beauty. Shrugging, Giles had replied that it was his father's pride and joy.

While Hugh headed out of the school, others were descending or preparing to descend upon it: Moira among them. Dead to the world, knocked out by sleeping pills, she had awoken dreamily to the telephone and ignored it. It rang and rang, and stopped, and then rang again. The caller was persistent.

Dragging herself out from under the eiderdown, she had padded down the carpeted stairs to the cold, parquet-covered hallway and picked up. It was Mary, her mother. Was she awake she wanted to know? A stupid question. Not even a hello or a good morning or an apology from her mother for waking her when her mother knew full well that Moira was not a morning person. Could she bring Frank to the phone, her mother demanded. Through the open door to the lounge, Moira surveyed the devastation wrought by Frank: the aquarium remained upended on the floor together with several large pieces of glass; the fish – the dead and the dying – she had flushed down the toilet the night before. She told her mother the truth: Frank was not at home.

Well, he can't be at work at this hour, Mary said with a petulant tone. In the background, her mother's small dog barked furiously. The Jack Russell demanded a walk. The dog had a way of making Moira feel tense and angry. Keen to end the conversation and return to her bed, she spoke plainly: what can I do for you Mary, she asked. There was always some kind of a favour to be asked. Over the yapping dog, her mother said that the school had been trying to get through. They called to speak to Frank or to you, she said, sounding shrill. But no one picked up, she said, in a tone which implied Moira was at fault.

Moira started to ask how the school had come to have her mother's telephone number, but then she remembered that the school had requested another contact name and details in the event of an emergency. Moira snapped properly awake.

"What's happened to Giles?" she said, urgently.

"How should I know," said Mary.

"They must have said something to you," Moira said, her voice rising. "Did you ask?"

Her mother told her to get a grip and get a pen and paper so she could take down the number. Ask for Anthony Richardson or David Scott. You will call me back, so I won't worry, won't you, Mary asked. Moira hung up and called the school

On the second ring, David picked up. Yes, it was about Giles. There is probably nothing to worry about. The police are involved. A precaution. Don't be alarmed. Could they come to the school as soon as possible? You and Mr Ashworth. He is not at home, she said for the second time in as many minutes. Can you drive? Do you have a car? Can you be here soon? Moira felt light-headed, out-of-body, drained of energy by the battery of questions. She would drive to the school immediately, she said, not knowing if the Escort had petrol in the tank, or if she knew the way. Frank had taken care of all those things. But yes, she would leave, right now, right this second: she would arrive within the hour. She was aware that her voice sounded shrill like her mother's and her beloved boy was missing, and she had sent him away, and she might never be able to say sorry, and hold him close again.

* * *

After a minute, during which Harry hung on his every word, David set the telephone down, and turned to the deputy housemaster and to the policeman who had joined him in Anthony's study in readiness for the call with the Ashworths.

"How did it go?" asked Harry, brow furrowed, aching for a scotch.

"Not great," replied David, with a heavy sigh.

"Did you speak to the father?" asked the policeman. Tall and burly with ears bent out of shape from years of rugby, the policeman carried with him an air of quiet authority, which made David feel a little better.

"I only spoke to the mother. Moira. The husband was not at home," said David, turning to the policeman. "She's driving over here now with some recent photographs, so they can be distributed to the volunteers ..." continued David. His voice trailed off. The request for pictures of Giles had filled David with dread, and the unnatural presence of two uniformed policemen at the school, had transformed the search from the simple case of an errant boy into the hunt for a missing child.

"I'd like you both to help with the search of the woods, if you feel things here can be managed by your staff?" asked the policeman.

The policeman was confident Giles would be found before the day was out. Transport police and authorities were already running checks on passengers travelling on buses and trains. Business owners in town were being tossed out of bed as he spoke, he added, with an instruction to thoroughly explore their premises in case the boy had got lost or hurt himself.

"I am better placed to join you. Linda Wallace, our matron, can manage here," replied David. "My wife Claire will help, and I've seconded a couple of staff from the kitchen to help steady the ship," he said tensely.

"Don't look so worried," said the policeman, clapping David gently on the arm. "Let's put you to work, you'll feel better doing something useful," he said, tugging open the study door.

In the lobby, the other policeman was waiting. Fresh-faced and anxious looking, he nervously tapped his feet on the spot. "All set?" he asked.

"Yes," said the older man, escorting David, and Harry outside, onto the driveway, where twenty or so people had gathered in expectation. At the sight of the policemen, their chatter died away; all faces turned to look at an enlarged photograph of the nine-year-old boy with dark brown eyes and a pale complexion framed by a pageboy haircut, which the younger policeman held aloft.

"Giles has been missing for twelve hours," said the burly policeman. "Some of you know the boy, others among you do not," he said. "Take a good look at his face," he continued. Giles had a solemn, almost hostile expression in the photograph. It had been taken on the first day at the school.

From the first-floor window overlooking the driveway, Linda and Claire listened intently to the words of the policemen and remained standing there for several minutes after he finished the briefing. They watched as people peeled off into small groups and started to spread out in different directions. Claire reached out and involuntarily squeezed Linda's hand. "It'll be ok," she said.

Linda had prayed before going to bed and when she awoke, although in reality, she had hardly slept a wink and now, to make matters worse she felt nauseous. "Deo volente," she intoned quietly, touching her crucifix. The thought of another day of worry was more than she felt she could bear. Surely, Giles would turn up soon. However, until he was safe and sound, she would not consider taking a break. The idea of a lie-down was alluring, but the house relied on her: she couldn't let her boys down.

Claire was looking at her strangely. "You've turned a funny colour," she said with concern. "Do you feel unwell?"

Claire had hardly uttered the words when Linda felt her knees buckle. "I feel quite faint," she murmured, grabbing on to Claire's arm for support. Claire took her by the arm and held her steady.

"Hold on tight," said Claire, leading Linda towards a sofa where she could sit down. Once seated, Claire fetched a glass of water.

"Thank you," said Linda, drinking slowly, the colour beginning to return to her cheeks. She smiled weakly, resting her hand on her belly. "I'm pregnant," she said.

Claire looked stunned. It took her a full minute to compose herself. "Oh, I see," she said, eventually, sounding awkward and looking slightly uncomfortable. "Congratulations, I mean. This is *good* news for you, isn't it?"

Linda had a soft spot for Claire. She was the only like-minded woman at the school, and although Claire was approaching forty years old, the ten plus gap in their ages seemed immaterial. However, she had quite forgotten that Claire belonged to the generation of women for whom having a child out of wedlock represented a stigma. "Yes, I am very happy," said Linda. "I have to keep pinching myself, actually.

Claire smiled and nodded thoughtfully, all the while her gaze remained transfixed on Linda's belly. "How far are you gone?" she asked.

"A few weeks, a month or so," said Linda, not wishing to go into details. She set down the glass and looked at Claire imploring. "Please don't say anything to David?" she begged. "I've only just found out. I haven't even thought about how to tell Anthony."

Claire gasped loudly, "I always thought there was something going on between you two. I said as much to David!" she exclaimed, her eyes widening in a look of surprise mingled with excitement.

Linda roared with laughter. "Anthony is *not* the father!" Claire looked at her open-mouthed: a picture of shock and befuddlement. "Oh, my goodness, you should see the look on your face," said Linda, laughing so hard that tears welled up in her eyes.

"Well, what on earth did you mean then by referring to Anthony?" asked Claire, looking embarrassed and confused.

"I was referring to my replacement," said Linda, "I can't very well stay on and bring up a baby here, can I?"

The idea about a life away from the house had started to occupy her thoughts ever since she had shared her news with Harry. Unable to sleep last night, the thought had crossed her mind that her preoccupation with her baby had blinded her to something she should have noticed about Giles or Isaacs. "Maybe you'd like the job?" Linda said, changing the subject.

"No, thanks," said Claire, no longer sounding quite so defensive. "It's difficult enough being married to a housemaster without taking on the boys as well," she said. "Anyway, forget them, I want to talk about you," she added, cosying up to Linda, so that she had no choice but to tell everything about Italy and Gio.

"Well, that's some adventure!" said Claire, when Linda had finished speaking. "I must say I rather envy you!"

"Really? I thought you were happily married?" said Linda, taken aback.

"I am," said Claire, flicking back her fringe, "It's just that I never got to do anything like that. We met young and got married before I'd even had a chance to meet anyone else."

"You should insist on a second honeymoon," said Linda, giving Claire a friendly nudge. "I'm sure David would jump at the idea of all that sun, sea and you-know-what."

"Jump? I'd have to push him first," replied Claire. The two women laughed at the thought. "You look better," said Claire, after the laughter had subsided. "Your face turned the colour of gone-off milk earlier. You had me quite worried."

"I suppose this will take some getting used to," said Linda, stroking her belly.

Claire shrugged. "You'll be ready, you have had enough practice with this lot," she said, pointing to the serried ranks of photographs that lined the walls: boys playing cricket, boys playing football, boys collecting prizes, pictures of boys going back over decades. "I often wonder what's become of them," said Claire, ruefully. "They spend their young lives here and then they're gone, out into the world, transformed into little men before you know it."

"One thing's for sure, I won't send any child of mine to boarding school," replied Linda, looking from one photograph to the next, her gaze finally coming to rest on the most recent photograph of the entire house, taken at the start of the new term.

Linda pulled herself up from the sofa and wandered across to inspect it closely. Fifty or so boys, some smiling, some frowning, others looking into the camera with bored or blank expressions. Harry was there in the middle dressed in a pale blue suit and sporting Raybans. She had sat to his right wearing a patterned summer dress. Anthony looked stern. The photographer had placed David to one end so that his height did not obscure the boys seated behind him. Claire stood to his left, arms folded. Jeffrey was absent from the picture: Anthony refused to count the gardener as a member of staff.

Silently, Linda recited the name of each boy in turn, her eyes travelling from row to row until her eyes came to rest on Giles and Hugh, sitting cross-legged on the grass. They were seated among the dorm one boys rather than with the rest of their dorm.

"The class of 1975," said Claire, coming to stand alongside Linda.

"Why did Ashworth and Burton sit there?" asked Linda.

Claire leaned in, studying the photograph. "I've no idea, perhaps they arrived late, and the photographer sat them there. David might know. Why do you ask?"

"Usually, the boys sit together by dorm. It just seems odd, like they have been outsiders from the start."

"I wouldn't read much into it," said Claire, studying the pair. "They do look alike. I'd never really noticed before," she said, staring at the photographs.

"It's the hair, the pageboy cut," replied Linda.

"No, it's more than that. There's a self-same expression on their faces, like they are thinking the same thing."

"You just told me not to read anything into where they were sitting!" said Linda, stepping up close to the photograph. However, she had to admit there was something to be said for it in the way they tilted their heads and grimaced at the camera. "How do they seem to you?" Linda asked, turning to Claire. "Do they look happy to be with us?"

Claire rested her hand on Linda's shoulders, "None of them ever are at the outset," she said, sighing. "At least, not one boy that I can remember, but things usually work out well enough for them all in the end."

* * *

Even as Claire spoke, Hugh had already made it out of the school, taking advantage of the lull in the search to slip out into the grounds while the policemen briefed the volunteers about Giles and organised people into groups.

Gingerly at first, taking care not to be seen, Hugh watched his step, cautiously threading his way through the kitchen garden towards the grounds. However, once he reached the lower playfields, he felt emboldened and began to jog towards the woods, carrying a plastic bag of hastily assembled provisions, and a thermos of water. His plan was to stay within the tree line and make his way gradually to the top field, and from there to cut across to the hedgerow and find the gap that led to the shelter.

Jim had seen Hugh come running across the fields. The boy had not tried to disguise his run. He had just kept his head down and bolted towards the trees. However, about halfway across the field, he had abruptly come to a halt. Like a startled rabbit, the boy crouched down and then stood up, all the while gazing in the direction of the woodland that lay to his right. He seemed torn about what to do next: something or someone seemed to have pricked his interest.

From his position at the crown of the hill, Jim could spy out the fields and the woods below. In the distance, the red brickwork of the main school building could be glimpsed through the trees. The search party that had scoured the area during the night had dispersed and returned to the school. Through the small hours, he had tracked their movements, following the path of their torchlight from afar, listening to their plaintive calls, which appeared to have gone unanswered. Whoever they sought remained yet to be found. Surely, he figured, there had to be a connection between the search party and the man and the woman. Were they part of the search, or were they the hunted? Jim had returned to the lane before first light that morning and the vehicle had vanished, only the indentations left by a front wheel remained visible in the earthy bank. Yet, he still had the uneasy feeling that the man and the woman remained in the vicinity. Did the boy feel that too? Had the child detected their shadowy presence and felt spooked, just as he had.

Jim turned his attention back to the boy. Hugh lay stock still, facing in the direction of the dense copse. In the dull morning light, the foliage and trees were of a uniform brown. With not a breath of wind in the air, the woodland had a solid, blank form, which belied the mysteries of the trees that lay within. Jim knew every twist and knot.

After five minutes or so, Hugh got to his feet and started to move off, keeping the woods to his right. In his brightly coloured T-shirt and shorts, he stood out like a sore thumb against the verdant grass. Suddenly, he stopped again and stared into the trees. Jim followed his line of sight. At that moment, the sun finally broke through the clouds and shone over the fields and trees. Jim caught the faintest of a reflection, no more than a flash of light reflected on a mirrored surface. Hugh saw it too and stepped back as though he had been seared by it. Except it was not that which had surprised the boy, it was the spectral image of the man who stepped out of the trees, beckoning the boy to come over. Dressed in the garb of a country man, Jim instantly recognised him as the driver of the red car.

"Hey," shouted Eamonn in a friendly voice, walking quickly towards the boy. Behind the man, in the trees, Jim saw the female occupant of the red car. She too called out to the boy, but the boy did not heed her words, nor indeed wait another second for the man to draw near. Hugh turned and ran as hard and fast as he had probably ever run, in the opposite direction, away from the strangers towards the top field. Surprisingly, the man did not give chase. Instead, he backed slowly away towards the woman. In an instant, he had stepped inside the woods and melted away right in front of Jim's eyes. Jim looked back toward the boy, who was now galloping headlong up the field, the plastic bag thwacking against his side. Then, the boy burst his way into the dense bracken, which fringed the top field and disappeared out of sight.

Hugh rolled over in the undergrowth, gasping for breath. His hands and knees were scratched and bleeding, but apart from that he was physically fine, but scared; the man had called him by his name. And then, the woman had signalled to him to come over. They were friends of his father, she said, with an inviting smile.

As a family, they had been drilled to use code words to cover every eventuality, including identifying friend or foe. "Curry or eggs?" shouted Hugh to the man, putting things to the test. The man looked mystified, and so the woman spoke.

"Eggs," she replied, peering from the trees.

"Wrong!" shouted Hugh. It was neither: the answer was ham – turning quickly and running away, knowing that whoever they were, they were hunting him down. He ran and ran, until his lungs were fit to fit to burst; until he was sure they were not following him.

Exhausted from running, Hugh eventually sank down in the thicket and weighed up his options: the man and the woman lay between him and the school, the shelter lay ahead; it was where he expected to find Giles. Hugh had a little speech planned in his head, which he hoped would win Giles around.

Deciding to remain in the woods until the last possible moment, Hugh took a path, which threaded its way towards the old assault course, near to the patch of ground where Giles had said he had encountered the weirdo. Hugh peered into the undergrowth. Briefly, he felt a flutter in his tummy at the thought of coming across the weirdo, or the man and woman. Plucking up courage he ventured inside: the further he went, the denser the wood became. The trees were taller in this part of the wood. He stumbled once or twice but ploughed on, the scrub becoming dense. It was disorienting: the thick canopy cut out much of the light, even though the morning sun was breaking through outside.

Taking the thermos from the plastic bag, Hugh drank slowly, pondering which way to head. The gnarly stumps had a familiar look. Had he walked in a circle? He was no longer sure of his bearings. When feeling lost, he had learned that the best thing was to retrace his steps. Taking another swig of water, he tossed the thermos into the bag and started to walk back the way he had come. A large tree lay shattered on the ground. Swinging a leg across the trunk and sliding to the ground, the thermos tumbled from the bag and rolled away. Hugh cursed his bad luck. Crouching down, Hugh spotted the shiny flask wedged under a branch beneath the broken trunk. The only way to retrieve it was to lie flat on his tummy and crawl forward. At full stretch he could touch only the cap – what he needed was a stick. Hugh tried a few different pieces, until laying spread-eagled on the ground he could get a hook under the bottle and bring it within range. Finally, he was able to grasp the cap. However, as he grasped the cap, someone grasped his feet and tried to drag him out. Instinctively, Hugh kicked out. But the person was too quick and too strong. As Hugh was jerked forcibly from beneath the shattered tree, the ground beneath him felt as though it was rushing up to meet his face, filling his eyes and choking his mouth. A dirty palm was around his mouth before he had a chance to holler out.

For a moment, Hugh felt unable to breathe. The man was behind him, his whole weight pressing against his body. Hugh could taste the soil on the man's fingers. He wanted to bite them, to scream and shout. He struggled but the man brought his left arm around his chest and held him tight. But still, Hugh resisted, thrashing around in the undergrowth, trying to smash his head back into the man, but the man was experienced in fighting. He avoided Hugh's blows by bringing his face up next to Hugh's, so they were cheek-to-cheek. The man's long dirty hair stuck to his face. "Shush. Shush. They'll hear you," he whispered.

Jim hauled Hugh away from the fallen branch, sweeping him back into the thicket with a hand clasped around his mouth. "Shush," he said again. Hugh had stopped struggling now, all his adrenalin spent.

First, one snap of a branch, and then another, growing ever closer; Jim tightened his grip around Hugh and pulled him down, deeper into the undergrowth. The noise grew louder as footsteps approached the fallen tree. Hugh felt his captor's muscles tense up at the sound of their approach. His breath grew shallow.

"What do we do with the boy when we find him?" asked Eva, resting against the broken trunk. Hugh immediately recognised the voice. Every strand of hair on the back of his neck stood up in fear.

"Keep quiet," whispered Jim into Hugh's ear.

The man did not answer the woman. Instead, he continued to look around, convinced that the boy was nearby. "Well, say something?" said the woman irritably.

Hugh felt the man close to hand, swishing his hands through the vegetation. With a loud tut, the man paused. Hugh sensed that the man was annoyed. The woman complained about a cut on her leg. The man told her to wrap something around it. On his knees now, the man searched below the large fallen trunk. In the scuffle, Hugh had to abandon the thermos. The man reached down and picked it up. He held it up to the woman like he had won a prize. "Why don't you come out, kid?" said Eamonn, trying to moderate the hardness in his voice.

The woman finished tying the dirty rag around her leg and stood alongside the man. Taking a pistol from inside his jacket, the man aimed it towards the bushes and inched forward, holding the gun at head height. The woman did the same. The man nodded to the woman to go right, to flank, while he took another step forward. The woman then crouched down and trained the revolver towards the bushes to Hugh and Jim's left. They could see the massy weight of the gun in the woman's hand.

"Come out now," said Eamonn, continuing to advance before sweeping forward into the bushes, whereupon he sank into the empty undergrowth. Cursing, he dragged himself out.

"I told you, didn't I? The kid is not here," said Eva. "We need to get out of these woods pronto, before those people from the school return."

The man shook his head. "I could have sworn…" he said quietly, looking around. Nevertheless, he knew the woman was correct. They could not take unnecessary risks. He waved his pistol in the direction he wanted to go, and the woman heaved a sigh of relief.

Jim watched them intently all the way until the sound of their footsteps had faded away and the people were no longer in sight.

"This place is not safe," he said. Hugh thought he had a soft and unthreatening voice. "We need to get you away, to somewhere safe." Jim removed his hand from Hugh's mouth. Hugh had no urge to cry out for help. The scruffy, long-haired man had kept him from falling into the hands of the man and the woman. They had come for him with guns, like the gang who had tried to kill his father.

"Will you take me back to school?" asked Hugh, meekly.

Jim shook his head: "I don't think we dare risk the woods or the grounds, not while they are still sniffing around," he said.

Hugh pulled his knees up close to his chest and buried his face into his shorts. "Don't worry, I'll look after you," Jim said, retrieving the thermos bottle and the food bag, which the man had kicked to one side in his fury. Jim handed the thermos to Hugh.

Hugh took a swig, wiping away the dirt from his lips. "What's your name?" asked Hugh.

"Jim," he said, rummaging inside the bag. He tore open a packet of biscuits and chomped into one and then another. "What's yours?" he asked.

"Hugh Burton," he said, before asking in a small, frightened voice, "Are you the man they call the weirdo in the woods who tried to grab Furnival and Mountjoy?"

He had been called many names in his life, but this one was a first. "They're those boy runners, I suppose?" he asked. Hugh nodded in reply. "I didn't mean to scare them. I was foraging," he replied, chewing his way through another biscuit. "Sorry about that," he added, brushing the crumbs from his mouth. "Eat these Hugh Burton, before I scoff the lot," he said, offering Hugh the biscuits.

"Thank you," said Hugh, eating hurriedly. Having skipped breakfast, he was starving now.

"Have this too," said Jim, giving Hugh the banana that he had stashed inside his jacket. The chef had tossed it away because it was going brown. "It's from your school," he said, with a shy smile. However, Hugh was too hungry to register the information. Jim watched him eat. He could see that the food was working its magic: Hugh seemed more relaxed and cheerful, while he was still feeling antsy and anxious, knowing they had to move on.

When Hugh had finished, he stood up and looked around before helping the boy to his feet. The only safe place for them was the shelter. "This is the key to our safety," he said, fiddling with the heavy black key tied around his neck by a thick piece of twine.

Hugh looked Jim up and down, hesitantly. He was about the height as his father, but whereas his father was thick around the middle and broad-shouldered, Jim was lean and wiry, and he also stank.

"It's up to you," said Jim. "But if you go back now, there's a chance they will get you." Hugh's eyes filled up. "Do you know why they are looking for you?" he asked, softly.

Hugh nodded slowly: "It's something to do with my father," he replied.

"In what way?"

"I don't know," he said, tearfully. "He's in the army. I think they want to hurt him and me."

Jim thought about his own father – a good man whose good intentions never came good because luck seemed never to be on his side – and then, about his own time in the army. He had been pleased to get out, but nothing much had gone right until he had come back here. "I was a soldier too before I came to work here at the school" said Jim

Hugh looked up at Jim, in a disbelieving manner. "Really?"

Jim nodded, "Yes," he said. "I liked being part of the school until…" He checked himself. There was no point explaining things to the boy. He wouldn't understand, unless Hugh too had made the same decision as he had, to leave it all behind. "Are you running away from school?" Jim asked, crouching down so he could look into the boy's eyes. "Is that why people have been out searching the woods, because they are looking for you?" Everything started to make sense now.

"They're looking for Giles," said Hugh.

"Who's that?" replied Jim.

"He's my friend," said Hugh, "and I've come to find him and tell him I am sorry."

"Sorry for what?" asked Jim.

Hugh scratched his head and shrugged. "For not believing in him," he said.

"And what makes you think he's out here in the woods?" asked Jim.

"He's not in the woods," said Hugh, brightly. "He's gone to the air raid shelter. We found it together. Do you know anything about that place?" he asked innocently.

* * *

Feeling much better, Linda decided to resume her regular, daily routine of giving the dorms a thorough once-over. The dorms would not tidy themselves and she thought dealing with the boys' mess would keep her mind occupied. The boarders had been packed off to chapel, primarily to keep them occupied while the search continued. Dorm one was neat and tidy, the little ones had scarcely occupied their bedroom in the last twenty-four hours. Bracing herself for the semi-permanent, ammonia-like smell that permeated dorm two, Linda pinched her nose and swung the door open so she could inspect things from afar. She was surprised to find her instructions had been followed to the tee: all the beds were made-up with sharp hospital corners, save the one where John Isaccs slept, which remained stripped to allow the mattress to air. Anthony had said he would deal with the boy later. In the meantime, he had set

Isaccs extra homework, which he was to do alone in Harry's study. When Linda poked her head inside the room, the boy had his face buried in a book. He didn't look up.

Dorm three: the middle years were spent here. The windows had been unlocked to let a breeze pass through. Declan, Douglas, Steven, and Varun: they had joined the school as seven-year-olds, passed through dorms one and two without too much trouble, just the usual childhood illnesses, which had resulted in stays at the san. Linda felt she knew everything there was to know about each of these four boys: their personality traits and behaviours, their hopes and fears. Part of her job was to shape the boys, to bring out their best side. But Giles Ashworth and Hugh Burton: they were unknown quantities. Linda turned back the covers on Giles' bed. There was something troublesome about the boy. In that respect, he was little different to Douglas. However, whereas Douglas openly displayed his mean streak to the world, Giles seemed more calculating. Linda plumped up the boy's pillow and brought it to her face: it had no smell to speak of.

She wondered what attracted one boy to another. What was it that made Declan and Hugh cleave to Douglas and Giles? Did they recognise something in them that they lacked or desired? Or was it altogether less complicated: an arbitrary choice, which once made, solidified and became unbreakable until the time came for them to go their separate ways. How many boys, she wondered, had passed through this old school making promises to remain friends forever, and then never once looked back. Is that all friendship brings, she asked herself?

Linda reached across Hugh's bed and opened his bedside drawer. Expecting to find the usual detritus of comics and flimsy paperbacks, Linda was surprised to discover the drawer contained just one item, a hardback edition of Jack London's White Fang. It was an exquisite edition. Linda had read it as a child, finding it impossible to put down, even though she had hated some of the passages and feared for the life of the wolfdog. She ran her finger over the illustration of White Fang's slathering mouth on the book jacket and randomly flicked through the pages. A neat little triangle indicated where Hugh had reached in the story.

Turning to the front of the book, she wondered what year it had been printed and how it had come into Hugh's possession: a family hand-me-down, perhaps. Instead, she was startled to find that the book belonged to the school. Pasted to the inside front cover was a yellowed library label listing all the names and dates of the boys who had borrowed the copy, from Nicholson, 17 October 1927 to the final entry, Covington, 26 February 1952. The book was not on the current syllabus list, nor available from the library, and yet Hugh had the schoolbook inside his drawer. Linda snapped the cover shut; the attic was the only place where teaching material was archived.

Linda stood up abruptly and walked briskly to Harry's study. This time Isaccs glanced round as she bowled in. "John, I want to ask you something about yesterday evening?" she said, pulling up a chair.

"Am I in more trouble?" he asked.

"No, not all," she said. "You might actually be the key to helping me solve a puzzle," she said.

Isaccs recounted carefully what he had told Hugh. "I only lied to Burton and said Ashworth was in his dormitory because he saw me going up to the modelmaking room," he said. "I didn't mean for him to get the blame for what I did."

"Don't get upset," Linda said, soothingly. "You never told me where you'd met Giles. Where was that?"

"Upstairs, in the corridor outside the modelmaking room," he replied, playing with the pen in his hand.

"Are you sure?" she said. The little boy nodded. "And then what happened, where did he go?"

"Downstairs, I suppose," he said, doodling on the corner of the book. "There's nowhere else to go, matron."

Except for the attic, she thought.

"Thank you, John," she said. With her heart beating fast, Linda hurried away in search of help. "Claire, thank god," she said, catching sight of the housemaster's wife at the end of the corridor.

Running towards Claire, she blurted out about the discovery of the book in Hugh's drawer and its significance. "It means Hugh must have been up in the attic, and if he has, you can bet your life it would be down to Giles," she said excitedly.

Claire however, looked sceptical. "Hasn't there already been a thorough search of the attic?" she asked. She thought that Anthony had left no stone unturned; every room, nook or cranny in the main building and out-buildings had been combed.

"I don't know, I suppose so. But people make mistakes all the time. I think it's worth looking again."

"Based on a hunch?" replied Claire.

"Yes, if that's what you'd call it," Linda said emphatically. "You don't have to come anyway," she said and started to walk away, heading towards the stairs that led up to the second floor.

But Claire understood the power of an instinct and ever since Linda had shared the news about her pregnancy Claire felt more strongly drawn to her than before. "I guess there's only one way to find out," she replied, neither sounding nor looking convinced. "We'll need torches. The place gives me the creeps."

Ascending the rickety ladder, Linda pushed open the hatch, slipping it to one side. Inside, the attic was pitch black apart from a pool of light, which came from the corridor below. "Come on up," she said to Claire.

"What's the plan?" whispered Claire, squinting into the darkness.

"I suggest we fan out," said Linda, directing her torch beam left and right, scanning the silhouettes of the boxes and furniture, old desks, and blackboards, all of which had seen better days.

The thought dawned on Linda that what they were conducting was a microcosm of the wider search; the scale of the area that the search party had to cover to look for Giles suddenly filled her with a sense of despair. Nevertheless, torch in hand, she walked forward peering into the assortment of dressers, storage boxes and desks, which had been heaped to one side. Opening a large wardrobe, she found herself face to face with a doctor's skeleton. "Jesus Christ!" she said out loud before chastising herself for blaspheming.

"What's wrong?" said Claire, training the light on Linda.

"This thing here just scared me half to death," she replied, shielding her eyes from the light, Claire trained the light on the wardrobe and laughed. "That's Eric," she said. "The previous headmaster kept him in his study." It had been the first thing Anthony had removed when he took over. Linda closed the wardrobe door and moved on.

Gradually, as their eyes adjusted to the conditions, they started to lose their fear. In no time at all, Linda discovered the open boxes of books from the library. Sifting through, she pulled out the same edition of White Fang that Hugh had in his belongings. There were ten or more inside. "Look what's here," she said, holding the cover up in the torchlight. "I told you he must have been up here," she said with a satisfied expression.

Claire nodded half-heartedly. She was more interested in something she had found, recent photographs from the renovation of the kitchen garden. In one grainy picture, Jeffrey stood erect and proud, shovel in hand. Alongside him was a much younger man with lank hair, smiling goofily into the camera. Judging by the works that had taken place, she guessed the photograph had been taken around the time she and David had come to the school. Claire examined the rest quickly. In another, the goofy man was resting his hands on his hips, smiling awkwardly while Jeffrey held some carrots aloft. They looked like they were having a good time. In all the years that she had known Jeffrey she could not remember seeing such a broad smile on his face. Claire tucked the photograph into the pocket of her skirt. She thought Jeffrey would like to see it.

Having explored the first section of the attic, Linda signalled for

Claire to come over to where she was standing by the main beam that traversed the roof. "Did you come across anything that appeared out of place?"

Claire shook her head. "Do you want to bother with the other side. It's just full of the boys' trunks." she said, shining the light into the area where they were stored. Approximately, half a dozen lay scattered around. "That's odd," she remarked.

"Were they left like this at the start of term?" asked Linda, picking out the brass buckle of the nearest one.

"No, never," replied Claire.

"Shall we?" asked Linda, sliding over the beam. Claire hitched up her skirt and followed suit.

The floor was uneven and badly laid, with the odd gap or two in the beams. Claire paused and looked through a slat. "You can see right into dorm four from here," she said, incredulously. They had to watch their step.

"That's where we keep dorm four and five trunks," pointed out Linda, circling the light on the trunks, which had been heaped messily to one side of the attic. Inspecting them closely, Linda could see that they were in some disorder, dorm four mixed with dorm five and vice-versa. "Where are the rest kept? she asked.

"Behind you, there," Claire replied. She shone the beam into the eaves at the far end of the attic. "At least, I think that's them," she said, nervously, hanging back while Linda advanced. "Why don't we wait for David?"

Linda glanced over her shoulder: "We've come this far, there's no point turning back now." Her concerns were only to keep her footing and to find Giles. "Is there any kind of overhead light?" she asked, frustrated that the torchlight only seemed to reach so far into the gloom.

Claire cast her torch over the ceiling. There was none that she could find. "Remind me to tell David to get the lighting looked at," she said.

Linda was now threading her way through the scattered trunks, edging closer to the eaves, to the point where the roof dipped abruptly to the brickwork. The air had a damp feel to it.

"Have you seen enough?" called Claire.

"The problem is I can't see!" said Linda, huffing and puffing. She had dropped to her knees to push her way forward through a space between several large wooden trunks.

"Shine a light into the gap in front of me, please?" Linda asked Claire, turning the dial on her own torch to focus the beam on the narrow crawl space.

"Wait, Linda, wait for me," said Claire, but Linda was already inching forward on her knees. Wordlessly, Linda pushed her way through. Inside the space was an upturned trunk. The lid had been prized off and set to one side. Linda felt her pulse quicken as she turned her beam on to the lid. Turned upside down, the lettering spelt out the name of the owner. Linda cocked her head and studied the initials: the trunk belonged to Hugh Burton. Instinctively, she reached forward to manoeuvre the upturned trunk into position, so that she could look inside, but then she suddenly stopped, sensing that it carried within it a large, unnatural weight. "Claire, come here, quick!" she called out, feeling paralysed by fear and a dreadful sense of foreboding.

"I'm here, hold on," said Claire, breathing hard as she crawled towards Linda. "What is it?" she said, kneeling beside Linda in the narrow space.

"I can't look. I think there's a body inside!" she whispered, turning her beam on the exterior of the trunk.

"Hold this," said Claire, handing Linda her torch. Edging closer, Claire took hold of the trunk with two hands. "Ready?" Linda nodded. "On the count of three."

"One, two, three," they said, together and slowly turned the trunk towards them, feeling the weight of its cargo but refusing to let their fear interfere with what they had to do. They saw the boy's shoes and socks, and then the pale skin of his hairless calves. Claire let out a high-pitched shriek. Giles lay stretched out inside. Reaching forward into the trunk, she touched the boy on the knee and recoiled instantly, "He's icy cold!" she exclaimed.

"What do you mean?" said Linda.

"Touch him," said Claire.

Linda knelt forward and reached inside the trunk, feeling for Giles's wrist to find his pulse. His hand was frozen, he didn't stir, and she could not find it. "Help me," she pleaded, urgently.

"Is he alive?" asked Claire in a panicked voice.

"I don't know. I need more light!" she cried out, demanding that Claire shone on Giles so she could feel all his pulse points.

Her hands felt again for his wrist and then for his throat, and as she did so, a fleeting image came to mind, a memory from another day, one which she had long sought to banish: the image of her dead father laid out to rest in a coffin for an open casket funeral, and she shuddered as she held Giles's freezing hands in hers.

11 - CONVERGENCE

David chose Chapel to share the news. "Before we start today's service, I am pleased to say that our prayers have already been answered. Giles Ashworth is safe and well." He smiled broadly and let the announcement sink in. "He's resting up in the san and he'll be back on his feet and rejoining the house in no time at all," he added, without providing any additional facts. A murmuring sound passed along the pews as the boys took in the news and whispered to one and another.

The picture that he painted to the boys was straightforward. The reality was more complicated. Having been stabilised by Linda and carried from the attic to the sanatorium, he had a high fever, which worried Sister. Hospital was briefly discussed, but Anthony decided that it would bring unwelcome publicity. So, with the news out of the way, David had to satisfy himself that God would forgive him for being economical with the truth. The Reverend thanked the Lord for returning their child to the flock. He cast his eyes around the church, assessing how the boys were reacting.

Ironically, it was Douglas who first noticed that Hugh Burton was not among their number. By rights, Hugh should have been sitting in the same pew as him and the rest of the dorm. Douglas craned his neck forward to study each pew. Dorm one, dorm two, dorm four, dorm five. Declan glanced sidelong and asked Douglas what was eating him. "I'm looking for Burton. I can't see him anywhere," he whispered, while pretending to sing the opening hymn.

What do you care?" muttered Declan, whose bandaged wrist was still causing him discomfort. "He's probably dashed off to see Ashworth. The little snitch."

Douglas mouthed along to the hymn while he commenced looking another time, quietly saying the name of each boy as his eyes travelled from face to face.

"Shush," said Declan, peeking nervously towards where the masters were sitting.

After Hugh's visit to wish him well, Declan had grown to dislike Hugh almost as much as he detested Giles. Either Hugh had pinched his comics or Ashworth had. They were both as bad as each other, and he wasn't convinced that it was an accident that had put him in the sanatorium. While he was lying in his bed, he had had plenty of time to think about what had happened when they were doing the washing up. It felt planned and purposeful. However, not even Douglas believed it was anything other than an accident. It didn't mean they shouldn't find a way to get back at him declared Douglas: of course, they should, and that made Declan feel a little better.

Douglas finished counting. "He's not here. You look!"

Declan quickly surveyed the church. "Ok, so what?" he said, after a while. "I hate him, so who cares."

"I can't stand him either," hissed Douglas, "but we should still tell Mr Scott or RD. It might land him in more trouble." He looked over towards the pew where the two masters were solemnly praying.

"So, you're going to sneak now?" snorted Declan.

"It's not the same!" said Douglas under his breath.

Declan used his bandaged arm to pull back his shirtsleeve and reveal his watch. Turning the face towards Douglas, he winked. "You've got an hour to think about that," he said, with a smug grin.

Douglas returned the grin. Whatever Hugh was up to, Mr Scott would blow his top once he learned that he had skipped Chapel. As soon as the final hymn had concluded and they were dismissed, he slid along the pew. Pushing Varun out of the way, he shot over to Mr Scott. "It's probably nothing, sir, but Hugh Burton's not shown up for Chapel and I thought you'd want to know," he said, smirking.

David tried not to look concerned, but he instantly felt that something was wrong. He leaned in to Harry and whispered instructions. "Thank you, Douglas," he said, dismissing the boy.

Harry dialled the sanatorium.

"No," said Sister, "she had not seen Hugh, and besides no guests were allowed."

A rapid search of the dorms and the house failed to turn Hugh up. "Marshall more people to search the grounds," he ordered Harry.

Jeffrey led a group of exhausted groundsmen outside, but a search of the playground, the skateboard area, the kitchen garden, the swimming pool, and the playing fields proved fruitless. Everything confirmed his worst fears: Hugh Burton was missing, presumed to have run away. Having stood one search party down, they would have to muster another. It fell to Anthony to inform the police and the parents.

Hector received the headmaster's telephone call in his lodgings. He'd barely slept since the attempt on his life, and he felt exhausted. "Are you sure?" he said wearily.

"We've combed the school," replied Anthony.

"So, he's up to his old tricks," said Hector, nonchalantly. "Have you spoken to his mother?" he asked. Anthony thought it was something that he would prefer to do. "No, she's all yours," said Hector.

"You seem quite relaxed about this," stated Anthony. Hector said that he had seen it all before.

"I've been thinking about coming to see the lad, after all the recent business," he said. "He'll have turned up by the time I arrive, but when you track him down let him know I am coming all the same," he added, promising that he would be at Frampton within a few hours. He dialled down to reception, requesting a driver. By the time he had changed clothes, the driver was waiting in the parade ground to drive him to Hugh's school.

"Where to, sir?" asked Private Colman, looking both flattered and flustered to have been given the task of acting as the Colonel's chauffeur for the day.

Hector looked the soldier up and down, he looked barely out of nappies, "My son's school. I'll give you directions," he said, slipping into the passenger seat. "How old are you?"

"Eighteen," replied Colman. He had passed his driving test six months ago.

"You look younger," said Hector. The private gave an embarrassed shrug. "I meant it as a compliment. This job will age you, trust me," he said, saluting the sentries as they waved the car through the new checkpoints. Since the attack, security at the barracks had been tightened. It was the first time he had left the base since Oakbury, the first time in a car since Harding. Today, he was in civvies. Today, was all about Hugh.

Up on the hill, Conor watched the scene below unfold, scarcely able to believe his eyes: Burton was on the move with only a driver for company and no visible escort. He ran for the car and took the same road out of town, catching up with Hector at the traffic lights. Reaching into the glove compartment, he grabbed the new comms device that Carrie had provided. It was US-manufactured, military-grade spec. Within a three-mile range, the calls were encrypted. They had the Yanks to thank for their comms and the Commie-backed Cubans for guns and bombs. It was a fucked-up world.

"I'm on the A-road out of town, heading south following our friend," he chirped.

"How many pieces are in transit?" she asked.

"Just the one! Our friend must be heading towards his son," replied Conor, feeling his heart pound as Hector's car started to accelerate towards the ramp for the dual carriageway.

"Stay in touch," she said, ending the call.

Carrie switched bands and punched in six numbers and three letters. After a few seconds, she was connected through to Eamonn. "Burton's on his way with just a driver. Any idea why?"

"Search me," he replied. He guessed it had to do with the boy and he didn't dare admit that they had had him in their sights and that they had blown it.

"Are you sure?" she probed.

"Yeah. Don't worry we'll be waiting on Burton," he said hastily.

"Don't do anything until I get there," she commanded.

Tom was hanging on her every word, listening intently. "Game on?" he asked.

"Yeah, grab your gear, we're taking a road trip to Frampton. Now, you're gonna settle the score for Brendan."

* * *

Veronica's blood was still up when she arrived at the school two hours later. She swept into Anthony's study with Gerry in her wake, scarcely noticing Hector and his driver. Instead, she went straight for Anthony, picking up a chair as she strode across the parquet floor and placing it directly opposite the headmaster. "What kind of ship are you running when you can't keep your charges from disappearing at the drop of a hat?" she fumed, banging down a small, tight fist on the mahogany surface.

Anthony Richardson gazed back with a non-committal expression designed to show that he would not be intimidated by her aggressive approach.

"Well, what do you have to say about my son's whereabouts?" she continued, narrowing her eyes, "or have you been too busy congratulating yourself on finding the other boy to give Hugh a second thought?"

To her left, Gerry shifted uncomfortably. With Hugh's track record for absconding from school, he thought Veronica was over-reacting. "There's no point in losing your temper," he whispered into her ear.

"Why don't you do something useful Gerry and leave this to me and his father," she said dismissively.

Hector and Gerry exchanged wry looks. Like a storm, it was better to duck for cover and let her do her worst. Eventually, she would blow herself out. "Over to you, then," said Gerry. Hector stepped aside to let Gerry pass. "Thanks," he said, wearing a sardonic smile.

"No problem," replied Hector, tilting his head towards Colman to follow suit. "Stay by the car," he mouthed to his driver as he departed.

Veronica bade Hector to pull up a chair and sit beside her. "He hasn't got the slightest idea where Hugh is," she said, referring to Anthony as though he was no longer present in the room.

Anthony looked at Hector for help. "We have fresh volunteers. They'll be out looking for Hugh right away!" he said. However, he no longer appeared quite so composed. His hands trembled while he cleaned the lenses of his glasses.

"The same ones who failed to find the boy in the attic after he'd vanished? That fills me with enormous hope!" she said sarcastically. Veronica paused for effect, glaring at Anthony, as though daring him to speak.

Continuing like this would get them nowhere thought Hector. He waited to see if Veronica had more to say, or whether the headmaster had a useful response to make. As neither of them spoke, Hector decided to pose a question of his own: "How's Giles getting on? I bet he's got a word or two to say about Hugh," he said, remembering how they had met on the first day of the new term. It felt like a lifetime ago after everything he had been through.

"He's recuperating in the sanatorium with his mother by his side," said Anthony, smiling weakly.

"Is he now? Well, that's nice," said Veronica, her voice still laden with sarcasm. "Still offering no clues as to why my son, his friend – his supposed bestfriend from what I gather – has disappeared into thin air?"

"There was some name calling in the dorm. A couple of boys were calling Hugh a tell-tale," replied Anthony. "We think that's why he stormed off." Veronica's persistent badgering was starting to wear him down. His nerves felt frayed. Someone had also left the radiator cranked up in the study and the heat was starting to make him feel quite ill.

"I think Hugh's made of sterner stuff than that," said Veronica, tersely. "Your housemaster seemed to think that Hugh's tore off to look for Giles. She turned to Hector. "That was the gist of whatshisface said, wasn't it?"

"Yes, Harry double-barrelled name …"

"Rhys-Davis," interjected Anthony.

"Yes, him," said Hector, irritably. "He told us that Hugh and Giles are very tight, do everything together, but that they'd had some falling out …"

"It was far more serious than that," said Anthony, cutting in.

"If you say so," replied Hector, feeling his temper starting to rise. "Anyway, my point is that once Giles Ashbridge was cleared of blame, Hugh took it upon himself to go and find him and…"

"Ashworth not Ashbridge," corrected Anthony, interrupting Hector for a third time.

Veronica stood up abruptly. "It strikes me that this Giles *Ashworth,*" she said, with added emphasis, "is key to locating Hugh. If they're best friends, then I am sure the boy will want to help. I want to see him!"

"That's not possible, only parents are allowed," replied Anthony flatly.

Veronica trained her sights on Anthony: "Why? My son's gone AWOL. The boy can help! Don't you agree?" she asked Hector, whose face was crimson with barely concealed rage. She knew how much he hated being interrupted. In his world, he gave the orders. However, a sharp ring of the telephone prevented him from replying.

"Do you mind if I take this. It might be important," he said, picking up the receiver before they had had the opportunity to answer.

"By all means," said Veronica contemptuously. Hector leaned across to whisper in her ear. She smelled of sandalwood, woody and warm. It reminded him of what he had lost. "He'll never let you visit Giles if we end up in an argument," he said quietly.

After a minute or so, Anthony terminated the call, promising that he would phone back shortly. His face had turned white. "I will have to ask you both to excuse me," he said uncomfortably after he had hung up.

"Important school business?" asked Veronica, arching an eyebrow.

"Something like that," Anthony replied impassively.

"None of this reflects well on you, Mr Richardson," she said, irked by his reply. "I don't feel you have provided any useful information during this meeting."

"I am sorry you feel that way," he replied with an apologetic shrug, "However, I can assure you that you know as much as me."

On his desk he had the paperwork on Hugh and Giles. Like David, he had been mugging up on their school records, looking for insights. Veronica's sharp eye alighted on the dark blue folders, one labelled Burton, the other Ashworth. She sprung forward and snatched them from the desk. Anthony lunged across the desk, but Veronica clutched them firmly to her chest. "They're private," he shouted, getting to his feet.

Hector jumped up and put himself between Veronica and the desk. "Let her read what's inside," he stated menacingly. Anthony sat back down like a petulant child.

From Hugh's file, Veronica removed a large colour photograph, a holiday snap from Bournemouth. Hugh had sand in his hair from where he had buried himself below her deckchair to hide from the sun. She wondered how such an uncomplicated boy could also be so unpredictable and difficult to manage. In her opinion, he was easily distracted, too eager to please.

Veronica opened Giles' school records. Anthony made another lunge for the folder. "Please don't, they're confidential!" he cried.

Almost toying with Anthony, Veronica tutted and scan-read the first page: Giles Ashworth —date of birth, place of birth, home address, previous school, school attendance record. A passport photograph was stapled to the top left corner. A solemn face. He wore his hair like Hugh's. She stared at the face again and then re-read the boy's name and his address. She grabbed Hector by the hand. "Can you see where Gerry has got to? I need him here, now!" she said urgently.

"I need to take that back," demanded Anthony, holding out his hand.

"Not now!" she exclaimed, snapping the folder shut and protecting it with both hands. After a minute, Hector returned with Gerry, who looked flushed and perplexed. "Gerry, read this," she said, handing him the folder.

"Will someone explain to me what's going on?" asked Hector in an exasperated tone.

Gerry turned to Veronica. "Do you want to tell them the story?" he asked.

"No. You!" she exclaimed, shaking her head. "You were *there* after it had happened, and you met the father. Tell them everything, tell them what he did to his *friend*," she said pointedly. Anthony and Hector both gazed at Gerry quizzically.

"Do you mind if I sit?" asked Gerry. "This will take more than five minutes to explain."

With a resigned expression on his face, Anthony picked up the telephone. "You'll have to tell the trustees to wait, something else has come up" he said. They could hear a woman's voice on the other end of the line objecting. Anthony put down the receiver and offered Gerry a chair. The room looked set for an interview.

"Well, let's hear it, then," said Hector, brusquely.

Gerry took a moment to gather his thoughts. As with any story, he had to decide where to begin: at the driving range tending to the boy's appalling facial injury, or the recent encounter with Giles' father at the other golf club?

"What are you waiting for?" asked Veronica impatiently.

Shooting her a knowing look, Gerry folded his hands in his lap and began his account of the Ashworths.

"A couple of days ago I met Giles' father, Frank. I play at several different golf clubs, and on this occasion I had been out on the course with some friends. There's a group of us, in fact, who meet regularly. I know most of the players in and around where we live," he said, clearing his throat.

"We'd played eighteen holes and by the time we had all gone round, the bar was busy. I looked up and saw Frank making his way gingerly through the throng with a tray of drinks. I recognised him instantly. He was worse for wear, having clearly had more to drink than he could handle," said Gerry.

"Anyway, as he pushed by, I stopped him. I could see he did not remember me. You see we had met before in quite unpleasant circumstances." He looked at them gravely.

"Go on," said Veronica urgently.

"A few months before, six or seven perhaps, I had visited the driving range at another club to work on my swing. It's by far and away the best one in the area. Very popular with pros and amateurs, and youngsters. That's why the Ashworths were there. They had brought Giles and two of his friends to play golf. It was a birthday treat apparently…" he said, his voice trailing off. Gerry realised that the room had become silent.

"They were a few booths down from me. I was concentrating on my game. But then came this blood-curdling scream. Everyone heard it. I raced over to see what was going on. It was a frightful scene, blood all over his face," he said, shaking his head unhappily. "There were signs everywhere warning players to stand back because of the dangers of the back swing."

Hector puffed out his cheeks. The image of Susan Harding bleeding out in his arms came straight to mind.

"People started to crowd around and get in the way, jostling for a view. Giles and his friend stood stock still, like statues," said Gerry, picturing the scene as though it was yesterday. "I asked them what had happened but they were both too shocked to speak, so I turned my attention to aiding the boy. Marcus. That was his name," he said slowly.

"At this point, people had finally stepped back to give me space. Frank arrived out of nowhere and began barking orders at his wife, ordering her to take care of the boys, to take them away. Giles still held the bloodied club in his hand. Marcus had taken the full brunt of the club in the face," he said, pointing to his right eye socket.

Although Veronica was aware of the bones of story, Gerry had spared her the details. She shivered visibly and clutched Gerry's hand in shock. Hector noticed immediately. It was the first sign of tenderness that she had displayed towards her lover.

"I remained with Marcus until an ambulance came," continued Gerry. "A few people went for a stiff drink to get it out of their system, but I just wanted to get home and put it behind me. Later, I heard the Ashworths had cleared off before the ambulance had arrived, which would of course have been a disgraceful thing to do if it was true. But by then another rumour had started to circulate of which I was unaware of, until the other evening when I chanced upon Frank." Gerry paused, swallowing hard. He still found it hard to believe. "Word went around that Giles had deliberately taken the club to Marcus, that he had swung out on purpose. The other boy had come forward and said so."

Anthony got up from behind his desk and closed the open window. The last thing he needed was this conversation to be aired outside the room. "You say you heard about this? So, you didn't see Giles do it?" he asked.

"The boys were playing on their own. It was one boy's word against the other, and Marcus couldn't help clear the matter up," replied Gerry.

"What do you think, now?" asked Hector.

Gerry shrugged. "Honestly, I don't know. *You* didn't believe a word of it when I first told you, did you?" he said, turning to Veronica, thinking back to the conversation they'd had in the morning after he had met Frank. It was on the same day that Hector's barracks had come under attack by the truck bomb. Veronica bit her lip and looked away.

"What a terrible thing to happen to a boy, to anyone," said Hector. "Did he lose the eye?"

"I believe so," Gerry replied, wringing his hands. The room fell silent again.

"You're unusually quiet, Veronica," said Hector after a while. She met his eyes. It was a look he recognised, one that spelt trouble.

"I'll tell you what I think," she said calmly but firmly. "If it's true that Giles could do this to one of his friends, who knows what influence he's had on Hugh or what he may have threatened him with?" She rose to her feet. "Maybe he turned on Hugh and that's why Hugh ran away!"

Hector baulked at her words. "Vero, you sound ridiculous!"

"Where did you say they found Giles?" she asked, her voice raised, her blue eyes blazing. "Laying down in Hugh's trunk, which had been bashed apart? That's correct, isn't it?" she said, rising to her feet. "Didn't you think there was something odd about that?" she roared, glaring at Anthony. "No?" she replied at his bemused expression. "Well, I do! The Ashworth boy sounds peculiar, obsessive!" she said, marching across the study floor.

"Where are you going?" asked Anthony.

"To get some answers from that boy, of course!" she said, flinging open the study door and rocketing off. Anthony looked from Hector to Gerry in horror.

"Come on, we need to put a stop to this nonsense before things get out of hand," said Hector, jumping up and making a dash for the door.

He and Gerry caught up with Veronica in the playground. Hector grabbed her by the wrist. "What's got into you?" he asked.

"Leave me be," she said, wrestling free. "I want to speak to Giles. The san is up that way. We passed it on the way in," she said, walking briskly.

"I know where it is. My driver is parked up outside," said Hector, keeping pace with Veronica. "You can't just barge in!"

"Hector's right," said Gerry, struggling to keep up. "And besides, no one will let you in, you are not family."

"We'll see about that," she said, striding swiftly on.

Outside the sanatorium, a handful of people had gathered together. Harry stepped forward to greet the trio. Veronica cast her eyes over the assembled group. "Are they all here to help find my son?" she asked.

"Fresh legs," said Harry. Word had gone around town that help was needed, and now their numbers had been swelled by more volunteers.

Veronica started to shake the hands of each member of the party in turn. "Hector, come and introduce yourself," said Veronica. However, Hector had stepped away from the group to talk to the pock-marked former chef, who was among those who had answered the call for help. "That's typical," she muttered, shaking the hand of the auburn-haired woman.

The woman smiled and warmly shook Veronica's hand. "Searlait," she said.

"And this is my husband Joseph," she added, introducing Tom, "and his brother."

Tom reached out and shook Veronica's hand. "Hello," he said calmly.

"Conor," said the reconnaissance lad, extending his hand. "Glad to help."

"You are all very kind," Veronica said, grasping Conor's hand.

Having met all the volunteers in turn, Harry walked Veronica to the entrance to the sanitorium. "Is Sister expecting you?" asked Harry.

"Richardson asked me to drop in and see Giles," she said, lying through her teeth.

"The mother is going inside," said Conor, angling his head to the sanatorium building.

"What the hell were you thinking just now?" hissed Tom under his breath to Carrie. "What if Burton had recognised you?"

"Keep your hair on," she replied, "I'd have made something up."

"That was unbelievable, you've got bigger balls than the two of us put together," said Conor under his breath. Carrie smiled thinly at the compliment, while keeping her eyes on Hector.

"Join the volunteering party. Be my eyes and ears," Carrie whispered to Conor. "Use the comms only if you have to, only if there's a problem. Ok?" Conor nodded in reply. Then she turned to Tom: "You know what to do," she said.

"What I was born to do," he replied, glancing quickly at Hector and the small knot of volunteers eagerly waiting to set off to search for Hugh.

She kissed him lightly on the mouth. "I know," she said.

"As do you," he replied, taking her hand. "You need to hurry if you're going to make that train. Send Sean my regards," he added, releasing his hand.

"Be careful," she replied, stealing one final look at Hector before casually walking away towards the main exit to the town and the railway station.

Outside the school gates, alone, she huddled up against a high wall and reached inside her jacket for the comms. She waited for it to purr into life "What do you have for me?" she asked, speaking quietly into the handset.

On the other end of the line, Eva and Eamonn sat hunkered down in a hollow in the top field. "According to the Ordnance survey there is some kind of structure in the grounds, maybe a small shed or a storage area for cattle," said Eamonn. "It has to be where the boy's hiding out."

"What makes you so sure?" asked Carrie.

"It's the only thing that makes sense," he replied evasively.

Carrie pulled her coat around her so she could be more discrete. "How far are you from this place?" she asked.

"Twenty minutes by foot through the woods."

"And you have a good feeling about this?" she asked.

"Yeah, like I said," he replied, hesitantly. They had exhausted every other option.

"You've only got this one shot. If the boy's not there clear out, and we'll complete what we came to do." She heard him curse in the background.

"Ok, understood," he replied grudgingly.

"Good luck," she said, ending the call. Carrie glanced around furtively before switching channels and pressing the handset to her ear. After a brief pause, she heard the distinctive cough as he picked up.

"Tell me," he said, wheezing.

"Everyone is here. Everything is as it should be," murmured Carrie.

Sean coughed loudly. "Good, I knew we could rely on you." She pictured him in the basement, with its yellow tobacco-stained walls and the solitary sofa which he slept on when he could not go home because of the patrols or his paranoia. "I'll see you soon," he said in his flat, emotionless voice, and hung up.

She thought about Tom and Conor, and Eamonn and Eva, and

the risks they were taking. They'd all meet again when the job was done. She tucked the comms inside her jacket and pulled a cap over her hair, a wind was getting up. The leaves rustled over her head, gold and red flourishes. Late summer was passing, autumn was banging on the door. A hard winter was coming, one that the Brits would never forget.

* * *

Hugh felt he knew the school grounds like the back of his hands: they were not far from the shelter. In his head, he went through what he would say to Giles when they were reunited. Then, with Jim's help, they would return to school and face the consequences for their actions.

As they nipped through the hedgerow, moving briskly and silently towards the shelter, Hugh whispered to Jim that he'd like to go in first. "Please let me. You'll scare him!" he said, without thinking.

"It's as black as hell in there," replied Jim. "Just don't go getting yourself upset if he is not there."

"Of course, Giles will be there," said Hugh, charging forward, racing towards the concealed entrance, and then dashing down the short flight of mossy stairs. "Giles!" he shouted, rushing into the dark space. However, before he could get his bearings a shape suddenly emerged out of the gloom, coming forward to greet him. "Giles, it's me!" he cried, excitedly. However, as the shape took form, Hugh slid to a stop.

"Hi," said the moon-faced woman, shooting out her hand. Hugh stepped back, but the woman was quick, and she wrestled him to the ground. Jim lunged forward. However, Eamonn was primed. Throwing a blanket over Jim's head, he struck him twice in swift succession with the butt of his gun. Jim swayed and dropped to his knees. Eamonn kicked him in the back for good measure, while Eva continued to press Hugh to the ground.

"Hold him tight, while I tie this one up," said Eamonn knotting Jim's hands with a rope, which he had found in the shelter. "Stuff a rag in the boy's mouth," he ordered.

Holding Hugh down with one arm, she yanked his mouth open and shoved it inside. "The little bastard tried to bite me," she cried.

Pushing Jim aside, Eamonn leaned over Hugh and peered into his face comparing him to the photograph that Carrie had provided. "That's our boy, alright," he said, congratulating himself.

Eva rolled off Hugh and rubbed the dirt and dust from her face and clothes. "So, who the hell is he, then?" she asked Eamonn, pointing at Jim's limp body.

Dragging Hugh to his feet, Eamonn pushed the boy towards Jim. "Well, who's this?" he asked. With the rag wedged in his mouth, Hugh could only give a muffled response. Eamonn let out a coarse laugh. "Don't make a peep. Just answer the question," he said, clamping his hand around Hugh's jaw before tugging out the cloth.

Hugh spluttered and gulped in air. "A teacher," he stammered. It was the first thing that came into his head.

"He doesn't look much like one," said Eamonn, eyeing up Jim

and pulling Hugh over to where he lay slumped. "Christ, he stinks! He looks more like a tramp and smells like one," he said with disgust, shoving the rag back into Hugh's gaping mouth.

"Let's hurry up and get out of here," said Eva.

"Not so fast, I need to call Carrie, and we'll need to do something about the fella," he said, kicking Jim.

"That's not part of the plan," said Eva.

"It is now," he snarled, pulling out his pistol and waving it in Jim's direction. "We can't have anyone recognise us," he said. Hugh tried to spit out the rag. "Don't fret boy, we're not here to harm you. You're coming with us," said Eamonn. He bent down and wrenched back Jim's head.

"He's out cold, let's go," implored the woman.

"Hold your horses while I call Carrie," he said, stepping over Jim. "Keep an eye on them," he added, darting up the steps to make the call.

Jim started slowly to come around. During his years in the ring, he had learned to absorb a punch. He understood how to go down and stay down, to conserve his energy and then to come out fighting. The wound on his skull didn't feel deep. He could taste blood from a cut on his forehead from where he'd hit the concrete. Squinting, he could make out the form of the woman. She had her hands clasped firmly around Hugh. The boy looked petrified. He wanted to reach out and reassure Hugh, but he feared what the Belfast man would do.

"Is the coast clear?" asked Eva on Eamonn's return.

"Kind of," he replied cryptically, looking around, staring into the shelter's recesses. Taking out a small pocket torch, he trained the beam on the walls and ceiling. "Give me the boy," he demanded. Hugh backed into the woman, afraid to go with the man.

"What's the plan?" asked Eva, pushing Hugh towards Eamonn.

"It's ok," said Eamonn, with a soft voice. "I'm going to take the this out of your mouth. I'll keep it out, as long as you stay quiet. Do you get me?" he said, directing the beam into Hugh's eyes. Hugh nodded, turning his face away from light. "Ok, then, we've got a deal," said Eamonn, withdrawing the gag slowly.

Hugh gulped in air and spat on the floor.

"What's in the other room?" asked Eamonn, shining the light at the outline of the doorway. Hugh shrugged. "We had a nose around before you arrived, so, you better tell me," demanded Eamonn.

"I don't know, I really don't," he said, stealing a glance at Jim.

"But he does, right?" asked Eamonn.

"He keeps a key on a piece of string around his neck." replied Hugh.

Eamonn shone the light over Jim. Momentarily, the beam dulled, casting Jim in a watery yellow. He shook the torch hard, the batteries jiggled inside, and the beam brightened and then dulled again. Eamonn cursed. Leaning over the slumped figure, Eamonn ferreted inside the folds of Jim's filthy overshirt until his fingers closed around the key. With a sharp tug, he tore it triumphantly from Jim's neck and prodded Hugh towards the partially concealed door.

Hugh felt his way along the walls of the shelter. Whereas the space had felt calm and welcoming when he and Giles had discovered it, it now felt cold and frightening. When they reached the doorway, Hugh looked up, recalling how the flames had licked the ceiling as the newspaper had burned down to his fingertips, and how they had fled. He ran his hand over the door until he found the keyhole. Eamonn stepped forward and turned the key in the lock. The door swung open to reveal a tidy bedchamber. "Isn't this homely," said Eamonn sarcastically.

"I guess," said Hugh.

Eamonn grinned at Hugh. "Make yourself at home, boy," he said, shoving Hugh inside and locking the door behind him. "Help me carry the teacher," said Eamonn.

"Why, what for?" asked Eva.

"It's what Carrie wants," he said irritably. "It's not safe to move the boy. There's another search party on its way."

"They'll find us, they are bound to!" she exclaimed.

"Nah, she's already taken care of that. One of ours is making up the numbers with strict orders to disrupt their plans."

"Jesus wept," she replied, as she helped take Jim by the arms, while Eamonn grabbed his feet. Together, they dragged him like a corpse towards the room.

"Back away from the door, boy," shouted Eamonn, opening up. Hugh pressed himself against the far wall. "Good lad," he said, shining the torch in his eyes.

Hugh watched in terror as they pulled Jim inside. In the yellow light, the man's face reminded Hugh of a hideous gargoyle that he'd once seen on the façade of the Notre Dame cathedral. Eamonn trained the beam one more time on Hugh and then closed the door. The room fell into total darkness. Despite that, Hugh scrambled over towards Jim. Stumbling forwards, he fell heavily on him. Jim cried out in pain. "I thought you were dead!" cried Hugh.

"I'll be ok, help me," he said, rolling on to his front so that Hugh could work on the knotted cord around the wrists. Tugging feverishly at the knot, Hugh freed Jim's hands. Instinctively, Jim threw his arms around the boy. Hugh collapsed into him. Jim felt Hugh's warm tears splash his face. "Don't worry. Just keep quiet. I know how we can get out of this," he said, rocking Hugh gently in his rams until at last he felt ready to release him. "Here's what we are going to do," he whispered in Hugh's ear and laid out exactly what Hugh would have to do when the time came.

"I can't do that," said Hugh, shaking with fear.

"You can," said Jim, bringing Hugh's face up to his "If you don't, that man will kill you."

"But what about you?" Hugh asked, his voice cracking and breaking with emotion.

Hoping for the best but fearing the worst, Jim lied: "I'll be fine," he said.

* * *

The sanatorium was cool and noiseless, as though existing in a vacuum sealed off from the outside world, which in some ways it was. "How is my little soldier?" asked Moira, parting her son's fringe and lightly caressing his cheek. She searched his face, feeling that there was so much to say which remained unsaid.

A week ago, her marriage had felt secure even if she had long suspected her husband's infidelities. Then, out of nowhere, Yvonne had re-entered her life and had laid bare the truth. Since that moment, Moira had been thinking about nothing more than bringing Giles home, not to the house in The Close, but to somewhere new where they would make a fresh start together. She had a plan for their future, and she wanted so much to share it with him. However, that could wait: Giles needed to rest for now. In a few hours, they would drive away together and leave all this behind.

Moira re-arranged the pillow and kissed him on the forehead and gazed fondly at him. Giles however, still refused to meet his mother's eyes. Instead, he let his gaze wander to the books and the board games arranged neatly on the shelves. His eyes rested on Colditz – it was one of his favourites. He always chose to be on the escape team.

At the gentle tap on the door, mother and son turned as one. Sister opened the door a crack and peeped through. "There is a guest to see you both," she said.

Moira had already met the headmaster and the policemen, and Linda and Claire, who had discovered Giles in the attic. She had got up to all sorts of high jinks as a girl; he seemed to take all these things from her. However, she shuddered at the thought of her son alone up there. Someone must have been very cruel and hurtful to make him hide away like that. "Who is it?" she asked, finally.

"Veronica Burton, Hugh's mother," replied Sister.

At the mention of her name, Moira felt Giles tense up beneath the covers. "Come in," said Moira.

"Thank you," said Veronica, passing Sister and walking purposefully towards Giles and Moira. "I'm sorry to meet again under such circumstances," she said, extending her hand to Moira. Reading Moira's baffled expression, Veronica said, "We've met before, at a New Year's dinner dance."

Moira shook Veronica's hand. "I'm sorry, I don't remember," she said awkwardly. "When was this?"

"Some time ago," replied Veronica. "It's a small world."

"Yes, I suppose so," said Moira, withdrawing slightly, feeling crowded by Veronica's unexpected presence.

"And this must be Giles, about whom I have heard such great things," said Veronica, pulling up a chair to his bedside.

Dressed in a blue and white striped pyjama top, Giles smiled nervously at Veronica and reached out to shake her hand. "Hello, Mrs Burton," he said, politely.

"Hello, Giles Ashworth," she replied, shaking his hand in return. The boy's palms were cold and sweaty. Despite that, Veronica continued to hold his hand in hers. The likeliness to Hugh was plain to see. However, there was a feline quality about Giles, which reminded her more of Belinda. "I'm very pleased to meet you," she said, formally, and then she cut straight to chase. "Do you know why I've come to see you?"

she asked.

Giles shrugged and glanced nervously at his mother. "Not really," he replied, pulling his hand away.

"I don't think he's up to talking, right now," said Moira, picking up a low-backed chair from the next bed and sandwiching herself between Giles and Veronica. "Perhaps another time," she stated impassively.

"It can't wait," said Veronica, leaning in towards Giles. She could smell his boyish smell; her stomach lurched. "Hugh's gone missing, and I think you can help us find him," she said, looking intently into his eyes, wondering how he would react.

Giles looked stung. "Did you know?" he asked his mother in an accusatory tone. Moira shook her head. "Since when?" he said, his voice moving up an octave.

"This morning, sometime before breakfast. Didn't Mr Richardson or one of the teachers tell you?" asked Veronica.

Giles grabbed the bed spread and pulled it around him like a protective shield against her words. "That's not possible. Hugh would never go anywhere without me," he said, shaking his head.

"What do you mean?" asked Veronica. Giles buried his head under the covers, wrapping himself into a ball. "I don't understand what you are trying to tell me," she said, becoming angry and exasperated.

"Stop this!" cried Moira, reaching across to cover his blanketed body with hers. She could feel Giles shivering and shaking. "There, there," she said, as she tried to embrace him.

Veronica threw back the chair and got to her feet. She'd seen enough of his theatrics. "Some best friend you are!" she said angrily.

At that, Giles kicked out from beneath the bedding and his mother, and wriggled free. "Has he really run away?" he whispered hoarsely.

"He's missing. I don't know if that is the same thing," said Veronica.

Giles sniffled and sat up in bed. "It's my fault that he's run away," he said. The two women glanced anxiously at one another. Giles took a deep breath and momentarily shut his eyes. When he opened them, his mother and Veronica were staring at him intently. "I told Hugh what happened on my birthday. About Marcus," he said, blinking hard. Moira gasped in shock.

"What did Hugh say to that?" asked Veronica, feeling her chest tighten.

"Nothing," he murmured, staring at Veronica.

"He must have said something. Think!"

Giles shook his head fiercely. "He didn't! I was at the window in the modelmaking room, and I was telling him everything because I knew he would believe me," he said, shooting Moira an angry look. "But when I turned around, he'd gone. He'd run off."

Moira reached forward and pulled Giles to her bosom. He briefly struggled and then let his mother hold him. "It's ok, it is not your fault," she intoned into his ear, all the while stroking his hair.

"Whatever went on between you and Hugh cannot be why Hugh is missing. You had your argument the night before Hugh disappeared. Correct?" Giles peeped out from his mother's arms and nodded. "Hugh took off sometime before breakfast the following morning. Today!"

"That was after matron found out that Isaccs was responsible for vandalising everything," interjected Sister, who had been eavesdropping from the corridor and had slipped in unnoticed. Veronica literally jumped up in surprise. So, too did Giles, who pushed his mother aside.

"I think Hugh went to find you," said Moira, wide-eyed.

Veronica took a sharp intake of breath, feeling certain that it was true. It was just the sort of thing that Hugh would do. "I'm so sorry for the things I said. I don't know what came over me."

Giles shrugged. "It's ok," he replied, sitting bolt upright in bed. An idea was already forming in his mind.

"But he could be miles away, anything could have happened to him," said Veronica, tearfully.

Moira wrapped her arms around Veronica. "Where would Hugh go to look for you?" she asked Giles.

"To our den, to the air raid shelter," he replied without a moment's hesitation.

* * *

Hector's driver Private Colman hugged the mug of tea to his chest. "You look like you needed that," said Harry with a friendly smile.

"You're not wrong. The CO sent me here to warm up," he replied cheerfully, looking around the wood-panelled lobby with the wide-eyed curiosity of a tourist. "It's an old school, is it?" he asked.

"Oh yes, centuries old. Founded in the 1540s," replied Harry, gazing at the old beams and wooden walls, and the banks of framed photographs of boys going back through the years. He felt a burst of pride, which he had not felt for some time.

"I'd prefer something more modern for my kids, assuming I have any," he said, depositing the empty mug on the parquet floor. "You got any?" he asked, staring at the recent photograph of the house.

"No, I suppose the boys are like my own children," said Harry thoughtfully.

"Look, it's young Hugh," said Colman, pointing at the picture. "Looks like the CO himself, same look and you know, presence. I bet he's the boss here."

"Mm," said Harry, bending down to pick up Colman's mug.

"Done another runner, has he?" asked Colman, removing his beret to scratch his head. "CO's not bothered. Reckons he will turn up when he turns up," he said, pawing at his scalp like a boy with nits.

Harry was intrigued. "Pray tell?" he asked.

"What do you mean?" said Colman, looking puzzled.

"Do you have an example?"

The private finally stopped scratching. pausing to reset his beret. "Too many to mention, but I'll tell you the one about Christmas. It's my personal favourite," he said, with an excited grin. "You know Hugh's got a twin, right? Belinda."

"Yes, yes," replied Harry, although he didn't.

"So, the Colonel and the Pocket Rocket – Veronica, Mrs Burton, I mean – take the twins to meet Santa at some fancy store or other. Well, Hugh sits on Santa's lap, all nice and that, but then the next minute he only goes and tugs his beard, and it comes clean off in his hands," he said, struggling not to laugh.

"Belinda promptly bursts into tears and runs to Mrs Burton, while Hugh takes one look at the Colonel and sees he's hopping mad, and then one look at dear old Father Christmas, who's trying to stick it back on his chops, and decides to leg it. Disappears like a jack rabbit under the giant tree, knocking off baubles and taking out the fairy lights." Tears of laughter started to roll down Colman's flushed face. "Anyway, the Colonel goes to fish out the little squirt, except he's nowhere to be seen. He vanished into thin air, just like that!" he added, clicking his fingers.

"Gosh, how amusing!" said Harry, sounding unintentionally pompous. "I didn't realise that Hugh had such a talent. No wonder that Colonel Burton's so calm and relaxed about things."

"Don't go believing that. He plays it cool to keep his old missus happy. But deep down, he's as worried as the rest of us," said Colman, drinking up the last of the tea.

Harry nodded sagely, making a mental note for the future. "As a matter of interest, where did Hugh get to?" asked Harry. Colman scratched his scalp again. He's got nits, thought Harry. With a boarding house full of young boys, he knew an infected head of hair when he saw one.

Colman chuckled at the question. "In the storeroom in the basement! The clever little sod took the service lift to evade store security. Mrs Burton gave him a right telling off, I can tell you. Colonel said Hugh was lost property and should stay overnight for collection!"

Colman's story made Harry feel more optimistic, and he found himself suddenly wanting to share it with Linda. "Do you mind if I slip away?" he asked.

Colman looked surprised by the question. "No, why would I? You're the guvnor," he said, mistaking Harry for the headmaster. "And besides, I can't leave the Colonel minding the car for too long, wouldn't be right."

"Minding the car?" asked Harry quizzically.

"You can't leave a vehicle unattended, rules are rules," replied Colman, straightening his beret. "Thanks for the cuppa and I bet you Hugh's already bored and making tracks. You see if I'm not right!"

Harry had not long walked upstairs to the staff room in search of Linda when the news came through that Giles had directed the search toward the abandoned air raid shelter. "That's the best news," he said excitedly to David, Claire and Linda, who had come together as soon as word had got out.

"Let's not count our chickens just yet," said David.

"Be positive," said Claire.

"I've a good feeling too," added Linda, playing with the cross around her neck.

"Me too," said Harry, telling them the story that he had heard from Private Colman. "Hiding out in the shelter sounds exactly the sort of thing that Hugh would get up to."

"We'll know soon enough," said David. "Anthony's going straight there with Jeffrey and the police, while the rest of have been told to stand down."

"No doubt, Anthony will be hoping to take the credit for finding Hugh," said Harry. Claire chuckled at that. "What did I miss?" he asked.

Claire and David shared a knowing look. "You can tell, Harry. Everyone will know soon enough," said David.

"Anthony's to be relieved of his duties. The trustees held an emergency meeting and voted unanimously to put David in charge," said Claire proudly.

"Congratulations!" exclaimed Harry. His day had just got better. "When is the coup taking place?" he asked jokingly.

"That's in poor taste," said Linda.

"I think it's rather too early for that sort of discussion, Harry," said Claire in a soft, soothing voice.

"Yes, all that'll be resolved in due course. The trustees want me to clear up this business, starting with removing Giles Ashworth from school. It's what his mother wants too, so there will no fuss," he said.

In truth, David was relieved about the matter. He had reached the same conclusion as Linda that there was something not quite right about Giles' behaviour. Even though Isaccs had admitted to destroying the models, he had sworn on his life that he had not been responsible for throwing things out of the window. Someone else was responsible for that – and in his view, Giles Ashworth had to be the culprit. Moreover, he felt that Giles was a bad influence on Hugh. "The Burton boy is a Frampton boy at heart. Once we get rid of the bad apple, Hugh will blossom," he said, mixing his metaphors.

"I'm so glad, you said that David," said Linda, jumping in. "I think Hugh's a decent enough boy, but Giles Ashworth is a law unto himself."

"Oh, come on, Linda, that's a bit steep isn't it," said Harry with a frown.

Linda shook her head sadly, "I don't think so. When Declan got scolded, I had the feeling Giles was behind it, even though I've no proof. And then, there's been all this nastiness with Douglas. I know he's mean boy, but there's an atmosphere in their dorm that is of Giles' making," she said, waving away Harry's attempt to interject, her voice growing louder.

"Linda, please," said Harry, trying to calm Linda down. He looked to Claire and David for support, but they were happy for Linda to continue.

"The Bulldog thing, the way Giles and Hugh went about playing the game, and then the howling and growling noises that the boys were making after lights out…Oh, don't pretend that you didn't hear the racket they were making!" she said, angered by Harry's plaintive expression. "And then, Hugh had a school copy of White Fang in his possession, which could only have originated from the attic. Don't tell me these things are not connected!" she exclaimed, clutching the crucifix, not for comfort or hope but as a shield. She looked almost possessed.

"And if you had seen the mess that Giles had made of Hugh Burton's trunk then you'd realise that we have a troubled, angry boy on our hands!" she said, turning toward Claire.

Suddenly, Linda felt a sharp stab in her stomach, and she shrieked out in pain, clutching her womb as she staggered to the sofa. "Please don't let it be the baby," she cried, holding on to Claire for dear life. "I must have this baby," she said, gripping Claire hard as another shooting pain wracked her belly.

"It'll be ok," said Claire, guiding Linda to the sofa. Linda let out a feral cry and doubled up in agony as she lay down. "Help me, please," she asked, squeezing the life out of Claire's hand. However, there was nothing Claire could do, except to comfort Linda, and hope and pray for her friend and her baby.

***

Cupping his ear to the door, Jim heard renewed arguing. The Belfast man was shouting, tossing things around; the woman was upset or angry. What sounded like a scream was followed immediately by a dull thump and a shuffling noise. Hugh gripped Jim's arm. Jim moved back from the door and knelt next to Hugh. "I think he may have hurt that woman," he whispered. "If the man comes to the door, we're on. Ok?" Jim felt Hugh's fingers tighten around his arm. "It's alright to be scared," he said, stroking the boy's hair.

Hugh loosened his grip and felt blindly for the box to his right.

The rubbery tube felt clammy like it had a life of its own.

"Can you feel it?" whispered Jim.

"Yes," replied Hugh quickly.

"Even with your eyes shut?"

"Yes," said Hugh, almost inaudibly.

"Be brave," said Jim, and he cracked his knuckles one more time and made himself ready. It was like stepping back into the ring.

At the sound of the key rattling in the lock, Jim set his position at two feet away from the door, while Hugh moved to one side of it, out of view. Jim glanced over his shoulder at the blanketed shape on the ground, to where they'd created a Hugh-like form by bundling together some old clothing. Hugh had had the bright idea to take off his distinctive Adidas top, so that the trefoil along the sleeves was partially visible. And now, he was shivering under the large shirt, which Jim had provided in return, in cold and fear.

Three, two, one: the key turned, and the door swung open. Hugh shrank back. Jim tilted his face forward, grinning like a lunatic. Eamonn recoiled, disgusted by the sight of Jim's rotten teeth and sour breath. Jim cackled and stepped back a foot, partly obscuring the bundled blanket, willing the man to step inside. Eamonn flashed the torch in Jim's face and over his shoulder. "Time to get up, boy," he said, casting the beam on the ground.

Jim spat on the concrete floor and stepped further backwards, keeping his hands behind his back as though his wrists were bound. "I'm not letting you take him," he said. Eamonn came forward, the torchlight bobbing around. Jim figured the Belfaster was half a head taller and a good stone heavier. In his army days, Jim had weighed in at welterweight. However, on his diet of surplus school dinners, he had shed pounds. He was probably closer to Bantam, a nine-stone weakling. He laughed out loud at the thought.

"Shut up and stop with the looney shit," said Eamonn. He was looking forward to putting a bullet in his filthy head.

Jim's mouth had always got him into trouble as a boy. That's why he had stopped talking when he had grown into a man. Now, he needed to find his voice. "I served in Londonderry," said Jim.

That had Eamonn interested.

"Did you now," he replied, shining the light into Jim's eyes. Hugh pressed himself into the shadows, as Eamonn walked further inside the room.

"Yeah. We used to love rounding up boys from the Bogside on a Friday night and giving them a proper kicking," said Jim, taking a big step backwards. "We'd keep them in over the weekend, just for fun, and then send them packing a Monday, all black and blue from our truncheons."

"You piece of shit," shouted Eamonn, darting forward, connecting his fist with Jim's jaw. The blow sent Jim spinning, but not enough to send him to the floor. One fall, but no knock-out, and Jim had free hands; the Belfaster wasn't prepared for that.

Eamonn came on, unable to restrain his anger. Jim waited until he was on him, and then weaved and jabbed as he came within range. Feigning to jerk forward while accentuating his shoulder as if to throw a punch, Jim suckered Eamonn in. The Belfast man tried to check his stride, stepping back, but as he did so, Jim nipped in. A one-two to the stomach and a devastating short right to the head. Eamonn reeled. Jim didn't hold back. A vicious straight right hand and another, and then he dragged Eamonn to the ground. "Now!" he bellowed at Hugh, as he put his weight on the man.

However, the woman was coming for them.

"Hugh!" he shouted.

Jim thought he had prepared the boy for this, but Hugh appeared to be frozen to the spot. Jim jumped off the man and grabbed the boy. Reaching into the box, he pulled out the mask and roughly shoved it over Hugh's head. Behind him, Eamonn was stirring. Ahead, the woman advancing, her moon-like face coming out of the darkness, the pistol in her shaking hand. Ripping the seal from the canister, Jim tossed it to the ground and dived forward as the smoke engulfed the room. The woman fired and dropped the weapon.

In the semi-darkness, Jim pictured her fumbling around; and then he saw her, up close, a look of blind fear on her face as her fingers clawed her eyes, as the gas swirled around them, as the bug-eyed monster with an enormous single eye and a thick rubber tube for a mouth slid forward along the floor of the shelter and over her flailing body. The adrenalin was with Hugh now, coursing through his veins as he crawled quickly for the light and the air, and the arms of his mother and his father, and his friend Giles who were coming, even then, at that moment, through the gap in the hedgerow to save him. Of that, he was sure.

"Run, run, run," mouthed Jim, the gas pouring inside the shelter, into his eyes and into his lungs. A golden colour to it that reminded him of the way the light fell on a winter's morning, when he had the woods to himself in the hours after dawn before the boys came out to play. He never tired of the beauty and majesty of the trees, the fields, and the sound of birdsong. There was always something magical to be found in those moments.

12 - EPILOGUE

Giles turned on to his stomach wondering when, or if, he would see Hugh again and, if he did, what he would say now that he had said what needed to be said. "Mum?" he asked, but Moira was miles away, plotting their escape from The Close.

"What's that?" she asked, after a prolonged pause.

"Nothing, it doesn't matter," he replied, closing his eyes.

"Do you want the door open or closed?" she asked.

"Closed," he said. His bedroom was plunged into instant and total darkness.

"'Night," said Moira from outside the bedroom door.

"Night," he replied. He listened to her soft footsteps, so light compared to Mr Rhys-Davis. He rolled on to his side, searching in vain for Hugh.

* * *

The tube pained Hugh's throat, while the patches over his eyes deprived him of sight. However, the army doctor said things were looking up. Gas boys, gas. He'd seen action, but his lungs were functioning fine. Hugh felt a warm hand reach out and touch him. "Giles!" he whispered, hoarsely. Belinda gave his fingers a gentle squeeze and lay her head alongside her brother.

"Hector would have over the moon to see the twins like this, usually they're at each other's throats," said Veronica, still feeling that she would wake up and find that everything had been a bad dream.

"Do you think he would have suffered?" she asked, picturing the fireball which had engulfed the car and Hector and the young private. The vehicle did a somersault. That was the enduring image. She would have never thought it possible, and when it landed, it was hollow. Everyone inside had been sucked out, rubbed out, vapourised, like they had never existed. Who would have thought?

"Let's go outside, into the garden," said Walters, remembering the last time he had visited it with Hector, just days before the blast.

Reluctantly, Veronica left Hugh's bedside. "I'm going for a chat with Uncle John," she said, following in Walters's footsteps. Belinda looked up quickly, her features a facsimile of Hugh's.

Veronica plucked at the dead heads and rested her head on Walters' chest. It was getting to become a habit. He did not seem to mind.

"The PM is pushing for a big send off," he said. It was a way of sending a message back to the Provos that the government remained resolute and steadfast. Walters could feel her anger rising with the heaving of her chest. He let her pound his back with her small fists until her rage was spent. She gave him one last thump and asked what the PM wanted. "A state funeral," he said. She laughed and said that he had to be joking. He assured Veronica that he was serious.

"They're trying to use him. They're abusing his memory. He'd despise you for this, John," she said, pulling up the flowers and tossing them aside. Walters sat down on the bench and watched on impassively, knowing that her fury would burn itself out. He smoked a cigarette while she plucked one flower and then another,

"Tell the PM, no! I'll consider a memorial service, but not now, not until I am ready," she said, without looking up.

"Thank you," he said.

Veronica glanced up. "Is that what you expected?"

"I had no expectations," he replied, his face a mask of inscrutability.

She cursed as she pricked her thumb. A tiny pool of blood bloomed on her skin. "One more thing. I'll decide who comes to the service otherwise there's no deal. Tell them that!" she said. Her voice sounded angry and belligerent, but her eyes spoke only of sadness and defeat.

* * *

Her mother assumed that Linda was leaving for Italy in search of the father. It wasn't the case. She wanted to put the boys, the school, England, the Troubles, all of it, behind her and start again. Linda decided to settle in Tuscany. Of the regions she had visited, it was the one where she had felt most at home. Linda had chosen the flat from a photograph. Her friend Jill knew the owner. If anything goes wrong, you can trust him to fix it, she had said. True to Jill's word, Mauro could be relied upon. He lived in a small basement flat in the building. His English was atrocious, her Italian was little better, but they muddled through. Mauro took care of re-decorating the flat, painting the walls to her taste. She chose yellow for the baby's bedroom.

In April, she gave birth to a boy and, by July, Mauro had left the basement behind and moved upstairs. Claire Scott said he was a fast mover. Her mother said it was simply, *too fast*. However, Mauro made a good father, and he was keen to be her husband. Despite her basic Italian, she found the right words to explain they did not need to rush things.

As spring turned into summer, she started to feel at home in the flat by the sea, with the man in her bed and her son. Harry. 'Ha-ree' - un bel nome, agreed Mauro's mother and father.

She explained the name was in honour of her friend. They frowned, imagining Harry must be the boy's father. However, when the foppish Harry Rhys-Davis arrived to meet his namesake, they understood that Mauro had nothing to worry about: he was no ladies' man in the traditional sense.

Harry was between schools. Like Linda, a turning point had come with that day. They tried to avoid talking about the subject, but it was impossible. The press had a morbid fascination with Hector and the Burtons. Almost one year after the atrocity at the school, stories continued to surface about their lives. One fine morning she, Mauro and Harry had been out pushing the baby in the pram by the quayside when Giles' face had leaped out of a newspaper. She had almost snatched it out of the hands of the young girl who sold the English language newspapers from the kiosk at the docks. 'Scarred for Life' ran the headline, describing how Giles had attacked another boy with a golf club. The article inferred that Hugh's life had always been surrounded by violence. "Basta!" Mauro had exclaimed: they had to move on.

The town provided more solace than any other place Linda had ever known. There was something comforting about watching the shadows settle over the quiet cobbled streets of the town in the late afternoon. In the distance, a cruise liner would occasionally slide into view, peerless and white against the deep blue sea and sky, a reminder that the outside world existed. When the sun dropped behind the tall apartment blocks, the streets filled with people. Always teenagers at first, signalled by the whine of Vespa engines, and then men and women returning from work or going out for drinks or dinner. From her balcony, she gaped in awe, transfixed by all the gossiping and flirting.

Harry's final visit of the summer arrived two weeks before he was due to start teaching at a new school. She could tell something was not quite right from the moment he walked into the flat. His expression was unusually anxious, and he seemed distracted. There was a new enoteca in town. Linda suggested they went there, while Mauro minded the baby.

The enoteca was dark and woody, not at all what Harry had in mind. The panelling reminded him of the old school lobby. Generations of the same family worked at the enoteca – Puglisi. They still spoke like southerners. Linda ordered for the two of them.

"It was good of Mauro to take the baby," said Harry, tucking into the bread and olives. The waiter left a flask of house red on the table. He poured a large glass for himself and a small one for Linda. "It's good," he said, relishing the berry notes. The alcohol seemed to calm his nerves.

"It's cheap too," replied Linda.

"Living here would be the death of me," he said, gulping down the red, and then refilling his glass. After a while, the edginess seemed to have left his behaviour, but she still thought he had a strange look in his eyes, like he had something to say but was afraid to say it. She decided to let it pass for now.

Over dinner, he told her about the new role as Head of Mathematics at a girls' school in the wilds of Somerset. Despite his initial reservations, he was finally beginning to warm to the idea. City life was too much. She nibbled on her meal, while he ate heartily. After dessert, he wanted a digestif. The waiter brought over grappa. Harry knocked back one and then another. Linda kept count: his drinking was becoming excessive.

After they had settled the bill, she suggested they take a walk along the canal. "The fresh air will do us good," she suggested. By which she meant it would sober Harry up.

The town was as quiet as a grave. They walked arm in arm along the wide pavement running alongside the canal leading to the medieval fortress and the old port, and then out to the open sea. The night air was warm and sticky, the kind of summers you only get in southern Europe.

After a while, Harry had to stop and remove his linen jacket. Underneath, his shirt was soaked through with sweat. "I thought I would be used to this by now," he said, parking himself on a low wall, facing out towards the sea, trying to catch the faintest of a breeze. From one of the boats tethered to the canal side, someone was listening to 'Ancora tu' on the stereo, on repeat. It was the song of the summer. Linda found herself singing along to the chorus.

"What is he singing about?" he asked, ruffling his shirt.

Linda smiled, "The usual stuff Italians sing about, love and romance."

Harry tried to sing along, but after stumbling over the words, he soon gave up. "You really like it here, don't you?" he asked.

She realised that she did: "You know I wasn't sure at first," she admitted, "but now I can't imagine being anywhere else."

Harry reached out and wrapped his wide arm around Linda's shoulder. She leant into him, feeling his warmth. A boat slowly made its way along the canal, its little outboard engine sputtering away. As it chugged along, the fisherman waved and whistled. "He thinks we are a couple," said Harry. Linda nuzzled up to him. He would have made a great husband, although some of his habits still infuriated the life out of her. Sensing that it was the right moment, she spoke her mind, "Ever since you've arrived, I've had the feeling you have something important to say," she blurted out.

"Am I that easy to read?" he asked, with a drunken, lopsided smile. However, beneath the half-smile, his expression was serious.

"Maybe not to everyone, but I can read you like a book. What's up?" she asked, feeling suddenly worried.

Harry unfurled his arm and patted down his jacket searching for the envelope containing the invitation, which he had brought over from England. "Please say you'll come," he said, handing it to her. While she opened it up and read the accompanying letter, he lit up. After the grappa, the nicotine went straight to his head and he felt as dizzy as teenager after a first tipple.

"When did this come?" she asked, glancing up.

"A couple of weeks ago. I wanted to wait until we were together. Will you?" he said, quietly.

"Who else is going?" she asked.

"David, Claire, Fran, Jeffrey too, I think…"

Linda turned the invitation over in her hands. "Anthony?"

"No. I don't believe so," said Harry.

"The Ashworths?" she asked with a frown-cum-scowl.

Harry had expected the questions. "Yes, of course, they're invited, although the parents are separated."

Linda read the address. City of London. "I know that it would mean the world to Hugh and Veronica if you came to Hector's memorial."

She turned the card over in her hands, running her fingers over the embossed text. Over Harry's shoulder, the streetlights outside her apartment were just visible, twinkling, calling her home. She felt happy and safe in the town. "Why does it matter if I come?" she asked. "What difference does it make? Nothing will change. Jim, Hector, and his young driver, they won't be coming back …" she said, her voice trailing off.

However, as she spoke, she understood why she had been invited. It was for the same reason as Harry, for all of them: to bring some closure by making sense of those days in September 1975, which had begun brightly, bathed in the warmth of the late summer sunshine, only to descend into something incomprehensible and dark.

Harry was staring out to sea. The little boat had slipped out of the centuries-old, Medici-built harbour and was crisscrossing the waves toward the lighthouse at Meloria, and the promise of a good night's catch. "I shouldn't have asked," he said. "I'm sorry."

Despite feeling woozy, he lit another cigarette, but the taste was acrid and made him feel sick. He flicked it into the canal, where it landed in the dense water with a sharp fizz. Linda reached into her purse and threw a coin at the floating butt. It plopped and sank without a trace. "What did you do that for?" he asked, bemused.

"A penny for your thoughts," she replied. "You should have asked me when you landed. You'd have had a more enjoyable time," and then she made room for herself on his lap and hugged him.

"Does that mean you'll come?" he asked, hopefully.

"The baby will be fine with Mauro for a couple of days," she said, and she hugged him again. Out to sea, the boat's taillight bobbled in the darkness. They sat watching it in silence until the night air finally cooled, and tiredness sank in and called them home.

* * *

The church of St Giles-without-Cripplegate welcomed lepers and beggars. Hector had specified in his will that this was where he would be laid to rest. Veronica thought it was an odd choice. One of the wardens at the door muttered darkly about a connection to Cromwell; she told him to keep his asinine remarks to himself.

"Hugh, smarten up please," said Veronica, reaching down and tucking his shirt in. Hugh pushed her away, looking embarrassed. "And don't forget to shake hands with our guests when they arrive, and when they depart" Although her voice was calm, she was visibly on edge.

Hugh smiled at his mother, "Don't worry. I know what to do," he said. She reached out and squeezed Hugh's hot and sweaty hand, and then led him into the cool interior of the nave to where hundreds of people had started to congregate for the service. Belinda and Gerry were milling around inside. Many of Hector's rank and file were present and had already taken their seats. The regiment's colours lay draped over the casket in the chancel.

"Look, there's Uncle John," said Hugh. Walters caught Hugh's eye and winked. "Shall I go and say hello?" he asked, but Veronica was not listening. She was too busy checking off the guests.

"Why don't you keep your sister company?" said Veronica, before bustling through the crowd to the doorway. Hugh thought Belinda did not require company. As ever, she was doing just fine, entertaining their guests with various stories about school and horse riding. Hugh hovered on the periphery of the conversation before he decided that he had heard enough. He was growing impatient waiting for Giles.

The pews were filling up fast, now: a sea of faces – servicemen, policemen, politicians, civil servants, family, and friends. A news crew stayed in the shadows waiting to broadcast the memorial service on World Service. Hugh glanced toward the wardens. Five minutes until noon, and still no sign of Giles. The old organist with whom Hugh had studied piano since leaving Frampton was already seated, fiddling with the sheet music. Hugh wondered what Giles would say, now that he had learned to play Yesterday.

"Hugh," whispered a voice from behind a pillar. He turned abruptly around and came face to face with Harry and Linda. Harry was no stranger to Hugh. Twice a week he home-schooled Hugh in preparation for sitting his eleven plus.

Hugh shot out his hand, "Hello sir. Hello matron," he said. They shook hands in turn. It struck Hugh that it was like the first day of term all over again. For a moment, he had the strangest feeling of being outside himself, looking in.

"How are you feeling?" inquired Linda. Hugh shrugged a Giles-like shrug. "We'll take our seat," she said, nudging Harry along so that they could sit with David and Claire. David winked at Hugh, which made him briefly shudder.

However, his attention was taken away from his former housemaster by a sharp tug on his wrist. Belinda. "The service is about to start," she said, frowning, and then leading him by the shirt cuff toward the front row to where their mother was seated among the VIP guests. Belinda took a seat on their mother's left. Hugh took the one to her right next to a man who introduced himself as Mr Mason, a friend of Hugh's father from the government. He leaned in conspiratorially to Hugh and whispered a few words into his ears about duty and sacrifice. Veronica pulled Hugh to her side and glowered at the man.

As the organist struck the first note of the hymn, Hugh wriggled free from his mother and stole a final glance toward the rear of the church. So many people were crammed inside. It was standing room only. He never realised that his father knew so many people, nor that so many people knew his father.

Veronica pinched him lightly on the thigh and hissed "Eyes front," as the vicar summoned the congregation to stand. Hugh rose and steeled himself for the long and difficult hours, which his mother had said were to come. Just think about how you want people to remember your father and behave accordingly, she had said.

As the rows stood as one, Hugh heard rustling footsteps drawing nearer and he turned abruptly, knowing in his heart to whom they belonged. The sight of Giles set his pulse racing. Butterflies fluttered in his tummy: nerves. excitement, happiness, sadness, all mingling as one.

Under the pew, he had a gift-wrapped Lancaster, the model that Giles prized. A peace offering. He still didn't understand fully why Giles had acted the way he did that day and other the other times, nor did he understand what Giles meant about John and Marcus. But in the many months that they had been apart, each living their own lives away from Frampton, Hugh knew for certain that Giles loved him in his own strange way, and that he loved him back, and he had missed Giles and he wanted to be his friend again. Giles caught his eye and held it, and smiled knowingly, and then he ducked along a pew to sit with his mother Moira and the rest of the mourners, and with that the service began.

* * *

The ten hard men and the one woman had gathered in the basement room waiting for this moment to arrive since early morning. In the corner of the room, a large black and white television set had been rigged up on a raised platform so that they could all enjoy an unobstructed view of the service. Sean studied the faces of the congregation, quietly mouthing the names of the faces he recognised. The camera panned to the coffin. "You did well, girl," he said loudly, so that every man among them could hear.

"All Tom's work," she replied, lustily over the tinny sound of the television. At the sight of the draped Union Jack, the Council rose to their feet and applauded, raising their glasses in a toast. "To Tom!" they said, turning as one to Tom.

"To Brendan!" he cried in return. They clinked their glasses and drained a shot. "To Eddie, and Robbie and Roy!" he hollered at the top of his voice. They poured another shot and solemnly turned to face one another and clinked and drained the whiskey.

"To Conor!" said Carrie, looking emotional.

Tom brought his glass to hers and looked Carrie straight in the eyes. "To Conor!" Life without parole. They locked arms and she drank from his glass and he drank from hers, and then they slammed them down.

"To Eamonn," wheezed Sean, with a respectful nod towards Eamonn's father, the beast of Belfast. The wiry commander raised his glass in memory of his son.

They clinked again. "Eva!" shouted Carrie at the top of her voice.

They banged their fists down on the table and cried out their names. "Martyrs!" boomed one of the generals, as the TV screen momentarily faded to black out of respect for Colonel Hector Burton, Private James Colman and Jim Farthing. No mention of Eamonn Flaherty, nor Eva Riordan. The IRA men swore at the screen and smashed their glasses to the floor. The building shook on its foundations, as rockets rained down from the Protestant side of town. Carrie called out for fresh glasses and they drank again until there was no more good whiskey and they had shouted themselves hoarse, and then dispersed, disappearing like shadows into the Belfast night.

"You've got the nimblest fingers," she said when they were finally alone in his mother's house. She threaded her hand into his, "Will you teach me?" she asked.

Tom rolled on to his back, watching the ceiling swim. "I learned it at Marconi. They taught me how to work fast," he said slowly, drunkenly. "He should have never sent the driver away for a minute like that... he should have never rushed away when his wife called out about their boy...he should have never let his guard drop." Tom closed his eyes and wished for the ceiling to stop spinning.

Carrie pinned him down and kissed him hard. "Tell me how you do it, so I can learn," she pleaded.

Like an incantation, he slowly recited the steps: Twist off the facia. Pull out the wiring. Pack in Semtex. Add in the nuts and bolts. Set the device to explode when the frequency is changed. Put back the facia. It sounded so simple and effortless – once set in motion, it was impossible to stop: a mere spark, that was all it took.

He pictured Burton fiddling with the radio, adjusting the dial from medium wave to long wave. A song might have started up, but it would have lasted for no more than a second, and then there would have been a huge flash, followed by a deafening roar and a searing heat the likes of which should never be inflicted upon another human being, not even upon a man like Hector Burton. He gazed drowsily at Carrie and closed his eyes. If he had sent Hector Burton to hell, then he knew that one day, perhaps soon, he would join him there.

THE END

ABOUT THE AUTHOR

Michael Saxton was born and raised in the Home Counties and boarded from the age of seven. After graduating from UCL, he has worked in the media and marketing industry as a consultant and editor. Married, with two children, he lives in London.

Printed in Great Britain
by Amazon

83743937R00251